THESE
LATTER
DAYS

THESE

LATTER DAYS

DAYS

A NOVEL

LAURA KALPAKIAN

Times
BOOKS

Books by Laura Kalpakian

Beggars and Choosers
These Latter Days

Copyright © 1985 by Laura Kalpakian

All rights reserved under International and Pan-American Copyright
Conventions. Published in the United States by Times Books, a
division of Random House, Inc., New York, and simultaneously in
Canada by Random House of Canada Limited, Toronto.

Library of Congress Cataloging in Publication Data

Kalpakian, Laura.
  These latter days.

  I. Title.
PS3561.A4168T48   1985   813'.54   84-40418
ISBN 0–8129–1154–7

Designed by Doris Borowsky

Manufactured in the United States of America

9 8 7 6 5 4 3 2 1

First Edition

For my father,
William J. Johnson

The author would like to acknowledge gratefully the assistance of Peggy K. Johnson, Katherine Frank, Perri Hale, and Ruth Stone and to thank the Virginia Center for the Creative Arts, Sweet Briar, Virginia, and the Montalvo Center for the Arts, Saratoga, California.

And it shall come to pass that the Lord God shall bring forth the words of a book and they shall be the words of them which have slumbered. And behold the book shall be a revelation from God, from the beginning of the world to the ending thereof.

Book of Mormon
2 Nephi 27:6, 7

THE FAMILY

Mason				Douglass	
Abel (1841–1899)				Buck (1823–1887)	
Afton (1846–1911)				Eden (1839–1870)	

Albert	Lily	RUTH	m. SAMUEL	Fred
1878–1946	1871–1926	1864–1940	1865–1933	1868–1937
m. Elyse	m. Arthur			m. Velda Cane
Farnsworth	Whickham			(1872–1897)
(1880–1955)	(1857–1938)			m. Mavis P.
				Anderson
				(1861–1909)

EDEN DOUGLASS (1890–1911)

GIDEON DOUGLASS (1892–1951)
    m. Katherine Tindall (1894–1956)
        Samuel b. 1914 - d. 1919
        Eden Louise b. 1920
        Ada Ruth b. 1922
        Ernest Fred b. 1925

AFTON DOUGLASS (1893–1965)
    m. Thomas Lance (1889–1969)
    Eight children

LILY DOUGLASS (1895–1976)
    m. 1st William Lance (1891–1914)
    Two children
    m. 2nd Mr. Walsh (1888–1939)
    One child

MASON DOUGLASS (1898–1970)
    m. Margaret Denton (1907–1975)
    Two children

NARCISSA DOUGLASS (1900–1974)
    m. 1st Zeniff Blankenship (1898–?)
    Two children
    m. 2nd Arnold Swenson (1896–?)
    Two children
    m. 3rd Thatcher Stout (1897–?)
    m. 4th Asa "Sport" Holliwell (1904–   )

BOOK ONE

The Unbelieving Wife

St. Elmo, California
March 1910

SOMETIMES THE WINDS reverse, and instead of blowing eastward from the Pacific, they come up off the yellow back of the desert and whistle westward down through the mountains. The valleys lie helpless. Twice a year the winds flatten the sunflower and ruffle the wild mustard; they chafe the skin and irritate the eye, and even the iron constitution of the railroad is not immune to them. In the desert the sands drift across the track like unbleached snow, and in the railroad terminus of St. Elmo the soot and ash dervish about the yard and congregate at the station door. The railroad's timetable has never taken account of these seasonal winds, and so today the train was late, but then so were Ruth Douglass and Dr. Lucius Tipton.

The doctor's aging Flyer, dripping oil and billowing fumes, trundled up to the front of the grotesque station. Moorish turrets were posted at each of its four corners, and iron grillwork latticed the windows. Ruth, dressed in black, her dark hair hidden beneath a dark hat, got out and waited while Doctor parked the car near a sagging hitching post. She was tall as a long-stemmed rose, implacably dried and varnished unto stiffness, but not so brittle as to fall apart under the touch. Doctor took her arm and they walked into the station.

Doctor bought their tickets while Ruth took a seat in one of the pews, which theaterlike all faced one way as if a grand drama were perennially about to unfold. The couple was without baggage save for the doctor's black bag and a large cutlery case, while Ruth carried a maroon carpetbag bulging with blankets and cotton bandages.

Doctor studied the tickets, put them in his breast pocket, and took his seat beside Ruth. "He said the train would be in soon. This is only the mail run, so it's not as reliable as some of the other trains."

"We're lucky it runs at all."

"Well, it's the only one that stops at Jackrabbit Junction." Lucius Tipton was middle-aged, like Ruth, and like Ruth he was tall, but his body betrayed both his sedentary profession and his fondness for good living. His face was mobile with expression, dominated by a bony nose and embellished with a mole. His hazel eyes were mottled like rain-pocked muddy waters, and a pendulous mustache disguised his generous mouth. He had immaculate hands. He inspected his hat for wind damage and then put it back on his head, where it protected a bald spot.

"How long will it take us to get there?" Ruth asked.

"Not more than a few hours. Jackrabbit is the second stop up in the desert, and we should be there by midafternoon. You don't have to come, Ruth. I'd rather you didn't. I don't know what we'll find in New Canaan."

"New Hell," she said, snorting.

"It might not even be the same group of heretics."

"Lunatics."

"Well, lunatic or heretic, revelation or hallucination, it all depends on your point of view, don't it?"

"Not on mine it don't. I know what I think."

"Well, I only know what that girl told me. Their leader was praying over her father's foot and it wasn't getting no better and she was afraid he would die. So I said I'd go have a look at him."

"Is that why you brought the saw?" said Ruth, eyeing the cutlery case.

The doctor regarded his hands and checked his pocket watch. "It sounds like gangrene to me. If it is and if I have to amputate, I don't want to do it with a kitchen knife."

"Did you tell the girl that?"

"No. I just said I'd come."

"I hate the smell of train stations," said Ruth, pulling her back away from the bench. "They're cold and they make my bones ache."

The station indeed seemed to have been constructed to wring the maximum dankness out of any day. Outside, the winds dappled the March sunlight over snowless mountains and brought the dry foretaste of summer. Ruth buttoned her black jacket and adjusted her high collar, stiff and ten years out of fashion.

"Ruth. You ought not to go. What purpose can it serve? What

good can it do? If it's Samuel, I'll find out. I'll tell you when I come back. Why do you have to come see for yourself?"

"Because I was married to him for years, Lucius."

"What if Samuel recognizes you? He may have lost his mind, but that don't mean he's lost his memory."

"Why do you think I wore the hat with the motoring veil?" She touched the hat swathed across its wide brim and crown with yards of black lace.

"Are you going to hide out behind that the whole time?"

"I've hidden out for ten years behind black veils and crepe, haven't I?" She took a deep breath and continued without looking at him. "I think—if only I could see him, see what he's become, know that I was right to do what I did, then I wouldn't be so afraid. If he wasn't a ghost, he wouldn't haunt me."

"Why must you see him? I tell you, Ruth, women confound me!"

"Then it's fortunate you've remained a bachelor, Doctor."

"Women confound even the men who marry them," he added unsympathetically. "Ruth, I implore you, let me do this. If it's Samuel and his Apocalyptic Apostles out there, I'll tell you. I'll tell you what he's like. I'll take his damned picture if you want! Blast it all, Ruth, I don't want you to do this!"

"Keep your voice down. The ticket man is looking at you."

"Let him look. What do I care? I'll never understand this, Ruth."

"That's because you've never been haunted. How could you know? You're an atheist and a scientist, Doctor, and people like you are never haunted. You can't possibly know what it's like." Ruth took off her gloves and rolled them in her lap. She tucked the thumbs in carefully. "For ten years I've lain awake at night, and I hear the rain gutter rattle beside my window or I hear a scratching in the walls and I think—it's him. Sometimes I feel like I can hear the dust roll around under my bed and I think—it's Samuel and he's come back to get me. He's come back to ruin my life and the lives of all my children. He's going to get me, show me up to be the maggoty sinner I am."

"You're not maggoty."

"I am in the eyes of the church."

"What the church don't know won't hurt them."

"What about God?"

"Bother God!"

5

"Please, Lucius. Your voice echoes." She touched his hand lightly, unobtrusively, and then folded her own hands back in her lap. "If it is Samuel," she went on, "and if I can see he's become everything I feared and if I know that whatever I did, however wrong it was, it was still right, then—well, when I hear the rainpipe, I'll know it's only the wind, and when I hear the scratching, I'll know it's only a mouse, and I'll be able to tell myself that the dust under the bed don't make any sound when it rolls. I want to be free of him."

"You're being irrational."

"That's the worst sin for you, isn't it?"

"I don't believe in sin, only stupidity and malice. And you're being both. What if his seeing you drives him into a vengeful rage? He might well come and rattle your rainpipe and scratch at your walls."

"I'll take that chance. Even if Samuel is crazy, he's still shrewd. He's always been shrewd. He's had enough trouble with the law. He probably don't set foot in a town bigger than Jackrabbit Junction."

"Jackrabbit's a depot. Not a town."

"I know what I'm doing," she maintained.

"You could do with knowing a little less and feeling a little more, Ruth. You could do with a little less courage and a little more insight. You could do with a little more—"

"Rubbish, Lucius. Let's go out on the platform. I hear the train."

The doctor sighed and rose. He would argue with her no more. When Ruth decided to do something the arguments of Socrates wouldn't deter her. She refused—and had for ten years—to be drawn into any sort of philosophical debate with Lucius Tipton. He always had the feeling that she could vanquish him with a single word such as "rubbish" because it was Ruth's nature to distill and reduce things down to graspable particulars and it was the doctor's nature to float among the more gaseous universals. "This is damned foolhardy," he said by way of having the last word.

The mail train to Las Vegas had only one passenger car, and they were the only passengers. The car was old, unswept, with hard wooden benches and heavily smudged windows. Ruth took a seat near the window, and Doctor sat beside her. The whistle shrieked as they pulled east out of St. Elmo, across the trestled bridge over Dogsback Ditch that separated the town from the mountain pass.

6

The town and the mountains had been named by an itinerant Jesuit priest who had stopped there briefly a hundred years before, discovered the mountain pass, and moved on.

Ruth had not made this trip in ten years, since she first came to St. Elmo, but she remembered the land. From the town they would climb up Jesuit Pass through the mountains and descend again into desert. She knew the desert lay on the other side of the mountains, but she could not guess what lay on the other side of time. The future was unknowable and the past unbearable, and the present could only be endured because it was so fleeting.

The doctor fell asleep as the train was making its long slow way up the grade. His head fell on her shoulder, and Ruth let him stay there, since there was no one in the car to witness the unsanctioned intimacy of the doctor's head on the widow's shoulder. She had never dreamed she would be riding eastward with a doctor's head on her shoulder, to a meeting, or a glimpse, or an apocalyptic encounter with a man who might be her own husband. There were many things she'd never dreamed. Dreaming was not Ruth's strength. She had good instincts but little insight and neither the time nor the taste for self-scrutiny, and so it was with the greatest personal pain that she admitted, as the train whistle shrieked through the mountains, that she should have listened. That first day. Twenty years before. Thunder had shaken the very foundations of her father's Salt Lake home. The thunder could have given her a revelation if only she'd listened. If only she'd heeded the thunder, she wouldn't be here now.

1

SHE COULD SCARCELY hear the bell for the thunder rattling the glass in the kitchen windowpanes. She was elbow-deep in bread dough, and she wiped her hands and face on her starched apron until she heard the bell once more. Then she went to the door.

Ruth Mason was tall, dark, and handsome, but it's not the same on a woman, and besides she was close (too close) to six feet and she walked with unstooped shoulders, her long gait inhibited only by sober-colored skirts. She conceded to fashion only by curling her bangs, inexpertly at best, with a hot iron. Most women of her generation smelled of singed hair. Ruth smelled of starch. She had—if such a thing is possible—a passion for starch.

Ruth could make out a man's figure, jigsawed by thick stained glass, on the other side of the door. Her hands were still floury, and bits of bread-flesh clung to the knob as she swung the door open. A cold breath of air preceded Samuel Douglass—who did not wait to be asked—into the hall. A dried leaf caught at his jacket collar, and he held a bunch of limp asters. He was clean-shaven, with fair hair, spectacles over his gray eyes, and a long mouth that turned up at the corners, but only at the corners. He handed her the asters. "Miss Mason," he said. He took off his coat and hat without being asked and hung them on the oak stand, regarding himself in the oval mirror.

Ruth watched him; Samuel Douglass was as tall as she was. They stood side by side in the beveled mirror, Ruth clutching the asters at her bosom. They looked serious but not unhappy. Like a wedding picture. As if fate had framed them from the beginning.

"Who is it, Ruth?" Her mother's voice floated down like audible dust from the dim lair where Mrs. Mason lived, prematurely retired from the world.

"It's Mr. Douglass, Ma," Ruth called back. "Mr. Samuel Douglass." Then she turned to the man in the mirror and said, "My sister is not at home, Mr. Douglass." She offered him back his asters.

"I didn't come to see your sister," he replied. (Though, she reflected years later, he did not say it with much conviction.) Samuel Douglass studied himself closely in the mirror, plastered his hair down against his skull, and took off his glasses, placing them in his pocket. Ruth noted that his ears stuck out. "I came to call on you, Miss Mason—Ruth, if I may call you so."

"You seem to have accorded yourself that liberty, Mr. Douglass," she retorted. She rather expected him to take his cue from Sir Walter Scott and beg her forgiveness for being so bold, or at least recoil from her rebuff.

"Yes," he said, "I guess I have."

"I'm working in the kitchen, Mr. Douglass. If you've come to see me, you'll have to come into the kitchen."

"Yes," he said, "I guess I will."

He followed her into the kitchen, where the windows were thick with steam and the dough had nearly risen out of its bowl. Ruth gave it a sharp, unmerciful punch and it fell back.

"I saw you in church the other day," said Samuel.

"I'm sure you saw a great many people in church."

"I saw you," he went on, "and I said to myself, that's a good-looking woman. That girl don't cringe or whimper, I said to myself. That girl's got faith and spirit. You don't find too many girls with faith and spirit. Sometimes one or t'other, but it ain't often you see both." He sucked imperceptibly at his teeth, and his cool gray eyes traveled from her face down her bodice, lingering at the asters, which she held at her breast. Ruth dropped the flowers to her side. "Yes," he said, nodding, "I said to myself, I envy that girl's husband."

"Then you envied no man, Mr. Douglass."

"That's what I hear. Just fortunate, I reckon. Covet not thy neighbor's wife."

Ruth pumped some water into a vase and crammed the asters in. She set them on the table and placed her arms on the rim of the bread bowl. She met his eyes without flinching. "I have no husband, Mr. Douglass."

9

"That's why I'm here. I already talked to your father. Just this morning, I went by his—"

"You talked to my father? How dare you! You asked my father if you could marry me?"

"Don't rush me, Ruth." He smiled slyly, and Ruth flushed crimson to her temples. "I told your father I'd make you a good husband."

"Don't you rush me, Mr. Douglass!"

"I got land up in Idaho Territory, land with a house near Healy, Idaho. You ever hear of Healy?"

"No."

"Well, I'm homesteading up there. I come to Salt Lake to get supplies and a wife."

"In that order?" Ruth applied herself to the kneading.

"I don't care so long as I get them both."

"Did you tell my father that?"

"No. I asked him if I could call on you," Samuel replied, taking a seat without benefit of invitation.

"And what did my father say?"

Samuel tilted his chair back so he could see her face without looking up. "Your father said he couldn't do nothing with you, couldn't speak for you, couldn't answer for you. He said I'd have to ask you all by yourself."

"Did he now?" Ruth squeezed the flexible neck of the dough till it popped and blistered. Samuel Douglass watched her without speaking, only making occasional noises over his teeth, but Ruth could scarcely hear them for the thunder which trampled in herds over their heads.

Ruth was the eldest child of Abel Mason, a well-to-do Salt Lake taxidermist and furrier, and she lived with him, her mother, her younger sister, Lily, and her errant twelve-year-old brother, Albert, in a large, comfortable home not far from the Mormon temple. The house gazed from numerous windows out to a street populated with houses very much like it, porched, gabled, impacted with so much rickety gingerbread they all looked like cobwebbed wedding cakes. The Mason home differed from its neighbors only slightly; inside they had the usual oak and rosewood furniture, red velvets and gold tassels (those emblems of security, stability, and well-being), highboys filled with knickknacks and the few necessary books: the Bible, the Book of Mormon, the *Doctrine and Covenants*, and a complete edition of Sir Walter Scott. They had a piano, which only Lily could play. But where most homes kept clusters of family portraits, the Masons offered up testaments to Abel's art. Two stuffed owls perched on the piano; a shaggy buffalo head, an eyeless moose, and a dusty stag kept watch over the Mason parlor. As a child these balding, moth-ridden bodiless creatures had frightened Ruth, but as she grew up, fear evolved into implacable—and impotent—hatred.

"If you hate them so much," her father once pointedly remarked, "then why don't you get married and have your own house?"

A rhetorical question. Ruth had not had a proposal in at least four years; she was six feet tall and growing into that weedy, unthinkable anomaly in the Mormon community, the unwed woman. Ruth knew she was well past the bud, very nearly past the blossom of her youth. When she went to church, the plump, usually pregnant young matrons she'd gone to high school with (class of 1882) eyed her with wonder and disgust.

"I haven't been asked," Ruth snapped back, sailing out of the room but not quickly enough to escape her father's half-despairing grunt.

She had in truth been asked, shortly after high school, but she had turned the young man down because she didn't love him, which seemed a perfectly legitimate reason for not marrying. Nonetheless, Abel Mason instructed his wife, Afton, to have a talk with Ruth. Afton Mason had scarcely talked to anyone in years, except to make a request—a little hot broth, a little cold compress, a fresh hanky. A hot-water bottle, perhaps. But she gave a gallant effort. As Ruth was plumping her many pillows, Mrs. Mason murmured that often love came as a result of marriage and not the other way around. Marriage was a holy estate, much to be envied, because Saints believed that souls entered the Celestial Kingdom only two by two, that the only way you could get into the Celestial Kingdom by yourself was if you died young, and then someone would have to go through the temple rites for you, marry you for the afterlife, someone you knew or were somehow related to, of course. The church would never force a perfect stranger on a girl, even in the Celestial Kingdom.

This speech wore Mrs. Mason out completely, and she collapsed back into her pillows and begged Ruth to draw the blinds and bring her a headache powder.

Ruth resolved to look more kindly on the next young man who might ask for her hand, but he was a perfectly odious boy from church who admired the stuffed heads about the parlor and thought he might like to go into taxidermy.

When she rejected this one, her father took a hand in things and in his bluff, well-meaning way extolled the virtues of marriage. He quoted from the Bible, the Book of Mormon, the *Doctrine and Covenants*, and other repositories of church wisdom, and recited the many spiritual blessings that accrued to one in the married state. Ruth asked him if he had studied up to have this talk with her, and he told her not to interrupt.

"Are you glad you got married, Pa?"

"What kind of question is that? Am I glad? I told you not to interrupt. Glad? What's that got to do with it?"

"Are you glad you married Ma?"

"That"—he drew a long, wheezy breath—"is none of your business. We are talking about you."

"No," Ruth corrected him. "We were talking about marriage in general."

"Am I glad? You're the one who ought to be glad! Yes, you, my girl! You wouldn't be here if I hadn't married your mother!"

"I might be," Ruth commented. "Doesn't the church teach us that we all have a preexistence as little spirit children waiting to put on our fleshly clothes and come to earth to test ourselves? If we only wait for parents, I might have got down here some other way. Don't you think?"

Abel Mason marched out of the room, as she had known he would. She always knew how to terminate unpleasant conversations with her father: she simply raised the ugly specter of debate, and he blustered out of the room.

But as the years rolled by and no more proposals were forthcoming, Ruth found that spinsterhood sat on her like a goiter. The older she got, the more pronounced—or pathetic, depending on your point of view—her spinsterhood became. Ruth grew more aloof. Her inherent reserve, if it did not protect her from the pity of her friends, at least allowed her to snip those friendships with little regret or qualm.

In the winter of 1885 she went to her last Christmas ball. She wore a dress of claret silk, tight over her bodice and broad shoulders, stunning with her high color, dark eyes, and thick hair. She danced four dances with Mormon swains before she realized she was taller and older than every boy whose name appeared on her dance card. She excused herself to her next partner, begging a sick headache, and left the steamy recreation hall for the gaslit December cold. She shredded her dance card and walked home.

The following spring the parlor filled with the fair Lily's suitors. Ruth served lemonade and wondered if they all had brass ears to tell Lily she played the piano like an angel. Lily had a practiced, soulful way of gazing into boys' eyes and saying, "Thank you, I shall treasure that always."

One night, in the bedroom they shared, Ruth asked Lily how she could possibly say such things, much less repeat them.

"Why! Boys like it!" replied the startled Lily.

"But it's degrading."

"Degrading?" Lily repeated the word as if it were Mongolian.

"Well, it's not the truth, for one thing."

"What difference does that make?"

"And it makes you look like—like you need them. How can you bear it?"

"You're just jealous," Lily retorted, studying the strata of a new pimple on her chin. "And next time I wish you'd put more sugar in the lemonade."

Ruth gave up her church activities one by one. She no longer went to the young persons' group because she was not a young person. Neither was she a young matron, so that effectively excluded her from the Relief Society. She bowed out of genealogy group because a woman without a husband wasn't likely to have a family, and a woman without a family was but a single, leafless twig and unlikely to understand the church's insistence on scrupulous record-keeping (on earth as it is in heaven) for all one's relations, living and dead (and in genealogy group, the distinction was almost moot).

Ruth spent her time reading Sir Walter Scott, and when she'd been through all the novels she suggested to her father that perhaps she might get a job. She was educated, after all. There must be some genteel occupation—

"What?" Abel Mason bellowed. "And have all of Salt Lake, the entire Church of Jesus Christ of Latter-day Saints, the whole world think I can't support my daughter? I am the breadwinner in this family, and let that be an end to it!"

It wasn't quite the end. The following Monday he fired the family's sole servant. He said he already had one able-bodied grown woman living in the house, why did he need two? He was desperate to be rid of her.

Ruth herself was a little desperate; she caught herself weeping in the kitchen now and then. Once Abel Mason caught her weeping in the kitchen. After that, Ruth decided desperation was unbecoming. Beneath a noble mind. She did not cry again. In the kitchen or anywhere else. She tended her father's house (though she refused to dust or otherwise sully her fingers with the stuffed animal heads). She cooked the meals, did the washing, starching, and ironing, looked after her mother, who required only frequent cold compresses, cups of hot broth, and changes of linen. Mrs. Mason had not asked for more of life for twelve years, since Albert's birth had left her—in the jargon of the day—permanently delicate.

And so, on that thundery November day in 1889 when her mother had asked her who was at the front door and she'd replied, "Mr. Samuel Douglass," and regarded herself in the mirror beside the first man who was as tall as she was, she knew from that moment she might just as well have called herself Mrs. Samuel Douglass. Samuel seemed to know it, too; his courting was pious and perfunctory. She would have to marry this one.

On her wedding day in December 1889, Lily did the serving in the parlor after the ceremony, which was sparsely attended (at Ruth's insistence) by the family, the officiating bishop of their local ward, and the ubiquitous stuffed animals. The bishop toasted the young couple with a cup of hot cocoa. Samuel Douglass said that God's will had brought him to Salt Lake to seek out Ruth. Abel Mason said that fortune would smile on their union and that the Celestial Kingdom was open to all who followed God's commandments, were married, and were fruitful and multiplied.

Ruth thought the reference to fertility indelicate on a wedding day. Indelicate and ominous. Ruth had not forgotten—even if Abel

14

Mason had—her mother's screams the two days and nights it took for Albert to get born. Ruth put her half-finished cup of cocoa back on Lily's tray and glanced at her mother, who, in honor of her daughter's wedding, had joined them downstairs in the parlor. For the occasion she had even shed her wrapper and was dressed in a faded peach-colored silk twelve years out of style. Ruth took her mother's hand and knelt by the side of the overstuffed chair where Mrs. Mason sat, staring vacantly into the fire.

Like all good Mormon girls, Ruth would have preferred a temple wedding with its secret decorum. This would have united her unto her husband for time and all eternity and endowed her marriage with an extra measure of sanctity. She was entitled to it, given her family's good standing in the church, and even Samuel agreed it would have been best. But, he added, if the proper recommendations were to come all the way from Healy, Idaho, it would take some time, and he was anxious to be wed. Ruth might have been willing to wait for the appropriate documents, but Abel suggested the parlor wedding with the understanding Samuel and Ruth could marry in the temple later; they could marry for time now, eternity could wait for a bit.

Abel, in fact, was generosity itself. He gave Ruth a dowry, handsome, but within his means, and a family Bible that optimistically included entries for ten under "Births." He allowed the young Douglasses to live in his house until spring, when they would set off for their Idaho home. He ordered young Albert out of his room, to sleep on a cot down in the kitchen in what had been the former servant's closetlike quarters. The newly wedded couple were then awarded Albert's room, between Lily's virginal chamber and Mrs. Mason's solitary space. Abel himself slept at the end of the upstairs hall.

So Ruth and Samuel Douglass took their wedding journey up a flight of stairs when the bishop had left and Albert and Lily were doing the washing-up and Mrs. Mason had been escorted back to her chamber. Abel sat in front of the parlor fire with the newspaper and said goodnight.

Albert's room was dark when the bride entered it, but her eyes adjusted quickly to the gloom. She could see her white nightdress on the bed, where she had laid it earlier in the day, its high trimmed

15

neck and long lacy sleeves starched within an inch of petrifaction. She passed the bed and walked to the window, pushed the curtains aside, and stared into the snow-covered street punctuated with buttery squares of light from the windows of neighboring homes. The view was no different from that of the room she'd always shared with Lily; she had thought it might be. She heard her husband come in and close the door behind him. She heard—rather more clearly than she ever had before—the funny noises he made with his teeth.

"You can come back in a few minutes," she said.

"Where am I supposed to go?"

"Anywhere. Out. You can come back in a—"

"I'm not going anywhere, Ruth. We're wed now."

"What difference does that make?" Ruth searched the darkness for his face.

Samuel turned up the gas, and it hissed angrily. "You read the Bible, Ruth. You know what it says about virgins past their flower." He chuckled. " 'Then let them marry.' And you know what the Bible says a man and wife are to do."

"Samuel, I can't—"

"They cleave together and make one flesh."

"I can't get undressed in front of you!"

"I'm your husband, Ruth."

"What difference does that make?" she repeated.

Samuel lounged against the door. "You're going to know me just like the Bible says. That's the way of marriage."

"Then I shall change elsewhere," she announced, sweeping the nightdress off the bed.

Samuel shook his head.

"Stand out of my way, Samuel."

He turned the key in the lock and came toward her. "We done it right so far. No bedding, no squeezing, no kissing. We're commanded to wait till we're wed, and we're wed. We'll do the rest of it right, too." He pulled her into his arms, drew her face up to his, and kissed her unyielding lips. "Thaw out your mouth, Ruth. Don't you know how to kiss?"

"Should I?"

"It don't matter. I know how."

He did know how, and Ruth found her lips thawed quickly, more quickly than she expected; she discovered tingling in a body that be-

16

came suddenly foreign, as if she had been given it anew and not lived in it for twenty-five years.

Samuel released her, sat down on the bed, and took off his glasses, placing them carefully in a case. He unhooked his shoes, newly bought for the wedding. He removed his coat and tossed it unceremoniously into a nearby chair. He unsnapped his collar and cuffs and threw them on the bedside table, unfastened his suspenders, and stripped off his shirt. Ruth noticed a great deal of short hair tufting out of his unbuttoned underwear: it had never occurred to her that men had hair anywhere but on their heads and their chins. Where else might he have hair?

"Now, Ruth, let's get you out of those clothes. There's only one way to do this, Ruth. You got to do it right the first time or it will always be wrong. You can be scared or not, it don't matter to me, but we're going to do this right." He moved toward her. "Now, let me unhook you."

"No."

"Why?"

Fruitlessly, she sought a response. He certainly seemed to have the unimpeachable fact of matrimony on his side. "You'll ruin my dress," she replied. "You don't know how to do it."

"What makes you think I don't?"

And while Ruth was trying to answer that, Samuel swiftly, surely unhooked her bodice and peeled it off her shoulders and down her arms; her skirt fell next, and in a matter of seconds her petticoat slid down her hips. Ruth stood, rooted to the rug with fear and still tingling in a body that wasn't quite her own, as Samuel unlaced her stays, effectively, efficiently, and not till she was standing half naked did she realize that it *was* her body after all, though she could not see her breasts because they were covered by a man's hands, and the heat from his hands penetrated her very tissues. Samuel fell back on the bed and pulled her on top of him, and then she could not see her breasts because he'd buried his face in them.

Ruth freed herself with one powerful shove, rolled off him, and clutched her nightdress to her bosom, quivering with shame. "No, Samuel." Her voice quaked; shoulders hunched, she murmured, "I can't. No. I won't. I can't."

Samuel put his hands beneath his head and sucked reflectively on his tooth. Ruth clung to her nightdress, plucking at the starched

17

lace, stammering, "I won't," and "I can't," not sure if she couldn't or wouldn't, and not caring.

She didn't even see him make the lunge, but the nightdress was torn from her arms and Samuel rolled on top of her. The flint and hardness of his body struck some tinder inside Ruth's bones. He said nothing placating, nothing tender, nothing soothing, only issued a series of hoarse instructions: which way to turn her head so he could pull the pins from her hair and loose it. She did what he said, and the dark hair spilled over the white counterpane. He kissed her throat and shoulders and lips until Ruth heard herself making hoarse noises that seemed to come from her guts. Her breasts burned and her arms burned as she wrapped them around his back, scraping her tender skin across his rough woolen underwear, and the blood seemed to leave her inner body and pulsate—every quart of it—up against her flesh. When Samuel told her to arch her back, she did, and when he told her to open her legs slowly, she did. A hard, foreign substance pressed against her where she was most vulnerable and had never known it. Samuel kissed her lips until they parted and he found her tongue and teeth, and then he said, "Take off your shoes."

Ruth did not say I can't or I won't. She said, "They're hooked."

Slowly Samuel slid down her body, kissed her as he went, leaving what seemed to be smoke down her skin and linen, and when he came to the fork between her legs, Ruth—eyes closed—found herself holding his head, not pushing, just holding and stroking his fine, fair hair.

He unhooked her shoes, and she heard them hit the floor one by one, heard him pad across the rug and turn out the gas, felt rather than heard him return to her and stand over the bed in darkness, felt rather than heard, certainly did not see, him remove the rest of his clothes. And her clothes. And after that, Samuel didn't have to issue any more instructions, because after that, Ruth's body knew what to do even if Ruth didn't.

In the early months of her marriage, those spent in Albert's room, Ruth permitted Samuel not just those intimacies a good wife relinquishes to her husband, but incursions, explorations of her body beyond the simple required act. And there were moments beyond simple pleasure, moments when Ruth cast off the shell of rational

18

being and became only sensation: quivering flesh and coursing blood. Samuel put his lips around words that Ruth had never spoken, and Samuel's hands discovered those places where her own hand never touched except in the interest of cleanliness.

She was troubled by difficult questions: could sin flourish even in holy wedlock? Was there some modesty demanded even in marriage? One afternoon she carefully consulted the Bible, the Book of Mormon, and the *Doctrine and Covenants*, but if the solutions were there, they were buried in parable and proverb, and Ruth hadn't the patience to sort through them. Ruth wanted to know hard answers: could a wife blamelessly caress what Samuel referred to as the rod or should she neither look nor touch? Ruth wanted to know if a wife ought to allow her husband to have her on the floor of the parlor where they were married, with an audience of stuffed animal heads and her semi-invalid mother upstairs and her brother due home from school any minute. Ruth wanted to know if a woman could sleep naked and still be decent. That's what Ruth wanted to know. After the fact, of course. These questions would never have occurred to her in a theoretical form.

She knew for certain she daily committed lust, albeit married lust, but she did not know for certain if lust was a sin one could commit without committing others. What Samuel did to and for her both satisfied that lust and begot new lust. She put an extra dollop of starch in the wash with her clothes, but that didn't keep them from sliding off her body the minute she and Samuel closed the door to Albert's room. At night, her wickedness was less troublesome. But during the day as she went about her daily round of keeping her father's house, she had occasion to think and blush alternately.

Without doubt, mornings and evenings were the worst. Family prayers. Abel insisted on them twice a day, and Ruth, who had always tolerated family prayers rather good-naturedly, discovered that her father was unbearably long-winded. It seemed to Ruth a waste of time and breath to tell God what He already knew; to discuss with Him the validity of the True Restored Gospel given unto Joseph Smith, the doctrine of baptism for the dead, the assumption of celestial estates, the powers of the priesthood handed down from father to son. To thank Jesus for not only having risen from the dead, but having come among the North American tribes before He retired to His Father's House. Indeed, Ruth reflected, listening to

19

Abel drone, not only did God know all that, but everyone assembled knew it, too. Ruth shut out her father's voice and used the time to implore God silently to quell her lust, grant her some modesty. Or both.

But God did not see fit to quell the lust. Throughout prayers Ruth could feel her very pores tighten as she looked across the family circle to Samuel, who was seemingly unaware of her, concentrating wholeheartedly on his devotions, oblivious to the flesh. Ruth's entire body began to spring leaks. Moisture pumped. The watch she wore suspended around her neck jumped and vibrated with her heartbeat. Ruth rounded her shoulders and leaned slightly forward so the watch would not betray her anxiety.

Or her anticipation. Because when they closed the door of Albert's room, Samuel—devoted Saint that he was—forgot all about God. He always wore the same smile at the corners of his mouth and his gray eyes gleamed and he was ready, at night or in the leaden light of a winter dawn, to spread what Ruth discovered were her wings, to expose that tiny mute tongue of flesh, pulsating before he ever laid his fingers to it.

One morning, still moist, warm, and swampy, Ruth put on her clothes and pulled back her hair and rushed downstairs to get the fire going. Breakfast, like prayer and everything else in the Mason household, followed a rigid schedule dictated by the undeviating taxidermist. The kitchen clock testified against her as Ruth blew into the fire and muttered her own prayers: "Please, God, let breakfast cook fast." She stoked up the oven to twice the heat she needed. She combined the lard, flour, and milk for biscuits, poured water over the oatmeal and set it on the back burner; she broke eggs into a bowl and seasoned them for ham cakes, and she was slicing white fat off a hambone when her mother unexpectedly entered the kitchen. Her mother had not been in the kitchen for ten years that Ruth could remember; Afton Mason never even got out of bed before her presence was required at family prayers, and even then she had to be roused and helped downstairs.

Afton Mason smiled weakly and closed the door behind her. Her fingers knotted around the ever-present hanky as she crept to her daughter's side. "Is he a beast, Ruth?" she whispered. "Is Samuel a beast?"

The knife slipped. Ruth cut herself, and blood spurted over the bone. She clutched her injured hand. "Please, Ma, go upstairs and wait for prayers, will you? Let me get breakfast on." She needn't have pleaded; Mrs. Mason was accustomed to doing as she was told, and she rustled slowly out of the kitchen in her voluminous wrapper.

The family gathered under the beady gaze of the balding moose at 7:00 a.m. sharp for morning prayer. Ruth was late, flushed and floury; she took her place and bowed her head. This morning Abel Mason took as his text the duties of Latter-day Saints with regard to prayer. Morning and evening and before every meal, of course, prayers were required, but the exemplary Saint should also pray before going to bed. Prayer before bed, he maintained, ensured that one would have only godly dreams. He cleared his throat and added that prayer before bed could also ensure that one approached one's duties and responsibilities in the proper frame of mind. And, he continued, if we enjoy our duties and responsibilities too much, do they not then lapse into something less laudable?

Ruth hustled back into the kitchen to find her particular prayer had not been answered. She brought out the soggy biscuits and underdone mush first. At the huge, heavy-legged dining table, Samuel sat, hands laced over his lap, glasses properly adjusted, staring at his empty plate. Equally taciturn at the head of the table, Abel Mason listened stoically to young Albert's vivid complaints about having to sleep on the kitchen cot.

Lily sighed, her face the hue of discolored porcelain, gray shadows under her blue eyes. Lily looked straight at her sister and said she hadn't been able to sleep a wink all night. Mrs. Mason wrung her hanky and said neither had she. Albert said if his mother and sister had to sleep where he did, they'd never get any rest, because there were mice in the kitchen and he never knew when one of them would run up the leg of the cot and leap into bed with him.

"Where's the rest of breakfast, Ruth?" her father asked.

"What's the matter with breakfast these days, anyway?" Albert piped up. "The eggs are always watery and the biscuits ain't done and the hash is still cold. I used to like breakfast. What's happened to it? Maybe if Sister Ruth can't—"

"Shut up, Albert," Abel commanded, and Albert shut up. "Your sister is a fine cook, and I'm sure the food will improve in the fullness of time." He consulted his watch. "We're waiting, Ruth."

21

Ruth had hoped for a little more fullness of time, but it was not to be had. She returned to the dining room with the half-baked dish wafting unconvincing steam and set it on the table. She took her place beside her husband and bowed her head, and as Abel Mason began his stentorian, well-rehearsed catalog of remorse and gratitude, Ruth opened her eyes to see her mother's face draped with unvarnished curiosity and her sister staring at her with a mixture of envy and contempt.

2

SAMUEL DOUGLASS BROUGHT his wife to Healy, Idaho, in the amber chill of a late-spring afternoon in 1890. At suppertime Healy's single street was deserted except for animals—a stray dog, a few chickens, some pigs wallowing in the drainage ditches that paralleled the dingy buildings and wooden walks. In front of the few stores and houses, planks crossed the muddy ditches. Dominating Healy, the Mormon church stood at the end of the street. Dismal and clapboarded like the rest of the town, at least it was painted and prim-looking, which was more than could be said for Fenwick's Farm and Home Supply right next door. Aside from the church, the most prosperous-looking establishments were Whickham's First Bank of Healy and Redbourne's Hotel, the latter having the distinction of Healy's only porch.

In front of this hotel Samuel called his team to a halt and jumped down from the wagon. His wife, dressed in a trim suit of traveling gray, sat in the wagon, staring into the sunset and the squalor. Samuel offered his hand and urged her down. "It ain't like Salt Lake," he said. "It ain't even National Falls."

"You said Healy was a town. You should have told me it was nothing but shacks in the wilderness."

"You go in. I'll bring your things. I got to tend to the horses."

As Ruth entered the hall of Redbourne's Hotel her hat very nearly brushed the ceiling. A long, imperfectly hewn plank served as front desk, and the walls were unfinished, chinked with plaster of Paris, one window of real glass, one of greased paper. Both doors opened on string latches. Over the makeshift desk hung a cheap picture print of Prophet Joseph Smith, founder of the Mormon Church, praying in the sacred grove, about to receive the golden tablets. The other wall boasted a picture of Smith meeting his death at the hands of the mob in the Carthage jail. Beneath the death scene, on a row of homely pegs, rough coats hung, suffusing the hall with the smell of too much wool, too long worn and too little washed.

"Well, you must be Sister Douglass!" A toothless woman with many chins and rolled-up sleeves burst in. "You're just in time for supper. You must be done under. That ride from National Falls, that's a rough one—and coming up from Salt Lake all by yourself! Ain't you the plucky one? And look at this." The woman fingered Ruth's jacket. "Velvet. My hands ain't touched velvet in fifteen years. Twenty maybe."

Ruth might have guessed as much. She flinched from Sister Redbourne, who introduced herself as she helped Ruth off with her jacket and hat and slung them on an empty peg. She led Ruth into another low-ceilinged room lit by a single overhead lamp that cast shadows into the faces of men seated at a table.

Sister Redbourne introduced her as Brother Douglass's wife. "Came by train all the way from Salt Lake to National Falls by herself, she did." The men nodded but did not stop eating. "Two years ago you couldn't do that, Sister Douglass. Two years ago there wasn't no railroad here at all. Why, just ten years ago we was a-still fighting off the Indians. Ain't that so, Brother Gibby?"

"That's so."

"That railroad is a blessing to this territory."

"A curse, too," Brother Gibby grumbled. "Lewdness, Chinese, and Gentiles go everywhere the railroad goes."

"Bishop Whickham told it true when he said we oughta be grateful the railroad went through National Falls and not through here. Healy don't need no more Gentiles than we got. Beggin' your pardon, gents." She nodded to the non-Mormon men at the end of the table. "Healy is a Latter-day Saint town. You mighta noticed, Sister Douglass." Her voice rang with confidential pride. "Healy don't have no saloon or fancy houses. The Word of Wisdom, the church's way, that's what we practice here. You can bring up your young ones here in the path of righteousness, the fear of the Lord and the light of the gospel. Now you just have a sit-down here on the bench, and I'll bring you some stew. You gents treat Sister Douglass nice."

The gents, six in number, ignored Ruth. She easily distinguished the two Gentile commercial travelers by their shiny black coats, frayed collars, and waxed mustaches, while the other four, Brother Gibby included, were rangy and bearded and themselves looked ramshackle and clapboarded.

"Throw me one of those 'ere biscuits, Sister," one of them asked, pointing to the plate in front of her. His beard, which was flaked with food, brushed the edge of the table. Ruth lifted the plate. "Just throw me one like I said."

Ruth had never thrown a biscuit in her entire life and did not intend to start at the request—or the demand—of an Idaho cur. She passed the plate down the whole row of men, who did not appreciate taking time from their troughs.

"Here you are." Sister Redbourne set a bowl of stew and a plate of biscuits before her. Thick puddles of grease floated in the stew, and as Ruth stirred it, bits of raw flour curdled at the top. She sipped tentatively. Peculiar and oversalted. "What's in the stew?"

"A little of this, a little of that." Sister Redbourne told Brother Gibby to move over and sat down across from Ruth. "Rabbit mostly."

Ruth set her spoon down.

"Brother Douglass says you graduated from high school."

"Yes."

"Ever been out of Salt Lake?"

"No, not till now."

"Well, it's pretty country up here, yes, it's that, but it can be hard, too. You, now you got good land. You just need some good weather and luck. Samuel Douglass is homesteading some of the best land in Monroe County. He's got water. Milk and honey don't flow out there, but water does, and that's the next best thing."

"Water's better'n milk and honey," Brother Gibby remarked.

"Yes, and I'll bet Brother Douglass has dug himself a nice little house."

"Dug himself?" Ruth's eyes widened.

"Why, Sister Douglass, all folks around here live in dugouts, least for the first six or seven years."

"Or ten or twelve," grunted Gibby.

"Some men got two dugouts," Sister Redbourne went on, "one for the stock and one for the family, and some got one for each wife, and some"—she winked at the local gents—"got a dugout for the old wife and a real house for the new wife! Though if you ask me," she collected herself, "the church is getting ready to leave plural marriage behind, disavow the Prophet's principle, and I say it was a revelation and we shouldn't be parting with it. Federal government or no federal government." Sister Redbourne scratched herself affectionately.

Ruth sat through this speech without hearing it. "I think you must be mistaken," she said, gently reprimanding Sister Redbourne. "Samuel has a house."

"A house in the ground." She snorted. "Now let's see, who's got a house? Bintons, they just built last—"

"You gonna eat that, Sister Douglass?" Brother Gibby asked.

"What?"

"You just taking a rest in between bites?"

"I guess I'm not hungry."

Gibby took her bowl and emptied it into his own.

"Biscuit, Sister?" said the unruffled Mrs. Redbourne.

Ruth sliced through the tough biscuit and buttered it in a way that seemed to strike everyone at the table into fascinated silence. When she brought it to her lips, the smell of the butter—old, strong, and nearly turned—assaulted her. She put it down untasted and said she wasn't hungry. Only tired.

The men left the table without excuses or regrets. Sister Redbourne leaned forward on her fat, bare arms, and they spread over the oilcloth. "In a year's time, Sister Douglass," she whispered, "you'll eat butter that crawls into your mouth. You mark my words."

"You should have told me the truth," Ruth murmured as she and Samuel lay in the spare, slope-roofed chamber in the hotel. "You said you had a house on that property."

Samuel rolled off her, and the coarse pillow ticking crunched as he lay back. "I think I'll build me a brick house. There's brick clay up there, least I think there is, and I got water, and I could do a good trade in bricks with a few ovens and a few—"

"You lied to me."

"That dugout is as good as a house."

"Not to me, it's not. I won't live in a dugout. You cannot expect me to live underground."

"I expect you to do your duty as my wife. Whither I goest. Don't forget your vows. You have your sacred oath to live with me and be my wife under God's holy ordinances."

"Not underground."

"If a dugout is good enough for every other woman in Monroe County, it's good enough for you. I heard of women up here been living in dugouts for ten years—and grateful for it."

"I'm not like them. I won't ever be like them."

"Maybe not." He shrugged. "You got no gratitude, Ruth. No gratitude and too much pride. You got to ask the Lord to deliver you from your pride."

"First I'll ask Him to deliver me from a liar."

Samuel suppressed a chuckle. "You got spirit, Ruth, I'll give you that. You got spirit and more fire than I woulda guessed. You got brimstone in your bones, Ruth, and I wisht I'da known that when I married you."

"I wish I'd known you were a liar when I married you."

Samuel rolled over, his lean buttocks pressed against her naked thigh. "It wouldn't have made no difference. You still woulda married me. And you know it."

Ruth lay awake, listening to Samuel make occasional noises with his teeth even as he slept. She crossed her hands over her bosom and closed her eyes. " 'I'm a pilgrim, I'm a stranger.' " She tunelessly intoned the old hymn. Cast upon the rocky shore indeed. She had never in all her life slept anywhere but under Abel Mason's solid roof, and here she lay in the wilderness beside a stranger whose roof was made of dirt, who had lied to her and who—she chilled at the marrow—might yet have other lies lurking at his heart or lips. He was her husband: the vows could not be unsaid, and she could not cast this burden upon the Lord. This burden would have to be borne until it was born.

She moved her hands down over her belly. Because she was this burden's vessel, her father had insisted that she ride the train from

Salt Lake to National Falls. He had said she should not have to endure two hundred miles in a springless wagon; he had said the jolting, smoky train was bad enough for a woman in the family way. Samuel had said that pioneer women crossed the plains; some of them even walked and pushed handcarts while they were in the family way. But since Abel was willing to pay Ruth's train fare, Samuel packed his supplies in the wagon and left by himself in early April.

Three weeks later Abel Mason took Ruth to the train, carried in her maroon carpetbag and her valise, and put them on the seat beside her. He kissed his daughter's cheek. "You're a grown woman now, Ruth."

"I've been a grown woman for a long time, Pa."

"But now you have a woman's duties, a woman's privilege. Motherhood is the greatest honor God bestows on a woman."

"Oh, Pa, stop it. God didn't bestow this on me, Samuel did."

Abel Mason broke into beads of sweat. "You must curb your tongue. You must learn to—" The train's whistle cut through his last admonition.

"Are you going to miss me, Pa?" She clutched at his hand. "Are you and Ma and Lily and Albert, are you going to miss me?"

"Of course, my girl. But don't you give us another thought. You're going off to your new life. You're a married woman now."

"All aboard!"

"You write when the little one is born." He wrung her hand. "I hope—I hope, Ruth—I hope . . ."

"What are you trying to say, Pa?"

He was a man accustomed only to speaking his mind, not his heart; the words strangled at the edge of his tongue. "I hope it's easier for you, Ruth. I hope you don't have it so bad as your mother did. I hope—" The train began to move. Abel released her hand, said goodbye, and bolted.

"Goodbye, Pa," Ruth said after him.

"Goodbye, Pa," she whispered into the darkness of the squalid hotel room.

As Ruth got out of bed and crossed the bare floor, Samuel groaned and tossed. She opened the maroon carpetbag and took out her nightdress, the one that had been neither washed nor worn since the day of her wedding. She drew it over her head, buttoned it to the

27

neck, and got back into bed. The starch in the nightdress smelled wonderfully familiar—redolent of the plenitude and stability of her father's home. But not quite comforting. Because with the first wash, the smell would be gone, of course, and Ruth's Salt Lake life behind her forever.

The next morning Ruth and Samuel breakfasted at the Redbourne table with some of the same men. Breakfast was equally unappealing, but despite her queasiness, Ruth managed to get down a few bites. Then she waited on the porch while Samuel brought the wagon around. A spring chill laced the air, but Ruth no longer wore her black velvet jacket, just a rust-colored shawl tied about the shoulders of a drab calico. She got into the wagon, spurning Samuel's aid, rode the ten miles north to the Douglass homestead, and then got out of the wagon without his aid as well.

"You'll want to come have a look at the dugout," Samuel said.

"What makes you think so?"

"You can't stand here till the conversion of the Jews, Ruth. You got work. You got mortal duties like everyone else." He went around to the back of the wagon and took out two heavy bags, one of flour, one of oats; he threw them over his shoulders and bent under the burden. His lip arched, and he sucked at the imaginary particle that had been stuck between his teeth for years. "The dugout's just over that rise."

She watched him walk out over land that did not look any improved for its being his. In the insufferable quiet Ruth heard Samuel's steps crack through the brush and the wind rustle through scrawny aspens just breaking into April green; it swayed the thick pines and rattled in the brush—sagebrush, greasewood, rabbit brush, and dirt dirt dirt as far as the eye could see. As Samuel disappeared over the rise, Ruth guessed that more of the same lay beyond that, too. A time and all eternity of work before her, and after that, to be laid in the same ragged ground. As she surveyed the terrain she'd married, she fervently hoped that Jesus would keep His appointment with mankind, usher in the last days, judge the quick and the dead. Very soon. Nothing less than Judgment itself would spare her the certain battle ahead. She hoped her family would never see what she had come to. If she must be humiliated, she preferred no witnesses.

The wind snapped at Ruth's hem and mud caked her boots as, clutching the maroon carpetbag, she followed Samuel up the rise. The earth did not give way underfoot, not in this unsoftened land with no human history. But Ruth recognized the moment for what it was. Henceforth she must shed all the genteel accessories of the young lady of the 1880s and fight Samuel on this, his own ground. If this was the beginning, it was also the end.

3

SAMUEL AND RUTH Douglass began their independent married life in a tiny two-roomed dwelling, six feet high and carved out of the hillside, supported front and back by unfinished timbers, the beams chinked with mud and sticks. Ruth was forcibly reminded of its squalor every time she had to stoop in the doorframe. The door itself was of indifferently slatted wood, and on good days, sunlight sprinkled through it to the packed-earth floor. On bad days, snow sifted in. A bunchgrass mattress tossed over a wood frame and leather lacings provided their bed, and two trunks the foundation for shelving. A small, inefficient iron stove, its chimney thrust through a hole cut in the roof, gave such heat as there was. It was not comfortable, it was barely sufficient, but it was better than the dugout Samuel had built for the horses, where the roof caved in twice in as many years. And Samuel and Ruth were not without amenities. They had two benches for the table, a porcelain washbasin, and several buckets; a rocking chair sat near the stove, a row of new earthenware jars gleamed in the dull light, and thrust in the corner, waiting for its moment, was a cradle for the child who was expected in October.

In front of this dugout the taxidermist's daughter skinned her first rabbit and vomited uncontrollably in the process. She fed her first chickens, checked them for lice, and wrung their necks with her own hands. She hung them up and let their blood drip into the dust. She kept a hog and fenced him out of her newly planted kitchen garden with barbed wire wound on stakes she pounded into the ground herself. She made renovating soap from alcohol, beef gall, and turpentine. She made vinegar from corn and dye from nutgalls. She fought roaches with hot alum water, rats with lime and tar, ants with cayenne pepper, and bedbugs with quicksilver and egg whites. She let her skirts out to accommodate the burgeoning baby and wore Samuel's flannel shirts instead of a bodice. When the fringed bangs on her forehead grew out, she pulled her hair into a knot at the top of her head.

She bowed her head and joined Samuel in morning prayers, but in the evening she was too tired. She simply knelt and listened to her husband, whose voice rang with conviction, not at all like Abel Mason's monotonous monologues. Samuel discussed salvation with the Lord instead of simply asking for it. He verified Scripture with Him instead of simply reciting it. No prophecy was too great, no proverb too small to merit Samuel's (or God's) attention. But eventually Ruth found that his prayers were composed of too many verily verilies and not enough amens. One night Samuel interrogated God on the meaning of Nebuchadnezzar's dream, but Ruth rose from her knees and fell into the bunchgrass mattress. She was asleep by the time Samuel called his wife's defection to the Lord's attention.

Ruth herself hoped God was not watching her too closely, though she explained to Him (out of Samuel's hearing) that she was a believing Saint, a practicing Saint, as good a Saint as ever, but she dreaded the Sabbath because she detested the Healy Saints. She found them dull, ugly, vulgar, and not as clean as they might have been. She feared it might be catching.

Samuel, by contrast, seemed to thrive in their company. After he baptized Sister Redbourne's eight-year-old grandson and Sister Redbourne swore she saw a white dove fly over his head, Samuel's reputation for patriarchal magnetism preceded him. He grew a patriarchal beard. The elders, and Bishop Whickham himself, counseled Sister Redbourne that white doves were neither possible nor desirable, but nothing would make her retract her testimony. Thereafter, Samuel was much in demand for baptisms and whenever illness required a family to call in the elders for a laying on of the hands. Samuel was one of three members of the priesthood who laid their hands on the head of Sister Evans as she and her baby lay dying after a breech birth. Sister Evans and her child died, but Brother Evans came to Samuel and brought with him a ham to thank Samuel for the inspired way he had prayed over the doomed woman.

And when Samuel rose to bear his testimony (as he did at every monthly testimony meeting) a hush descended over the Saints. Samuel removed his glasses slowly, braced himself against the pew, and lifted his sonorous voice, imploring God to visit His mercy and bestow His blessings on Healy, Idaho, and thanking God for the many blessings they all enjoyed. Among his own blessings, Samuel always counted his wife, his forthcoming child, and the water that flowed through his land.

His wife, for her part, never offered testimony. Answer not a fool according to his folly, she thought, lest thou also be like him. Who but fools would be grateful to live in dugouts and skin rabbits? A life of degradation and thankless servitude. She would keep her own counsel, thank you. But the Bible offers many lessons, and it was not long after this that Ruth, to her great bitterness, was reminded of another Biblical proverb: As it happeneth to the fool, so it happeneth even to me.

On a hot Saturday afternoon in August, Ruth stood at the counter of Fenwick's Farm and Home Supply. Smells of leather, seed, cheese, and stout cloth pervaded the store. Brother Fenwick was busy with Sister Gibby, so Ruth waited patiently with her broken harness and her list of supplies.

"What can I do for you, Sister Douglass?" asked Fenwick. He was a skinny, officious man, about fifty.

"I need a new harness. Just like this one."

He inspected the harness. "I'll have to climb up and get one. You rest yourself, Sister Douglass. A woman in your condition should rest whenever possible."

Ruth was sitting on a nearby barrel, scraping the dried dung from her boots, when over the sea of inflectionless voices she heard Sister Redbourne call her name.

"No, don't stand up, Sister." Sister Redbourne bore down on her. With her huge, flapping fat arms, she reminded Ruth of a fleshy crow. "That little one is coming right along, isn't he?"

31

"Yes," said Ruth wearily, rising all the same. She reminded herself of a pregnant scarecrow.

"I saw your husband in the bank the other day, and I said to him, Brother Douglass, why don't your wife join us for Relief Society meetings? And your husband said to me, I've asked her that myself, many times, Sister Redbourne. That's what he said. The Bible tells us a godly husband requireth a godly wife."

"I don't recall anywhere in the Bible where it says that," Ruth retorted.

"I expect it's the spirit of the thing, Sister Douglass. But your husband says it's so, and he says you should go to Relief Society meetings, but he says it would take the tongues of men and angels to make you do it."

"Did he?"

"I said that just a little common sense would bring you around. You don't do nothing for the church, Sister, but come on Sunday, and the church asks more of—"

"I haven't been well." Ruth could feel the gaze of every Saint and Gentile in Fenwick's Farm and Home glued to her.

"Not well!" Sister Redbourne patted Ruth's belly, blooming under one of Samuel's flannel shirts. "A little one don't mean you're not well!"

"I am too busy."

"Remember, you always want to think about storing up your treasures in heaven as well as on earth."

Treasures indeed. "Thank you," Ruth replied crisply. "For reminding me."

Ruth started past her, but the older woman did not budge, and rather than turn or back away, Ruth pulled herself to her full height and stared down into Sister Redbourne's face, which gleamed with sweat and righteousness. Half-moons of sweat darkened her clothes at the arms and collar, and her neck was dusky with dirt. Her hair, matted and oily-looking, was wound in a knot at the top of her head, and she smelled of grease—animal grease, axle grease, and lard. "Excuse me." Ruth pushed her aside and made her way toward the bolts of new cloth at the other end of the store.

"The Bible tells it true," Sister Redbourne called after her loudly. "When pride cometh, then cometh shame."

A general assent rippled through the room. How dare they?

32

Dirty, squalid little souls. She stalked back to Sister Redbourne. "If you are referring to me, you sanctimonious, vulgar, dirty—publican!—then you are wasting your foul-smelling breath. I have absolutely nothing to be ashamed of."

Sister Redbourne inspected a new cast-iron fry pan. "That's true, Sister Douglass. But you got nothing to be proud of anymore, either, have you?"

Ruth drank in the smug glances of the other customers, their dusty, grim faces, soiled cuffs, and sweat-stained hatbands. Their hateful, reflectionless eyes.

The harness clattered on the counter behind her. "Your harness, Sister Douglass," said Fenwick.

Ruth paid cash and bought nothing else, nor did she wait for him to wrap it. She marched out of the Farm and Home Supply with her pulse pounding in her ears, her very bones constricted with loathing. She eased her ungainly body into the wagon and directed the team up the north road out of Healy. She bit into her lower lip until she was halfway home, then she dropped the reins and wept into her calloused hands till trails of dirt and tears ran down her wrists. She wiped her nose on the hem of her skirt. Vulgar. It was vulgar to wipe your nose on your skirt. She had grown every bit as dull, ugly, and vulgar as the people she despised.

Ruth was composed, however, and sitting in the rocker that evening when Samuel came back from the would-be brickyard, his boots caked with clay, his hands full of figures scratched on cheap paper, his guts rumbling for supper.

"I am not going to church tomorrow, Samuel," she announced, "nor the next Sunday nor the Sunday after that. And I won't go into town anymore either. If you need supplies, you'll just have to get them yourself."

Samuel ladled out some water and splashed his face and neck. "Remember the Sabbath and keep it holy."

"I'll keep it holy, but I won't go to church or anywhere else until after this baby is born. I will not be seen in public wearing skirts I have to hold up with suspenders and a man's shirt and a man's hat to keep the sun off my face. It's humiliating and I won't do it."

"Vanity and vexation of the spirit," Samuel replied. "The Saints know what it is for a woman to be with child."

"I don't give a pig's whistle what they know. I'm not going anywhere until after the baby is born, and there's an end to it." She recognized her own voice delivering one of Abel Mason's decrees.

For prayers that Saturday evening Samuel took as text I Corinthians. "Knowledge puffeth up, but charity edifieth," he said. In his petition he stressed his own charity and forbearance, his goodness of spirit in dwelling with Ruth despite her willfulness and vanity. "The unbelieving wife is sanctified by the husband." Though he rattled on, Ruth remained unmoved. The following day he went to church without her.

Ruth spent her Sunday mornings in devotions of her own. She pulled the rocker outside in the sun and sang her favorite hymns softly while she sewed things for the baby. She had a strong, flat voice; the chorus was often picked up and carried by the wind.

One Sunday in September while Samuel was detained in Healy for a priesthood meeting, Sister Binton came to call to offer her services as midwife when Ruth's time came. "I know you'd rather have your mother with you at such a time," Sister Binton began, "but God grants us what He knows is best."

Ruth threaded her needle judiciously and knotted her thread. "My mother would not come to Idaho if I died, Sister Binton. She hasn't been out of her room, hasn't lifted more than a hanky to her lips, since my brother, Albert, was born twelve years ago. My mother almost died with Albert. I was there. I heard her. She wanted to die."

"You won't die, if that's troubling your heart," Sister Binton assured her. "All women fear death their first time, but it gets easier with each child. Less pain. Less fear."

"What about Sister Evans? That baby was her third."

"When God calls us, we must go. But that was a very great tragedy. Still, I've had five of my own, and I've birthed many times that in this county."

"Is it terrible, Sister Binton?" Ruth dropped her needle and the flannel she was hemming and fastened her eyes on Sister Binton's plain freckled face. "Is it as terrible for everyone as it was for my mother? No one tells you, do they? They should tell you how terrible it's going to be."

"The pain of childbirth is our penance for our sins, Sister Douglass, our penance for being human."

"I thought death was the price we paid for being human."

"There is no death in the Lord."

"Hmph." Ruth took up her sewing again. "It seems to me that childbirth is our penance for being female and fools. Better a felon than a fool."

Sister Binton gathered her skirts around her lest Ruth's words fall nearby and soil them. "You will feel differently when your little one gets here. A baby touches its mother's heart as nothing else. Children are worth any sacrifice. They are a blessing."

"Even if they're born underground like beasts?"

"Remember, Sister, Jesus was born in a manger."

"Yes, but He didn't live there."

Sister Binton took a deep breath. "God don't send us any burdens we can't bear, and besides, Sister Douglass, I heard your husband talking in church this morning about his brickyard. He says he will build the first brick house in Monroe County. Brother Douglass is such a—"

"—fool. Why does everyone in the county think he's turning water into wine just because he says he's going to make bricks? It's a fool's errand, all this brick business. He ought to plant cash crops, wheat and sugar beets, but no, he puts in a few turnips and some corn and then goes off to squat in the mud and watch the horse churn up clay like it was going to turn to butter. And now he's gone to Whickham's bank and put up the corn crop, the wagon, the horses, the hog, and every cent my father gave me when I married him against a loan for some ovens and molds. We'll be living in the fields next summer. And if that ain't enough—" Ruth coughed and corrected herself. "If that's not enough, he takes the other cash-crop field and plants fruit trees that won't bring in anything for years. He says there's a Timber Culture Act—if you plant more trees, you get more land. Who wants more land? Who wants more trees? What are we supposed to do? Eat apples till they dribble from our—"

"I have to go, Sister Douglass. Lars will be expecting me." Sister Binton rose and made her way quickly to the door. "But when your time comes, you just send Brother Douglass over to fetch me and I'll be here."

When Samuel went to fetch Sister Binton, Ruth's labor had only just commenced, but Samuel said she should come right now, because he had to leave for National Falls. The ovens and molds he'd ordered from Chicago had come in. As she rode back to the dugout with Samuel, Sister Binton remarked that it seemed mighty heartless to leave his wife at such a time.

Samuel sucked on his tooth so hard his face gave a tic. "I done my part for this baby, Sister Binton. The rest is up to Ruth."

Ruth did her part. Sister Binton did her part. Samuel's daughter, Eden, was born while he was in National Falls. Eden was born healthy, but not till thirteen hours of labor had passed and not till Ruth herself had passed blood, urine, and excrement and fainted twice from the pain, and had to be revived so she could get on with it. Then was Eden born.

She entered the family Bible in Ruth's own flourishing, still-schoolgirl hand: Eden Douglass (so named for her paternal grandmother), October 23, 1890.

Sister Binton was right; Eden touched her mother's heart in ways Ruth had never expected. She wondered if as a baby she, Ruth, had ever moved her mother to such love and delight. She could not remember Afton Mason ever demonstrating either. Ruth was so smitten with her daughter, she was dismayed, then sorry, then angry to discover she was pregnant again when Eden was not yet six months old.

But Sister Binton was also wrong: each birth was not easier. Ruth suffered a painful miscarriage, but the following year she bore Gideon Douglass (named for his paternal grandfather). She was months recuperating from Gideon, especially since none of her other duties could be delayed or transferred to other hands or shoulders. So it was no surprise to Sister Binton that the following child—Afton, entered in the family Bible February 17, 1893—brought her mother to a pitch of agony Sister Binton in all her years of midwifing had never witnessed.

Sister Binton damped a cloth and mopped the perspiration from Ruth's brow. "Hush," she said futilely. "It gets easier with each one. You must believe that. Less pain. Less fear."

"Don't say that again!" Ruth shrieked. "I'd rather die and take this child with me than to hear you say that again!" She took deep convulsive breaths and lay back on the bed awaiting the next surge of pain. Fleetingly she thought of her mother's camphor-smelling chamber, her mother lying prostrate for sixteen years. Afton Mason would never leave that bed alive. We get born in bed, Ruth thought, grinding her teeth as the contractions began anew, married off and borne to bed, brought to childbed, and leave the bed only for the grave.

Afton Douglass, named for Ruth's mother, was born five hours later.

For all the agonies of childbirth, Ruth found motherhood rewarding. She would not have believed that duty could be sweetened with purpose or diluted with love. Her pleasure in her children— Eden, dark and serious like Ruth, Gideon, and baby Afton, with Samuel's fair hair, gray eyes, and long mouth—grew as her children grew. Though Eden, Gideon, and Afton were often dressed in outgrown, worn-out, or cut-down clothes, they were fearfully clean. Ruth saw to that. When they went to church, they smelled of starch.

When Ruth went to church, not only did she reek of starch, but she flaunted her black velvet jacket even after it had become threadbare. She still refused to bear her testimony, and she maintained her distance from the Healy Saints, who, in Ruth's eyes, continued to be dull, ugly, vulgar, and not as clean as they might be. She never again spoke to Sister Redbourne or acknowledged her presence in any way, even when the woman stood before her. Samuel apologized to Sister Redbourne for Ruth's lack of charity and forbearance. Ruth did not speak to Samuel or acknowledge *his* presence for a week after that.

During evening devotions, Samuel often commented pointedly on Ruth's shortcomings, not only her lack of charity and forbearance, but her lack of delight in a wife's earthly duties.

"Render unto Caesar," she retorted angrily one night as she got up off her knees. If God wasn't bored with Samuel's litany, she was.

Samuel put his glasses back on. "What has Caesar to do with—"

"You heard me," she snapped. "You talk it over with God and maybe He'll explain it to you!" Ruth had discovered that Samuel was best fought with Biblical injunction, however random, much as her father had been best fought with the prospect of debate.

But if Biblical injunction closed Samuel's lips for the time being, it did not still his hands. He continued trying to get and beget upon Ruth. He had very persuasive hands.

Ruth Mason Douglass never forgot that she was not meant to live like this, but her days assumed a rhythm that dulled her pain, leav-

37

ing her pride intact. She lived in perpetual process, her obligations never complete, seldom savored, rarely relished: beans soaking, bread rising, irons heating, soap cooking, dyes setting, flannels stretching, the ever-boiling caldron just outside the dugout door continually filled with laundry, her own family's and that of other people. She did a brisk trade in laundry and hated it. Even without the laundry, there was vinegar fermenting, rain collecting, eggs and fruit to be preserved, water to be hauled, hogs to be slaughtered and smoked, their feet and ears and heads boiled till the flesh fell from the bones. There were whooping cough, croup, thrush, and worms to be fought off in the children, and the incessant demands of stomachs—her family's and the hired men's—stewing, steaming, baking, pickling, plucking chickens and skinning rabbits, process without product, all of it circular and incessant, performed without hope of reward or achievement.

4

RUTH RAISED HER eyes from the caldron of cooking clothes to see a figure walking up from the Healy road, a man, framed in fire by the sunset. She squinted into the glare, but smoke from the laundry fires rose up and clouded her vision. Behind her, shirts, flannels, and petticoats swung from stout lines that stretched between the pines and a half-dozen buckets lined up single-file. She wrung out muslin sheeting by the yard and draped it over the line. Probably another drifter who wants a job, she thought. Samuel was forever hiring men to help in the brickyard, but he would hire only the godly, and most drifters quickly proved themselves ungodly.

The stranger was a big man whose shoulders seemed too narrow for the rest of his frame; a gray beard shrouded his otherwise youthful face. He surveyed her from behind thick glasses, approached with his hand out, and took her hand without waiting for her to dry it. "You must be Sister Ruth. Yes, you must."

"And who might you be?" she asked, taking her hand back; he had wrung it with alarming power. He sucked his teeth and smelled of licorice.

"I'm Fred Douglass, Sister Ruth, Samuel's brother, Fred. I'm pleased to meet you."

"I didn't know Samuel had a brother."

"I didn't know Samuel had a wife till I come to Healy."

"Hmph, Healy," Ruth grunted. She stirred the clothes with a stick. Fred Douglass took off his jacket, walked to the woodpile, and picked up the ax; standing the logs on end, he split them in sure, rhythmic strokes. Ruth noted that the brothers had the same bad vision, though Samuel now wore his glasses, inexplicably, only for prayer. But where Samuel was lean, Fred was rounded; Samuel's beard grew stringy and untended, and Fred's, by contrast, was clipped and curling, though his hair was unkempt and his hands— great, powerful hands hanging from arms that were too short— were seamed with dirt.

"Where do you want these, Sister Ruth?" He stood in a pile of split logs.

"Inside by the fireplace."

"That's a fine-looking chimney," said Fred, regarding the neat brick structure, sturdier than the entire dugout. "Samuel do that?"

"Who else?" She threw some cotton goods in a bucket of salt water to set the colors before washing.

"Samuel always did have a way with things. He was always real clever, Samuel was."

"You have any other kin?" she asked, afraid that Fred might be the first of many hungry Douglasses.

He shook his head. "No, me and Samuel is orphans. Our ma died long ago, and Pa, he's dead, too, I reckon. We had some half brothers and sisters once, but we don't know nothing about them. I ain't even seen Samuel since—well, since a long time."

"You come from Idaho, too?"

"No, Montana, mostly. Mostly Montana." Fred studied the blade of the ax, testing it with his fingers. "Samuel has done all right for himself. Nice chimney. Nice wife. Nice—you got young ones?"

"Three of them."

"Yes, Samuel has done all right."

"Hmph. You must be a bigger fool than he is. You'd better leave the logs here after all. I want to finish by sundown. Looks like rain tonight."

Fred scanned the sky, where the clouds themselves resembled mounds of unwashed laundry piled high against the sunset. "It's a nice chimney, that one. Looks to be a nice-drawing fireplace, too. I don't believe I seen one like it around here."

"You won't, either. Samuel tells me I ought to be grateful for that fireplace. Build me a brick house, then I'll be grateful, and not till then." She rummaged through the basket and pulled out a pair of men's pants.

Fred watched her pick up a sawed-off broom and whip the dust out of those pants as though the man might still be in them. She was a handsome woman, he decided. Her face was smooth, but neither young nor old, her eyes were black as two coals in flour, and her mouth was pinched as a piecrust. She's as tall as Samuel himself, Fred thought, and when she unpins that black hair, it's probably a sight to behold.

"I told him, don't expect any gratitude out of me as long as I'm still hanging over this laundry pot. What do I care that they might be putting up a brick schoolhouse or that the Saints want a brick church or that National Falls thinks they deserve a brick railroad station? What do I care as long as I have to wash other people's clothes? It's not as if I don't have enough to do. I got three children and my brother, Albert, visiting besides. That's an extra mouth." She didn't mention Fred's extra mouth, but he worked his licorice just the same. "It would be a whole day's work just cooking for them, let alone taking in the clothes of newcomers, Gentiles who never cleaned a kid glove, let alone got chicken blood out of wool."

Fred was ready to pick up the ax again when the narrow slatted door of the dugout opened and out came a man, tall and broad-shouldered with dark hair thinning at the top. But Fred's bad eyes deceived him, and as he peered more closely, he found the man had a boy's beardless face with darting, inquisitive eyes set too close together. He had a piece of pie in one hand and a chicken leg in the other.

"You shouldn't take things in trade, Ruth," he said, eyeing Fred dubiously. "Cash. Cash on the barrelhead, that's what I say."

40

"He didn't come here to get his clothes washed," Ruth replied, resting her hands on her hips.

The boy ambled up to Fred. "You come here to work? I hope so, because if Samuel don't get another hired man soon, I'll die before September. He'll work me to death."

"Not if you keep eating the way you do," Ruth said.

"Well, I'd rather die than spend my days working for Samuel Douglass. Work and pray, that's all he knows. He don't quit praying but to work and he don't quit working but to pray. You wonder when he eats and pees."

"This is Fred Douglass, Albert, Samuel's brother. I don't think Fred cares when Samuel eats and pees. Albert is my brother, just up here paying us a little visit. My father sent him up for the summer, for a corrective holiday, you might say, but Albert's not saying what he did to get sent up here, are you, Albert?"

Albert flushed, sat on the log pile, and applied himself to the chicken leg. "They could empty out the prisons and send them up here, and in a week they'd all shriek to go back behind bars. Prison's better than working for Samuel Douglass and living underground like animals. And not no noble animals either." Albert gnawed on his pie. "Sniveling little burrowing ferrety animals."

"You better watch your tongue, Albert." Ruth took the cotton goods out of the bucket and put them in the tub. "The last time you went on like that, Samuel boxed your ears for you."

"Can he hear me now? Can he? Ain't he down in the brickyard hip-deep in mud? How come everyone in these parts thinks Samuel Douglass is so smart? Can you answer me that?" He tossed the chicken bone over his shoulder.

"Samuel always was real clever," Fred replied helplessly. "Had a way with things, Samuel did."

"What's clever about mud and water? What's clever about a bunch of fruit trees? If he's so smart, why don't he turn it all into capital? It's capital, that's the way the world is going."

"Capital what?" asked Fred.

"Shut up, Albert," said Ruth, sinking her arms back into the laundry tub.

Albert wiped his hands on his pants. "Well, all I can say is, if you think Samuel'll give you an easy deal because you're his brother, you can walk right back to Healy—you are walking, aren't you? You

41

don't have the look of a man with a horse—and not trouble my sister for supper."

"That'll be enough, Albert. I see you helped yourself to some supper already."

"If I'm going to get worked like a Chinee, I got to eat."

"I don't see you working."

"The Sabbath begins at sundown."

"Today's Tuesday. Now go in and check the baby and make sure she don't fall in the fire and send Eden out here with the renovating soap."

Albert groaned and got up, and after he left them, Ruth turned to Fred. "Don't mind Albert," she said.

"Oh, I wouldn't. I can see he's just a boy. He don't mean no harm."

"I'm not sure of that, but don't pay him any mind anyway, and don't be telling Samuel what he said."

"Oh, I don't tell Samuel nothing, Sister Ruth. I never have."

"Why?" She stirred the laundry pot and stepped back from the steam. "Has he always been like this?"

"Like what, Sister Ruth?"

She shrugged and turned her back to him.

A small, shoeless girl came out of the dugout. She was pale, with crisp, curling dark hair, and she carried the jar of renovating soap. A toddler dressed in a long, coarse sack followed her. "And who have we here?" Fred put on his jacket as though he had to be formally attired to greet them.

"That's Eden and Gideon," said Ruth.

Fred's eyes lit. "Why, that's just like—"

"Yes, yes," Ruth replied wearily, "like your ma and pa."

"Well, well." Fred squatted down to their height. "Eden and Gideon, it is a real pleasure to meet you. Why don't you just come here and have a look in my pockets and see what you find. Come on. Well, look at that. Nice licorice bits." Fred took a piece himself, and the three of them stood face to face, eyeballing each other, chewing.

Ruth put a glop of renovating soap in the wash water. When she looked up again, Fred had swung both children to the top of the woodpile and their lips were black with licorice, their eyes wide with admiration. Fred picked up the ax again, chips flew, and the blade flashed as Fred split logs and the evening quiet.

* * *

Fred's story emerged gradually, the unsavory facts surrounding his departure from Montana. Fred had left his wife. He had just walked out one day after he had beat her around a little bit. (After this came out, Ruth reassessed his grip on the ax and the effortless twist he gave the chicken's neck.) He had beaten Velda up—blacked her eyes and broke her nose—just after beating her lover within an inch of his life. Fred had left Montana not knowing if the senseless, naked man he'd thrown in the corner was alive or dead, but figured him to have lived, since there was never a warrant out for Fred's arrest for murder. All of that within some twenty minutes after he had caught them in the throes of adultery in his own bed.

It took the whole summer of 1893 for this story to come out, bit by bit, and by that time Ruth was certain that young Albert had an earful of it and would take it back to Salt Lake along with the grim picture of the hardscrabble life his sister led. No use telling young Albert to keep his mouth shut; Albert's mouth was seemingly never shut, not eating, not sleeping. It was hard to say who was the more intolerable, Albert or the slow-witted, slow-footed Fred.

In September of 1893, Albert took his unshakable sneer, his snoring, and whatever stories he cared to tell back to Salt Lake, and Ruth would have insisted that Fred leave, too, but she found his presence convenient. Ruth refused to let Samuel lay a hand on her while that owl-eyed Fred lay behind the ragged blanket partition. She assumed that God would understand that no decent woman would lie with a man—even her own husband—with that great lug Fred lying sleepless and watchful nearby.

Sometimes Samuel simply growled his disapproval, rolled over, and went to sleep. Sometimes he got out of bed to pray because he wanted God to know that Ruth had refused to perform her earthly duties. Occasionally, however, Samuel leaned over her so she could see his long mouth and his gray eyes even in the unlit dugout. His hands, his lulling, insistent hands, traced the swell of her breast and the slope of her neck, and her mind fell into the morass of her body. He tugged the nightdress up over her head and it fell to the packed-earth floor.

After those nights when she succumbed, Ruth tasted bitter brick dust on her lips for days. She hated Samuel because she knew he enjoyed her chagrin as much as he had enjoyed her body. But she

43

hated Fred, too, because Fred was the half-blind and silent witness to her weakness and Fred, she was certain, kept his gaze more firmly glued to the ground, grew quieter and more unobtrusive yet. Like all truly proud people, Ruth despised the meek.

Fred was so meek he asked for nothing, save his bits of licorice and a few pennies now and then to use in magic tricks he performed for the children. He drew the pennies out of their ears. He did whatever the children asked of him, whatever Samuel asked of him, whatever Ruth asked of him, and he did it doggedly. He sat in awe of his sister-in-law's energy, her sharp tongue, and her cooking. He lived in awe of Samuel's business intuition, his seeming intimacy with the Deity, and his inspiring prayers. Sometimes Samuel's prayers, particularly those that stressed our sin-riddled nature, moved Fred to an anguished examination of his own past, which, save for his beating up of Velda and her lover, had been virtually blameless. He thought maybe he ought to leave his brother's family and go find his wife, but Eden and Gideon wept when he talked about going, and so he said he would stay till the Healy church was built. Until the peaches were in. Until the apples were in. Until the National Falls railway station was built. Until the grain elevator was finished. Until he couldn't stand his own sinfulness any longer.

"It was wrong what I done," he said to Samuel one night after evening prayers while Ruth was putting the children to bed.

"You had cause to do what you did," Samuel replied, running his fingernail between his teeth. "A woman who takes another man into bed is an adulteress. Velda deserved to get beat up. She was a whore."

"I won't have that word spoken in my presence," said Ruth, pulling the blanket partition behind her. She walked to the fireplace, and lit a match, and it burned blue till she put it to the wick; the smell of sulfur and kerosene floated briefly overhead, and then Ruth rolled up her sleeves and poured hot water over the dishes.

Fred was whittling a wooden doll for Afton, to match the one he'd made for Eden. He popped an extra bit of licorice in his mouth and kept his eyes on his hands.

"A whore is a whore," Samuel said solemnly. "The Bible says a woman who fornicates is a whore."

"And what about the man?" Ruth bit back. "The man caught in adultery. What is he?"

"The Bible don't say nothing about him."

Fred intervened quickly—as he had learned to do. "I wasn't speaking of that per-ticular sinfulness, not when I raised my hand against—when I beat Velda up like I done, though I prayed for forgiveness for that one, Samuel, and I think God might be willing to let that go, though He don't give me any kind of sign like He does for you. But I was meaning the sin after that—I shouldn't have left. The church says marriage is for time and all eternity, a—what did you call it?"

"A solemn ordinance. A covenant. An oath. A vow." Samuel spoke as though he were spitting his words in a cup, the better to see them.

"Yes." Fred whittled furiously. "That's what I mean. You got to be true to your vows. You give your word when you get married, and if you break your word, why you're shamed ever after. Ain't that so?"

"Giving vows and living vows are two different things," said Ruth as she scrubbed a ten-pound fry pan. "One is easy and one isn't. You give them because you don't know any better, and you have to live with them because you do."

"You got to speak more plainly, Ruth," Samuel cautioned her. "God don't understand that kind of talk."

"God don't have to, Samuel. He isn't down here living like a gopher because you'd rather build churches than a house for your family, now is He?"

"I got the foundation done. What more do you want?"

"The house, Samuel. The brick house you promised me, that's what I want." She set the fry pan near the fire to dry and began on the dishes.

Fred cut himself whittling and sucked on his bleeding finger. "Well, maybe after the house is built, maybe then I'll go find Velda. I'll ask her to forgive me and maybe we can—"

"She should beg your forgiveness." Samuel sucked at the offending tooth. "Velda ought to beg your forgiveness on her hands and knees before you live with her again."

"Well, Samuel, I don't think Velda'd do that. No, she never did beg me for nothing, 'cept a new hat once. She wanted that hat real bad."

"You never shoulda married Velda anyway." Samuel knelt and

stirred the embers. "You jumped into holy marriage with the first person who gave you an itch where you didn't even know you had a place to scratch. You just shoulda bedded Velda and been done with it. God don't smile on that, but He woulda understood."

Crockery rattled, plates cracked and chipped as Ruth slammed the dishes, one after the other, into the rinse water. She dried her hands on her skirt and turned to her husband, her face bone-white, eyes narrowed to slits. "How many women did you bed and be done with before you married me?" She hoisted the bucket of dishwater and walked toward the door with it.

Samuel brought his gray eyes up from the fire. "I've atoned for my sins."

"Have you?" she demanded. She could not bear the sight of them, one smug with holiness, one abject with humility; she could not bear the earthen squalor she had lived in for four years or the man who had brought her to it. "He hath cast me into the mire," Ruth said, trembling, "and I am become like dust and ashes."

"What's that mean?" Samuel eyed her as though through a rifle sight.

"It's from the Book of Job, Samuel; it's what you've done to me. What about the sins you committed against me? Can you ever atone for those?" Ruth flung the bucket of water into the fireplace. Soot billowed out and cinders flew over them, the flames hissed, whispered, but did not die, and smoke settled on their lips.

Fred scurried out of the dugout without another word and without bothering to brush himself off. Samuel wiped his eyes with his sleeve, took the bucket out of the fire, and stood it upright. He walked to his wife and wound his fingers around her arms. "We're all sinners, puny and loathsome in the eyes of God, Ruth. Don't forget that. You got sins to atone for, too."

Her fists and teeth clenched as his hands tightened over her arms, but she neither winced nor retreated. "I atone for my sins, too, Samuel, but not on my knees, not like you do. I atone for them on my back. I pay with my body. I pay for your sins, too. For your lust."

A smile flickered across his lips. "You're going to have another little one. That's it, ain't it?" He pulled her face so close to his she could smell the wet ashes in his beard. He nodded to himself mechanically. "You got another one cooking, don't you?"

Ruth licked the soot from her lips and shook herself free. "Let me

46

go. I'll never let you lay your hands on me again," she said, rubbing her arms where she could still feel the imprint of his fingers.

"You'll change your mind. You always change your mind."

The walls of the brick house were up, the fireplaces in, the floors laid, and the staircase almost finished, but the next baby, Lily (entered hurriedly in the family Bible, April 2, 1895), was born in the dugout just the same.

Lily was so small and sickly that Sister Binton told Samuel she didn't think the baby would live and she could only pray that Ruth would live, because something had gone wrong this time. You had only to look at that scrawny baby that took twenty hours to get born and blood everywhere, more blood than any mother should lose— and was still losing—to know that something had gone wrong and that neither mother nor child could survive. Samuel called in the elders to pray for his dying wife.

But if Sister Binton or Samuel or the elders or Death himself expected Ruth Mason Douglass to surrender, they were wrong. Time lost shape and dwindled to an all eternity of pain that coiled around her body and sucked her downward into a cold white well. Were those the bony fingers of death on her brow? She fought to open her eyes. Perhaps she was already dead, and though her vision was furred, perhaps dead, she could see with her eyes closed. The disembodied fingers belonged not to Death, but to Bishop Whickham, Brother Binton, and Samuel. She wasn't dead. She turned her head from the ministering palms and saw Fred, underfoot and penitent, and Sister Binton holding a bundle of rags that gave feeble, inconstant cries.

> *I knew I'd die like this. Life pouring out of my body, baby's life and my life and my blood everywhere. They'll lay me out like they did Sister Evans. Dead baby at a gray breast.*

"Oh, God, the Eternal Father." Bishop Whickham brought Ruth's forehead back under his cool fingers. "If it pleases Thee to take back Thy handmaiden Ruth, then Thy Will be done."

No. My will. My will be done. Mine.

"But we pray, Oh, God, the Eternal Father, that she might live to further serve Thee on earth, live to Thy greater glory. And if it please Thee to take Thy child Lily Douglass unto Thy bosom, then Thy . . ."

> *It does not please me. Lily can't die. Won't die. My . . .*

". . . Will be done, but we pray she may yet live to serve Thee. Have mercy, Oh, Lord, on Thy child Lily . . ."

> *My child Lily . . .*

". . . and Thy daughter Ruth. We pray that their lives may be spared, but Thou knowest all things, yea from the beginning unto the end. We bow to Thy Infinite Wisdom. We . . ."

> *. . . won't die. Even if God wants me I won't die. Neither will you, Lily. You hear me? You do what I tell you. I am your mother and you do what I tell you. Don't listen to them. Don't listen to God. Listen to me. Live. You live. Live. I will . . .*

". . . say this in the name of Jesus Christ. Amen."

> *. . . live. I won't die. Not now. I won't die in this mud and be buried in it, too.*

Ruth and Lily were still weak in early July when the family moved into the brick house. The first brick house in Monroe County. Eight rooms, two stories, six perfectly drawing fireplaces, a separate room for the bath, an iron stove all the way from Chicago, and an indoor pump in the kitchen. Fred moved the chickens to the dugout.

Samuel helped Ruth up the stairs, and Fred stood at the top. "See here, Sister Ruth?" He pointed to his handiwork. "I built the stairs so they won't creak and bother you." Ruth smiled and let herself be ensconced in her new bed.

Samuel hired a Gentile girl to help out, a buxom girl who—he failed to tell Ruth—was thought to have endangered her Gentile soul with more than one of the railroad men who came through town and who had been thrown out of a respectable boardinghouse and now lived at the edge of town in the worst circumstances imaginable to the Mormon mind—alone. Fred warned Samuel that when Sister Ruth found out the girl's background, she'd be in a fury, but Samuel said he didn't care where the girl lived or what she did nights as long as she took care of the house, the cooking, and three children and one squalling, sickly infant who intruded on his time, which was otherwise spent in praying, in the proliferation of bricks throughout Monroe County and beyond, and in the erection of a barn where he intended to house livestock.

Ruth took pride in the eight-room house, the marvel of Monroe County. The windows were draped with lace curtains; the parlor boasted a rug, a sofa, and two upholstered chairs. She had a clock in the kitchen and chairs for the table. She took pride in the new barn, the livestock, and her newly acquired servant (though she fired the Gentile girl the minute she caught her flirting with the hired men; Ruth did not countenance so much as the suggestion of sin). She had three healthy children and one delicate but lively baby, and because the new state of Idaho needed bricks and more bricks, her husband was richer than banker Bishop Whickham himself. Worldly pride, all of that, but Ruth took especial pride—spiritual pride—in not dying. She began to believe that she had cheated death and thwarted God Himself, that at the moment when she fought back the hand of death, she had struck a bargain, a deal that excluded Samuel, the bishop, even God, all of whom might have been content to let her die. She promised herself that if she did not die, she would never have another child; she would never again allow Samuel entrance to that corridor of her body that had brought her such pleasure and such pain.

In the months following her recovery, the exercise of her will became itself a source of pride for Ruth. Privately she affected a mixture of pity and scorn for women who allowed themselves to be brought to childbed year after year because they hadn't the will to resist their husbands. She scoffed at her younger self, who had so

49

pandered to her body that she let go of her senses. She repudiated the bride she had been. She forgot that that woman had ever existed, and when Samuel sought to remind her—with his hands or his lips—she loathed him all the more, and it became easier, always easier, to rebuff him. She retreated behind the inseparable equation of body and honor that women have always been taught: her honor is dependent on her body. Men are taught differently; they can sunder their bodies from their honor, and so their progress through the world is made simpler.

Ruth became increasingly adroit and vigilant. Even Samuel came to expect and accept her refusals; his assaults on her were churlish, short-lived, and futile. Samuel would often pray till everyone was asleep and then leave the brick house, riding to the former hired girl at the edge of Healy, creeping from her bed just before dawn and meeting the silent, sad, bespectacled Fred in the kitchen, where he was firing up the stove.

As for Ruth, she would never have dreamed that Samuel would be so base as to seek another woman's body. She congratulated herself on her freedom from him and from childbearing. The brick house freed her from low-ceilinged squalor. The brickyard (ten kilns by 1896) freed her from other people's laundry and the thrall of poverty. And whatever these freedoms cost her in tenderness, compassion, or charity, these were never her strong points anyway, and so she scarcely noticed their erosion and demise.

5

DESPITE HIS OCCASIONAL bouts of restlessness and remorse, Fred stayed on, quietly stinking of licorice, past the time when sickly Lil was up and about on sturdy little legs and golden hair curled around her sunny face. "Oh!" Fred would cry, sweeping her up and making her laugh. "You're such a dandelion puff! Dandelion Lily! A real beauty!" He stayed past the time when Eden learned to sass (and subsequently the taste of soap), when Afton learned to swing on the gate, when Gideon, young as he was, was a prize pupil at the Healy School (the new brick Healy School) and the teacher thought he should not only go to high school, but go to college as well.

Fred was lacing up Lil's boots for her one afternoon in the spring of 1897 when Eden came running, breathless, all the way from school with Gideon right behind her. She felt very important, since the telegram had been delivered to her right in school and she had been personally instructed to take it to her Uncle Fred Douglass, though Gideon had fought her for the honor; he stood pouting and panting beside his sister.

Fred read it, and to the children's open-mouthed amazement, he burst into tears: Velda Douglass had died, decapitated by a runaway trolley in Chicago.

Velda had lied, committed adultery, and broken her vows, and yet, Ruth reflected on hearing the news, if heaven was big enough for Velda Douglass, Ruth ought to be able to say her name in charity, and she did so, expressing her sorrow to Fred. Privately, however, she wondered if there was room in heaven for Velda, or if her many sins wiped out the spiritual endowments she'd acquired when she was baptized into the Church of Jesus Christ of Latter-day Saints. Saints, after all, believed that souls entered heaven's gate only two by two, husband and wife, and Ruth wondered if when Fred died he would be dragged down to hell on the sins of his wife, or if Velda would be elevated to spiritual grandeur. Either alternative seemed equally unfair.

If the afterlife puzzled Ruth, Fred's earthly grief for Velda mystified her completely. He should have been overjoyed to be released from a woman who had spurned him, heaped ridicule on him, trampled his pride, driven him to violence and out of the state of Montana. But Fred took the train the next day to Chicago to see that Velda was properly buried. His whole face sagged from the cheekbones, and a mourning band fluttered from his arm. He blew his nose on his newly dyed black handkerchief and bent to kiss Gideon goodbye. "I loved her, Gideon," he sobbed into the boy's narrow shoulder. "I did love her."

51

Ruth watched Fred wipe his eyes and readjust his steamy glasses. How could he have loved such a woman?

If that surprised her, she was downright astonished when in July 1897, still grieving for the luckless Velda, Fred married a widow he'd met when he and Samuel were contracting for a grain elevator near National Falls. Ruth would not have believed that Fred, with his big paws and bad vision and the everlasting stink of licorice about him, could have mourned his first wife or had a second one all picked out.

Ruth had not thought to miss Fred, but she did. She'd never counted the numerous onerous household tasks he silently assumed. She'd never realized how his shaggy person and imperturbable nature sheltered them all from the sharpening edge of Samuel's religiosity. Samuel now called on God to justify his every act, whether he was fighting lice in the chicken coop or taking the strap to Gideon, likening Gideon to Isaac and himself to Abraham. Samuel drew on the Divine Will like an endless bankroll and took to conducting private devotions after family prayers concluded. He bolted the parlor door and supplicated the Lord in solitude.

Well, let him, Ruth thought, listening to him exhort about Bloody Lambs as she completed the day's last task, cleaning the lamp globes with carbonate of ammonia. She rested her feet on the stove's friendly fender; the house was quiet save for Samuel, the children sleeping; even the autumnal winds had died. She was tired, too, and had scant patience with lambs that weren't in the form of chops, and she would have far preferred Samuel beseech God to give His favor to their brickyards, their orchards, their livestock and machinery and contracts, none of which Samuel could attend to when he was entreating the Almighty to share with him the secrets of these latter days.

"God can't be sugared up," she muttered to the soapy globe, "and even if you spend your whole life on your knees, you're still just mortal, Samuel." She added his name as an afterthought.

"Revile me! Reproach me!" came the cry from the parlor. "Humiliate me, Lord. Cast me down and trample me with Thy battering feet. Let me suffer the sting of Thy wrath, Lord, before Thou comfort me with the balm of Thy mercy. Smite my sins. Thrust me from Thy sight."

The metronomic swish of her brush lapsed; she tossed it into the ammonia and it sank.

"I am viler in Thy eyes than the smallest worm, yea more corrupt than the maggot who from the rotting carcass creeps. Pluck my soul, temper it in Thy forge, make me Thy servant. Make me to know joy, that the bones which Thou hast broken may rejoice." His voice broke into short, moist spasms.

Ruth took her feet from the fender and tensed her vertebrae one by one, or so it seemed, because something she did not recognize crawled up her spine.

Samuel gave a gratified cry, and a long silence ensued before he continued. "Thou took Joseph Smith from us. Thou took Brigham Young. The prophets are as fools. The Saints are become abominations in Thy eyes. But Thy new prophet and Thy great day are coming! Blow ye the trumpet! Sound the alarm. Let all the inhabitants tremble." His voice gained velocity and conviction. "God will blow the coals. Heat the fiery furnace! Give us a new revelation and a new prophet and let him go blameless among the people! Scorch the earth with his feet and leave the wicked as stubble!"

Ruth attacked the globe energetically, hoping to drown out his voice, which had sunk back to a whimper punctuated by little shrieks.

When he finally emerged from the parlor, Ruth was almost finished with the last globe, the others lined up on a towel laid across the table. He lounged at the door, sucking his teeth. "God's unhappy with you, Ruth. He told me so."

Ruth snorted.

"God chooses who He will reveal Himself to. He told me He is unhappy with you."

"Well, you tell Him to come to me and say it." She sent the brush furiously over the opaque globe.

Samuel took the chair across from her. His long mouth pressed into a seam; he stared at her with glimmering gray eyes. "God would never reveal Himself to a woman."

"Are you making God's choices for Him these days?"

"God says a man should have many sons. One son is not enough. It's God's commandment."

"You show me where God commands any such thing."

"God don't justify Himself to women. A patriarch must have

53

many sons, and his wife must do his bidding. You should obey God."

"You should obey Him, too, Samuel, and not go about taking His name in vain and saying that He spoke to you."

He scooted his chair closer to her. "You have to do as God says. A woman who will not lie with her husband, who don't give that husband what God wills, don't deserve to be a wife."

"Not your wife anyway."

"A man should have as many children as he can."

"As many as he can! Well, you just tell me the next time a man has one of his own children, and I'll get down on my knees to whoever is telling you all this nonsense."

He stood and moved behind her. "God don't like to hear you talk like that about Him. The man shall look to God, and the woman shall do as she's bid. All women. Even you." He grasped the back of the chair. "Especially you. You been too proud too long. No other man but me would have you for your pride, and you haven't gotten no better. Pride goeth before destruction, and a—"

"You go straight to the devil!"

Samuel snapped the chair back, and the globe flew from her fingers as she went down on her back. Samuel clutched her arm and rolled over her, pinning the arm beneath her. He lay beside her like a lover, but no lover wraps his big hands around the jaw, contorting the lips.

"God don't like to hear you talk like that."

His ashen eyes were so close she could see black threads spinning in his irises. Samuel made noises with his teeth and the tongue he tried to plant in her mouth. She thrust away from him, but he pulled her back and threw his body over her, holding her flailing arms to her sides. "You get off me, Samuel! You hear? You get off!"

He inched his legs up, pinning her wrists with his knees, and brought his hands up to her hair, smiling so that the edges of his teeth were visible. He pushed the stray hairs, almost tenderly, from her face as he bent toward her lips. She spat at him and brought her feet up into his back. He grabbed her hair and shook her head from side to side till the hair spilled down, and he knotted his fist around it and pulled her face up to his as he sat astride her. "The rod chastiseth, Ruth. The rod chastiseth the unbelieving wife." He fumbled with the buttons on his pants.

"You lunatic! You filthy swine! You get off me!" She heard the crack of flesh before she even knew he'd hit her; her head snapped, her ears rang. "I'll kill you!" She twisted, squirmed upward so she could bring her feet into his back or his groin or wherever she could find to kick. She freed her right hand from the pressure of his knee and aimed for the gut. He dropped her hair and her head hit the floor, and he caught her hand and brought it down over his exposed, extended penis. "Oh, God! Oh, Samuel! Let me go!"

"Feel the rod, Ruth. Feel it. You used to like to feel the rod."

She screamed before she remembered she had four children who could wake at any minute. She bit her lips shut, gave a terrific upward jolt, threw him off balance, scrambled free and toward the door. He caught at her skirt and pulled; the skirt shredded, and her clothes fell from her. She was almost to the door when his hands clapped around her ankles and dragged her backward, kicking, clinging to the tumbling chairs and the tottering globes that smashed all over the floor.

He dragged her back beneath him, and using one hand to hold her down, he ripped open her blouse and corset as if he were tearing open her ribs. He crawled upward on her chest and told her to kiss the rod that stood upright from his open pants.

Ruth slid between his knees; he grabbed her hair again and threw his whole weight on top of her. Rolling over in the broken glass and powerful ammonia, they struggled across the floor, one of Samuel's hands crushing her breasts, one clawing at the underclothing till he found her flesh, the leg, the thigh, the hip he had not touched in years. He pressed her head to one side so his lips and teeth were at her ear and his beard alongside her neck. "Scream, Ruth, so God can hear and know you've repented of your pride."

And then Samuel impaled Ruth, thrust himself up her again and again and commanded her in whispers to scream. Ruth's mouth opened in a wordless shriek, but she kept her screams locked at the back of her throat, and she never unleashed them as long as she lived.

Samuel rolled off her. He found an overturned chair and pulled to his feet. "A wife shouldn't think she can deny her husband," he said calmly, though he was still short of breath. He buttoned his pants, and his boots crunched over broken glass. "It's God's will that a man and wife should be one flesh." He stumbled over fallen chairs on his way out of the kitchen, leaving her on the floor with the cold, soapy water that dribbled toward the door and seeped through the cracks.

Ruth rolled to her side, pulled her knees up, and wound herself into a human skein of flesh and hair. She wiped her face on the petticoat still left to her, reached for her skirt, and tied it shawllike around her bare shoulders. She pressed her legs together as tightly as she could, as if to form a solid pedestal on which she could rise, and still teetering, she brought herself to her feet. She made her way around the room, gathering up every piece of cloth, every thread, every pin, button, and hook, and dumped them in the knotted remant of her petticoat. When her feet would not support her, she crawled. The hair was the worst; the hair Samuel had pulled from her head clung to her wet fingers. Finally the only maimed and broken things on the floor were of glass, wood, and water, none of Ruth's clothing or hair. None of Ruth. She went to the cupboard where she kept her washing supplies and pulled out the benzine and some matches.

The dogs woke when she opened the kitchen door and stepped into the autumnal chill. They sniffed at her mournfully, but she kicked them away. If she had to endure anyone's pity, even the pity of a dog, she would dissolve. A moonless, star-whorled night closed in around her as she left the porch and walked across the yard, dogs padding after her to the back of the barn, where she dropped her bundle to the ground. She uncorked the benzine and poured the entire contents over the clothes. She struck a match against the grain of the barn wall and protected the flame in the cup of her hand.

The benzine exploded with the first match and sent up a deep hollowing vacuum of noise, singed the hair hanging over her shoulders and licked the rags that still hung from her hips. She could smell the leather of her shoes cooking and felt the starch in her petticoat melt. She did not step back. She untied the skirt from around her shoulders and dropped it into the fire. Her corset clung to her ribs by a few strings and habit only; she slid it off and fed it to the fire, then she stepped from the smoking petticoat and dropped it into the flames. Smoke swirled about her shoulders and into her eyes. Her drawers, though still tied at the waist, were shredded open, exposing blue veins branching from curling, hairy moss. She untied the drawers as if they were unrent and stepped from them, then dropped them in the fire while her white skin burnished orange.

Ruth Mason Douglass wrapped her arms over her bruised breasts and looked past her flat, broad hips to the fire at her feet.

Wisps of charred rags blew about; she kicked the embers till they died and the smoke, exhausted, allowed itself to be borne away on the wind. With her arms at her side, this big-boned, angular woman, naked in her high-button shoes, walked back to the house and closed the door behind her.

She found an old calico dress, stained with vermilion dye, hanging in the pantry and slid it over her head. She pumped water into the washpan and plunged her face into it till she grew faint. She splashed her legs but could not bear to look at the region of her own violation. She dropped her skirt over her legs without drying them and buttoned the cuffs to the wrist and the collar to the neck. She dried her face, knotted her hair, and then took a stranglehold on the broom and swept up the broken glass. She mopped the spilled ammonia, righted the metal basin, brought the chairs up to the table. Although her hands bled from the glass and stung from the ammonia, she did not stop till she was certain that no hook or hair or splinter had escaped her or could testify to this night's violence. Then she put more wood on the stove and wrapped herself in her rust-colored shawl. She snuffed the overhead lamp, pulled the rocker close to the fiery furnace, and sat down in darkness.

Mason Douglass's entry into this world late in July 1898 was complicated not only by the dry, fierce, unjoyous union of his parents, but more immediately by the fact that he was a breech baby and owed his life to the skillful hands of Sister Binton.

The ordeal of Mason's birth left Samuel Douglass assured of God's continuing favor, for God had blessed him with a son. It left Sister Binton utterly exhausted. It left Eden, Gideon, Afton, and Lil terrified by their mother's unearthly screams. But it left Ruth with the conviction that she would gladly spend time and all eternity in hell, that she would kill or be killed, that she would slit Samuel's throat or her own rather than allow herself to be split asunder again.

6

GOD TOLD SAMUEL to do strange things. He told him to chop down all the apple trees in the orchard because they offended Him. And Samuel did. He told Samuel that wicked books were filling the children's minds with sin and that Gideon's addiction to the adventures of Ragged Dick, the Rover Boys, and Frank Merriwell would plunge him into hell. Samuel forbade them. God told Samuel that secular music was blasphemy to His ears, and Samuel threw away his harmonica; and then God told him all music was an abomination, and Samuel forbade his family to sing in church. God told him not to dance. God told him to cut his hair short and let his beard grow long and to require the same of the men he hired to fill Fred's place, but few of these men stayed longer than a month, so there was no opportunity to test God's satisfaction. God told Samuel that the seventh seal was taut unto breaking and that the latter days were closer at hand than anyone had reason to believe, and He told Samuel not to sell bricks to the wicked, unconverted Gentiles.

Bishop Whickham talked Samuel out of that. Bishop Whickham had a long discussion with him, and when Samuel left his office, he'd agreed with misgivings that the Gentiles might purchase his bricks, but at a higher rate than the Saints. Eventually even the Saints (barring the bishop, Brother Binton, and a few others) came under the bludgeon of God's displeasure, and though Samuel did business with his unregenerate neighbors, he quarreled with them constantly, weighed them in the balance of holiness, and found them wanting.

In September 1899 God commanded Samuel to take another wife, to resurrect the Saints' old custom of plural marriage, which had fallen into disuse because of the Woodruff Manifesto of 1890, wherein the church did not altogether forswear what was after all a revelation given to Joseph Smith and recorded in the *Doctrine and Covenants,* but agreed to forgo the practice, to submit its members to the law of the land.

Ruth was plucking a chicken when Samuel made his announcement.

"It's God's ancient law and modern revelation," Samuel declared. "The Saints have spat on it, reviled and denied God."

"The Manifesto says no more plural marriage," said Ruth levelly without taking her eyes off the chicken.

"The Manifesto! Filth in God's eyes! The Manifesto was a sop to the Gentiles. God said if ye abide not, ye are damned."

Ruth kept up her neat pattern over the body of the dead chicken while she listened to him invoke the patriarchal law, the highest orders of the priesthood, the blessings of heaven, the assumption of Godhood and the kingdoms thereof. He directed her to the Old Testament and the *Doctrine and Covenants.* He said that God was absolute and unequivocal and anyone who doubted God was either a fool or a Gentile. "If we wish to live as gods ourselves, we must do His bidding. Only by following His commandments can men have everlasting powers, have the angels kneeling at their feet. Practice God's law or be damned."

She finished with the chicken, and it lay plucked and stubbly across the table, its feathers in neat piles. "The Manifesto didn't say Joseph Smith was wrong, it just said we weren't going to practice plural marriage anymore."

The right side of Samuel's face twitched, and he sucked at his teeth. "You don't understand what God has told me. God commanded me. God gave me a blinding revelation! He hath chosen me to glorify His name." His eyes glowed like coals.

Ruth rubbed a spot of chicken blood that stained her skirt. "You'll go to jail," she said. "They put the president of the church in jail once, and they'll put you in jail, too."

"No jail can hold God's anointed."

"Carthage jail held Joseph Smith. He died in that jail, or have you forgotten that?"

"That was God's will. The Prophet was too holy, too pure, to live on this foul earth any longer. Now God has put the holy mantle of prophecy on my shoulders, the awesome revelation before mine eyes. I will not forsake Him."

59

"You're mad, Samuel."

"Do not speak to me like that or you'll be visited with the vengeance the unbelieving wife deserves." His eyes narrowed as if he were contemplating that vengeance.

Ruth moved to the pump, close by the carving knife; there would be no reenactment of what had happened on this floor once.

His sun-streaked beard rose from his chest as he threw his head back. "No one can thwart the prophet. The Lord hath girded me, commanded me to seek the alien desert, to taste the alien corn, to sell my possessions and take my wives and sons and daughters and servants and oxen into the wilderness and there secure a place for the Lord to appear. We are going to leave this iniquitous valley. We are going to Mexico."

"Mexico!"

"That is where He will appear to me next."

"Leave Healy and all we've worked for here? Leave this house? Leave the brickyard and the orchards and everything they've brought us? Go to Mexico? Are you mad?"

"God hath spoken. It is better to live in the wilderness than with a contentious woman. It is revealed that I shall take another wife and go into the wilderness to await His next command."

"Hmph. Have you scouted out the Healy girls? Can you find anyone who will be your polygamous wife? You get crazier by the day."

Samuel stepped closer to her, and Ruth rested her fingers on the knife. "The unbelieving wife will smoke in hell, Ruth. Only the good wife can enter God's Kingdom with her husband."

"I'd rather go to hell. And besides, who will perform this marriage for you? Have you thought of that? No one in the church will do it."

"Marriage is God's own sacred ordinance, and He will perform our marriage."

"Our marriage?"

"Elda's and mine."

"Elda?" The name dangled in the air between them.

"Elda Allred will be my plural wife by God's decree."

Ruth swallowed her consternation that this celestial wife had a name, and thus a face and no doubt a body. "Samuel, you are crazy. You are a crazy, lustful old goat, and if you think I'm leaving this brick house to go live in a Mexican tent, then you're even more

60

crazy." She did not flinch from his glare nor quail at the twitch contorting his face.

"You are a speck in God's eye, Ruth. The Prophet's wife, Emma Smith, obeyed him, and you will obey me, even as Sarah obeyed Abraham, calling him Lord. I am the prophet, thy husband, and God hath commanded me: on the first day of the new century, sell thy earthly increase, for they are as chaff before Me, take Elda Allred to wife, and go unto Mexico, where you will see Christ and the Last Judgment." He turned on his heel and left.

Ruth prodded the fire. He was crazy. Of course he was crazy, but he could do it. He could uproot her and her children. He could pull them from their eight-room house with its indoor pump and the only lace curtains in Monroe County and send them back to squalor more degrading than the dugout. Squalor in a foreign country. Squalor she would have to share with another woman and another woman's children.

Ruth said her prayers in the kitchen that night. They were modest prayers. She did not pray for the conversion of the Jews or ask Him how many trumpets would sound on Judgment Day. She did not discuss the covenants, contracts, bonds, obligations, and oaths that once made in this world will be binding in the next. She did not invoke the prophets or apostles. She said: dear Lord, save me from this. Whatever you do or say to Samuel, save me and my children from this travail and disgrace.

Ruth did more than pray. The next day she took down *Dr. Chatton's Medical Receipts* from her kitchen bookshelf, where it shared equal prominence with the Bible, the Book of Mormon, and the *Doctrine and Covenants*. She studied Dr. Chatton for symptoms of brain fever. She made sage and mint teas. She fed Samuel onions in various forms. (Dr. Chatton was a great believer in the restorative and protective powers of the onion.) She ransacked Dr. Chatton for tonics and added them to the evening milk. She slipped Samuel alteratives and more than one purgative and a couple of emetics, believing, perhaps only hoping, that the devil in his soul could be expelled through one of the body's ordinary orifices.

She suspected him of drink. Dr. Chatton warned that people who drank in their youth (yea, though they swore off the stuff for twenty years) paid the price later, that the brain fermented in its own iniquitous juices. But there was another possibility suggested by Dr.

61

Chatton, worse than drink, because it implicated Ruth in Samuel's madness. She read several paragraphs on the follies of self-abuse and the penalties extracted. Men who, in the cold language of Dr. Chatton, masturbated ran the risk of impotence in later life, blindness, and cancer of the hand, but most prevalent was madness. Further:

> The man who succumbs to this evil practice is ever prey to nature's reprisals against those who misuse her gifts. His ulcerated brain dooms him to madness and more than one is the man who, having destroyed his mind, destroys his home, leaving his little children weeping and his wife in rags.

There was no cure for this. Dr. Chatton had cures for cancer, consumption, stuttering, and hydrophobia, but not for this.

She closed the book with a snap and laid her hands over it. Could she have driven him to this? Had she, by virtue of her will and pride and resolution, condemned herself and her children to this destruction? Lacking the ministrations of an affectionate wife, might he have resorted to his own hand, roused up all that bad blood and sent it coursing and inflammatory to his brain? What else did he do in the parlor, Ruth wondered, besides pray?

Samuel Douglass accepted the return of his wife's physical affection without comment or acknowledgment or even surprise. Ruth cherished some hope that she had done the right—the only—thing, because he did not mention Mexico or plural marriage or the first day of the new century for months. But revelations die hard, and one morning in early December he announced he was not going to the brickyard; he was going over to Woodrull to spend the day in prayer with Elda Allred.

That night Ruth dosed herself with a tonic, cursed Dr. Chatton, put her children to bed, and awaited his return.

Samuel came home singing the praises of Elda, her piety, her respect for the Lord, her joy in Samuel's revelations, her understanding of the holiness of plural marriage, her certainty that Samuel would smooth her path before God and raise them both up to everlasting glory. She wanted to have many children and raise them up to everlasting glory, too. She was seventeen and a virgin.

62

Elda Allred, Ruth gleaned from the nuggets of actual information Samuel gave her, limped by on a dry farm over near Woodrull, living with her mother. The men of her family were gone: father kicked in the head by a horse, one brother bolted to California, and the other wasted by disease and put in the ground last spring. Elda's mother was a shrewd practicing Saint who, Samuel claimed, would have insisted that the late Brother Allred practice plural marriage so as to assure them all of God's favor, but the Allreds were too poor for the celestial luxuries. If she couldn't assure such blessings in the storehouse of the Lord for herself, Sister Allred was only too happy to see Elda inherit them. The wife of the prophet, after all—and that wife's mother—would enjoy the highest fruits of righteousness in the afterlife and some of its blessings right here on earth, especially when that prophet's farm and orchards and brickyards and eight-room house could be sold for a tidy sum. It was clear to the Allred women that Samuel was God's chosen successor to Joseph Smith. Sister Allred was anxious to accompany Elda and her prophet-husband—and his first family, of course—to Mexico for a new life in the new century, because the dry farm was too much for a woman alone and too little for anything else.

As Ruth listened to the litany of Elda's virtues, she knew she'd lain with Samuel, lied to herself, been a fool, for nothing. She was going to lose this house and the worldly wealth it represented. She was going to lose everything, and there was nothing she could do about it.

"Come to bed, Ruth."

She raised her eyes to his ashen face and glittering eyes. So his afternoon of celestial love with the virginal Elda had left him with more carnal desires, had it? "I'll never lie with you again, Samuel. You'll never touch me again."

He shrugged. "There'll come a time when you'll be happy to hear my boots by your door."

She could hear the thud of his boots on the bedroom floor as she sat in the kitchen, and in the awful stillness she even heard the bed creak under his weight.

Ruth snatched the Bible and the Book of Mormon and the *Doctrine and Covenants* off the shelf. If she had to fight God she would see for herself what God had to say.

She read them diligently. They were not easy books, though the

63

exalted language was familiar. (You never heard such language over a corn crib, of course, but you heard it often enough that sometimes it floated through your dreams, a second tongue with its own vocabulary and grammar.) They were difficult to fathom, but Ruth came to the conclusion that Samuel was wrong and God was pretty equivocal on this matter and hard to understand after all. All that Old Testament coupling, all that blather about Abraham and Sarah and Hagar and Jacob and Leah and Billah and all their domestic arrangements, made it hard to see exactly what God had in mind.

The Book of Mormon further confused the issue. There God said that more than one wife was an abomination to Him. And the *Doctrine and Covenants* (those revelations God gave to Joseph Smith before He spoke with Samuel Douglass), they were worse. Samuel had marked one portion with clumsy stars: the adulteress shall be damned and destroyed. Further on, God revealed, and Samuel underlined, that if any man espouse a virgin and desire to espouse another, even ten or twenty virgins, that was not adultery. But the virgins, Ruth read on, the virgins had best watch their tender steps. They could commit adultery. Ruth shook her head, picturing the virgin Elda Allred (for Ruth, Elda was short and potato-faced), who couldn't wait to go to Mexico and replenish the earth.

The *Doctrine and Covenants*, however, gave Ruth some unexpected solace. She was not the first woman to doubt the wisdom of God's revelation, not the first woman brought to this impasse by a man who wanted to sleep with virgins. God addressed Himself to Emma Smith, the Prophet's wife, and told her if she didn't like the principle He'd revealed, she'd be the one cast out and destroyed. Further, God admonished Emma to forgive her husband his trespasses, and Ruth reckoned Emma had a lot to forgive, and it wasn't till she closed the book that she realized she was having these thoughts about a prophet and a seer.

She blew out the lamp. Leaving the books on the table, she went to the window, pressing her warm cheek to its cold pane. The dying moon draped the yard with gauzy banners, rendering the ordinary—the chickenhouse, the barn, the windmill, the sleeping dogs—beautiful, slathering cold magic over the fence posts and the tufts of brown grass in the balding yard. She took Samuel's jacket off the hook, no hat or gloves, just the heavy jacket with its pall of brick dust, and closed the door behind her. At the edge of the porch she breathed in a bright stab of cold air, billowed out her own foggy warmth, and started walking.

One dog joined her. The other, less adventurous, sidled up to the kitchen door and lay back down. She walked past the privy and the windmill, its blades stiff, creaking, resisting the encroachment of yet another winter. She walked over her own grievous past: past the dugout (now sheltering chickens) where she'd once lived and borne four children, past the yard where she had bent over other people's laundry, past the barn where she had burned her clothes. She folded her arms and walked faster.

The fragile shell of frost cracked under her feet and trimmed the branches of shivering, unclad fruit trees. She came at last to the brickyard, where round ovens squatted on the warm ground and retained heat. No frost could form and no snow adhere where the embers glowed. The ember-red ovens and the amber-red brick dust gave the yard the appearance of a little patch of purgatory, hell's outpost.

She held her cold hands out to the brick oven, and then Ruth opened her mouth to the blasphemy that had been slowly collecting in her heart for years and opened herself to death and destruction. She railed against God's commandments and men's wishes and declared that Sarah and Abraham were a pair of meddling old fools, that she had no sympathy for Jacob and his seven-year stints, that Leah was dim-witted and Rachel deserved everything she got. And if God didn't punish Lot for begetting children on his own daughters, what right had He to threaten poor old Emma Smith with destruction? What right had all those men to go about espousing virgins and begetting and begatting? She laid her dry palms close to the cozy oven. Joseph Smith and all the rest of them were just as mad as Samuel. All prophets were as fools, and Ruth Douglass was not going to be cowed by a maundering madman who thought he had God on his side.

Maybe he did. Ruth held her breath against the cold wind and the half-formed fear that the little oven would erupt into another burning bush and God would tell his handmaiden Ruth that she had best apologize and cease this blasphemy. But God ignored Ruth. Or at least He did not deign to speak through the oven or anything else.

She walked through the brickyard, the dog still at her side; the

65

dog was not at all concerned that Ruth was committing murder in her heart: she wished Samuel dead. As the Widow Douglass she could inherit everyone's condolences and the property, too. Considerable property: the brickyard, the orchards, the eight-room house. But short of Samuel's death and under the prevailing laws and customs, she was powerless. If she left him, if she deserted his bed and board—even if that bed was reduced to a board in Mexico—she would be neither wife nor widow nor virgin, and those were the only three things she could possibly be. She would have nothing and no one would take her in.

She brushed brick dust from her skirt like flecks of dried blood. Embers winked at her from all the grates, as if the ovens winked on blasphemy and encouraged desecration. She had slandered God and the Prophet both, but she still believed in the church. The church was more than the teachings of one man, more than prophecy. The church took care of its own, and Ruth was one of its own and always had been, and even Samuel might yet listen to an appeal from the church. Bishop Whickham, after all, had talked Samuel out of withholding bricks from the unsanctified Gentiles. The bishop was persuasive, and even if he could not bring Samuel to his senses, perhaps he could dissuade him from the folly of plural marriage and moving to Mexico.

She walked back to the house knowing she must put her pride in her pocket and tell Bishop Whickham her plight. He would summon the whole body of the church to rise and unite behind her, support her through this ordeal, and convince Samuel that these latter days would have to be more latter yet before the world was ready for another prophet. Bishop Whickham could convince Samuel that if men could not comply with God's perfect plan of celestial marriage, at least they should live in terrestial peace with the imperfect laws of men. Ruth was determined to enjoy whatever terrestrial peace there was while she lived in her eight-room house with its indoor pump and lace curtains and not allow Samuel to expose her and her children to humiliation, to drag them off to the Mexican wilderness so he could live like an Old Testament patriarch or a New Covenant prophet.

7

RUTH TIED THE team to the rail in front of Fenwick's Farm and Home Supply. She helped the younger children out of the wagon and lined them up in the snow; they sniffed and stomped their feet; they huddled close to the steaming horses. "I want you all to go into Fenwick's and have a look around. Just a look. I'll be there shortly. Gideon, you keep hold of Mason's hand and don't let go. I don't want to hear of any trouble." She locked her sons' hands together and smiled at them. Gideon had the strong frame and the weak eyes of the Douglass men, and Mason, too, seemed to have the Douglass body, but he was too young to be much of anything except ruddy and underfoot.

"Now, here's a nickel, Eden. You can buy yourselves some candy, but not licorice. I can't stand licorice." Afton punched Eden's ribs in an effort to snatch the nickel, but Ruth insisted that Eden was the eldest and she should have the money. Ruth thought Eden was too somber for a child only nine years old, and she wished Eden shared some of Afton's high spirits. In their childish games it seemed to Ruth that it was Eden who finally prevailed, but it was Afton who dominated. Certainly Afton dominated lovely little Lil, who at four mimicked Afton's every word and gesture and did whatever Afton told her.

Ruth watched them march into the Farm and Home Supply before she repinned her hat firmly to her head and walked up the street to Whickham's First Bank of Healy. In the ten years she'd lived there, Healy had changed considerably from a collection of stick-and-mud buildings to a self-conscious little burg with aspirations and pretensions and an underground sewage system in place of the old open ditches. There was more of everything now: more brick buildings, more wagons, more Saints, more Gentiles, a sprinkling of Jews, and some Chinese left behind by the railroad. There was even a touch of luxury in Mrs. Dodd's Millinery Palace, where you could finger the only aigrettes in the whole state of Idaho, if you had time for that sort of thing.

A woman whose husband's gone mad did not have time. Ruth arrived at the bank flushed, her throat dry, palms moist. She was shown to the bishop's small, overheated private office, and he bade her welcome. Bishop Whickham sat at an elaborately carved rolltop desk with enough pigeonholes for the woes of the entire Healy Ward. Bishop Whickham was corpulent, blue-eyed, and powdery —as though he were continually showered in a fine white dust— graying, devout, and approachable.

She sat opposite him, and he began with the usual placating inquiries. The children? Fine. The brickyard? Fine. And Brother Douglass?

"Ah," said Ruth, "he is not fine."

"Is his body ailing him?"

"I wish it was, Bishop. I wish he was sick unto death." Ruth cleared her throat. "I mean, I wish I could bring him back to health. I wish it was anything but what it is."

The bishop's chalky right eyebrow shot up. "And what is it?"

She could not launch herself into the painful truth, so she mentioned the obvious. How Samuel was not himself. How he was more and more neglecting the brickyard for solitary prayers. How his worship of the Lord had taken a fearful turn.

"I don't know what a fearful turn is, Sister Douglass," said the bishop, crossing his hands over his waistcoat.

"He's dangerously pious, Bishop. You surely know that. You remember he wouldn't sell bricks to the Gentiles."

"Yes, yes, but I don't know what you regard as dangerously pious."

"He wants to practice polygamy," Ruth said flatly. "He wants to take a second wife."

"That's impossible. Plural marriage is against the laws of the land, and the church no longer condones it. The Manifesto—nine years ago now."

"I told him all that. It don't seem to matter."

"Well, it should. The church forbids plural marriage."

Bishop Whickham's retreat behind the picket fence of legality was not what Ruth had hoped for. "He says, Bishop, that God has given him a new vision, a new revelation."

"That God has given Samuel a new revelation?"

"Yes."

Bishop Whickham shook his head; dander dusted his shoulders. "If the church says polygamy's wrong, it's wrong."

"So is murder, but people still kill each other, even Saints."

He assembled his thoughts in a cough. "Being a Saint means being obedient. When the church says no plural marriage, we obey. When they say only Joseph Smith and his successors can enjoy revelations, we obey."

"Well, Samuel don't obey. God tells him to do all kinds of things, and I've stood it all I can."

The bishop busied himself with a penknife as if honing his thoughts down to a fine point. "I can see where your husband might have alarmed you."

"Alarmed me! He has scared me within an inch of my mortal life! He's mad!"

"Have you ever reflected, Sister, that perhaps it is not altogether his own madness?"

"What?"

"Have you ever—let me say this. The bond between husband and wife is a sacred one, the most sacred on earth, the closest earthly thing we have to that bond which seals us to our Heavenly Father. When one person in the marriage bond is unhappy, such as Brother Douglass—"

"I am unhappy, Bishop. Samuel is mad."

"—unhappy, as I say, the other party, person, cannot be wholly extricated from the implications of—"

Ruth squinted, as if peering through an unexpected fog. "What are you saying?"

"Perhaps you should concentrate on being a better wife to Brother Douglass. Are you certain that his home is all a man could wish for? Perhaps his wish for another wife does not mean that he is, as you say, mad, but rather that his home and his present wife— you—are giving him less than a wife should." He broke into a brief, flat rendition of the old hymn "There Is Beauty All Around, When There's Love at Home."

69

"He wants to marry Elda Allred," Ruth snapped. "Do you know her?"

The bishop's face altered perceptibly, telling her only that he did indeed know Elda Allred. But before Ruth could speak, he began, "Sister Douglass, have you given your husband enough children? There are many little spirit bodies waiting at God's knee to receive earthly raiment from loving mothers."

"I'm not here to talk about children, my own or anyone else's. Samuel wants to marry Elda Allred because he says it's God's commandment. He says God Himself will perform the ceremony and then he's going to sell everything we own and go off to Mexico with Elda and her mother, and he wants me to trot after him into the wilderness. Now, that is mad. Fanatic. Samuel has lost his mind. You should hear him! Discussing the conversion of the Jews with God, giving God advice! Samuel clamors in tongues!"

"God's plan is not always easy to live by."

"What has God's plan to do with lunacy?"

"Only in the fullness of time—"

"Bother the fullness of time! He says he is going to marry her on the first day of the new century, which is less than a month away. I need your help."

"You haven't heard me out."

Ruth lapsed into an anxious silence; she had not come to hear him out.

"Revelation is a special gift, given only to the few, the chosen. For those not chosen to say they have been appointed for revelation is—"

"Madness! That's what I'm trying to tell you. He thinks God's chosen him!"

"No one but the president of the church or the apostles is entitled to revelation."

"You tell Samuel that. He'll listen to you. He respects you."

"For Samuel to claim that God has divinely touched him, given him a modern revelation . . . well, Sister, there are worse things than madness. There's rebellion, for instance." He lifted his powdery eyebrows as if they might help carry the weight of that statement.

"There's no worse thing than madness. Not when you're married to it. I'd rather see him dead and buried"—in fact, she would have *preferred* him dead and buried—"than let him humiliate me and my children."

The bishop brought his steely blue eyes to rest on her. "Humiliation is not the issue here, Sister Douglass. Humility is. Humiliation is the offspring of pride, and pride is the serpent we must crush under the heel. Pride is to be suppressed. Humility is to be cultivated. Pride goeth before destruction. Perhaps you should look to yourself. Perhaps you should uproot the rebellion in your own heart. Have you ever thought it may be you, yourself, you who gave Samuel such ideas?"

She peered at him through the gathering miasma. Perhaps the bishop had lost his mind, too. Perhaps after the age of thirty, all men lost their minds and women just lived around them.

"What lies at the root of rebellion, Sister?" Bishop Whickham continued. "Pride. Crass, secular pride. If you are convinced that the home you've built is the kind of married life two Saints should enjoy, then of course you may be at peace, but on the other hand, in the matter of pride—"

"I came here because I want the church to help me with my crazy husband."

"Sister Douglass, your husband is not crazy. He has a heart full of rebellion, and a heart full of rebellion is a heart full of pride. To set himself against the laws of the land and the church, to claim God's revelations, that is the worst sort of pride. The worst. And wherefore has he eaten of the fruit of that pride? Could it be at your own table?" He leaned forward as if to speed his words toward her. "You have many blessings, Sister Douglass. Blessings should make you humble, not proud."

"Is it a blessing that my husband wants to marry a second wife?" she demanded. "Sell everything we've worked ten years for and run off to Mexico to play Abraham in the desert?"

"You have more education than your husband. You have more wealth than any family in Monroe County. Vanity and vexation of the spirit, Sister. You are known to be a proud woman, and if your fear of humiliation is what's driven you here to talk to me, then I suggest that you look into your own heart before—"

"You have no right to talk to me like that," she said. "I won't have it."

"You only prove what I've been saying. I am happy to counsel you, Sister Douglass, but your pride won't allow you to heed. The way of the fool is right in his own eyes, but the wise man harkeneth to counsel."

"I didn't come here for counsel. I came here to ask you to stop Samuel from this horrible folly."

"I only suggest that if you were a more perfect wife, it follows that you would have a more perfect husband."

"There isn't time for perfection! You have to stop him!"

The bishop shook his head at a Job-like tempo. "For all your education, Sister, you cannot see wisdom when it lieth before you. Perhaps you are at fault in this matter, perhaps not. I won't judge you, but the church, the church, Sister Douglass, will thrust your husband from its sight if he claims to be receiving revelation from God, unsanctioned revelation. He is breaking the rules the church has laid down for the conduct of the Saints. The church don't hold with unsanctioned revelation. The *Doctrine and Covenants* tells it true. Revelation is forbidden. Only to Joseph Smith and his appointed successor shall God reveal Himself. Others—the rebellious—shall be cast out. It's gone too far, Sister Douglass. His polygamous marriage, of course that's against the church's rules, too, but"—he held up his hand when she began to interrupt—"it's rebellion that can't be forgiven. The rebellious shall be cast out of Zion and live in the dry land. If you told me that Samuel wanted to take a plural wife, though it's been forbidden, perhaps I could have talked to him. But if he says that God's revealed Himself unto Samuel Douglass, that Samuel Douglass is the new prophet with a new God-given vision, then there's nothing I can do."

"But the bricks! You talked him out of the bricks!"

"He never said that was a revelation from God. He never said God told him not to sell the bricks to Gentiles."

"But God *did* tell him!" Her fingers flew to her mouth; she'd substantiated madness, and if she stayed she might further betray herself to this comfortless Pharisee. She rose and put her hand on the brass doorknob. "We could stop him, Bishop. Me and you and the church, we could stop him."

Dust or salt or dander seemed to agitate and flutter around him as he shook his head. "When a man has his heart set on rebellion, Sister Douglass, only God can stop him."

8

RUTH MASON DOUGLASS was born well on the other side of the last century and she lived well into this century, none of which is to say that she lived well. She married when she was older, but her age gave her no added insight, and she married a man who, with a jigger of scrutiny, she would have rejected even at the cost of spinsterhood. She feared childbirth, but bore six living children. She cherished her education, but she had no imagination. Ruth Mason Douglass never planted so much as a flower; she never wasted so much as a wish or an ounce of bone marrow. She saw no paradox in her lifelong reverence for the institution of marriage, which she detested, or her adherence to a church in which she had no faith. She brought up her children as Saints, attended services, paid her tithing, and practiced the Word of Wisdom, eschewing all spirits, coffee, tea, and tobacco. After 1899 she did everything required of the good Mormon except believe it.

Riding home from Healy, Ruth ignored the quarreling children and beat the horses unnecessarily. She spoke to no one until she stopped in front of the brick house and the hired man came out to help her unload supplies and warn her that Samuel was plenty mad that supper wasn't only late, but not even started, and that he'd gone back into the parlor to pray. "So he'll neglect his soul when his stomach beckons, will he?" Ruth said. "Well, you just wonder what God thinks about that."

She could hear Samuel droning prayers when she stepped into the house and wondered if he was praying louder or if the walls were getting thinner and the partitions that separated her from his madness were weakening.

Samuel came out when he smelled supper. He chided her for its lateness, then spent ten minutes thanking God it was there at all.

Afterward only Mason was excused from family prayers and sent to bed. Everyone else, by custom including the hired man if he valued his job (and there always came a day when he did not), went into the parlor and knelt. In deference to Lil's childish fears, Samuel allowed a candle on the floor, but no lamp.

They formed a circle around the candle, on their knees, backs straight, thighs tensed, hands folded, heads bent. All heads except Samuel's. His was cast back following the wavering beam of the candle on the ceiling. "Oh, Lord," he began, "we implore Thy mercy. We grovel before Thy magnificence. We groan before Thy power. We pray to be snatched from our erring ways."

> *I am past praying. I cannot afford to err. I must think. I must leave. Flight. Leave my lawful wedded husband and eight-room house, because if I stay I'll lose the house anyway and live in the wilderness with his madness and his plural wife, and I would rather die. It's wrong. Betraying everything the church holds dear and everything I've ever been taught or believe in. Of course it's wrong, and two wrongs don't make a right. Two nickels don't make a dime either. They make ten cents, and that will do.*

"Look into our hearts, Lord, and purge them of their evil. Cauterize our wickedness, Lord. Smite it, burn it, and leave us clean and white in Thy sight."

> *White as burnt bones, you fool, Samuel. You mad fool. He's gone daft with Sainthood and now the Saints have tossed him back to me like he was a bad coin given in tithing. If he'd just deserted me without revelations, if he'd just taken his virgin Elda and run off, if he had bedded her and been done with it, I could have been the wronged wife, I could have had the rags of righteousness to cover*

74

me. Now I am the wrongdoer, the sinner, the breaker of vows.

"Help us, oh, Lord, to know Thy mightiness. Give us a glorious display of Thy sovereign Will. Take our vile desires and purify them. Let us know Thy tempered steel. Strengthen us in Thy flame. Chastise us with fire. Cast us into fathomless waters. Renew our salvation by drowning our sins."

> *Maybe he's going to build an ark and float down to Mexico. Maybe it's not enough to play Abraham in the desert with a seventeen-year-old virgin, he's got to be Noah as well. Noah and Abraham and David and Solomon and all the blabbering fools, including Nephi and Moroni and Joseph Smith, too. Taking what they wanted and calling it God's Will. So God told Joseph Smith he could take ten virgins without committing adultery, did He? Yes. And He told Emma she could like it or lump it.*

Eden sniffed, wiped her nose, and sank back down on her thin haunches. Samuel heard nothing over the tide of his own voice. Ruth glanced at the hired man; he'd be gone in a week, she could tell from the look on his face. Maybe she'd be gone in a week, too, but she feared it would be longer than that, because Ruth knew that the worst of her plight was that a woman with five children and no man was powerless and penniless.

She stared at Samuel, whose gray-streaked beard gleamed in the puny light of the candle and whose head was thrown so far back all she could see was the eggshell-white rim of his eyes. And it was then that she understood how and why Fred had laid his great mitts around the thin neck of his adulterous wife and how he could have beaten her lover insensible and then just closed the door on them both and left.

"Amen," said Samuel.

"Amen," said Ruth.

* * *

75

She began secret caches. She could not pack in advance without arousing Samuel's suspicion or the children's curiosity, so she began little bundles of clothing for each child, stashed under their beds or behind the washstand. A change of clothes, extra underwear, heavy stockings. In the cellar beneath the straw-packed potatoes, she hid another bundle of dried apples, pressed beef, cheese wrapped in muslin, and hard gingersnaps, which traveled well and kept a long time. She awaited her opportunity, fearing that it would not come and that she would have to move without opportunity and her control would crumble into desperation.

Opportunity appeared some weeks later on a Saturday, two days before Christmas, in the big blond body of Brother Lars Binton, who arrived before Samuel had locked himself in the parlor for his morning devotions. Brother Binton was one of the few Saints Samuel deemed worthy of conversation on anything so trivial as the weather, let alone the new dairy house Binton had in mind. He asked Samuel to accompany him to have a look at the site, and Ruth was glad that revelations, plural wives, and mad or not, Samuel was still the best builder in Monroe County.

"Can you ride in Brother Binton's rig?" she asked, not raising her eyes from the knife she slid through the flesh of slabby bacon. "I have to go into Healy for supplies."

Samuel cocked his eyebrow at Binton, who wasn't happy about the extra ride there and back, but he wanted the new brick dairy house and he agreed.

Ruth heard Binton's rig leave and saw the hired man go off to the brickyard, but for a full ten minutes she continued to scrub the scorched oatmeal in the bottom of the pot, then she dropped it and left it where it lay. She called Gideon and smoothed the lank hair from his face. "How would you like to visit Fred for Christmas, Gideon? Would you like that?" His little face lit. "You think the girls would like it?" He nodded. "We're going to take a nice jaunt out there, so you go tell the girls to get their warmest clothes and hats and scarves, and have Eden dress Mason, and when you're all ready, go out on the porch and wait for me."

When Gideon dashed out, Ruth went down to the cellar, brought up her stash, and put it in a basket with two loaves of day-old bread. She collected the bundles of clothing from around the house and shoved them into a valise and the maroon carpetbag. Then she went up to her bedroom. For a moment she sat at the edge of the bed, clutching the post, fighting the nausea that assaulted her when she realized the irrevocability of what she was about to do and the impossibility of any other course. Her resolve did not desert her, but everything else had. She had learned, much to her bitterness, that her husband was a man, that the church was man-made, that the world was man's handiwork, and that men were untrustworthy.

She pulled a valise from under the bed, the same valise she had brought from Salt Lake ten years before. She undid the leather straps, and the smell of stiffened paper and old glue and mildew rose up. Besides a change of linen, a fresh blouse, heavy stockings, and a nightdress, Ruth packed what cash she could find, and her family Bible and her marriage certificate, because she did not want to lose those records that testified that she was once a woman with a husband. She exchanged her household nub-colored skirt for her Sunday black alpaca and a crisp starched blouse and jacket. She took her coat off the hook, wrapped the rust-colored shawl over her head and neck, and with a firm grip on the valise, she opened the door and heard the latch close behind her for the last time.

She banked the fire in the stove (serve Samuel right to come home to a cold house; this was his doing). She closed the kitchen door behind her, marched out to the barn, hitched up the team herself, drove it around to the front, and put the children, the basket, the two valises, and the carpetbag in the back. She tied up the dogs so they wouldn't follow, slid her gloves on, and was about to tell the horse to get on up when, on second thought, she jumped out of the wagon, took the key from her pocket, locked up the eight-room house with the indoor pump and lace curtains, and put the key behind a loose brick. Then she told the horse to get on up, and the dogs howled mournfully after her.

She was quite certain that should she ever need to, she could look back to this moment and know that the rest of her life unfurled from it. The wagon tracks that threaded over the winter landscape took her south, away from Healy, away from Samuel, away from Idaho and the nineteenth century altogether. What she did not know was that there were beliefs, predilections, and assumptions that were part of her baggage just as surely as the underwear, the day-old bread, the ten-year-old marriage certificate, the nine dollars and fifty cents in cash, and the five bewildered children.

77

9

THE JOURNEY FROM Healy filled the short December day. Ruth stopped at the National Falls blacksmith's because the forge looked inviting and asked after the Douglass place. The smith scratched his lean cheek and shook his head. He'd never heard of a Douglass place near National Falls, though there was a Douglass builder and brickmaker over near Healy. One of the inevitable loiterers around the forge said, wasn't Douglass the man who had married the Widow Anderson? Oh, yes. Well, the Anderson place was about three miles east; take the north fork and you couldn't miss it. Ruth wondered on her way out of town how little imprint Fred had made if in two years he had not succeeded in replacing Brother Anderson.

She couldn't miss the place, because the name Anderson still swung from the gatepost. About a quarter mile up the rutted road she saw a clapboarded house crouched under the blood and cold-milk colors of winter twilight. The windows were all dark.

The children were quarrelsome, confused, and hungry, and Ruth was sharp with them. Anxiety gnawed at her resolve. What if Fred would not help her? Getting out of Samuel Douglass's house she had done by herself, but henceforth she would be beholden, dependent on others. Beyond Fred lay the only possible course: back to Salt Lake City and the ignominious return to her father's house. She reflected bitterly that if she had no pride, if she were not troubled with free will, she could have lived out her days in Mexico, stupid and invincible.

Dark as the house was, she knew someone was home, because the smell of smoke wafted over them, and after it the smell of supper. No sounds. Only the ringing hooves of her team and their snort of surprise when she finally called them to a halt.

She ordered the children to stay in the wagon and jumped down. Before she even knocked, she could hear footsteps down the hall and see the glimmering approach of a lamp. She found herself face to face with her sister-in-law, the erstwhile Widow Anderson, a plain, plump woman about forty with tiny little pig eyes and a face set about with bristling ringlets. She was many inches shorter than Ruth, who drew herself up to her full height and announced who she was but not why she'd come.

The other Mrs. Douglass moved the lamp closer. "Fred's in the barn with the cows," she said tersely.

Ruth glanced back to the wagon full of children. She'd come too far to be intimidated. "I'll just send my boy around to tell Fred we're here." She ordered the children out of the wagon and unloaded the carpetbag, the valises, and the basket.

The other Mrs. Douglass filled the doorway with her body, and Ruth realized she'd forgotten the woman's name except for Widow. Widow said her name was Mavis, and they followed her lamp down the dark hall to the kitchen, which in contrast to the rest of the house was brightly lit.

"This is my boy, Lafayette," said Mavis, pointing to a boy about sixteen, who except for his britches was the image of his mother. "And this here is Dorothea, my girl." The girl probably resembled the late Brother Anderson, because she had neither pig eyes nor ringlets, and at thirteen she was sprouting in all the wrong directions. "Dorothea costs me a fortune in skirts," Mavis added.

Ruth asked Eden to help Lil with her coat.

"Eden was Fred's ma's name, wasn't it?" Mavis scrutinized the little girl carefully. "Strange name. It's Christian, though, I guess. Your girl don't look like no Douglass, though."

"I look like Mother," Eden offered. "Everyone says so."

Mavis grunted and told Lafayette to skip down to the cellar for more potatoes and bacon.

"Would you mind . . ." Ruth paused. "Could they have a little warm milk before supper? I think they're chilled clear through."

"Long ride from Healy."

"Yes."

"We'd been ready for you if we knew you was coming."

"There wasn't time to write."

"No? Where's Brother Samuel? Dorothea, you go down there and get some of yesterday's milk and tell Lafayette not to be all day."

Ruth busied herself changing Mason, laying him out on the rag rug and undoing the labyrinth of buckles and snaps on his clothing.

"Brother Samuel didn't come with you, I see."

"Not this time."

Dorothea came up with the milk, and Mavis stirred it into a pan. "Fred told me how you took him in after that sin-loving wife of his run off. He said you were a Saint and a God-fearing woman."

Ruth buttoned Mason's britches single-mindedly and did not reply. She was not prepared for the happiness and relief that flooded over her when the door opened and Fred stood there, unchanged, his features still all but hidden under the beard and thick glasses. Gideon held his hand, and Eden and Afton and Lil fell into his arms. He hugged them and wiped his eyes.

Fred pumped Ruth's hand and made a fuss over Mason. He said that Ruth was the best cook in all of Idaho and probably Utah, too, and that Eden was the best little girl ever and that Afton was braver than any ten boys. Lil tugged at his pants, and he laughed and gave out licorice all around and said that Lil was the flower of the family, a regular dandelion with her golden hair.

Both women grew increasingly uncomfortable at this recital. Mavis believed that in praising his brother's family, Fred was slighting the merits of Lafayette and Dorothea, and that he waxed on about Ruth to the detriment of his wife. Ruth cringed because she knew that these were sweetened, condensed memories and that in truth she had soured many of Fred's days.

Fred bounced Mason on his knee. "Where's Brother Samuel, Sister Ruth?"

At that moment, Ruth didn't know. Samuel would certainly be back from the Bintons' by now. He would have come home and found the house cold and the family gone, and he wouldn't have worried too much because he had known they were going into Healy, but when suppertime came around and the fires stayed banked, he might have cut short his nightly congress with the Lord to do some thinking about his family. He wouldn't know that their clothes were gone and wasn't likely to check for the valises. But he would know something was wrong. Still, his delusions probably would not permit him to recognize that he had been deserted.

The younger ones didn't make it through supper; their heads drooped, and they snoozed at the table. It was decided that Eden and

Afton would double up with Dorothea, and Gideon with Lafayette, and that Ruth, Lil, and Mason would sleep in the parlor. Fred sent Lafayette in to fire up the parlor stove and take the chill off the air.

"That's a waste," said Mavis. "They're just going to sleep anyway."

"That room gets pretty cold, Mavis."

"No colder than the others, and we don't light fires in there."

"Well, it can't hurt to warm it up this once. It ain't every day we get Ruth and these young ones to visit. Get on, Lafayette."

The boy stood motionless till Mavis shrugged. "Waste not, want not, I always say."

That much was clear, Ruth thought. She reckoned that Fred's tidy little widow had married him to heat up the bed so she wouldn't waste fuel.

When the children were abed, Mavis began on the supper dishes, and Ruth offered to help, but Fred wouldn't let her. He said she didn't look well. Her broad back to them, Mavis asked if Brother Samuel was going to join them tomorrow. Fred's chin sank to his chest, and he plucked at the balls that had gathered on his wool shirt. Behind his glasses his eyes were full of pain.

Mavis finished the dishes and took her seat, mending in hand, her needle pricking viciously at the cloth. She asked again: when would Brother Samuel join his family?

Ruth knotted her hands and cleared her throat. "I've brought the team and wagon for you to sell, Fred. I need the money. I'm taking my children to my father's in Salt Lake, and I don't have enough cash for the train fare. You can sell the team and wagon. They're good horses, you know that, Fred. We always take care of our animals."

"They're good horses." Fred plucked at his shirt.

"Don't your husband need that team and wagon?" Mavis bit her thread with a flash of her pointy teeth.

Fred raised his bleary blue eyes, and his long mouth sagged. "You're leaving Samuel, aren't you, Sister Ruth?"

"I am, Fred."

Mavis clucked. Fred sucked reflectively on a piece of licorice. "Now, Mavis," he said.

"Marriage is a sacred ordinance for time and all eternity, commanded by God. If you don't think that's so, Fred Douglass, you just have a look at them wedding vows you and me took, even if they was only for time—I'm pledged to Mr. Anderson for all eternity," she added. "No man and no woman is to put marriage asunder. That's for death alone to do."

"Now, Mavis, we should hear Sister Ruth out."

"Did you hear out that man Velda run off with?"

"I'm not running off with any man," Ruth declared. "Samuel's gone mad, Fred. He's getting revelations from the Lord, each one crazier than the last. He's mad, and there's no living with him."

Fred blinked uncontrollably and sucked at his teeth, as if they might otherwise desert his mouth.

"He's your lawful husband, and you're his lawful wife," said Mavis firmly.

"Fred, he says he's God's new prophet, Joseph Smith's successor, and that God wants him to take a plural wife, sell everything, and go to Mexico."

"The church don't hold with polygamy anymore," said Mavis.

"Samuel don't care about the church. Don't you see, Fred? God tells Samuel everything. He doesn't need the church. He doesn't need anybody except to do his bidding, and what he says is God's will." Ruth took a deep breath and continued more calmly. "Well, I don't care who gives him revelations or who gives him his supper for that matter, so long as my children don't have to suffer and I am not dragged through the dirt of another country."

"You can stay the night, but you better go home in the morning," said Mavis.

"Now, Mavis. I don't think Sister Ruth's come here for our advice. I think she needs our help."

"That advice is the best help we can be."

"Samuel's gone daft, Fred. He don't talk to anyone but God and he don't listen to anyone but God, and he says he is going to marry a girl from Woodrull on the first day of the new century, which isn't but a week away. I couldn't stay there and stand for it, could I? I couldn't let him do that to me."

Fred's Adam's apple bobbed, and he wound his powerful hands together as if to subdue them. "I mighta seen this coming. I mighta seen it, but it wasn't my place to say anything, so I just stuck with the children and didn't say nothing. But maybe it wouldn't have done no good anyway."

"It don't change what's right and wrong," Mavis contended. "Marriage is right and desertion is wrong."

"Well, Mavis, I don't know. I don't know if that's always so. I think me and Samuel might've been different men if our ma coulda taken us away. I think we might've, all right. Our ma was Pa's plural wife. We was her only living children. They'd get born and they'd die, poor woman, and Pa's first wife was always telling her—and telling Pa, too—that it was God's vengeance for her having stole away another woman's husband. She didn't steal him, but she was young and Pa's first wife was old, and she hated us. We had our own house, but it was on the same scrap of land as Pa's first family's, and it was just awful living out there after Ma died. Pa went crazy. He tried to get back in his first wife's bed, but she wouldn't have him. She'd feed him now and then, but she wouldn't feed us. We wasn't allowed to cross their threshold, me and Samuel. We had to live with that terrible old man. He was a terrible old man." Fred scraped his hands along his pants. "Me and Samuel, we got up and git as soon as we could. One morning I woke up and Samuel was gone, and I left pretty quick after that. I never went back. I wrote Pa to tell him me and Velda was married, but I guess he musta died by then, because I never heard nothing from any of them and I never wanted to." Fred popped a piece of licorice and swallowed it in one gulp. "So, Mavis, I think Sister Ruth is right in taking those children from here. It ain't right for children to be around the crazed. Yes, I have to say I think she's right no matter what the church says about marriage vows. Sometimes they just ain't to be lived."

"You should know. Look at Velda."

"Well, me and Velda was too young to marry, but she was just the prettiest little sixteen you can imagine."

Mavis brought her sights up to the needle's eye and jabbed the thread through. "You'd have been better off if she'd been less pretty and more modest."

Fred blushed to his temples. "Well, I guess that's true. Your people know you're coming, Sister Ruth?"

"No. There wasn't time. I'll be on the train out of here tomorrow morning, though, no matter where it's going."

"Well, it's going south. Yes, I think tomorrow's train goes to Ogden, don't it, Mavis?"

"Sister Ruth can't leave tomorrow anyway. That team and

wagon can't be sold on the Sabbath, and the day after that's Christmas. You'll just have to wait."

"I can't wait. Samuel's not that crazy. He'll come after me, Fred. Just give me the money for the train fare, that's all I need. You can have the team and wagon for whatever they'll bring."

"We can't do that!" Mavis cried. "We can't go around giving people our cash. Cash is hard to come by. We need every bit of cash we can get from Mr. Anderson's farm, and we're not going to be giving it to strangers."

"I don't think Sister Ruth is a stranger."

"Well, I never laid eyes on her afore today."

"I'll give you a bill of sale, Fred."

"That wagon ain't yours to sell, missus. When Samuel gets here he might just say, 'Gimme back my team and wagon,' and he'd be right. That's the law of it, and we'd be out our cash and them horses, which is probably no great beasts either."

"I'll pay you back the money for the fare, Fred. I'll send you the money from Salt Lake."

"Oh, no, you won't." Mavis jabbed her needle into the pincushion. "Because there's nothing to pay back. It's against God's law to leave your husband, and you'd be an aider and abettor, Fred, if you do this, and the law won't stand for it, and me neither."

"Now, Mavis. I don't think we can turn Sister Ruth and the children away when they need us. I'm sure that wagon alone is worth the fare."

Under her breath, Ruth prayed that Fred could exert himself against this niggling little woman, though Ruth had never seen him exert himself against anything except a shovel or an ax.

"I'm not giving cash money from my farm to a criminal and a stranger."

"We're wed, too, Mavis, don't forget. It's our farm now." Fred played with the licorice stuck in his teeth.

"I was a fool! Better I had just hired a man till Lafayette got good and growed, but no, I have to marry a man who might just as well take my money out to the fields and cast it to the winds as give it to a runaway wife who don't have no legal rights."

"Now, Mavis."

"You'd give away the clothes from your back, Fred Douglass, if there wasn't a commandment against nakedness. Somewhere."

"I've got nine dollars fifty," Ruth implored him. "If you could just make up the difference for the fare."

"You go home, missus, and make up your differences with your husband, and maybe he won't want a second wife."

"Now, Mavis. I think we're just going to have to give Sister Ruth that money. We'll sell the team after Christmas."

"Not if Samuel comes to claim it, we won't. You'll be the doom of me and Lafayette and Dorothea."

"Now, Mavis, if the tables was turned, if it was you in trouble, I don't doubt for a minute that Sister Ruth would help you."

"You mean if you got revelations from God and turned prophet?" Mavis hooted.

"Well, I mean if anything happened to me. If I was sick or couldn't work the farm."

"Well, your brother's not sick. He's crazy!"

"Maybe it's the same thing. Sister Ruth gets that money, and there's an end to it."

Ruth wilted in her chair, relieved, but not convinced. She'd have to have the money in her hand, or perhaps be on the train or out of Idaho or standing by her father's side in Salt Lake City, before she'd be convinced of her escape. She met Mavis's angry pig eyes and knew that if the tables were turned, she would not have lifted a hand to help Mavis. But she put these thoughts behind her. She did not intend—ever—to explore the domain of regret.

The new National Falls railway station, constructed of Douglass bricks, was a fine building that glowed like an ember in the snow from a distance. It stood well outside of town, surrounded by snow-drifted empty hog and cattle pens and white-wheeled mail wagons. The ticket office and waiting room were small and stuffy with the winter smells of wet wool and coal oil and the perennial odor of travel: poorly printed tickets and disinfectant. Unpolished cuspidors sat glumly in the corners, and varnish peeled off the floor. Two long pews faced each other, and except for the teller that afternoon, the station was empty. The train was miles and hours away.

Fred roused the teller from the *Police Gazette* to buy their tickets. He handed them to Gideon and told him to keep them safely in his pocket. They left smudges on the boy's fingers.

"I'm the oldest," Eden said. "I should have them."

85

"I want to hold my own," Afton added.

"Quiet, all of you," Ruth snapped. She was in no mood for childish spats.

"Now, Gideon." Fred knelt and drew him into the warm circle of his arm. "When the conductor asks you for the tickets, you give them to him, because you're the man on this trip and your mother and sisters and young Mason here, they'll all look to you."

"Where's Pa?"

Ruth ground her hands together till her gloves squealed.

"Now, Gideon—you think your pa can just up and leave the brick business because he'd like to? He'll be along, but here you are, you and your sisters and mother and little Mason, going down to Salt Lake to see your grandparents, who you ain't never seen. Oh, Gideon, don't I wish I was you! Just think, if you're seeing Salt Lake when you're only eight, just think how many places you'll see by the time you're old as me. You are real lucky children, all of you."

Gideon nodded, his eyes shining with self-importance and rosy prospects.

"Well, I better get back. Mavis won't like it if I'm late. I just hope you're not too big, any of you, to give old Fred a hug." Gideon threw his arms around the tall, bearded, bearish Fred, and the girls clamored into his embrace, and he kissed their cool cheeks and pressed their shiny heads to his. He said maybe Lil ought to have a look in his pockets, and what was that? "Licorice bits! Now, Eden, you have a look in the other pocket, and Afton, you, too. Gideon, there's enough there for Mason." He pulled a piece of licorice out from behind Eden's ear. "Now what are you doing keeping licorice behind your ears? What will your ma think when she goes to wash your ears and finds licorice?" Fred rose and turned to Ruth. "You better reach in the top pocket of my coat here, Sister Ruth."

"I hate licorice, Fred. I always have. It makes me sick."

"I know that. This is something else."

She reached into his breast pocket, and her fingers touched the thin bodies of fifteen silver dollars. "Oh, Fred! I'll pay you back."

"This ain't for paying back, Sister Ruth. This is for keeping. This is mine to give, and it ain't Mavis's or have anything to do with her."

Ruth began to cry and apologize through her tears.

Fred patted her back. "Now, Sister Ruth, you'll give young Mason ideas and he'll start to cry." Mason sat wide-eyed and happy on the bench, his nut-colored curls shining even in the dim light of the station.

Ruth blew her nose. "Thank you, Fred. You can't know what this means—"

"No thanks needed. What? After all those years you put up with me?" Ruth started to interrupt, but he hushed her. "Don't you worry about anything. Don't worry. You're doing the right thing, Sister Ruth. The church thinks they thought of everything. The church thinks they got every floorboard nailed down, but they don't. There's things that can happen between folks, between men and women, that just can't be nailed down or lived with."

He gave the children hugs all around and finally disentangled himself from their small arms and hands. He said again that Mavis would be waiting and he had to go, much as he'd like to stay and wait with them till the train came. Against his protests, Ruth accompanied him to the snow-powdered platform. She watched him climb into the wagon, where he stood, took off his hat, and saluted her. Then he hit the horses with the cold reins and left.

"Why isn't Pa going with us?" Afton demanded when Ruth returned inside.

She moistened her handkerchief and wiped the licorice off Mason's face. "Because we're going to see your grandparents. It's high time for a visit."

"Will Pa come later?"

"Yes," she said tartly. "Maybe later." Maybe in the afterlife. Maybe on the day after the Last Day. Maybe when Elda Allred had five living children and had borne them in shelters dug out of Mexican hillsides. Maybe when God quit conversing with Samuel. Maybe then. But not before. "Anyway, don't you want to go to Salt Lake and see the streets lit up and have a toilet in the house?"

"No thundermugs?" said Gideon.

"Thundermugs are a thing of the past in Salt Lake."

"Aunt Mavis didn't empty her thundermugs as often as she should," Eden said seriously.

"And not enough salt in her biscuits," Afton added.

Ruth's mouth opened to laugh, but she heard only an unpracticed cackle, and she closed her lips. Once she escaped, perhaps she'd get her laugh back and some bloom in her cheeks, and surely she'd feel better, less drained, once they got to Salt Lake. Oh, it was Christmas, and there would be the Z.C.M.I, the church's own store, that sprawling testament to the Saints' material prosperity, lit up and bustling, and there would be parties and dancing, lots of dancing, because Mormon men could step with the best of them, and maybe she hadn't forgotten how to dance.

A thirty-five-year-old woman who has left her husband and run away with five children has no business dancing, an inner voice told her, *and isn't likely to find anyone to dance with either.* Well, she didn't have to dance. Never cared much for dancing anyway. It would be enough to have people all around, hear hooves ring on pavement instead of the horses' dull thud on the backroads of Idaho. Gaslight and trolley bells on Temple Square! The Mason house was on a street not far from Temple Square, and it was lit with gaslight, too. The ice was delivered in wagons and not cut from the heart of winter and stored against the spring. She longed to hear the neighbors or their servants bickering over back fences. Imagine having people so close you could just call to them. She longed to see women in store-bought clothes of lemony yellow and robin's-breast red, colors other than the nutgall, black, and drab of her own repertoire. She longed to be a girl again and feel the claret silk she'd worn to the Christmas party of 1885. She longed to sit next to her father and tell him how hard it had been for her, what with Samuel's mind going the last few years, and hard even before that, living in that filthy dugout and washing other people's dirty clothes. Imagine a woman of her refinement transplanted to so barren a wilderness. It was unthinkable. And it was over. She would breathe in her father's chemical odor, not like Samuel's smell of brick dust and righteousness. Those smells were past. Father would say that Samuel had never deserved her in the first place, and he'd find a way to get her a divorce—unendurable word!—but Father would help her divorce quietly so that no one would ever think the less of her for leaving her husband. Everything would be fine in Salt Lake. Broken bits of hymn rolled to her tongue. " 'In the furnace God may prove thee,' " she whispered. " 'Thence to bring thee forth more bright.' "

The harrowing at her heart eased, but the smell of licorice was making her sick. She put Mason in Eden's charge and walked out to the platform, where the snow thickened and the wind funneled it into multitudinous cones. She looked up the tracks into the future, and even though it was December, some of the old seductive spring stole over Ruth. She tilted her face to the snow. A blast of wind from the north blew snow off a nearby cedar, and it fell like powdered glass. She listened for the train's jarring, unharmonic shriek, but the train was miles and hours distant, and even straining her ears, all Ruth could hear was the sound of the station roof, creaking and contracting in the cold of Christmas Eve.

10

"WELL, JESUS, JOSEPH, and Emma! You're a little late, aren't you, Ruth?"

"What's that black wreath doing on the door, Albert?"

"Didn't you get my wire? Don't they deliver wires in that slog bog Healy?"

"What's that black wreath doing on the door, Albert?"

"Didn't you know? What are you doing here if you didn't—"

"What's the black wreath for?"

"Pa, Ruth. Pa died. He went quick, two days before Christmas, and I wired you to get down here for the funeral, but you didn't wire back or nothing, so we buried him this morning. If I'd known you were going to come, I would have—"

"Pa?" Ruth blanched white as a new ledger. "Where's Pa?"

"He's dead, Ruth, he di—" Albert explained no further, because Ruth fainted at his feet. He carried her into the parlor and stretched her out on the sofa, and when Lily walked in and saw her sister, she began to scream that she, too, was going to faint, and Afton Mason, hearing the commotion, padded softly down the stairs to see her five wide-eyed grandchildren surrounded by their valises standing in the hallway and both her daughters prone. She began to whimper. So that just at the moment when Albert thought the worst was over, the Mason home was filled with weeping women. Again.

Albert had had his hands full for the last few days: his father's sudden death, the necessary arrangements to be made, both sisters to be notified, and his mother to be sedated. In fact, the same doctor who had pronounced Abel dead had given Albert a fresh vial of laudanum for his mother, a vial now nearly empty. If his father's death had been an unexpected blow and his mother's breakdown thoroughly predictable, Albert had not been ready to deal with the hysterical Lily and her husband, Art Whickham, who had caught the first train out of St. Elmo, California, to come to Salt Lake for the funeral, and he was certainly unprepared for his eldest sister to arrive trailing a pack of little children and faint on the doorstep.

Albert unfastened Ruth's collar, fanned her face, and chafed her hands. "Effie!" he hollered. "Effie, get your fingers out of the larder and come in here and help me! Bring the smelling salts!"

"Bring a cold compress," Afton Mason suggested, hovering in the doorway, eyeing five grandchildren she'd never seen. The strain was too much, and she made her way to the chair and gnawed her hanky.

Effie, whom Abel Mason had hired to replace Ruth, slouched in and gave the smelling salts to Albert and the compress to Mrs. Mason. "No," she demurred. "It's for Lily."

"It's for me." Lily signaled Effie from the chair where she'd collapsed.

"She's coming around," Albert announced, still chafing Ruth's hands. "There, there. It's all right."

Ruth opened her eyes before she should have; they seemed to roll back into her head, and she thought she might faint again, but instead she began to cry. She ground her palms over the hot tears and took deep, unrefreshing breaths. She had never cried in front of her children; she did not intend to start now. "Take the children out of here, please."

"What, Ruth? The children, you say? Certainly. Effie. Effie, take those children in the kitchen and give them something to eat. And keep them there," Albert added, sizing them up; the little Douglasses had grown in size and number but not improved in the six years since Albert had been in Idaho. They were still stringy and slack-jawed, with runny noses. "There, there, Ruth. The children have gone with Effie. Now you just have a good cry if you want."

She didn't want, but the tears and her story bubbled forth anyway; she'd been telling the story all the way from National Falls, readying it for her father, who would understand and sympathize and make it all bearable. The unbearable story spilled forth with unrehearsed tears and gasps, and Ruth heard herself repeating, "What could I do? What could I do?"

"Oh, Sister, no!" Lily exclaimed at every pause.

"There, there," said Albert, donating his handkerchief.

Ruth blew her nose and sat up slowly, noting, much to her horror, that a stranger had overheard the whole ugly tale. "Who is that?" she asked, pointing to the man leaning against the mantelpiece.

"That's my husband, Ruth," Lily said. "That's Art Whickham."

Art Whickham was a man of medium stature, dwarfed in the Mason household by every adult except Effie. He wore a natty checked suit with a thick gold watchchain across his paunch, and his lips had petrified into dyspeptic disapproval. As Ruth composed herself, she sorted back through the tale she'd heard from Albert, how Lily Mason, the belle of Salt Lake, had married a widower from St. Elmo, California, one of the numerous tribe of Whickham, a man fourteen years her senior. Both her parents had been against the marriage, until they were apprised of the gravity of Lily's situation, whereupon they had not only condoned the marriage but had hastened it. Lily and Art had been married in the same parlor as Ruth and Samuel and had apparently committed equally inappropriate acts in that very room. Ruth and Samuel had been married when they first enjoyed each other on the parlor floor; Lily and Art had not been.

The parlor itself, Ruth realized as she planted her feet on the carpet, was as oppressive as ever, perhaps more so with Mrs. Mason and Lily swathed in black and regarding her with a lack of comprehension that had not changed in ten years. The red velvet drapes had faded and the gold tassels dimmed, but the heavy hand of convention seemed to squeeze Ruth at the temples, except that something was missing. Abel Mason was dead, so he was missing, but so were the taxidermist's monuments. "Where are the stuffed animal heads?"

Albert gave her a warning look, which she didn't heed, asking again after the baleful, balding creatures, and then Mrs. Mason's furtive eyes darted to the piano, where the owls were missing, and the walls, where dust rings testified that once heads had hung there.

"Where are they?" Mrs. Mason whined. "Your father won't like this, Albert. He insisted on those heads. Your father will be very angry with you."

"Jesus, Joseph, and Emma, now you've done it!" Albert barked at

Ruth. He rose and took his mother's arm, escorting her out of the room as he explained that he had removed them only because he thought they might be too painful for her—reminders of the dear departed and the glorious happy past, now lost to us forever since Abel Mason had left Salt Lake and taken up residence in the celestial estates.

Ruth regarded the dust rings as she listened to Albert's explanation, and then, against the dictates of good taste and conscience, she broke into laughter, harsh, crackling laughter, like dry paper put to the match. She fell back against the sofa laughing, laughed till she wheezed and tears ran down her cheeks.

"Sister Ruth don't feel well, Art," Lily explained. "She's had a bad time of it."

"I can see that."

"She must have the brain fever, don't you think, Art?" Lily took Ruth's hand in hers. "Please, Ruth, don't laugh like that. It's not right. You shouldn't laugh. Pa is dead and Samuel's gone crazy and you've run away from your home and your husband and you don't have anything and you shouldn't laugh."

Ruth wiped her eyes. "What should I do, Lily? What do you think I should do?"

"Well, you should just have a nice lie-down and let Effie bring you some broth and a nice cold—"

"Damn broth and compresses! Damn them!" Ruth snatched her hands away from her sister. "Spare me a life of broth and compresses!"

"Come, Lily." Art took his wife's elbow and urged her to her feet. "Let's leave your sister in peace."

"Peace! How can you leave me in peace? Where is there any peace to be left in?"

"Oh, Ruth," Lily wailed. "You're not yourself."

"Oh, yes, I am," she said wearily. "I wish I wasn't, but I am."

Art and Lily left Ruth, if not in peace at least to herself, and she moved to the fire, warming her hands against the chill that had started in her bones and was inching outward.

Albert bustled in. "I told Effie to take the children down and show them the temple grounds before supper. That ought to hold them for a while."

"Yes," Ruth replied mechanically.

"I don't know why you had to call those stuffed heads to Ma's attention. You set her off again. I'll have to call that expensive quack in for more laudanum before the week's out."

"Did you let Pa get cold before you took the heads down, Albert?"

"I meant no disrespect," Albert snapped. "There's enough death around this house without dead animals on the walls!"

Ruth smiled. "I've always hated them, too."

"And taxidermy! What kind of life is that? Stuffing dead animals? I say, let the living get on with it. I'm the man of the family now."

"Did you have to wait for Pa to die before you could say that?"

"Don't take that tone with me, Ruth. You've seen Ma and Lily. They haven't gotten no better. Someone's got to take care of things."

"I'm sure you've taken care of everything." Ruth collected herself slowly. She buttoned the collar back tightly and tucked the stray hairs back into the bun at the back of her neck. "You've probably got it all in hand, the will, Pa's money. I'm sure you know exactly what you're going to do with the money."

"It's no sin to be rich, to be comfortable."

"I didn't say it was."

"There's a future in Salt Lake, in America, for a Saint with some capital in his pockets and some brains in his head. I'm buying into the insurance business with some partners, if you must know. I'm selling the taxidermy business and going into insurance."

"What are you going to do? Convince people that they can buy off the Grim Reaper?"

"You ain't changed either, Ruth. Same nasty tongue as ever. I would have thought your afflictions would have taught you a little humility, anyway. Here you are, a runaway wife with a crazy husband and no place . . . no place . . . no place to . . ." Albert watched his sister pace the room. Her skirt rustled, the fire crackled, the clock ticked incessantly, and Albert heard his own increasingly heavy breathing. He didn't have to be Daniel or Nebuchadnezzar to see the writing on this wall. "You, uh . . ." He pinched the bridge of his nose. "You planning to stay here, Ruth? You and the children?"

"Well, I'm not going back to Idaho."

He cleared his throat and tried to imitate his father's resolve.

93

"Well, Ruth, you can't do that. You see, I'm getting married real soon. Me and Elyse Farnsworth, we're getting married. I'm twenty-two, after all, and she's nineteen, and we're not getting any younger, and it's time for me to make my way in the world."

"What does that have to do with me?"

"We're going to live here. In this house."

"There's plenty of room."

"Not enough for me and Elyse and Ma and you and five snot-dribbling children!"

"You dribbled snot once, Albert. Everything in its season."

"Well, excuse me, Ruth, but I don't fancy starting out my married life with my sister and her five children. No, I don't. I got plans."

"I have five children. They need a home. Is that clear?"

Albert wrung his hands. Sweat needled him under his collar and beaded at his balding forehead. "Don't misunderstand me, Ruth, I have every sympathy for your afflictions."

"I can't abide sanctimonious codswallop, Albert. Just tell me what's on your mind."

He didn't dare. What was on Albert's mind at that moment was the sole Biblical injunction he had taken to heart: What profiteth it? "Well, Ruth," he began more slowly, "it don't surprise me that Samuel Douglass don't know polygamy's been outlawed. Slavery's been outlawed, too, and that didn't stop him from working me like I was deeded, stamped, and delivered, and I got to admit, I'm happy to see someone pull a good one on Samuel Douglass. It must have been Job's own job to get out of Healy with five children. I admire that. Too bad you couldn't have took more cash—but that don't matter now, Ruth. You're right. We have to think of the children. Those little ones have to be protected from Samuel. He's crazed, Ruth."

"Get to it, Albert."

"He's crazed, but he's not stupid, no, you never could say that of Samuel, and sooner or later he's going to know that this is the only place you had to go, and he's going to come looking for you. He'll know where you are. He could show up any day now, crazy as a loon, with his new wife in tow." This vivid scenario made Albert bilious; he lived in the very shadow of the Mormon temple, and the scandal that his brother-in-law could bring down on him could ruin him. Only death was more final than scandal. Ruth quit pacing and stood by the fire. Albert wished she would sit down. It would be easier to be firm with a woman he didn't have to look up to. "You've had a time of it, Ruth. You have. No one knows that better than me. I was there, don't forget. I know what Healy was like. Yes, I've often felt for you. Here you are, taller than most men, smarter than most women, and you married this—"

"I know who I married. I don't need you to tell me that."

"No, of course you don't. But—marriage, now that's not easily undone. Ever. The church teaches us that a woman don't get into heaven but on the arm of her husband—"

"Yes, and that's the only way she gets into hell, too."

"Well, Ruth, you've had it hard up till now, but I think I can provide for you. I'm the man of the family now, and—"

"If you say that again, I'm going upstairs and unpack. If you have some other suggestion, let's hear it."

Jesus, Joseph, and Emma, he thought—struck with inspiration, as if the Lord had cracked the golden tablets over his head. "Well, Ruth," he said confidently, "the Lord provideth. Indeed He does. Even though we've been afflicted here with death and its dominions, it's brought us the very answer for you, Ruth. And for your young ones, too."

"Well?"

"Well, Lily and Art, of course. The Lord has given us Lily and Art, all right. There's the answer. You go back to St. Elmo with them on the train, and no one needs to be the wiser. Samuel's so crazy he probably don't even remember you got a sister, much less that she's married or who she married or where she lives."

"And what am I supposed to do in St. Elmo?"

"That Art Whickham is rich, Ruth. Rich! He holds mortgages on half the town. He's president of the bank down there, a real pillar of the community, the son of St. Elmo's founder, Madison Whickham."

"The Mormon scout?"

"The very one, though if you ask me, it ain't any great honor to be one of some hundred children, because old Madison, he sowed his seed all over the West and left it to his thirteen wives to reap it. Madison Whickham did more begetting than Abraham. But Art, now, he's made money, not babies. He's rich. Why, he and Lily, they were just telling me ten minutes before you got here about their

95

big house, so big they just rattle around in it, them and their two boys. They got plenty, Ruth, and don't you let them tell you any different." He placed his hand on her shoulder. "I'm only thinking of you and the children. If you stay here, Samuel'll come for you sure. Why, if it wasn't for that, I'd say, you stay, Ruth. This is as much your home as mine. Only a beast would throw his sister out."

Ruth shook off his hand and began to pace again. "But only a fool would keep her here, isn't that what you mean?"

"You certainly have gotten small-minded, Ruth. I never thought you'd say a thing like that to your own brother. And here I am, thinking of your welfare. Samuel will know you had to come here. The law might be on his side, Ruth. You did desert him, and if he was to show up and want his children back—"

"Over my dead body."

"Yes, that's what I say. That's why you should go with Art and Lily."

"And what if Art says no?"

"He can't say no." Not unless he wants to be shown up, Albert thought, for the cold-hearted, snake-skinned, two-bit toad I've always known he was. "He's a Latter-day Saint. A man of honor."

"Just like you, Albert."

"You can go or not," he said with more bravado than he felt. "But St. Elmo is your only salvation. Samuel will never find you there."

Ruth stood before him, and Albert felt his resolution shrink under her hard gaze. His hands began to shake, and his mouth grew dry. "You ought to be grateful to me, Ruth. It's not every brother who would look out for you like I'm doing."

"You've gotten real smart since I saw you last, Albert," she said, appraising him with what he recognized was shrewdness equal to his own and a toughness of spirit he could not hope to emulate. "You've gotten smart, all right, but I don't want you to think I've gotten stupid. I know what's happening. I know what you're doing. I want you to know that I don't mistake it for brotherly love."

"If Pa was alive, Ruth, he'd tell you the same thing I'm telling you. He'd say—"

"Oh, shut up, Albert. If Pa was alive, he probably would have sent me back to Samuel. I must have feathered my brains to think anything different. He would have sent me back to my lawful wedded husband. Till death do us part. I wish I was dead. I'd trade places with Pa if I could, but it don't matter." She took the poker and knelt in front of the fire. "Whether I live or die I'm going to spend my life in hell. And I could even bear hell"—she jabbed at the logs—"except that I'll have to show that I'm grateful for it. I'll always have to be grateful." The fire collapsed, and a shower of sparks fell at her feet.

11

 RUTH PRESSED HER forehead to the window as the train pushed south and west. Sometimes her head fell back on the seat, stained with the oil of many such heads, and she fell asleep with her mouth open. As long as the train moved, its rolling, incessant clack reassured her: an ordeal behind her, an ordeal before her, the track was a long shallow trough that held the wheels in their place and kept her—for all her forward velocity—in an immutable ever present.

Arthur Whickham spent the journey fortified behind a newspaper, adjusting his specs now and then, sometimes crumpling the paper's edge to glance at the seat across from him, where Ruth gazed mutely outward, somber, sallow, and pensive. She had seemingly forgotten her children, and they ran wild in the aisles and were reprimanded by the conductors. She allowed herself to be moved like freight. She resisted Lily's attempts to draw her out, to "talk about something else." Art didn't try to talk to her; he didn't believe in talking too much to women.

Art Whickham cursed Albert in particular and the Masons in general. He'd gone to Salt Lake to see one soul out of the world and was returning home with six extra souls—six extra mouths, twelve grabby hands, and five runny noses. He wished he'd had the presence of mind to refuse, because if what he'd heard about Ruth was true, he didn't fancy Lily's learning any lessons from her older sister. Lily was just fine the way she was, even if she spent half the year claiming that the St. Elmo heat destroyed her, lying on a hammock on the screened porch trying to "catch" a breeze exactly as if it were a fly or a moth or a cold.

The St. Elmo Valley lies on the western side of a jagged spine of mountains connected to the deserts by a long natural pass called Jesuit Pass, which winds up from the bleached, bone-strewn desert floor through the mountains and thence down into the town. St. Elmo owed its existence to the Mormons and its life to the Gentiles. The Mormons, under the leadership of Madison Whickham with five of his thirteen wives in tow, first established themselves there as part of Brigham Young's grand plan for the Saints. Whickham and his band of faithful were to establish an outpost, a corridor to the sea, because whoever controlled Jesuit Pass controlled the southern access to the Pacific.

The Mormons, with their solidarity, their industry, their self-denial, and their women, prospered, built a mill, and laid their town out in a dull foursquare grid radiating from the courthouse. When it wasn't dried up, like everything—and everyone—else in St. Elmo, water flowed through a natural sluice, which the Mormons named the River Canaan but which everyone referred to as Dogsback Ditch in honor of its mangy color.

In 1857, Brigham Young challenged the United States government to what amounted to a duel and called all the settlers back to Zion to defend the homeland against the Feds. Whickham and his followers deserted their homes, their gardens, their mill, their collective efforts and retreated, much to the leftover Gentiles' delight. Not everyone, however, responded to Brigham's commands. Among those who stayed was the tenth wife of Madison Whickham, who said that the Lion of the Lord could fight his own battles; she would not leave her home and all she had worked for because Brigham Young was so cocky as to invite the wrath of the U.S. government. Madison Whickham invoked every prophet and patriarch in a half-dozen holy books, but to no avail. She stayed, and her children stayed with her.

After the Saints left, the Gentiles went on the rampage, burned the Mormons' church, ransacked their storehouse, destroyed their abandoned homes, and would have pulled the mill down and torched it, too, but that the tenth wife of Madison Whickham stood her ground there and with her two oldest sons threatened to blow the head off any Gentile who came near the place. She moved her family into the mill to protect it, and it was there that Arthur Whickham was born, a humble beginning for such a pillar of civic rectitude.

For a quarter century after that, St. Elmo limped by while other nearby communities discovered the politics of irrigation, formed themselves into land and water companies, planted acres of citrus groves, sold false stock, and prospered. St. Elmo could pride itself only on the cathouse and courthouse, and save for those two sturdy institutions, the town would have blown away with the desert winds except that in the mid-eighties, the railroad saw the wisdom of Brigham's vision. Indeed, St. Elmo *was* the perfect link between the southern deserts and the sea. They built their yards and terminals there, established headquarters, and brought with them men, money, and a necessary infusion of enterprise and responsibility.

Arthur Whickham found himself facing the new century from the second-story window of the spacious St. Elmo National Bank and Trust Company building. He looked out over a maze of trolley wires, electric wires, and telephone wires and the courthouse clock. His ample, high-ceilinged home on Salt Lake Avenue (also known as Silk Stocking Row) sheltered his delicate second wife, the former Lily Mason, his two boys, three overworked servants, and now his sister-in-law and her five children, and unbeknownst to him, a sixth, because by February, Ruth suspected the worst.

She told Lily as they sat on the broad porch, rocking and sewing. Lily's mouth puckered into a round O of surprise and sorrow. "Oh, no, Ruth."

"Oh, yes, Lily." Ruth ripped out a hem savagely. "It's so. I'm sure of it."

"What will you do?"

"What do you mean? Have I any choice?"

"I meant without your . . . without a husband, what will you do?"

"I'll do just fine. Better than if I had Samuel around, I'll tell you

99

that. You're not to breathe a word of this to a living soul, do you understand? Not even Art. Especially Art."

"Oh, but Ruth, I tell Art everything."

"Well, you just keep your mouth shut about this, Lily Mason, or you'll be sorry."

Lily nodded slowly. Ruth didn't realize the sacrifice she was asking. Lily had no secrets from Art. It was easier that way. She told him everything, and he made it all better. Art took care of things. But even Art could not take care of this. "When will it be born?" she asked.

"Too soon and not soon enough," Ruth replied grimly.

"Oh, Ruth, was he a beast?"

"Shut up, Lily. I wish it would die or miscarry so that I could be rid of it and rid of Samuel."

"Oh, Ruth, that's a terrible thing, a sinful thing, to say."

Ruth had no reply. She knew her sister was right. There didn't seem to be any path or any thought that didn't lead Ruth to sin, and maybe her heart was naturally corrupt. Why not shred the veil of pretense and indulge in unrestrained, unchristian hatred?

Ruth hated Samuel. He'd brought this on her with his madness, his lust, his revelations. Why didn't he bed Elda Allred and be done with it? If he'd done that, Ruth wouldn't be lying now in an attic room in Arthur Whickham's house with the fruit of her own folly and misguided hope growing inside her. Listening, at the dark core of midnight, she was certain she could hear Samuel laughing at her, his ragged, crazy laughter welling up inside her and echoing down the dry conduits of her bones, laughing from the womb where the child took shape and girth. Triumphant laughter, because he knew she'd never escape him. If she traveled to the earth's ends, Samuel would make certain she never forgot: he was her husband and she was his wicked, unbelieving wife.

12

April 18, 1900
Salt Lake City

Dear Ruth—

I thought you ought to know that your fool husband
showed up here last week and threw Mother into a
nervous fit. It's taken me three days and an arm's-length
doctor bill to get her calmed down again. I came right
home when Effie rang me at the office, and you can thank
Jesus I did, because if I hadn't gotten here, Samuel would
have had Mother so rattled she'd have come out with it.
The truth, I mean.

I got Effie to take Mother back upstairs and told them
both to stay there. I closed the parlor door and I said,
well, Samuel, how's the polygamy business? How many
wives you got now? Had any revelations lately? I thought
he was going to come after me with the poker, but he just
stands there with that tic jerking his face around and
starts to blabber out all sorts of Biblical nonsense like he
hasn't even heard my question at all.

I don't need to tell you the names he called you. I
listened, not saying anything, till I couldn't stand no
more, and besides, time is money, and I wasn't about to
waste more of either. I said to him, my sister left you at
Christmas. How come it's taken you till April to come
after her if you want her back so bad?

It's plain enough why. Even though God told Samuel
that Christ's about to come back any minute now, he only
just now sold the land and the brickyard and is on his way
to Mexico with his new wife and mother-in-law, and you
can just imagine what he's been doing in between
prayers. So I said, why bother with Ruth? You got a nice
new wife. Why not let the old one go?

He got hopping mad at that and called on God and all the prophets and swore he'd have the law after you, and I said the law don't smile on polygamy no longer and a person that commits it might just find himself in jail.

Samuel swore he'd find you and make you kiss the rod and lots of other nonsense and demanded to know where you were, so I told him you went to Canada. Your little brother is a pretty smart man.

I'm sure he's out of Salt Lake now, because no man with a polygamous wife wants to stay around this city. The church is getting real touchy on the subject, and they surely don't want to see it on their doorstep.

I have sold the taxidermy business, and good riddance. There are many opportunities in the twentieth century for a Saint with some brains in his head and some capital in his pocket, and I don't intend to spend my days stuffing dead animals. I and some partners have formed the Providential Mutual Insurance Company, which reminds me, you should buy some insurance, because if anything should happen to you, it would be the orphanage for your little lambs. And if nothing happens, insurance gives you a nice nest egg when, as they say, you are full of years and want to rest by an untroubled hearth.

Elyse Farnsworth and I are getting married in May. We would have done it sooner, but her father passed away last month. I am sorry for the delay, but Elyse was his only living child, and now the house is hers. I never did fancy living with Mother when I am a married man, and the Farnsworth house is much grander and newer than this old barn, and in the insurance business, it's not enough to be prosperous, you got to look it.

I am sorry that the enclosed check is all I can afford to send you. You and Lily have left Mother as my sole responsibility, and she can get real tiresome and expensive. Please don't ask me for any more money, because I can't afford it. Arthur Whickham roosts on piles of money.

Give my regards to Lily, but don't give Art a thing.

Your loving brother,
Albert

Ruth read Albert's letter behind the closed door of her tiny room in the upper reaches of the Whickham house. She laid it in the fireplace and put a match to its corner. She leaned against the mantel and watched the fire lick the words, destroy the pages, and die back to glowing ash and curling cinder. If only she could burn her past as easily. If only there were a forge from which she could emerge malleable once more.

That evening Ruth Douglass cut an onion and squeezed its juices into a handkerchief. She called her children into her room, closed the door, and piled them on the bed. She pulled the baby, Mason, into her lap and surveyed the faces of the other four, who had followed her thus far with scarcely a query as to the whys and wherefores of their extended visit with the Whickhams. Even now only Eden betrayed a bit of concern at Ruth's unusual display of tenderness as she stroked their heads and cheeks and felt their collective childish warmth. Eden was so independent and so reliable. Ruth felt a gush of gratitude to her children for their unquestioning love and loyalty. Gideon and Afton were visibly Samuel's children, with Samuel's eyes, fair, lank hair, and long mouth. Lil was the family beauty, with her golden halo of curls and bright eyes; Lil snuggled close to Afton. She never got too far from Afton.

Ruth took a deep breath and daubed her eyes with the reeking handkerchief. Hot tears sprang forth. "I have some terrible news, children. I've kept it from you as long as I could, but I think you must now be told, and you must be very brave," she began as tears spilled down her cheeks. "We only came to St. Elmo for a little visit with Aunt Lily, but now we won't be leaving. We're going to stay here now, because we don't have anything to go back to. Your father's dead." She clutched Mason to her and waited for the gasps of the others to subside. "He died in a fire in the first days of this new century. He died when our house burned to the ground. The barn went, too. Everything—everything went up in flames, the chickenhouse, the windmill, the barn, everything."

In her mind Ruth set the torches herself, first to the house and then the barn, the windmill, the past decade of her life; and the sound of the flames roared in her ears, and the screams of the chickens and livestock echoed as the ravenous, exuberant flames lit up the black sky and the white earth and melted the snow for miles and miles around. Billowing black smoke veiled her past.

Eden wept into her hands. Lil leaned against Afton, who moaned and clutched her sister's hand, and Gideon's eyes wobbled with tears, and he made little whimpering noises.

"No one knows how it started," she continued, rubbing the hanky into her eyes. "A faulty flue, perhaps, a broom or benzine left too near the stove, but it doesn't matter, not to us, not anymore. Everything we had is gone, lost, burned to the ground. Your Uncle Fred, dear Fred, wired me when it happened, and we would have gone back for the funeral, except—you're going to have a new baby brother or sister soon, and my health, the new baby . . . I had to think of the new baby and the future."

Eden fell face down on the bed and sobbed, and the others, save for Mason, seemed to tumble into a heap of fair heads and unrestrained tears.

"Your Uncle Fred buried your father, and all Healy came to mourn. They said there never had been a Saint like your father. Never a man like him. You mustn't mourn for him now, because he's gone to the Celestial Kingdom, where all good Saints go, and we should rejoice for him as we look to the future. We may be alone, but at least we are together, and we must look to the future." She patted Lil's hair and held tight to the restless Mason.

Eden brought her tearful face up and reached for Ruth's handkerchief, but Ruth snatched it back. "Go ahead, Eden, honey, wipe your nose on your skirt. It's all right, just this once. No one's going to mind." Ruth used the onion-drenched hanky once again on her own eyes till they stung and tears gushed, and she drew her children into her embrace and slid the handkerchief under the pillow.

Killing Samuel off, while it gave her some degree of satisfaction, had not the palpable quality of sweet, raw revenge, nor did it diminish her hatred of him. Indeed, her hatred increased, gained weight and girth as her body gained weight and girth with his child, and she sometimes felt she was expanding not with a quickening child at all, but with hate itself that would push her very body beyond its corporeal limits and explode. Her hatred ignited at the mere thought of her brother, Albert, who had turned her out to graze in Arthur Whickham's lean fields. She came to hate her sister, Lily, for the look of simpering pity that so often draped her face. She had threatened Lily with eternal vengeance if Lily so much as cracked her lips about the truth, and probably Art Whickham had threatened Lily with the same thing, because Art Whickham, the very sight of whom consumed Ruth with unreasoning hatred and rage, would not have wanted it known in St. Elmo or anywhere else that his sister-in-law was an unregenerate liar, a murderer in her heart, and a runaway wife. Not when she was already plainly pregnant with no husband in sight.

Ruth's wrath grew in her burgeoning body until it came to include and extend to every man who ever drew breath, beginning with the inoffensive Bishop Myles, who came to offer his condolences when he heard of Sister Douglass's loss, and ending with Joseph Smith and Brigham Young and all the long list of begats and begots and the men who chronicled those begats and forgot or failed to heed or didn't give a damn about the bornes. Who was borne by whom. There was nothing in the begetting. A dog could do it.

A dog could do the borning, too. She sat shelling peas on the Whickham porch, and her hands fell useless to her lap as she watched a pregnant bitch lug her bones across the dusty street, fur falling out, head down, sore swollen dugs suspended from her bulging belly. Ruth watched the mute, soulless beast sniff at trees and evacuate on bushes. She'd have her pups in a shelter provided by a man, if she was lucky. If not, under a hedge, or in a bog or a ditch. Ruth shot out of the chair, and peas danced over the porch and blood drained away from her head, and she fainted clean away.

"Well, Mrs. Douglass," said a voice, moving closer. Dry, disinfectant-smelling hands chafed her face till she turned and saw a knee covered in broadcloth. Then she looked back to the pink-bouquet wallpaper. The voice said, "Everyone out now. She's come to. Everyone out." Ruth looked back to the knee and up to a round, mustachioed face with a big nose and a sad smile, wreathed in the unfamiliar odor of tobacco. She turned back to the wall.

The door closed, and the man cleared his throat. "Look here, Mrs. Douglass, I'm Dr. Tipton. I'm your sister's doctor, and you and I have to have a little talk. Don't overestimate the attractiveness of the back of your head, Mrs. Douglass, it won't do. What are you, five, six months along? Don't look at me like that. I'm a doctor. I'd be a fool not to know. And I know a case of strain when I see it, too. What's that old heathen Whickham doing, having you scrub floors for your keep? No? Exhausting yourself, are you? Except that you're so run-down, you appear to be a healthy woman, and there's no rea-

105

son why you shouldn't have a healthy baby. You've had five already, your sister says. Why kill yourself having the sixth?"

Ruth closed her eyes and grasped at the counterpane, twisting it in her fingers.

"Now, Mrs. Douglass, I don't want you to worry about a thing. I won't hear of any more fainting or crying in the night." His brows bobbed like corks on the broad expanse of his forehead. "Your sister told me that."

"What else did she tell you?"

"The obvious, Mrs. Douglass, the obvious! That you'd fainted, that you're pregnant, that you're not well. Now, you follow my orders and forget what's troubling you, and if you can't forget it, then pack it in camphor and fret after this baby is born. You rest and let Lily take care of you. Do her good to get up and about and look after someone else. We all have to toil, Mrs. Douglass, but we don't all have to weep. Now sit up. Slowly."

Ruth took his hand and put her feet on the floor. She gave an involuntary gasp when she saw her dress was unbuttoned halfway down.

"The first thing you do after I leave is take off that corset," he said, snapping his black bag shut. "I don't know how women stand it or why they do it. This is going to be a modern, scientific baby. No corsets. No hocus-pocus. You're to exercise moderately, eat a few light meals a day, watch out for the heat, and get some fresh air. My prescription for you is no more crying or exhaustion. This is going to be a child of the twentieth century."

Dr. Tipton took his leave of the Whickham household and drove his horse and buggy back the short distance to his combined home and office. He put the horse up and threw a blanket over it despite the heat. He avoided the office entrance, where he knew Emily Hurst waited with her colicky son, and went directly into the house. He washed his hands in the kitchen, and on his way through the study toward the office, he gazed at the bald, eyeless head of Blanche, the skeleton who hung behind his desk. He rested his hands on her clavicles and stared into her sockets. "Was it ever that hard for you, old girl?" And for a man committed to the universals, the doctor found himself wondering, more curious about Ruth Douglass's particulars than he would have thought possible.

13

DR. TIPTON'S METICULOUS records testified that Baby Girl Douglass was born on August 3, 1900, and weighed in at a healthy six pounds, four ounces. He noted that the mother had a severe but normal labor. It was a spare account and did not so much as indicate that as the gravid womb began to bring forth its contents, so the gravid heart of Mrs. Douglass rumbled and from her lips poured a volley of oaths.

The doctor was aided in the delivery by the patient's sister, Lily Whickham, who was of no use whatever and who actually fainted during the pitch of her sister's agony. Dr. Tipton carried Mrs. Whickham out of the room and dropped her less gently than he might have on her bed. He called his usual assistant when these matters grew difficult, Mrs. Nana Bowers, an experienced midwife, a black woman, born the slave of Madison Whickham.

Ten days later the doctor came to call on Mrs. Douglass, and the patient's sister answered the door, a task she usually left to the long-suffering servants. She asked the doctor to step briefly into the parlor if he would. The parlor was still, shades drawn, the air redolent of decorum and death. Hair wreaths of the family's deceased festooned the walls, along with pictures draped in black. Sentimental funeral tokens clustered on the rosewood tables. No breath of air stirred, and so weak was Mrs. Whickham's voice that her hands made more noise as she wrung them. She told the doctor she feared for her sister's recovery. She kept her gaze glued to the flowers in the carpet and said that the new baby stirred no maternal chord in her sister's bosom. The doctor said that was not infrequent among women who had borne children who would not have been their choice; he said Ruth would come around.

Lily folded her hands against her breastbone and licked her lips.

She said that as yet the child had no name, that Ruth showed no interest in giving her a name. "She's got to have a name, Doctor. I don't know what to do."

The doctor did not know what to do either. He adjusted the dry brush of his mustache.

"Ruth won't listen to me," Lily murmured. "She thinks whatever I say I've been put up to it by Arthur. She won't come out of that room. She won't talk. I've told the children their mother isn't recovered yet from her ordeal, but I can't keep it from them forever."

"Keep what?"

"Well, I don't know what, Doctor. That's why I'm asking you to talk to her."

"If she won't talk to you, it's unlikely she'll talk to me."

"She might listen to you, though, and I don't think Ruth even hears me." Lily peered through the dimness. "Besides, it's a terrible burden on me, Ruth being sick like this. I'm not used to it, and I'm not well myself, and it's a strain. I mean, all those children, and I'm not used to it, and I don't think I can keep it up. You know, Arthur and everything." Lily's tongue flew over her lips, and she returned her gaze to the floor.

"Have you any suggestions as to what I might say to your sister, Mrs. Whickham? Have you any idea why she is so indifferent to this baby?"

"Ruth never was real warm or affectionate. Not that she don't care, she does. She feels things deeply, Ruth does, she just never says them. She never has."

"Has she behaved this way with her other children?"

Lily's hands flew to her cameo brooch. "Oh, Doctor, I couldn't say. Honestly, I couldn't. Ruth was living up in Idaho when the others were born. I never went there. I was too sickly."

"Do you think she neglects the child because of the obvious, I might say unusual, animosity she bears for her husband, the late Mr. Douglass?"

Lily stroked her earbobs and pursued an itch across her forehead. "I'm sure I couldn't say, Doctor. He's dead, you know."

"Perhaps if you could tell me something about him, I might be able—"

"Oh, Doctor, I don't know. No indeed. I don't know anything. All that was in Idaho, like I said. I never saw Samuel Douglass after he took Ruth away from Salt Lake. Albert spent some time up there, and he said Ruth had a hard life, but—"

"What did Samuel Douglass die of?"

"Die of?" Lily's eyes filled with curiosity. "Oh, he died this year, yes, just this year, and he burned to death, Doctor. Died in a fire. The eight-room house burned to the ground, and the barn went, too."

The doctor regarded the agitated woman before him and wondered fleetingly how two sisters could be so different. "You say she hasn't yet named the child?"

"No. Sometimes she don't even pick it up when it cries."

"All right. You bring me the family Bible."

"Mine or Ruth's? She has her own."

"Where is it?"

"I don't know. Ruth keeps things to herself."

"Very well, then. I want you to bring me a pen and some ink. Your sister and I are not to be disturbed under any circumstances. Is that clear?"

Lily nodded.

"I don't care what you hear from up there, you're not to come in unless I call you. And if you'll permit me, Mrs. Whickham, this parlor is barbaric. There's no reason to keep a room so utterly ill-ventilated, useless, and populated with relics."

"Why, Doctor, I . . . I shall treasure that always."

He grunted and took himself up the stairs, leaving Lily in the grip of the August heat, wondering what a relic was and what made her parlor barbaric. She had always thought it was rather nice.

The blinds in Ruth's room were closed as well, but afternoon sun dappled through the leafy elms anyway. Without a word to Ruth, the doctor went to the baby's cradle. The unnamed child was sleeping peacefully, with nothing on her wizened face to indicate discontent. The doctor did not speak till Lily brought the pen and ink. She left it on the bureau, muttering apologies, and left. The doctor stared at Ruth Douglass, whose hands were folded across her breast as if in rehearsal for the grave.

Dr. Tipton had evolved his own bedside manner over the dozen or so years he'd practiced medicine. It was not all confection and gentleness; it was not all of one piece.

Lucius Tipton was a man of contradictions: both passionate and shrewd, painstaking and impulsive, brusque and convivial. Active by nature, he was often indolent by choice. He was, above all, a scientific man, a rationalist and a thinker. He had watched people drink themselves to death, drug themselves to death, work themselves to death, but he had never seen anyone will herself to death quite like Ruth Douglass.

He parted the curtains, and the thick sunlight patched across the floor to the bed and cradle. He stood at the foot of Ruth's bed. In brightened sunlight her skin was the color of bruised green apples; her lips were cracked, and her dry, disheveled hair hung loosely about her face. "This baby needs a name, Mrs. Douglass."

"You've done your duty, Doctor. Leave me be."

"I'm not leaving the room, and neither are you till the baby has a name."

"You are impertinent, Doctor."

"And you are a willful, malicious woman, visiting your own sufferings on an innocent child." He drew a chair up by the bed. "Whatever you may have suffered, it's ignoble to punish a child."

Ruth blinked against the sunlight, closed her eyes, and tightened her fingers around one another. "Please go away. I never wanted you here. I've had my other children with no doctor in a hundred miles."

"Do you expect me to believe that if you'd had some hawk-nosed housewife attending you, you would have named your baby?"

"Believe whatever you want. I don't need a doctor. I don't need anyone."

"You need someone, Mrs. Douglass. You are getting ready to die. Shall I ask Lily to call in the Mormon elders so they can lay their hands on you and call on God to—"

"Don't you dare!"

"Ah, no elders. But you are a Latter-day Saint, aren't you?"

"Get out."

"What did your husband die of, Mrs. Douglass?"

"Get out! Lily! Get this man out of here!"

"Lily won't come, and if she did, what good would she be? She can barely take care of herself. It's time for you to be up and do your duty."

"What do you know of duty? I did my duty for years."

"Did you get this child by doing your duty?"

Ruth raised herself to her elbows. "You have no right to speak to me like that. Get out of here."

"So you can die by yourself? No. I won't stand for it. Not when you have six children who need you. Now, let's get down to business. Lily tells me you have a family Bible. Where is it?"

"Get out!" Ruth sat bolt upright. "You don't know anything. You and your duty. I'm sick unto death of duty. Duty was invented by men for women."

"Really? I'd always heard it was invented by God for mortals. An equally odious proposition, I grant you."

"Damn you, Doctor."

"Damn yourself, Mrs. Douglass." Dr. Tipton rose and took the sleeping child from her cradle, and as she broke into the erratic high-pitched squall of newborns, he put the child in her mother's unwilling arms. "Forget the man, Mrs. Douglass, whoever he was."

"I am a married woman, Doctor."

"I don't care what you are to any man, you're mother to that child, and she needs a name."

"Take her away."

"No, you hold her and tell me where your family Bible is."

The baby filled her tiny lungs with air and bellowed in a scratchy contralto. Ruth hushed her and rocked. "In the top drawer of the dresser."

He found the book and brought it to the bedside with the pen and ink. The first page said "Births" in a rolling script a full half-century behind the times. He dipped the pen in the inkwell and poised it over the page. "Why not call her after your own name?" he offered.

"I hate Ruth. I've always hated Ruth and her story. They try to make you believe she aroused love in Boaz's heart, but it couldn't have been love. It could only have been pity or lust."

"Pity's not an ungenerous emotion."

"I hate pity and I hate lust. They're both indecent."

"To feel pity is not the same as to be the object of it."

"You're full of observation today, aren't you, Doctor?"

"You must hate Arthur Whickham very much."

"I do hate him." Ruth met the doctor's eyes. "I detest him. I live under his roof, we eat at his table, and I detest him."

"Then you must get out from under his roof, but you can't begin to get your strength back till you name this baby girl."

111

"I tell you, I don't have a name for her."

"What about a flower's name? I always said if I had a daughter, I'd name her after a flower. What about Rose? Or Lily, after your sister?"

"I have a daughter Lil."

"What about Narcissa? Narcissa . . ." He lingered over the name. "The narcissa is a lovely, a fragrant flower."

"It's not a Christian name."

"All the better. You don't like Ruth, after all."

"Oh, all right then." Ruth took the baby's hand in her fingers. "Narcissa. But no middle name. They're a useless frippery."

He dipped his pen and wrote in his small, neat hand so different from Ruth's Spencerian schoolgirl flourish: "Narcissa Douglass, born August 3, 1900, St. Elmo, California."

"You can get up now, Mrs. Douglass. You put on your wrapper and change that baby and come downstairs. You are weak, but you're not sick, and you're not going to die even if you want to."

"I'm not strong enough to get up yet."

"You're not Lily Whickham, Mrs. Douglass. She is indulged in her little vapors and whims, but you can't afford to be. You're going to come downstairs and have a cup of tea."

"I am a Saint, and I don't drink tea."

"I don't care if you drink Burning Bush whiskey, just so you come downstairs."

"It's too soon."

"Mrs. Douglass," he said, strolling to the bedroom door, "if you don't get out of that bed promptly, it may well be too late."

It was not too late. In early September, Dr. Tipton noticed a clapboarded house for rent at the corner of L Street at the northern edge of St. Elmo. L Street was unpaved, one of those that turned to mud in St. Elmo's brief, violent rainy season and parched unto dust during the long, dry summer. Pepper trees, a single palm, and an abundant lemon grew in the untended yard, along with wild mustard and the small, stubborn variety of sunflower. The back porch opened on a wide, unencumbered view of the St. Elmo mountains, and the front porch looked into an empty field waving with the same wild mustard and sunflowers.

Dr. Tipton called on the Widow Douglass at her brother-in-law's home and drove her in his buggy that afternoon to have a look at it. The rent, he said, was ten dollars a month. The Widow Douglass said she did not have ten dollars, and the doctor said he did. If he expected her to protest, she did not. She asked only how much interest he wanted on his loan. She said a loan from him was preferable to Art Whickham's interest-free charity, and the family moved in the following week.

A low gap-toothed fence surrounded the house and kept out the pigs, which rooted through the neighborhood at will until 1904, when Art Whickham became mayor and passed an ordinance forbidding wandering livestock. The furniture in the house was motley, the rooms badly painted, the screens broken, the roof in need of repair, and the front-porch step proved untrustworthy. Lucius said the last tenants were probably Goths. Eden asked if the Goth family were Saints. The house's deficiencies could be remedied, and at least it was fitted with indoor plumbing and gas, which Lucius said was the final step in evolution and at last man could be distinguished from the apes. Eden asked what evolution was.

When school started, the elder Douglass children, carrying their dinner buckets, marched to school every day. All except Eden. On Eden fell the responsibility of getting breakfast for her brothers and sisters and caring for Mason and Cissa, because Ruth got a job serving meals in the Brigham Cafe in downtown St. Elmo. Ruth rose well before dawn and worked the breakfast shift, returning home at nine or ten so that Eden could go to school. The teacher would have objected more strongly to the arrangement except that Eden did not fall behind, and her grades, like those of her brother Gideon, remained at the top of the class.

When Ruth returned to the Brigham at noon for the dinner shift, she took Mason and baby Cissa with her, and they learned to amuse themselves in a corner of the cafe. The proprietor would have objected more strongly to this arrangement except that he, too, was a Latter-day Saint and a widower and knew the tribulations of rearing one's own children. In fact, he had been twice widowed, and his children were all grown. Still, he thought he might like to be married again and thought the Widow Douglass a handsome woman, and he was shocked when she declined his proposal. He pointed out to her that if she were married she would only have to serve breakfast to one man instead of many, and some of those Gentiles, commercial travelers, railroad men, and other unsavory types. Ruth failed to be persuaded by his arguments, though she thanked him for the offer.

Within her first year in St. Elmo, two other widower Saints proposed to Ruth and were similarly rebuffed, much to the surprise of the other church members, who thought that a widow with six children would be only too happy to share her many burdens with a man. Ruth Douglass shared nothing. Not only did she spurn proposals of marriage, but she resisted all offers of friendship as well, save from Lucius Tipton, on whom she bestowed a rusty smile when he came into the Brigham for breakfast.

Her contact with her sister and brother-in-law chilled to a polite nod as the two families were filing in or out of church on Sundays. Lily would not have had it so, but Art assured her that only harm could come from involvement with a woman—even her own sister—who had deserted her marriage vows, committed verbal murder, lied to the world, and felt, or at least demonstrated, no remorse for that lie, and who further took as her only friend an atheist doctor. Art contended that a decent woman would not associate with such a man, except professionally—he was, after all, the best doctor in St. Elmo—let alone cultivate any intimacy with him, and what could you call it but intimacy when the doctor went to the widow's home every Sunday for dinner? There was, Art maintained, something fundamentally indecent about a relationship that lacked the sanctifying possibility of marriage, and the unchaperoned friendship of two unmarried people (even if one of them had six children) was an affront to the community in general and the Saints in particular.

In those early years the Douglasses hadn't a ribbon or a button or a bone to spare, but their attitude, in the eyes of St. Elmo, suggested a totally unwarranted sense of superiority. Ruth and her children were clannish, inhospitable, and rather aloof. The Widow Douglass was crisp, efficient, a little less than cordial, a little more than cold, and her daughters Eden and Afton followed her example, growing into responsible, well-mannered girls who came to school in starched-stiff serviceable clothing and moved with a starched-stiff grace well beyond their years. Lil continued in frail health, always Afton's shadow, and Gideon grew into a studious boy who was never without a book. The Douglass children made friends slowly and shyly, because their mother cautioned them against low associates and added that mere Sainthood was not enough to insure one against the ultimate invective: vulgarity. Vulgarity, she told her children, was worse than sin; you could atone for sin. And, too, Ruth rather exaggerated the worth of a stainless reputation. She demonstrated her point with matches: she struck a match, let it flare and hiss in front of their young faces, then blew it out with one breath. "You see, your reputation is like this match. Once it has been burned, it will never again light with its old glow or usefulness."

After she performed this ritual, she sat in the kitchen rocker, her rust-colored shawl about her shoulders and her lips curled slightly over her own stainless—if unsocial—reputation: the hardworking Widow Douglass, bereft by a fire that had leveled her eight-room house, though her love for her husband must yet smolder in her heart. She accepted the Saints' condolences and won their grudging respect, but she never forgot that she was tethered to the truth by lies, tethered to the living Samuel Douglass by the lie of his death. And because she never winced when she told that lie, never flinched at being called the Widow Douglass, she knew that she would go to hell. The Saints did not believe in splitting the marriage bond even after death, so she and Samuel would certainly meet in hell. She prayed they wouldn't meet till then. Better a time and all eternity of flames than one moment's reckoning on earth.

14

DR. LUCIUS TIPTON came from an old Philadelphia family who began as Quakers, degenerated into Freethinkers, and emerged in the late nineteenth century as Darwinists with a greater faith in Progress than in God. Like his father, who was also a doctor, Lucius believed that men could be good without religion, that religion incited men only to slavish imitation and instilled in them only fear while ignoring the impulses to good implanted in every human being by virtue of his being simply human. Like his father, too, Lucius was scrupulous, learned, an alumnus of the University of Pennsylvania Medical School, and he might have found his eccentric religious beliefs better tolerated in a city like Philadelphia than in a small town like St. Elmo, where society was dominated by the Methodists and Mormons, who detested one another and everyone else besides. He would have stayed in Philadelphia, but for his weak lungs, which were further undermined by long hours spent in drafty dissecting rooms and chill lecture halls. He contracted consumption, and when none of the prevailing cures worked, he was told another Philadelphia winter would kill him.

He came to the arid St. Elmo Valley in 1890 and never suffered another moment's physical discomfort or another moment's intellectual ease. He took up cigars and rigorous reading and maintained a discreet professional distance from the niggling civic disputes of St. Elmo. He was spared the attentions of the female population because of his unorthodox religious beliefs and his undisguised advocacy of a snort of brandy against chill, pain, and sorrow.

For ten years Dr. Tipton pursued his appointed rounds as faithfully as possible, given the exigencies of his profession: babies that will be born at dawn, the appendix that must come out at midnight, and death, which knows no time and needs no call but its own. These circumstances sometimes forbade his rising when the courthouse clock struck six. The courthouse had long since passed its heyday, the doctor noted on his short walk from his combined home and office to St. Elmo's central district. The courthouse cupola sagged, and the plaster blew away in the seasonal winds, and the doctor often asked himself what larger moral could be gleaned from the observation that the courthouse was structurally unsound while the cathouse remained well preserved.

Passing the courthouse, he found the newspaper stand and shoeshine parlor, and exchanged his customary pleasantries with the attendant, who was one of Nana Bowers's many grandsons. He had his shoes shined, read the paper, and then walked to the fashionable Ferris Hotel and bought the six Havana cigars he smoked daily. Before 1901, Doctor had also taken his breakfast at the Ferris Hotel, but when Ruth Douglass went to work at the rather less fastidious Brigham Cafe he began to frequent that place for breakfast.

He often remarked to Ruth that no Mormon ever made a decent cup of coffee and suggested that the Brigham hire a heathen for this task. He removed the rind from his ham surgically, and Ruth inquired if maybe he'd like a side order of chloroform. "You're a mighty picky eater for a man who don't live with a woman, Lucius," she added.

"And you're mighty tart for a woman who don't live with a man, Ruth," he retorted.

They were Ruth and Lucius to one another from the beginning. Otherwise they were universally known as Doctor and Widow. They were the only two people in St. Elmo (barring the Mormon bishop and the Catholic priest) who wore their titles much as nobility might, to keep themselves separate from the St. Elmo herds. They had a life separate from the St. Elmo herds. Every Sunday afternoon Doctor arrived at the Douglass home for dinner. He usually carried a bunch of half-wilted wildflowers, which he presented to Ruth with a flourish. Ruth put them in a small vase on the dining-room table. Lucius sat at one end, Ruth sat at the other, and the children lined up between them.

Lucius enjoyed the Douglass children. Though they were each quite different, the girls in particular seemed to share something of their mother's aplomb. Eden certainly had inherited Ruth's stately carriage and capable hands, Afton her mother's unquenchable sense of rightness; and Lil, though she trotted continually and quite happily in Afton's shadow, had a sturdy little nature beneath her frail, pale exterior. Golden Lil was the beauty, no doubt of that, though Cissa might one day rival her. Doctor liked to study their young faces as they chatted during supper; he liked their piping voices and their unclouded eyes. Behind a curtain of cigar smoke, he liked to watch Ruth, the long stem of her throat swathed in a high black collar, the firm chin, the strong hands, the mouth that was more expressive than she knew. Professionally he liked to imagine the well-wrought bones of her skeleton; personally he liked to imagine the tiny tarp of flesh between her collarbones, which could sometimes be seen to throb despite the high collar. He liked the way Ruth moved—without haste or waste or even quite grace, a long stride continually at odds with her black skirt.

Dr. Tipton encouraged the studious streak in Gideon Douglass, urged him to avail himself of the doctor's bountiful library. Gideon, however, was very much a child of his church and stuck to Saint-sanctioned books. Doctor kept his eye on Mason Douglass, because of all of them, Mason alone seemed to have a penchant for craftiness; even at the age of four he was secretive and petulant.

On the first Sunday of every month the Douglasses piled into the doctor's buggy after dinner and he drove them back to the Mormon church for afternoon services. The doctor knew all of St. Elmo goggled to see the Douglasses pull up in front of the church in the company of the cigar-smoking atheist. He assumed that Ruth was equally aware of the Saints' tight-lipped stares, but they never discussed it. Indeed, Ruth seemed to regard St. Elmo and its approval or disapproval as beneath her contempt. Hers was a stainless reputation. Perhaps that was why in the spring of 1902, the doctor— who was a man of regular habits—did a very irregular thing.

The six children tumbled out of the buggy in a welter of long legs and arms, cuffs and sleeves that were too short, high voices, and crackling starch. Lucius put his hand over Ruth's and held it. "Let them go to church by themselves this afternoon, Ruth. You come with me. Please."

She regarded the doctor's large, immaculate hand. "I have to go."

"Go next week."

"They only have afternoon services once a month."

"Then go next month."

The children stood restlessly beside the buggy, and the other Saints tied their horses, shooed their children, and filed into the prim church, casting covert glances toward the Douglasses and the atheist doctor.

"Let the Saints be damned for once, Ruth," Lucius said, with more passion than he'd intended.

Ruth withdrew her hand. She might well have stepped from the buggy, but at that moment Art Whickham's motor car chugged into sight, frightening the horses and riveting the jealous attention of every Saint who was there to see it. Art shepherded Lily and their two boys toward the church. He touched the brim of his hat with unaffected disdain as he glanced at Ruth and Lucius. Lily hurried past her sister with only a fearful nod.

"Eden," said Ruth, "you keep Cissa with you, and the rest of you

118

mind Eden and behave yourselves. You go on into church. I'm going with Lucius."

"Where?" asked Afton.

"I'll be home by the time you get there. Drive on, Lucius. Just this once," she added as they pulled away from the Church of Jesus Christ of Latter-day Saints. They had passed the courthouse before Ruth asked him, "Where are we going?"

"To hell, my dear, if the Saints have their way."

"The Saints always have their way."

St. Elmo has an illusory spring. For two weeks the air is tender rather than parched, flowering trees shoot forth blossoms, which blow away like snow petals before the wind, trees sprout tight green fists of new leaves, and small, curling stems of grass appear in little congregations around fenceposts as if together they might ward off the sun that will ravish them in a few weeks' time. Outside the town itself, cacti bloom shyly and the leathery hills seem to be covered in soft green suede.

Ruth and Lucius drove up the narrow track north of town toward Urquita Springs into the foothills. The road had dried since the winter rains and had not yet hardened into the brittle dirt-ribbon it became in the summer. Up near the springs they found a point, cluttered only with hip-high sage and some desultory brush and wild mustard. From here they could behold the entire St. Elmo Valley with the church steeples and courthouse cupola sticking up like needles in a pincushion of complacency. Jesuit Pass threaded through the mountains, and Dogsback Ditch lay at its feet, still flowing with a thin brown seam of water. Wind ruffled the mustard at their feet, and the desert sky was a bleached blue.

"I never dreamed St. Elmo could look so puny," she said, unpinning her hat and stepping down from the buggy. "It's nothing but a bunch of wooden tents and railroad track camped in the desert. It could wash away tomorrow." The eastbound train shrieked in the distance, and they watched it pull across the Dogsback bridge. "I feel like a truant child. At least, I guess I do. I never was a truant child, of course."

"You never skipped school, Ruth? Not even on a spring Friday?"

"I was too afraid of getting caught."

"I can't imagine you afraid of anything."

119

"Can't you?" Her dark eyes met his, and then she looked back toward the train vanishing into the St. Elmo pass. "My father was very firm about duty. It was my duty to go to school."

"Was it your duty to marry Samuel Douglass?"

Ruth took a deep breath. Lucius could hear it whistling through her nose. "It was my duty to get married."

"Do you regret it?"

"Regret! What's that but excess baggage? I can't waste my time with regret. Can you?"

"Of course, my dear. I don't have six children."

"You should have married."

"I used to think I would, and then I regretted that I hadn't, but now—well, I have my rounds to make, a good library, good cigars, a bottle of Burning Bush, and a half a dozen out-of-town newspapers. I'm happy. Besides, I've got you and Blanche."

"A fine wife that bony Blanche is."

"At least you and Blanche don't try to reform my bad habits. Just think, if I'd married I'd be a paragon of civic virtue." His hazel eyes mottled with humor. "No cigars or skeletons, no alcohol, no books of questionable morality. If I'd married, I'd be down in that valley right now at some church or another along with every other upright citizen swallowing medicinal doses of guilt for my bad habits and fear for my soul."

"You don't care about your soul?" She caught blowing strands of hair and tucked them firmly back into the bun at the top of her head.

"Ruth, my dear, I have studied every one of the body's processes, stem to stern. I've poured over the anatomy books and dissected corpses, and I know where the heart and liver and spleen and the adenoids are; I could name you every bone in your foot. But in all my physiological investigations, I've never run across a soul. Not a one. Now, I don't dispute that there may well be one somewhere, maybe lurking down in the further marrow of the tiniest metacarpal, but I don't believe what I don't see." He bit off the end of a fresh cigar.

"You're lucky to be free of all that codswallop."

"Codswallop?" He turned his back to light the cigar out of the wind. "Codswallop coming from the Saintly Widow Douglass?"

"I'm up here with you, not down in the valley looking after my soul. Does that make me Saintly?"

"No, it makes you truant." He puffed reflectively. "Momentarily."

She licked a bit of grit from her lips. "Why did you ask me up here, Lucius?"

"Impulse, my dear Mrs. Douglass." As she walked to a nearby boulder and sat down, the starch in her skirt creaked. He stood before her, blocking the sun with his body, and played with his cigar. "I reckon I wanted you to come up here so I could ask you to marry me without all six kids standing around. Besides"—his mouth drooped into a half smile—"I figured if you left with me in full view of every Saint in town you'd have to marry me. I've compromised your virtue now."

"My virtue," she scoffed, "is hardly worth compromising."

"On the other hand, virtue's a sort of negative state, isn't it? You can't be actively virtuous, only passively hold on to it, clutch it."

"You make it sound like day-old bread."

"Well?" He grinned at her over the cigar. "Tell me how this is done, Ruth. I've never had the experience. Do I go down on one knee and say: my dear Widow Douglass, I esteem you above all other women. I shall never rest till you pledge your troth to mine."

"Troth, sloth, Lucius. Can't you be serious?"

"I am serious, Ruth."

"I know."

"I love you, Ruth."

"I love you, Lucius. You're the only man I know who's not a coward or a hypocrite or both. I love you and I expect I always shall love you, but I can't marry you."

He sat beside her and smoked; the wind fanned the end of his cigar, and it glowed. "Samuel's alive, isn't he? You left him and lied about his being dead."

"What makes you think so?"

"Because you're not a coward."

"But I am a hypocrite and a liar. How did you guess?"

Lucius removed a bit of tobacco from his tongue. "If Samuel were dead, you would have forgiven him whatever it was he did, but you never have forgiven him."

121

"No. And yes, he's alive. Somewhere. Mexico, maybe. He's alive."

A deep, unhappy sigh escaped from Lucius; he regarded it as flatulence of a sort—it gave him some relief, but it was unpleasant all the same. "I hoped I was wrong. I hoped enough to ask you to marry me, but I have suspected ever since Cissa was born. Your hatred for him was so violent even then, I knew he couldn't be dead."

"I should have murdered him. That's what I think now. I could have. I could have done it more than once, and now I think I should have. If I'd murdered him I'd only have to fear death and going to hell, but as it is I've got hell right here in the midst of life, and death is the least of my fears. Samuel will burn in hell, but so will I." She took his hands in hers and held them fiercely. "Samuel went crazy, mad with religion. By the time I saw it for madness, it was too late to stop. I couldn't have stopped it anyway—how can a mere woman fight the word of God? God started talking to Samuel, giving him revelations, telling him he was the New Apostle, and finally God commanded him to take a plural wife and sell his earthly possessions and go to Mexico to wait for the Last Trump. Samuel was a beast and a lunatic. But," she added, meeting his eyes levelly, "he was a smart beast and a rich lunatic, and I stayed with him till I knew I'd lose everything no matter what I did. I couldn't endure that, not after everything else I'd been through."

"Who knows about this in St. Elmo?"

"Only my sister—the fair Lily—and her snake husband, Art."

"Well, you're safe there. Art Whickham would swallow whole toads before he'd let it be known he was related to a . . ."

"Runaway wife? A liar?"

"I only meant—"

"Oh, it's all true. Sometimes I can forget I'm a runaway wife, but I never forget I'm a liar. Every time I meet a Saint on the street or in church I remember what a liar I am. I tell myself, you need the church. Your children need the Saints. They have to grow up like everyone else or they'll be lost. They have to be the poor fatherless children of the Widow Douglass, not the offspring of a lunatic and a runaway wife. I have to be the perfect Saint, because the less than perfect Saint's a sinner."

"The perfect Saint wouldn't keep company with me, Ruth."

She released his hands, and he pulled her into his arms, her head against his shoulder. "I think of you as my one vice. You're the one person who keeps me from going mad as Samuel, because even though I bring my children up in the paths of righteousness the Saints have all marked off, picketed everywhere with dos and don'ts, I loathe them. It's true. I am a liar and a hypocrite, and I am reminded of it every time I pass a Saint on the street, because I'm seized with loathing. I loathe their smugness and their narrowness and the way they dress it all up in piety and charity and that smothering sweetness. I think I'll choke to death on their smothering sweetness."

"You wouldn't consider adding bigamy to your sins, would you, Ruth? It wouldn't bother me."

"I love you, Lucius, I love you with whatever's left in me to love, but I'm like Blanche. The fire I invented to kill off Samuel burned me to a stubble, too. Everything except my bones. If you dissected my body, all you'd find is bones." She stood and let the wind wash over her like water.

"I can think of other things I'd rather do to your body than dissect it," he said, stamping out his cigar. "I often wonder about that little space between your collarbones. I watch it throb. Like it is now."

"Widows don't throb."

"You did once, though, didn't you? When you were first married you must have throbbed. It's your nature to be passionate and to be loved."

"There never was any love between Samuel and me. It was just what you said about the soul, something physical like the liver or spleen. I called it love then, because I didn't know I had a liver or a spleen, much less anything else."

Lucius stood and enveloped her in his arms; her hair blew into his face, and she caught it with both hands, but he held her hands. "Let it blow, Ruth—we're up here, not down in that valley. Don't underestimate yourself. You still have love left to give. Underneath the starch and the widow's weeds, you are a woman with love still to give. You could give it to me."

"I'm a woman with six children and a past. The children will grow up and leave me, but the past never will. Fear never will. I live in constant fear."

"I know. I can't change that, but I still—" He slid his hands up her throat and into her hair, and it loosened and spilled, and then

123

his hands, kneading slowly, moved over her shoulders and her back and around her ribs to her breasts. He closed his eyes as if he had to commit her body to memory through his hands. He held her face and kissed her open mouth. "There'll come a day when you're ready," he whispered, "if not for bigamy, then for adultery."

"I thought you didn't believe in sin."

"I don't. I'll wait till you don't either."

The sky was dipped in the first pale rinse of sunset as they walked, arms around each other, back to the buggy. Ruth regathered her hair and knotted it and pinned her hat back on with a particularly determined jab, as if she had to secure more than her hat, as if to repair the unraveling fustian of her soul. Lucius slapped the horse's back idly, and she sat beside him as she always had: shoulders straight as a T-square, her gaze as flat as a carpenter's level, though her skin prickled with desire she'd all but forgotten was possible. She gave him her hand, and he held it until they crossed the St. Elmo city limits. Widow folded her naked hands in her lap. And Doctor found himself throbbing in places whose anatomical names were familiar enough, but for all his physiological knowledge, he also experienced unusual, elusive sensations, more befitting the soul than the body. But then, he did not believe in souls.

The doctor and the widow did not leave St. Elmo again, except for an occasional picnic to Urquita Springs in the company of all six of the children. They remained together, but the only union they entered into was a business partnership in 1906 when the owner of the Brigham Cafe was called to his greater reward.

The Brigham remained shuttered for a month, and when it reopened, it had a new name, the Pilgrim Cafe, and it smelled of new paint, fresh bread, and fine cake. Gideon Douglass painted the walls a creamy yellow and the tables an appealing blue. Eden Douglass sewed up muslin curtains, starched and ironed them, and placed a vase of sunflowers by the cash drawer. Afton Douglass, even at thirteen, already demonstrated her God-given knack for the baker's art, and the cakes lined up like frosted dreams. Ruth did the accounts and the cooking and kept her eye on the cash drawer. Three times a week at dawn she was at the St. Elmo markets down by the railyards and loaded the doctor's buggy (and later, his Flyer) with provisions for the Pilgrim. She fingered everything she bought, and anything less than fresh did not interest her. She drove her bargains the way she drove the doctor's Flyer: fearlessly. She hired impeccable young women who complained that she insisted on too much starch in their collars and inspected their fingernails with a doctor's scrutiny.

The medical meticulousness should not have surprised them, because Dr. Lucius Tipton in partnership with Mrs. Ruth Douglass now owned the Pilgrim Cafe. And that really was too much for the St. Elmo Saints.

Bishop Eldon Whickham himself called on Ruth and said it wasn't seemly. Ruth replied that she wasn't aware that the church had any strictures against making money. The bishop said it wasn't the money; it was the principle. Ah, said the widow, if they're any good at all, principals collect interest. And with that she excused herself, because she was a busy woman.

The Pilgrim Cafe under Ruth's benevolent tyranny set a reputation for clean linen and light biscuits throughout the St. Elmo Valley and beyond. Ruth served the first omelettes in two counties; she "frenched" her toast in a way that no one could quite duplicate; she used a tad of ginger in her rice and created a custard that a wandering professor declared was better than anything he'd tasted in the court of the Second Empire, thus dubbing it forever. The Ferris Hotel at first lost customers and then tried to buy her out, but she refused. She took pride in what she did, but she didn't overestimate it either. She might have cut her operating costs had she allowed her children to work at the Pilgrim, but she kept them clear of the place except for the delivery of Afton's cakes. She told them there were better things one could do than stuffing the guts of paying customers, though one could do no better than to stuff one's guts at the Pilgrim.

There were those in St. Elmo who said that if the widow watched her children as closely as she watched the cash drawer, the stockpot, and the greengrocer, they would be better off, though in fact the elder ones could be faulted for little except a taciturnity the Saints thought unbecoming in children. In his first year in high school Gideon won the School Prize for Best Essay for a piece entitled "A Reconciliation of the Prophecies of the Book of Mormon with the

Course of American History." When they made the award, Gideon's history teacher predicted a great future for him, and the Saints were pleased because a Mormon boy hadn't won the prize for five years. They announced his honor in church, and Gideon blushed.

In 1907, Eden graduated from high school, winning the prize for Best French Student, and at her mother's urging she began the course at the Blakely School of Business, where she learned the elements of typewriting, the new shorthand, and bookkeeping. "A woman with skills can do as she likes," Ruth maintained. Eden would have liked to go to Paris, but she contented herself for the time being with picture postcards stuck to her wall and invested her graduation money in an atlas of the world so she'd know all about the places she would one day visit.

Afton Douglass grew more efficient every day and gradually took over the management of the house on L Street. Afton was an electrified version of Ruth. Lil, though she was Afton's pale shadow, had wide, watchful eyes that took in everything, whereas Afton only glanced around quickly to make sure things were running her way.

Mason and Cissa, well, Doctor had seen it before: the youngest children in a large family seemingly have no need of parents; there are too many others willing to wait on them and fuss over them, straighten and scold, pamper and protect. Privately Lucius thought that the crafty Mason and Cissa (whose vanity was insatiable from the time she could walk) could do with a bit more of Ruth's attention and affection, though he mentioned this only in passing.

"They get plenty of attention," Ruth snapped back. "I don't miss a thing." And for that Lucius had no reply, because it was true, of course. Ruth knew it was Mason who filched one of the cakes destined for the Pilgrim, though he denied it fervently. She caught him the next time; the frosting on his collar gave him away. Ruth knew when Cissa had lied and when Lil covered up for her. She figured that Gideon was in love with Arlene McClure when he was still referring to her decorously as "my classmate." And she knew that Afton and Eden would be a handful of trouble each if they ever set their wills contrary to her own. And Lucius knew, even if Ruth didn't, that one day they certainly would.

15

CASSIE LAFFERTY DID not have a heart of gold. In 1905 she was thirty-five or thereabouts, and she had come to St. Elmo with a railroad man with whom she had been living more or less virtuously if not legally for several years. The man left her one morning to go to the railyards, and on his way out the door he accused Cassie of giving him the clap. Cassie declared that wasn't possible, but when he didn't return, she began to believe it entirely possible that he might have left her with a little venereal keepsake.

In examining her, Dr. Tipton could find no evidence that this was so, but he gave her materials and instructions for a douche of sulfate and quinine anyway. He washed his hands, listening to the snap of Cassie's garters. She was of medium height, full-girthed, and topheavy, and had a freckled face with a wide mouth. Her dark eyes contrasted with her hair, a brassy color seldom found in nature. Her petticoat fell back, exposing the white band of flesh above the stockings. She said she had no money at the moment, but he needn't worry, she'd pay soon, as she was going back to work. "Don't you want to know what kind of work, Doctor?"

"Mrs. Lafferty, every trade has its hazards."

"You mealy-mouthed men are all the same. You'll probably call the sheriff the minute I leave here."

"I may be a mealy-mouthed man, but I am a doctor as well." He dried his hands calmly. "As a doctor I think every woman in your profession should be certified to check the spread of disease. As a man I think it would be ideal if every man could cleave unto his wife forsaking all others, but we're human and not made that way."

"Are you married, Doctor?"

"No."

"It figures," said Cassie, jabbing her hatpin into the resistant straw.

The doctor never quite knew what or how it figured, and when his appointed rounds took him to the famous St. Elmo cathouse, he asked the proprietress if she had hired a Cassie Lafferty. No, the woman said, but Cassie Lafferty had come looking for work, and she'd had experience, you could say that for her, but you had to plan ahead in this business; it was a young woman's trade, at least it was in her house, and Cassie Lafferty was just about the last rose of summer.

"What happens to a woman like that?" he asked.

The proprietress shrugged, sending the silken layers of her clothing into whispers. "What happens to all of them, Doctor. They drink or die or go to jail."

Cassie was neither drunk, dead, nor jailed when he saw her some months later. He was finishing a late-evening drink at the Ferris Hotel as she came down to the lobby. He tipped his hat to her, and under her dark veil he noted blood trickling from her nose. He took her elbow and escorted her out, much to the snickering delight of the bellboys. Cassie protested it was nothing and he ought not to be seen with her, but the doctor said that a man who didn't fear God couldn't be expected to fear the St. Elmo matrons, could he?

"Who did this?" he asked as he settled her in his office and untied the veil. Cassie's lips were cut and her left eye swollen, and the soot from her eyelashes coursed down her face with tears.

"It wouldn't do no good to tell. The hotel won't let me come back if I brung the sheriff down on them. It wouldn't do no good anyway. He'd just say I lied, and what could I say?" She wept, and he staunched the blood from her nose.

"Hush, hold still now." He brushed the cuts with salve. "Did he hurt you anywhere else?"

Cassie burst into fresh tears.

"Where else?"

"My back."

Doctor unfastened the hooks at her blouse and slid it down her shoulders. He peeled the cotton camisole away from her bruised back and wiped it gently with warm cloths. Cassie wept into Doctor's handkerchief, and then she wept into his arms, and he comforted her with his hands, not only the cool, professional hands of

128

the doctor, but the tender hands of a lover, a man moved past simple indignation that anyone could beat up a woman like Cassie, knowing she was legally, morally, and physically powerless to stop him. The doctor suffered a compound fracture of the heart.

Dr. Tipton made love to Cassie Lafferty that night in the quiet tobacco-smelling study in full view of Blanche. Made love to her gently, kissing her bruised mouth, and she touched his face and murmured his name, which he was surprised she knew at all. His self-control deserted him for the first time in years, and the hungers he had so successfully raised to the level of cerebral pursuit reasserted themselves, and he felt not like the university graduate and medical school alumnus that he was, but like a peasant and a seducer and a damn stupid fool, and anyone who was such a peasant that he would seduce a half-reformed whore was even more a damn stupid fool.

The doctor drove her home in his buggy and declined to spend the night. Guilt assailed him, invaded even the inner sanctum of his study. Lacking Christian convictions, the doctor always felt it somehow essential that he be morally intact and rainwater-pure. After Cassie Lafferty, or pity or lust, eroded that purity, he was forced to conclude that even an atheist must subscribe to the old tribal code, much as he might repudiate the tribe. He went to Cassie again the following Saturday night.

The doctor still spent his Sunday mornings reading the week-old out-of-town papers, drinking coffee laced with brandy. He still spent his Sunday evenings with the Widow Douglass and her six children. But he spent his Saturday nights in Cassie Lafferty's bed, because if after 1905 he could no longer deny the needs of the flesh, he could at least regulate them. He continued to scoff at religion and keep his professional rounds, and if he ever perceived that St. Elmo would surely find him out and just as surely never forgive him, he ignored it.

Saturday nights the doctor reached Cassie's place about ten o'clock. She lived in a house some ten miles north of town on unirrigated land that had once been part of a sheep ranch, but the sheep were long gone and tumbleweeds clogged their pens and troughs, and periodically Cassie tore them up for firewood.

On Saturday night Lucius Tipton took off his clothes and put on a robe and sat by Cassie's fire drinking Burning Bush whiskey, which warmed him inside while Cassie warmed him outside. In summer he didn't bother with the robe; Cassie opened the windows, and the sounds and smells of the foothills blew over them as Lucius stretched his white legs out in bed beside Cassie's and she rubbed his shoulders. Sometimes Cassie had the kettle hot and the water buckets ready, and they filled the tin tub and took turns in it because it was too small for the both of them together. Lucius admired Cassie's generous body, unsupported by stays, unbound by garters, unsheathed by stockings, and uncluttered with clothes. His affection for her and for her body even touched him professionally, because a doctor, after all, is best acquainted with the body as a charnel house, and Dr. Tipton would not have believed the body could provide such balm to the mind and soul, such ease to the heart. They should have mentioned that in medical school, he thought as he watched the firelight illuminate the blond hair on Cassie's legs. At least they should have mentioned it.

Anyone watching the doctor return to St. Elmo in the last flush of Sunday's dawn would have thought that he was returning from a late-night call up the valley and not that he had just left Cassie Lafferty's bed and tin tub or slept with his head on her heavy, stretch-marked breasts.

More than one night the doctor lay awake in his singular bedroom above the office, cigar glowing, unable to sleep. He tried to rationalize, to balance, to understand his involvement with two such different women as Cassie Lafferty and the Widow Douglass. Though she had a bracing intelligence, Ruth lacked curiosity and imagination. Ruth's company was astringent, but for all her tempered edges, the doctor decided there was something to be said for the elastic smile, the practiced embrace, the spontaneous flesh of Cassie Lafferty. As he lay there in the dark he concluded that these two women were not so very different from each other after all. Cassie also lacked curiosity and imagination, and both women knew that the world was a complicated enough place all by itself and that curiosity could teach you things you did not want to know and imagination was a waste of time. While this knowledge allowed the doctor to put his cigar out and get some sleep, he knew it did not fully explain his attachment to Cassie or Ruth, because he was a man of ongoing curiosity and unstinting imagination and high principles he broke with weekly.

Lucius Tipton had little acquaintance with love. Before Cassie and Ruth he had never felt love except in the universal sense of human brotherhood. He was committed to those universals which are fine on a spring morning when he could stand on the valley floor and smell the sage and the distant orange blossom, listen to the wind carry the train's whistle, see the last of the snow softening the peaks, and watch the bandito bluejay flit from pepper to palm. But it's only the particulars that have smiles and hands and backs and buttocks and are any good at all on a cold winter's night.

16

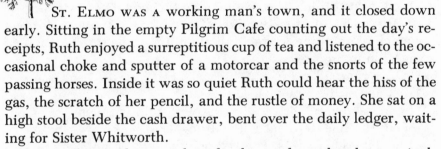

ST. ELMO WAS A working man's town, and it closed down early. Sitting in the empty Pilgrim Cafe counting out the day's receipts, Ruth enjoyed a surreptitious cup of tea and listened to the occasional choke and sputter of a motorcar and the snorts of the few passing horses. Inside it was so quiet Ruth could hear the hiss of the gas, the scratch of her pencil, and the rustle of money. She sat on a high stool beside the cash drawer, bent over the daily ledger, waiting for Sister Whitworth.

Sister Whitworth ran a boardinghouse down by the terminal. Twice a week, unbeknownst to her boarders, she came to the Pilgrim's back door for Ruth's leftover cakes and breads and pastries. She paid for them in cash. It was a happy arrangement all around.

When a knock sounded at the back door, Ruth put the teapot and cup beneath the counter and walked back through the immaculate kitchen and unbolted the door for Sister Whitworth. Ruth found Sister Whitworth rather unappealing and less than fastidious; she was a large woman whose arms bulged through the seams of her clothes and whose skirt was invariably stained with food.

"Sorry I'm late, Sister Douglass, but I got three new railroad men at my place and they all had to work late, so I had to feed them before I could come. You know how men are."

"I've forgotten."

"Ain't you the lucky one. Well, what have you got tonight?"

Ruth went to the bread bin and pulled out half a dozen half-used loaves and then to the pie cooler for the remains of a few pies. Sister Whitworth put them carefully in her basket. "The cakes are out front," said Ruth.

"Your Afton sure can put together a cake," Sister Whitworth said, following Ruth into the dining room. "I don't know no one, young or old, who can do what she can with a bit of flour, sugar, and orange peel. One of my new boarders was saying just tonight that Afton Douglass could bake fit for angels."

"And who might that be?"

"A young man, new to St. Elmo. You might have seen him. He comes in here sometimes for his breakfast. He's not bad-looking, but for a scar all along one side of his face. He might be real good-looking, but for that."

"I don't notice the men who come in here."

"Well, I don't think he comes here for the food, begging your pardon. He likes a look at Afton, though he don't say as much. He don't say much of anything, come to think of it. But he surely does hold your Afton in high regard."

"Is he a railroad man?"

"He's one of the new boarders."

"I don't allow my girls to step out with railroad men."

"Well, this one steps out with Afton—least he knows who she is, least he knows her cakes. I served one the other night, and he says right away, this come from the Pilgrim, didn't it? Well, I just said, no indeed, everything at this table is fresh-baked in this kitchen."

"Well, he can come here all he wants, because from now on I'll have Mason deliver the cakes. I don't let my children work here."

"You ought to have Eden keep your accounts now she's so good at it."

"Eden has her own job."

"Nice of your brother-in-law to give her that job at the bank, wasn't it?"

"Eden graduated first in her class at the Blakely. She deserved that job."

132

"Don't no one argue with that. Why, Sister McGahey was just saying to me at Relief Society the other day that her boy Jack couldn't do no better than to marry your Eden."

"Marry Eden?" Ruth held the cake remains in midair.

"You should tell Eden to say yes, soon as she can. Jack's not going to wait forever, and she could do a lot worse. Brother McGahey's got that nice blacksmith business, and it'll come to Jack in time."

Ruth bit her bottom lip and wrapped the last of the three cakes. Sister Whitworth peered at her. "You knew about Jack's proposing, didn't you, Sister Douglass? I thought every girl ran home to tell her mother the minute she got proposed to. Mine all did."

"That'll be two twenty-five."

"Ain't that a bit steep?"

"Charity has its place, Sister Whitworth, and it's not at the Pilgrim."

A rhythmic knock sounded at the back door, and Sister Whitworth jumped. "I hope that ain't one of my boarders."

"It's Lucius. I can tell."

"Let me give you a word to the wise about the doctor, Sister, because a woman that runs a boardinghouse hears things a widow don't."

"I don't want no words to the wise or anyone else, thank you." Ruth drew herself up to her full imposing height. "And a woman that runs a boardinghouse should learn to keep her mouth shut. Gossip-mongering is beneath a Saint."

Ruth left to open the kitchen door for Lucius, and Sister Whitworth packed up her cakes, covered her basket, and sailed past Lucius Tipton. She was nearly out of the kitchen door before Ruth reminded her of the two dollars and twenty-five cents.

Ruth and Lucius sat at one of the tables, where she had carefully folded back the cloth so it would be fresh for the morning. "That woman's tongue ought to be cut out and pickled in brine," she said, bringing the teapot and another cup.

"None for me, Ruth. I'll just pour some of this in the cup, if you don't mind." He drew a small bottle of Burning Bush out of his coat pocket.

133

Ruth studied him in the harsh gaslight. "What's the matter with you, Lucius? You don't look well."

"Well, I thought a little snort of this might help."

"Help what?"

"Help me. Help you, too, if you want it." He pulled a newspaper clipping out of his pocket; it was crumpled and three weeks out of date. "Does this sound like anyone you know?"

PROPHET EZEKIEL HELD ON
CHARGES OF MAYHEM

Federal authorities in Arizona Territory have arrested a man calling himself the Prophet Ezekiel, leader of the Apostles of the Apocalypse. He is being held in connection with destruction of the town of Cupid, Arizona Territory.

Witnesses say that Ezekiel and his followers settled near Cupid some months ago, in August 1907. The man calling himself Ezekiel has continually prophesied the immediate approach of the Last Days. Last week, fired by his preaching, the people of Cupid went on the rampage. They burned their goods and their furniture. Some even set fire to their homes. He told them anyone holding worldly goods on the Last Day would be smitten with God's wrath.

The town of Cupid was reduced to rubble and ash, despite the efforts of some of the more sober citizens. Ezekiel is not charged with arson, only mayhem and the willful destruction of property. Witnesses say he did not light the fires himself. The Apostles of the Apocalypse are also being investigated for bigamy and lewdness. The identity of the man calling himself Ezekiel cannot be established. His followers and his wife, Elda, refuse to cooperate with the authorities. They say their leader is answerable only to God, but there is hope that the Apostles of the Apocalypse will disband while their leader is in jail.

"Care for a drink of Burning Bush, Ruth?"

She shook her head; her face was bloodless and her lips dry. "I'm not done with that man. I can feel it in my bones. He'll be here one day. You mark my words. He'll destroy me."

"I don't think he can harm us, Ruth."

"Us? You needn't be destroyed."

"Oh, but my dear Mrs. Douglass." Lucius's eyes gleamed with something of their old light. "I would insist on it. It's the least I can do."

"You don't know what you'd do."

"What would you do if things were reversed, if it was me who could be destroyed?"

"If! Only a man has time to ask questions that start with if!" She closed the account books and slammed the till and took the clipping to the stove. "I wish it was Samuel himself," she said, opening the grate and throwing the clipping on the embers.

"You ought to consider the ifs now and then, Ruth. Thinking about if sometimes prepares you for when."

If became when in the fullness of time, which was about eight months later.

During those eight months, Jack McGahey proposed three times to Eden Douglass and was three times denied. Eden informed her mother (and anyone else with the temerity to inquire about her marriage plans) that she had no intention of marrying; she was leaving St. Elmo as soon as she could. Eden vowed she'd marry only *after* she'd been to Paris. Afton Douglass, with equal determination, informed her mother that she intended to marry Tom Lance as soon as she possibly could. Ruth forbade her from seeing Tom on the grounds that he was a railroad man and five years Afton's senior. Afton only retorted that nothing could make her stop loving him. Gideon Douglass indicated that maybe he'd one day like to marry Miss Arlene McClure. Gideon seldom made up his mind to anything; he was happy when things went his way and sad when they did not. His languor occasionally annoyed even Miss Arlene McClure, who was just as prim and studious as Gideon. Lil, who was only thirteen, after all, didn't have anyone in mind to marry. And Mason and Cissa learned from all this to keep out of Afton's way on a bad day and not to ask Eden to unknot their kite strings right after Jack McGahey had proposed.

Mason and Cissa, in fact, both had the whooping cough when

135

time reached its fullness and if became when. Lucius Tipton checked in on them on Saturday night, pronounced them on the mend, then got back in his Flyer and drove to Cassie Lafferty's. Wally Hurst also paid a call on Cassie Lafferty on November 14, 1908.

Wally Hurst was the son-in-law of Judge Avery Patterson, Sr. The Pattersons were Methodists, but Wally Hurst was a ne'er-do-well. Emily Patterson had married him on the assumption that love cures all, but it did not cure Wally. He was often drunk, frequently unemployed (despite his status as the judge's son-in-law), and always an embarrassment to the Pattersons. He was troublesome to the rest of the town, too. He had, in fact, been forbidden from the premises of the St. Elmo cathouse for being drunk and disorderly. The proprietress there did not care if he was the judge's son-in-law.

Wally Hurst had on more than one occasion paid for and received the ministrations of Cassie Lafferty, meeting her in cheap railroad hotels down by the terminal. On November 14 he could not find her in town, so he drove his father-in-law's motorcar out to her little shack and banged on the door.

Cassie answered clad only in a light blue wrapper. Her hair was down and her house lit only with firelight. "What do you want?"

"What do you think?" Wally shoved a dollar at her.

"Not now. I'm busy."

"My money's as good as anyone's."

"Not now."

"Now." And with that Wally kicked the door open. He knocked Cassie backward and beheld the naked Dr. Lucius Tipton pulling on his pants in front of the fire.

Within the week the story had percolated among the Methodists and Mormons, and the Baptists, all the way down to the heathen Chinese who had come to St. Elmo with the railroad and stayed to wash the town's dirty linen.

17

 AND DIRTY LINEN it was. Eden Douglass heard it from no lesser personage than Arthur Whickham himself. She came into work one morning at the St. Elmo National Bank and Trust Company to find a note signed "A. W." requesting her presence in his office.

Art Whickham, having an indelicate nature, was hard pressed to put the news delicately, but he tried.

Eden heard him out and then said: "I won't hear another word against Dr. Tipton. Where is this woman? Let's ask her if this is the truth. I'm not afraid of the truth."

"You can't ask her. Cassie Lafferty is gone. She left in the dead of night on the eastbound train."

"The eastbound train don't leave in the dead of night."

"She's gone, anyway. Maybe she left on foot just to get away from the scandal."

"It takes a whole lot more than one person to make a scandal, Uncle Art." She had not called him Uncle Art since she'd lived under his roof, and he cringed. "It takes lots of dirty minds and wagging tongues, and I don't think Latter-day Saints should lend themselves to such low pastimes."

"Don't tell me my duty, young lady! You just tell your mother that I said the truth will always out, and the dirtier the truth, the more likely it is to come out."

"Tell her yourself," Eden retorted. "I don't sully my lips with malicious gossip, and I am shocked that you, an elder in the church, would call me into your office 'specially to hear something I could have heard in any saloon if I was a man or any old cat's kitchen if all I had to do was sit around and tell nasty tales about others!"

With that Eden left. Art Whickham spent the rest of the morning staring out his second-story window, cursing Ruth Douglass and wringing his hands.

Jack McGahey told Eden he'd still marry her, no matter what Doctor had done, and Eden said she still wouldn't marry Jack, no matter what Doctor had done.

Gideon heard it from Arlene McClure. She added that lots of folks had had their suspicions, only kept it to themselves because Lucius was a doctor. "But I don't think a person's situation on this earth has anything to do with his standing in heaven, do you, Gideon?"

"I don't know," he said miserably. "I don't know anything."

"Oh, Gideon, don't it just give you the creeps to think that all those Sundays Doctor sat at your mother's table, he had just that morning arisen from a bed of sin? And who knows"—Arlene shivered—"he might not even have washed his hands! Well, I am sorry to be the bearer of bad tidings, but it's best you should hear it from someone who holds you in the highest regard as I do. I guess you won't be keeping *his* company anymore."

"I don't know." He took off his glasses and pinched the bridge of his nose till it hurt. "I don't know anything."

"Well, Gideon, a girl is known by the company she keeps, and I prefer those who are clean of body, mind, and spirit. The tiniest bit of taint, even by association, why it could ruin you. If you and your family are going to keep company with a . . . a . . . whoremonger"—she felt free to use the word because it was Biblical, after all—"then I don't see how I can associate with you." And with that Arlene flounced off, warning Gideon not to see her or call her cousin Gloria.

Lil Douglass was confused by all this, because she usually counted on Afton for her opinions, and Afton was confused. Afton said she didn't believe it, but Lil knew better. "What if it's true?" she asked her older sister. "What'll we do then?"

"Well, we'll just have to see what Mother does," said Afton, who did not generally rely on anyone for her opinions.

Ruth for her part heard by indirection, whispering innuendo in the Pilgrim Cafe and not so whispering innuendo from Sister Whitworth. "Is that all?" said Ruth grimly when Sister Whitworth had finished her agitated recitation. "Because I don't want you coming back in here next week with some little morsel you forgot."

"What else can you expect from an atheist and a cigar smoker?" Sister Whitworth concluded.

Ruth charged her double for the baked goods and told her she could like it or lump it. Sister Whitworth didn't like it, but she bought just the same.

By the first Sunday in December the gossip had spread, like chicken pox, into every home where English was spoken. The Douglasses went to church, where everyone treated them as if the doctor's transgression might be infectious. One of the hymns chosen that Sunday was "Do Not Feel Inclined to Censure," which, of course, everyone did.

The bishop himself came up to Ruth to offer the sympathy one reserves for the afflicted. "The church never forgets its faithful, Sister Douglass. We want you to know our hearts are with you in your hour of need. It is always distressing to lose a friend."

"Someone you know die, Bishop?" said Ruth as she walked away.

Doctor had not appeared for two consecutive Sunday dinners, nor did he appear for this one. His absence was more keenly felt than his presence had ever been. His empty chair seemingly glowered at them. Ruth asked Gideon to give the blessing, but Gideon, who had just seen Arlene in church on the arm of Lloyd Whickham, said he couldn't. "I'm sick."

"Too sick to eat?"

"No, but too sick to pray."

Ruth gave the blessing herself and then picked up the plate of parsnips and helped herself and Cissa.

"I hate parsnips," said Cissa.

"Hate sin," replied Ruth, "not parsnips. After supper we're going over to Doctor's. We'll take what's left of dinner, and Lil, you can slip next door and pick a few of the neighbor's mums. This is a social call."

"But we can't!" Gideon cried. "Everyone in town will see us."

"That's the point."

"But, Ma . . . you know . . . you've heard, haven't you?"

"We've heard a lot of cheeky bull," Eden answered for her mother. "And personally I think it's the work of the Methodists. The Pattersons are Methodist."

139

"But Ma—" Gideon turned to Ruth. Gideon had his father's sticking-out ears and sandy hair, and his long mouth was twisted with despair.

"Gideon, when we were in need, the Saints were very nice to us and all that, but it was Doctor came to our aid. The Saints was never happy unless we groveled with gratitude, but Doctor, he never asked of us, nothing but our friendship, and that's what we're giving him. You might as well learn it now, boy—it's not always easy to do what you think is best and stay on the right side of the world. Either you are someone's friend or you're not. It's that simple. And that hard."

"Yes," added Afton. "Who would you rather face, Gideon, the disapproval of this pea-brained town or God Himself when you get called up at the Last Judgment?"

"But that's a long way off," Gideon pleaded.

"It might be sooner than you guess, and anyway, God don't forget."

"That's right," said Lil, relieved to know that Afton had made up her mind. "God don't forget."

In the late-afternoon chill the Douglasses marched down St. Elmo's Silk Stocking Row toward the central district. They walked in formation, the girls leading the way, Ruth holding Cissa's hand and Gideon bringing up the rear. They passed the Whickhams' ample house, and Mason dawdled in front of their fence gazing at his Aunt Lily in the parlor window; her hair was the color of old lace, her face the color of cornmeal. "Get a move on, Mason," said Ruth. "The Douglasses are too busy for the Whickhams, and the Whickhams are not busy enough for the Douglasses."

When they arrived at Doctor's they found Lucius Tipton in his customary place behind the desk with Blanche peering over his shoulder. A half-dozen empty bottles of Burning Bush, glasses, and cigar butts littered the desk. A sparse beard darkened his jowls, and his eyes were as flat as coins lying in sockets as big as Blanche's. "What are you doing here?" he said, scowling.

"Just what it looks like. Bringing Sunday dinner to you, since you didn't come to it."

"You've heard, I assume."

"We've heard the Methodists are trying to run you out of town because they have their own doctor now," Eden offered.

Lucius's lips curled around a fresh cigar. "That's not the whole bucket. You've heard whole buckets of vileness, and you're skimming it off on the Methodists. You want to tell me what you've heard?"

"No, Lucius, I don't," Ruth said unequivocally.

"Shall I tell you the truth?"

"The truth is overrated." Displaced moths flew out of the chair as she sat down. "Benzine is good for moths," she announced. "The place stinks for a few days, but benzine gets rid of the moths."

"They keep me company." He puffed a blue cloud of smoke that settled about his shoulders like the arms of a friend. "You shouldn't have come. You're not touched by any of this, much less accountable. We're not necessarily connected."

"We are now."

"Yes," he said tiredly, "we always have been, haven't we? Connected like tissue and sinew and blood and bone, but you could still leave."

"Let's leave," said Gideon, taking his glasses off.

"You could still say to folks—can I help it what that old fool of a doctor does?"

"You're not a fool," said Eden.

"Oh, yes, I am, and your mother's a fool for coming here."

"My mother's no fool," Afton snapped.

"I expect you to drive us all home in the Flyer, Lucius," said Ruth, "and I expect you to be at my house next Sunday."

"They'll come after you next, Ruth. You could lose the Pilgrim."

"Eyewash. There are enough hungry bellies in this town who don't care about either of us, and there are enough broken bodies who don't care what the doctor did on Saturday night. No, Lucius, I don't condone whatever it was you did—or did not do," she said, condoning with the codicil, "but I've lived too long to start being wormy now. It's wormy to desert your friends, and I won't have it. Now, Afton, you take that chicken into Doctor's kitchen and heat it up, and Eden, you make Doctor a cup of coffee. He needs it."

"I don't know how to make coffee."

"You just throw some in a pot of water and boil it up. Vile stuff, coffee. Mason, you gather up these plates and glasses lying around, and Cissa, you get rid of the cigar butts, and Gideon, you—"

"I want to know if it's true." He sat on the overstuffed sofa with his long arms dangling between his knees. "I have to know."

"We're not here to poke and pry."

He coughed and cleared his throat. "I have to know. Arlene. I have to know for Arlene. And"—he gulped his voice back to its usual timbre—"I have to know for me. I prefer those clean of body, mind, and spirit, and I can't bear to be tainted by association. You're known by the company you keep."

Ruth wilted visibly. "Don't do this, Gideon."

"I have to know."

Lucius put his cigar out and pushed the chair back, bumping into Blanche, who rattled consolingly. "What have you heard, Gideon? Not all of it's true, you know. There's something about a loathsome disease, and that's not true."

"What is?"

Lucius never took his eyes from Ruth. "I took part in, I enjoyed a liaison with, a woman who lived north of town. I paid her for her affections, which were really freely given. And accepted."

Ruth knotted the black silk of her Sunday skirt in her fingers. "Lucius, please don't." She wiped her eyes quickly. "Please."

Lucius's sad face sagged. "I'd do anything to spare you pain, my dear. How I regret the pain this must cause you, but you're not the only one with—well, we all have our secrets. Mine was certainly"—he plucked his words from the thistles of the obvious—"blacker and more culpable than anything you could imagine, Ruth." He added her name almost tenderly as the tears spilled down her cheeks and stained her skirt.

"How long?" said Gideon, hating himself for wanting to know what could only defile him. "How long did this go on?"

"A few years. Two or three. I've forgotten. I got used to it. Like any other sin. Listen to me—sin! I'm worse than the wool-mouthed Mormons."

"We're not wool-mouthed!" Gideon cried. "We're Saints, and we know wickedness when we meet it, and we won't have nothing to do with sin and foulness."

"Oh, Gideon, stop!" Ruth begged him. "You don't know what you're saying."

"I know what my church teaches me!" He put his glasses back on, carefully placing their thin stems over his ears. "You're going against the Bible and the Book of Mormon and everything we hold holy, Mother. You're going against your own teachings. You're the one lit the match! You're the one said it would never light again once your reputation's been tainted."

"I expect you to do what you're told."

"You want me, want all of us"—he motioned to his speechless brother and sisters—"you want us to be liars and hypocrites? You want the world to think we're—"

"The world can go to the devil," she shot back, "and the church, too!"

And with that Gideon bolted; he shot out as fast as his long legs would carry him. He stumbled over the ottoman and ran through the office door, not pausing till he reached the street, and then he ran to Arlene McClure's house. Her little brother answered his frenzied knock. "Please tell your sister I'm here," he said, breathing and shaking.

The boy ambled into the house, and Gideon waited, mopping the sweat from his upper lip and hands. The boy came back and eyed him cautiously. "She said to tell you she won't have no further intercourse with you till you've freed yourself from unwholesome associates. That's what she says."

"Tell her I'm free!" He shook the boy's shoulders. "I'm free!"

He did not feel free. The boy left, and Gideon put his handkerchief away. He composed himself, as he often did, by reciting the dates of the Punic Wars. He did not feel free, but it was only taint by association, he told himself, and it would pass in the fullness of time.

18

REASON GOT THE best of Lucius. Self-pitying hibernation was, after all, contrary to the principles of nature and his profession. He returned to as much of his practice as would have him, and he found among the ranks of the poor, the black, the brown, and the yellow families of St. Elmo, enough birth, death, and broken bones to keep him professionally occupied. Still, he was surprised one morning to answer the office door and find a girl with blond hair tangled into a mat of dirty braids. Underneath the grime streaking her face, Lucius reckoned her young, Afton's age perhaps, about sixteen.

"You Dr. Tipton?" She wore a man's jacket, hat, and boots, and her skirt hung in tatters near her feet.

"I am."

"I'm Sister Rachel. I come about my pa." Sister Rachel entered tentatively; she seemed uncomfortable in the pristine office. "It's his foot. It was three weeks ago he cleaved it with an ax, and it ain't getting no better. It stinks, and he don't have no more feeling in it. Our prophet's been praying over him, and still it don't get any better. Our prophet says God will cure my pa and make him whole again, but I don't see God doing no such thing. So I come to you. I been to one doctor already, but he won't have nothing to do with my pa. He said I should come to you."

"Gracious of him. Well, Rachel, where is your pa? Let's have a look at him."

The girl's mouth wrung with tears, and she twisted her leathery brown hands in her lap. "He can't be moved."

"Well, where is he?"

"We're up in New Canaan, up in the desert, fifteen miles east of Jackrabbit. Oh, I know it's a long ways, but you got to come. My pa'll die otherwise. I know it. He's getting worse, and for all Prophet's praying, God don't seem to hear or heed, and I know God'll smite me for bringing a foreigner to New Canaan, but I don't care so long's you'll come save my pa. I know Prophet and God, they don't like no meddling with their miraculous ways, but I don't see no miracles. All I see is my pa's foot getting sicker and sicker. Prophet says God only cares for Prophet and don't trust doctors, but I'm scareder of my pa dying than I am of God—or even Prophet—so I . . ." She faltered. "I stole the one horse we got in New Canaan and come down last night."

"You came over Jesuit Pass by yourself at night?"

She nodded vigorously. "My pa's all I got, Doctor. If he goes, I'll have to marry Prophet. I'll be all by myself, and Prophet don't allow no unattached women." She wept in her dirty hands.

Lucius dampened a towel in the washbasin, wrung it out, and handed it to her. "Here, Rachel," he said. "You calm yourself now."

Rachel wiped her eyes, leaving streaks, but she showed no signs of calming. "Rachel's not my real name," she declared. "I'm Addie Young, but Prophet makes all of us change our names when we join up with the Apostles. He says we have to forsake the things of this world and get Biblical. We joined up with Prophet in Cupid, and we all had to change our names—me and my ma and pa and sister, Caroline. But they're all gone now, all 'cept Pa, and I can't lose him."

"Are they dead?"

"Mostly. Esther—that's my sister, Caroline—she run off last year just 'fore she was going to marry Prophet and First Apostle Jeremiah."

"Both of them?" said the doctor in a rather more horrified tone than he'd intended.

"We, all of the women, we got to marry Prophet and sometimes someone else besides, but Caroline—Esther, I mean—she said she'd sooner die than bed down with Prophet and First Apostle. Even Pa couldn't talk no sense into Caroline. She said she'd rather die, and then . . ." Rachel broke into fresh sobs. "She ran away, and Prophet said a vision come over him that Caroline had died, run over by a trolley in Chicago and her head cut off. Oh, Doctor, my pa's all I got left!"

Doctor knelt beside her chair and took her damp and dirty hands in his. "What's your prophet's name, Addie?"

"Ezekiel," she said through her tears. "He'll kill me when I get back. He'll kill you, too, Doctor. I got to warn you. Prophet said he'd kill any foreigner who meddled amongst us."

"Hush, Addie. You go into the study for a few minutes and have a lie-down." He ushered her into the study, but when she saw Blanche hanging behind the desk, she screamed and would not move. "Blanche is quite harmless," he assured her, but Addie would not be budged until Lucius got two blankets out of the cabinet and gave one to Addie and draped the other over Blanche's head.

He went into the kitchen and rang up the Pilgrim Cafe and asked to speak to the Widow Douglass. "Ruth, I need some food sent over here. Some bread and ham and pie and milk and whatever else you got there. I got a girl here's who's ridden all night from Jackrabbit. I have to go up there. I think there's a mail train at noon."

"What's in Jackrabbit?"

"It's her pa. He can't be moved. They're living in a place called New Canaan. And Ruth . . ." He put his lips to the mouthpiece as tenderly as if it were her ear; he chose his words carefully, because the St. Elmo operators often enlivened their days eavesdropping. "This girl belongs to the Apostles of the Apocalypse, and their prophet's name is Ezekiel."

The wires crackled as if they smoldered at the mere mention of Samuel Douglass. "I'll send the basket over," she said in a low, hollow tone. "And you can pick me up at the Pilgrim before you go to the train station. I'm coming with you."

"No, you're not. This is business."

"So it is. My business as much as yours."

"No."

"I'm ready now, Lucius. I have to put fear behind me sometime, and I'm ready to do it now."

Addie Young or Sister Rachel devoured the food that Ruth sent by way of one of the cooks. Doctor gave her some money and instructed her to go to Sister Whitworth's and show Sister Whitworth the color of her money before she asked for a room. He said she was not to mention the Apostles or her pa or Lucius Tipton at all. He scribbled Addie's directions to New Canaan on a scrap of paper and put it in his pocket.

146

"I'll need to know your father's name, Addie."

"Brother Hosea."

"His real name."

"John Young," she said, stuffing the last of the pie in her mouth.

"I'll do what I can for him."

"Oh, Doctor, bless you! But you best watch your step around Prophet. I seen him do some terrible things to unbelievers. I seen some awful things in my time."

Doctor returned to the study after she left. From the bookshelf he pulled a volume of Manilius. He felt around behind the books and found a small revolver, a gun more suited to a woman than a man. It had, in fact, been Cassie's parting gift to him. He cleaned the gun methodically and loaded it and put it in his pocket.

He pulled the blanket off Blanche, whose jaw drooped with sadness, as if she knew she'd been momentarily forsaken. Lucius assured himself, however, that skeletons could not express emotion, it wasn't possible, at least not in the material world, which was the only world Lucius Tipton recognized. He packed up his medical bag and briefly considered driving straight to the station and not picking Ruth up at the Pilgrim at all. A form of protective treachery. He dismissed the idea, finally. Ruth had said she was ready. Lucius wondered if he was.

Jackrabbit Junction was as forlorn as its name, surrounded by dry land like cracked leather, tufted with sage and chaparral and populated within a fifty-mile radius only by a few daft miners, broken-down sheepherders, a handful of religious zealots, and lizards, and even they stayed out of the noonday sun. Low hills rose in the distance, scaled with boulders, rather like the once-shed skins of old dinosaurs, Doctor reflected as he and Ruth stepped off the train. The depot itself was little more than an unpainted, splintering shack. Inside it was lit by sunlight falling through the chinks, and the stove was cold; paint peeled off the benches, and a water barrel with a tin lid stood in the corner. It smelled of unemptied cuspidors.

"Mr. Emery," Lucius called, peering into the stationmaster's tiny, empty office. "Mr. Emery!"

Mr. Emery came in buttoning his fly. "Oh, begging your pardon, ma'am," he said, blushing, when he beheld Ruth. "I wasn't expecting no one but the doctor." Mr. Emery was small, wizened,

147

with sparse red hair thatched across his skull and eyes puckered from extensive experience of sizing things up and whittling them down. "I got your wire, Doctor. I got the wagon for you, too. Out back. Horse and all," he added, as if the horse were luxury. "That'll be five dollars hire. Now, you might think that's a bit steep, and if you want to find another wagon in twenty miles of here, you just go right ahead."

"I'll pay it."

"You didn't say where you were taking it."

"That information will cost you," Doctor replied, handing the stationmaster the money. He held back one dollar. "How curious are you?"

"You just better have my horse and wagon back here by tomorrow morning when I get in, or it'll be another five."

Lucius and Ruth went around back to find the wagon—as splintery, unpainted, and springless as the depot—and the horse, which seemed to be in an equally dilapidated condition. Ruth put her foot on the wheel to hoist herself up, but Doctor stayed her arm. "Please, Ruth, wait for me here at the depot."

"And suffer the company of that old lizard Emery? I'd rather face Samuel."

They found New Canaan where Addie said they would, fifteen miles east of Jackrabbit. They found the Apostles in a shallow, saucerlike ravine where a few stunted trees grew. They were protected from the worst of the wind by gnarled hillsides covered with coarse scrub. In this, the short-lived, tender early spring, a few cactus flowers bloomed flamboyantly. Some undernourished greenery sprouted in the ravine, fed probably by an artesian well or underground stream. Ruth was reminded of her first sight of the Healy homestead; this place had the same spare, grizzled visage, as if Samuel could never bear to live where the land had been defiled by mere humans and their history. She lowered the motoring veil from her hat, and it lay around her shoulders like a shroud.

The Apostles lived in squalor so degrading that the Apocalypse might have been a welcome relief. Huts and tents dotted the ravine floor; some were mere blankets strung together, or lean-tos with roofs of tin or walls of tarp. One family lived under the shell of an old wagon. Ruth figured they had probably eaten the horse. The few shelters of wood or gathered stones were windowless, and the

Apostles apparently believed the Last Days so near at hand they had made no provision for sanitation. Flies hung bloated, heavy, almost motionless in the air, and fleas jumped visibly across the ground. Dogs whose ribs could be counted barked at their wagon. The dogs' eyes were as yellow as their sparse fur. Cooking pots hung over cold fires, and slack-breasted women with waxen eyes hovered near them. The erratic cry of babies broke the air, and hollow-cheeked children dressed in flour sacks eyed the wagon suspiciously as they scratched themselves.

Doctor handed the reins to Ruth. "Hello! Anyone here tell me where I can find Brother Hosea?" His voice reverberated off the nearby hillsides; it seemed to hang like the flies in the afternoon air.

A few men emerged from huts and tents. One rolled out from underneath the wagon. Some of them were conventionally if poorly dressed in pants and flannel shirts, some were in Biblical robes. They all wore long flowing beards, matted and untrimmed hair. Dirt filled the crevices of every face young and old, male and female. "Who wants Brother Hosea?" said an older man in a coarse robe, his sandals strapped to his feet with leather thongs. "I'm first apostle here."

"I come in peace," Lucius assured him. "I got business with Brother Hosea and no one else."

"Brother Hosea is with the prophet."

"Well, your prophet's had him a long time. Now I'd like a little time with him."

"Prophet dispenses time in New Canaan."

"Does the prophet dispense direction as well? Just point me to Brother Hosea's."

"Who be you?"

Ruth touched his hand before he could answer. "Tread lightly, Lucius," she murmured under the veil.

"I'm just passing through," Lucius announced unconvincingly. Then he brightened and added, "I'm a drummer, and I got some news for Brother Hosea. Sad news, I'm afraid. So sad I reckon I ought to give it to him in person, and if your prophet's with him, then so much the better, because Hosea's going to need all the comfort he can get when he hears the news I brung."

"What news is that?"

"It's his daughter, Caroline."

149

"She is no longer among the Apostles."

"Well, she's no longer among the living either. Died in Chicago. Got her head cut off by a trolley. Saw it with my own eyes—trolley cut her clean across the neck, and the scream was still on her lips when her head went bouncing down the track."

"Praise God!" The man turned to the others. "It happened just like Prophet said! Sister Esther got her head cut off by a trolley." The man pointed toward a shack of scrap board with a faded red blanket for a door. "You go tell Brother Hosea yourself—he'll believe it, if it come from a stranger. Amen!"

"Much obliged. You wait here," he said to Ruth. "Let me go in first." He patted his coat pocket to make sure Cassie's revolver was there, and then he dismounted and walked toward the red blanket that twitched in the wind.

Ruth stayed where she was. She surveyed the Apostles from under the motoring veil, wondering which of these women was Elda Allred, or indeed if Elda Allred was still alive after ten years of life with the prophet. She figured that one of the stone huts was Samuel's; he always had been a good builder, and he would have one of the best. And yet, how could these people believe themselves chosen by God? Blessed? Beatified? How could they harken to a prophet whose visions included severed heads and whose voice had led them hither? And then she remembered the power in Samuel's eyes and voice and the Healy Saints enraptured in his prayers. And then she remembered his strong, competent hands. And then she shuddered.

A small girl with dingy eyes approached the wagon carrying a tin cup. "Ma wants to know if you want some water." She held it up to Ruth.

"Thank you." Ruth brought the cup under her veil and drank. The water tasted strongly of alkali.

"Ma wants to know if you want to wait over yonder." She pointed to a lean-to where a woman and three other children waited in the shade of their tin roof.

"No, thank you. I'll stay here." Ruth returned the cup.

"Ma wants to know if your dress is silk."

"No. Cotton."

The little girl looked back to her mother and shook her head. The mother stood and walked into the flat sunlight, which cut across her face like a scalpel, revealing a woman not yet thirty who looked

150

more like fifty; her eyes were drained of life, and her mouth was eroded by the loss of her teeth. She reached up and fingered the edge of the veil and lifted the hem of Ruth's skirt to touch the petticoat.

"That'll be enough," Ruth said, pulling her skirt close to her ankles. "That'll be just enough."

"We all of us come naked before God at the Last Trump, Sister," said the woman, cuffing the girl's ear and shoving her back toward the lean-to, where a dog gnawed on the body of a mouse and where, Ruth could just discern, a single brilliant cactus flower floated in a bowl on a rickety table.

19

LUCIUS ASSUMED THE stench would be overpowering, and he was right. Seven lamps burned, placed at intervals around the sufferer, who lay on two tables pushed together in the middle of the hut, which was otherwise furnished with a few hand-hewn stools, a small pallet, and shelving that held cookpots, simple tools, a wreath of rope, a bag of flour, a bag of beans, a huge Bible, a washbasin, and a water bucket.

The patient was covered with a blanket of the same cut and texture as the one that hung in the doorway. His face was ashen and pinched, and beside him sat a man whose features—except for the eyes—were swathed in a cloud of stiff, graying hair. His eyes were closed, and his lips were close to Brother Hosea's ear. "How hast thou offended God, Hosea? God would not visit this on you if you had not offended Him. God will not be denied. Lay your sins at God's feet and confess to His prophet. How hast thou sinned with thy foot? Cast off sin as you would cast off maggots, or God will afflict you further." His voice was thick with insinuation, toxic and seductive at the same moment. The Prophet Ezekiel looked up and beheld the doctor. "Get out. God will not suffer interference of unbelievers."

"Please God," whimpered Hosea, "spare me. Let me live."

Lucius pulled the blanket away from the foot. It was as he feared, gangrene of the gaseous variety, resulting from the dirty laceration from the ax. The foot had putrefied, and the black skin seemed to drop away.

"The girl sent for you, didn't she? Rachel. Rachel the horsethief. Rachel the maggot. Rachel the unbeliever."

"Rachel?" Hosea wept. "Where's Rachel?"

"She's in hell with Esther and all others who prefer the fruit of unbelievers to the Apostles' dry bread."

"She's not in hell. Rachel is alive and safe. Listen to me. I am a doctor."

"You are a serpent, a vile worm. No one can go against the will of God. If God wishes to take Brother Hosea, then God will."

"Then why do you bother his sins?" inquired Lucius coolly. "What difference does it make?"

"He must admit his unworthiness before God."

"I am unworthy," Hosea moaned.

"He must throw himself on God's everlasting—"

"Everlasting gallstones! John Young! Listen to me!"

The man opened his eyes, which were so sunken as to have dropped into the abyss of his head.

Lucius chafed his hand. "Listen to me, John. Your foot is dead. I'm going to have to cut off your foot or the rest of you will die, too." John Young began to thrash and scream, but Lucius held his shoulders. "If you let me take that foot off, you'll live. Otherwise, you'll die."

"He'll die in God's time and at God's will and when God wants his soul."

"God can have it! I don't give a damn about his soul. But his body, that's my terrain. His foot"—Lucius pointed to the hideous, humid blackened foot—"what's that got to do with his soul?"

The prophet rose. He was taller than Lucius had expected, and dressed in a robe that could not conceal his spare, powerful frame. In the light of the seven lamps the shadows of his wild hair writhed on the walls like snakes, and underneath the heavy beard his mouth twitched.

152

"John Young," Lucius insisted. "I have to operate. I can save your life."

"Let this man cut you," the prophet said with the assurance of the Almighty, "and you won't be resurrected in all your flesh. Your foot will search for the rest of your body throughout eternity. This man wants to separate you from the flesh God hath given you. He is a vessel of wickedness. Trust God. Trust your prophet." He stretched his huge, hard hands out over the body. His eyes were the opaque gray of smoked glass. "Can these bones live, Hosea? Ask of me and I shall restore you. Corruption will fall away, and you shall be whole again."

"This man is no more prophet than I am," said Lucius, still holding the patient's hand. "Your name is John Young, and his name is Samuel Douglass. He's an ordinary man like any other."

The prophet took his attention from God and gave it to Lucius. "Who are you?"

"Do you want to live, John?" Lucius ignored Samuel. "Better alive with one foot than dead with two. If you want to die, I'll leave."

"Don't leave." John Young began to weep. "Don't leave me to die. Please, don't let me die."

"All right, then. Maybe I can't save your foot, but Samuel Douglass can't save your soul either."

Samuel peered at Lucius as if they were not simply divided over the body of a sick man, but over a body of water, thick with fog and pestilential vapor. "If you lay your knife to Brother Hosea's flesh, Doctor, you'll die before sundown."

"And who will kill me?"

"God and his anointed. God girds the righteous host. The smiter of wickedness is pleasing to the eye of God. Your flesh will rot in the desert and be torn to bits by vultures."

"You're a bloody fool lunatic, Samuel, and if there was a God and if He had a lick of sense, He'd have seen you drowned at birth. I'm going for my instruments, and I'll be back."

Blinking against the harsh sunlight, Lucius walked quickly to the wagon as Ruth got down and handed him his bag. "You must not say a word when we're in there, Ruth. You're not safe here. No one is safe here."

With dogs sniffing at their heels, as if they smelled both fear and

153

blood, Lucius and Ruth walked to the hut, where they found Samuel standing at Hosea's head, his thumbs pressing into the patient's eyes and his head thrown back, speaking in tongues. The sick man shook with whimpers and chills.

Beneath the black veil, Ruth regarded her husband. He was as she remembered him: gaunt and hard and hairy, with the unchanging embery eyes of the mad. His voice had coarsened, but there was no mistaking it. He had haunted her in the spirit; he was haunting in the flesh. Her loathing of him had always been rooted in a fear too terrible to name or recognize, allied somehow to her refusal to name or recognize Cissa ten years before. The stench of the rotting foot and the stench of the fear, rotting for ten years, overcame her, and she thought she might faint.

"You've brought your own angel of death," said Samuel, eyeing Ruth. "Oh, my people!" he cried. "My brethren! My holy anointed! Fall upon the unbelieving! Smite the heretics! Save Brother Hosea from the knife! Destroy these wicked devils!"

The blanket burst aside, and the Apostles crowded in, led by First Apostle Jeremiah, who grabbed Ruth's arm while two women tore at her skirt. Across the body of John Young, another lunged for Lucius, who ducked, and when he came back up he had the revolver in his hand, and he aimed it at the prophet's head and cocked it quickly. "Let go of that woman," he croaked, "or I blow out the prophet's brains. You hear me? Take your hands off her and get out. Do as I say!"

Jeremiah's huge paws remained tight on Ruth's arms; he looked to Samuel beseechingly. "Command me, Prophet."

"Tell him to let go of that woman, Prophet, or you'll be picking your eyeballs off the floor. You'll be next, Jeremiah. I'll blast your guts to hell. Where they belong. Tell him, Prophet." He shoved the gun into Samuel's ear. "Are you ready to meet this great God you're so intimate with? Are you?"

Samuel's brown teeth emerged as he drew his lips back in a smile. "You may release the woman, Jeremiah."

"Tell them to get out. All of them."

"You may leave us, my children."

Whimpering and fearful, the Apostles backed out of the hut. The blanket fell forward, and Samuel and Ruth and Lucius stood once again in the meager lantern light. "We will kill you before the sun sets," Samuel declared. "Do you hear me? My people! My Apostles!" he shouted. "They shall not leave New Canaan. We shall kill them in God's good time."

"Get the rope," Lucius said to Ruth, "and wrap it tight around his arms. Get over there," he commanded Samuel. "Sit on that pallet."

"No rope can hold the anointed," said Samuel as he shuffled, the gun still at his temple.

Ruth wound the rope around his arms, binding them to his sides. The smell of Samuel was worse than the smell of fear and rotting flesh, or maybe it was all the same smell. She knotted the rope around his wrists and tested it.

"We will stone you to death," said Samuel calmly.

Lucius put the gun in Ruth's hand. "Make certain he feels it. Keep it right against his head." Then he went outside and ordered the milling, moaning Apostles to bring him boiled water and every blanket they could find. "You'd better obey me for the time being or you won't have a prophet."

They brought the blankets and the boiled water in buckets and basins. They hovered outside the flap; their collective rough breathing, their tearful mumbling, crept into the hut like the drone of insects.

Lucius took off his coat, hat, and vest. "You can keep the gun at his temple, or the ear," he said to Ruth. "The bullet will plow furrows across his brains in either case. On the other hand"—he unsnapped his cuffs, rolled up his sleeves, and washed his hands— "the throat's not a bad place either. Takes longer to die when you're shot in the throat, so if you get tired of holding it at his brains, you can lower it to the throat." He uncorked his bottle of disinfectant, and the smell of it filled up the hut.

Lucius arranged his instruments but did not remove the saw from the case. He'd learned never to remove the saw from the case until the patient was out. Under surgical conditions, Pirogoff's amputation—foot coming off at the ankle—would not be that difficult, but these were hardly surgical conditions, and Ruth's presence made him even more uneasy. Her silence and the thick motoring veil did indeed make her look like an angel of death, and though Lucius did not believe in angels, he did believe in death.

155

He opened the bottle of chloroform, held it to John Young's nose, and told him to breathe deeply, until the patient fell unconscious.

"Murderer," said Samuel.

"Fake," retorted Lucius.

"I am God's anointed and ordained. No man can kill the prophet. When I die my flesh shall be made perfect before the eyes of mine Apostles. I shall die and be resurrected in a single moment. And besides"—he regarded Ruth from the corner of his eye—"no woman could ever—would ever—kill me."

Ruth jammed the gun into his ear. Slowly the mucilage of hate and fear that had held her silent for ten years thinned, and she said in a low, coarse voice, "Don't tempt me, Samuel."

He whirled around to confront the gun's muzzle, to peer past the black, smoky veil. "By all the fires of hell! The Whore of Babylon hath come. The unbelieving wife!"

"The Witch of Endor to you, Samuel. Think of me that way, as the bearer of bad tidings. The Lord is departed from thee and become thine enemy. I should have killed you after what you did to me on the kitchen floor that night. I should have stabbed you in your bed. I should have poisoned you, and now—maybe I'll kill you now and be done with it. I'm already going to hell."

"Ruth Mason," he muttered as if tasting salt upon the name. "Ruth Mason, Ruth Mason, you and your foul butcher friend will lie in fleshly rags on the desert floor this night. God will smite you. Almighty God!" he cried out, and on the other side of the blanket partition the Apostles shouted his name. "Smite this woman and this butcher, shred their souls before mine eyes!"

"By the bowels of Christ, if you don't shut up, I'll kill you myself," Lucius told him. His hands were thick with blood, and he mopped his forehead with his arm.

Samuel kept his beaded gaze on Ruth and the gun, smiling into its round, deadly funnel. He chanted and muttered under his breath; he filled the sweltering hut with sweat and hate and acrimony. The gun trembled slightly in Ruth's moist hands; the sound of the saw grinding through bone, the blood cascading from the table, weakened her. She retched, and the gun faltered slightly. Samuel's craggy mouth coiled into a tight smile. "A dog and his vomit," he said and chuckled.

156

"Prophet!" came the cry from outside, a woman's cry. "What wouldst thou have us do?"

"Stone them as they leave! Kill them! Fell them! They are devils!"

"Shut up, you damned fool!"

"Kill the man first. Leave the woman to me."

Lucius dropped his instruments and quickly grabbed some of the cotton wadding he'd brought for bandages. He stuffed it into Samuel's mouth till his cheeks bulged. Then he returned to the operation.

"Prophet. Lead us. Feed us. We will lick your blood and sweat," came the chant, in unison as if rehearsed. "We will stand by you at the Apocalypse, clothed in robes of righteousness. The wicked shall be cast into the pit, but we shall be suckled as lambs. The wicked shall smell their own flesh burning," they recited. "Our flesh shall become as angels."

Inside the hut, the table was covered with blood, and it dripped audibly to the dirt floor. Lucius's hands shook as the chanting dribbled into tongues, moans, and whispers.

It took him longer than he had expected. He had to put the chloroform to John Young's nose twice before he sewed up the stump. He bandaged it with yards of cotton rags and elevated it by placing the huge family Bible underneath. Samuel groaned and twisted, and his breathing became forced and heavy.

Lucius wrapped the severed foot in one of the old blankets and took it outside, where he found Samuel's flock on their hands and knees. "If you want your prophet's rotten carcass back in one piece," Lucius commanded the first apostle, "you'll take this foot and bury it. Deep."

The apostle's eyes rolled backward. "Prophet!" he cried.

"Don't ask him. Ask me. Because if you don't do what I say, I'll bring him out here and shoot him in front of you. Now take this."

Lucius returned to the hut and poured the bloody water into two buckets. He carried these outside and ordered another prostrate apostle to get up off his knees. "Dump this somewhere."

"Only women touch blood," said the apostle.

"Do what I say, or I swear by Almighty God, you won't have a prophet."

Two women scurried forward and took the buckets. "It's the blood of the prophet," someone shouted, and the women dropped the buckets, and a thin pink stain spread over the desert floor.

157

Lucius returned to the hut, feeling as if he had gangrene himself. Contaminated. This day had reduced him to a level of brutality he would not have believed possible: Lucius Tipton surely would not threaten a man's life, or endanger a woman's, or call on God to witness his oath. Would he? Physician, heal thyself.

He washed up and checked John Young's pulse and heartbeat. He said, folding the stethoscope, "We'll have to move him before he comes to, or the pain will kill him." He packed his instruments and, in the wavering light of the seven lamps, concocted soft pills with tincture of opium. He wrapped them in a paper and slid them into his pocket. "Are you ready now, Ruth?"

She did not reply. She still held the gun in both hands, still pointed at Samuel's head.

"We're done here, Ruth. At least," he added, "I am." In Samuel's glimmering eyes, Lucius perceived the flickerings of fear, the first avowedly human emotion the prophet had evinced. "We have to go now, Ruth." Beneath the black veil, which she had never raised, he could see nothing of her face, and he was afraid to touch her, afraid the gun would go off if she so much as moved. If Lucius Tipton had been a praying man, he would at that moment have asked for guidance, but instead he pursued the rational course. "Of course, it's all the same to me. If you want to kill him, kill him." The prophet's body twitched as if he'd been threaded with electric current. "The poor bastards out there would be better off with him dead. You'd probably be better off, but it's all the same to me." He turned back to John Young and readjusted the bandages and checked his pulse.

Finally she said, "I'm done here, too."

He took the gun from her and yanked Samuel to his feet. Ruth tore down the blanket partition, and they walked into a semicircle of squatting Apostles, who chanted under the first stars and the heavy moon, which hovered like an overripe peach on the lowest bough of the horizon. Lucius shoved Samuel before him. "If you want your prophet in one piece, you'll do as I say. You," he said to the man who had buried the foot. "Go take one of those blankets and lay it in the bottom of the wagon. And you two, you get in there and carry Brother Hosea to my wagon. Carry him like he was your own mother, or I'll blow your prophet's head off."

"God will—"

Lucius fired into the air. "Just do as I said, and bring that Bible with you."

They put Brother Hosea in the wagon, but they would not touch the Bible, because it was bloodied. "I'll get it," said Ruth. She carried the Bible, the carpetbag, the cutlery case, and Doctor's bag to the wagon. She climbed in and picked up the reins.

Keeping the gun at Samuel's head, Lucius dragged him toward the wagon. He climbed in the back beside the patient. He flung Samuel to the ground, then fired three times randomly as Ruth slapped the horse's back and the horse bolted forward, spraying dust and rock. And for the second time in ten years, Ruth put wagon tracks between herself and Samuel Douglass. But this time she left no brick house, no lace curtains, no indoor pump. This time she left behind only the invisible: fear, ghosts, rage, and regret. And this time she had no need to invent a fiery furnace of destruction for her past, because before they'd gone a mile, the flames of New Canaan lit the sky as the enraged Apostles torched Hosea's hut. Ruth looked back only once; she drove that horse toward the future, because the past had finally cremated itself.

20

JOHN YOUNG GROANED as the wagon bounced and ricocheted over the sage and rock, through the moonlight and the cold desert night. Ruth's hat flew off and her hair fell down as she drove that horse within an inch of exhaustion back to Jackrabbit Junction.

She halted the wagon in front of the depot platform and threw a blanket over the sweat-crusted, frothing horse. The depot was dark and locked, but she kicked the door open, and it swung noisily on dry hinges. "I'll bring a lantern and be right back," she said.

"Here," Doctor said to John Young, sliding one of the soft tincture of opium pills between his lips. "Chew this. It will help the pain."

Ruth found a lantern and lit it, but the station offered no place for the patient, save the stationmaster's desk. She cleared it of everything—telegraph key, papers, pens, tobacco, tickets, and unclaimed mail.

Together and with great difficulty, they lifted John Young from the wagon and carried him inside, laying him as gently as possible on the table. Doctor held the lantern over the bloody bandages, frowning. "I'll have to change the dressing again. Would you boil up some more water while I go out and get the things out of the wagon? I'll take care of the horse, too."

Ruth fired the stove and lit another lantern, and with the heat and light, the depot seemed almost cheerful, certainly in contrast to New Canaan. She ladled some water out of the barrel and put it on to boil. She took a long draft of water, undid the first three buttons of her blouse, and rinsed her face.

Lucius returned with his bags. "Give me the lantern, and you go lie down."

"Is there a blanket that isn't bloodied, Lucius?"

"I think so. Look in the bottom of the carpetbag."

Lucius went into the stationmaster's office, and Ruth could hear him shredding more cotton bandages. She spread the blanket on the waiting-room floor in front of the stove's friendly grate. She took off her boots and rubbed her stockinged feet. Resting her chin on her knees, she watched the moonlight seep through the cracks in the depot walls, and without quite knowing why, she wept, until she fell into a sleep troubled with dreams of black hats and veils strewn across the desert floor and fires and wind that blew both hat and fire, urging one to escape and one to pursue till the fire licked the veil and the veil became smoke and the hat ignited and still the wind pushed and pursued the cinder and smoke, which woke her, and she coughed.

"It's just the stove," Lucius said, putting a few more sticks in. It blazed and warmed them once again. Lucius was shoeless and in shirt sleeves, and his hands and arms reeked of antiseptic. "I've given him enough opium to get him through the night, and if infection doesn't develop he'll survive."

Ruth sat up. "Take off your shirt, Lucius. I can't bear the sight of any more blood. I hope I never see that much blood again."

160

"There could have been more." He slid out of his shirt. "Could you have shot him?"

"I don't know."

"Don't suppose you want a little snort of this?" He handed her a small flask.

"I guess if I'm going to hell anyway, I might as well have a little Burning Bush along the way." She took a brief swig, and it warmed her all the way down. "I knew he was mad, but . . ."

"Are you free of him at last, then?"

"I'm free of hate and fear. I guess that's the same as being free of Samuel. You only hate what you fear and fear what you hate, and I'm free of all that. What will I do without hate and fear, Lucius?" Her shoulders shook. "They've been my whole life."

Lucius lay down and pulled her into the circle of his arm. She rested her hand on his chest, where she could feel the rhythmic, comforting beat of his heart. He put his hand over hers. "You can love now, Ruth. It's time. Time for both of us. I've loved you for ten years. There never would have been a Cassie if—"

She put her fingers to his lips. "Hush, Lucius. That never mattered to me. I knew. I knew for a long time before anyone else knew. One day a woman came into the Pilgrim all alone. She was wearing a hat with a heavy veil, and she ate her pie without lifting the veil, and she never took her eyes off me. When she came up to pay, she said to me, you're a friend of Lucius Tipton's, aren't you? And I said yes, and I figured then that no one called you Lucius but me. And her."

"But you never said anything."

"What was there to say?"

"She was not a bad woman. She was a good woman, really."

"You're a good man, Lucius." She raised herself on her elbow and studied his well-known homely face, craggy and clean-shaven, the mustache hiding his full upper lip, and the hazel eyes, devoid now of mirth. "I've done everything wicked there is to do today, Lucius. I've drunk whiskey, and I've held a gun to a man's head and very nearly shot him. And yet I don't feel sinful or wicked."

"That's because you're free of hate and fear, Ruth, my dear, and that is the worst sin of all. There's no religion that can toler-

161

ate that for very long—why, once free, you might start to think. Then you'd be dangerous. So you've cast your lot with the wind now, Ruth."

"I've cast my lot with you, Lucius." She brought her lips down to his and kissed him as his arms encircled her back.

"Shall I compromise you, Mrs. Douglass? You'll never be the same."

"I never want to be the same."

"Will you marry me now?" His hands moved to the compliant hooks on her blouse, and he drew it from her arms. She lay down beside him, and he kissed her throat and the smooth, fragile pulse at its base.

"Will you take me instead as your lover, Lucius, from this day forward till death do us part?"

"No death, Ruth, only as we've ever been: for richer and poorer, in sickness and health, as long as we both shall love. That'll do. Will you have me?"

"I do. I have. I will."

Mr. Emery arrived at Jackrabbit Junction early in the morning. He found his horse and wagon. The horse, which was spavined and ill-tempered to begin with, had his ears thrown back and a collar of salt crusted on his neck. He wheezed and took a nip at Mr. Emery. The wagon had bloodstains on the floor.

When he went inside, Mr. Emery found the Widow Douglass sitting on a bench rolling bandages. She was hatless, and her clothes were torn and streaked with dust, but her hair was wound up tight against her head, and Mr. Emery reckoned that woman could use her heart for a whetstone. She said hello, but Mr. Emery only snorted by way of greeting, because pride in women offended him.

In his office Mr. Emery found a man with one foot only, the bloody stump of the other on a bloody Bible, lying across his desk. The man was barely conscious, and Dr. Tipton was just folding his stethoscope.

"Good morning, Mr. Emery," said Doctor. Doctor's eyes were bleary and his face was pale, but he looked remarkably fit and not at all apologetic for having strewn the office with bandages and blood.

162

"What in hell's name do you think you're doing?"

"Checking my patient, Mr. Emery, checking my patient." Tipton's vest was splattered with blood. He buttoned his coat over it. "I think he'll survive this. What do you think?"

Mr. Emery didn't give a damn about the patient and said so. He demanded more money for the abuse of his horse and wagon.

"Would you be good enough to wire up the line somewhere so one of the westbounds will stop here and pick us up?"

"Will you be good enough," Emery mimicked him, "to get that bloody stump off my desk?"

"Not till the train comes." Doctor checked his watch. "I'm afraid I can't move this patient till the train comes." Doctor grinned.

A westbound train stopped at Jackrabbit at 1:14, just long enough for John Young to be carried on. Ruth carried the cutlery case and the bloody Bible. Doctor put the Bible beneath the stump and took a seat beside John Young as the train lurched westward. Ruth sat across from him. They smiled.

When they arrived at the St. Elmo terminus, Lucius brought the Flyer around, and together they helped the injured man into the back. Doctor drove Widow to her home on L Street. "Shall I see you to your door, Mrs. Douglass?"

"Please stay with your patient, Doctor. Good day, Mr. Young. Good day, Doctor." She rested her hand lightly on his, and he very nearly bent to kiss it.

"Thank you for your help with the operation, Mrs. Douglass."

"You're quite welcome, Doctor."

The Flyer smoked and protested as Lucius returned to his home and installed John Young in the small anteroom just beside the office, where there were a small cot and washbasin, fresh sheets, and clean water. "You want something more for the pain, John?"

"Yes."

"You try to rest, and when you wake I'll call Addie, and she can look after you."

"Bless you, Doctor." He seized Lucius's hand and kissed it. "You are an angel, a vision of mercy."

"No, John, you won't find no angels or visions in St. Elmo. Just lots of men and women, some of them with small minds and big mouths, some of them with big hearts, but most all of them curious, so you and Addie, if you're wise, you won't mention angels and vi-

sions to these folks, not prophets or apostles either. You understand?"

John Young nodded and fell back on his pillow. He was still pale,
but his eyes had lost their milkish cast.

Lucius brought other pillows to elevate the leg, but Young protested. "I'd druther it was the Bible keeping me up, Doctor, if it's all
the same to you."

It was all the same to Lucius. He left his patient supported by the
Bible and went back through the study. He poured himself a short
glass of Burning Bush and put his hat on Blanche's head. "The body
is a marvel of processes, Blanche, my girl." He caressed her lower
mandible. "You wonder if it's the flesh rekindles the spirit or the
spirit reconstitutes the flesh, don't you wonder, Blanche?" Blanche
did not seem to wonder, and he felt sorry for her, pitied her the loss
of her flesh, the loss of what flesh could experience and express.
"Maybe the poets are wrong, Blanche."

He patted her clavicle and started wearily up the stairs. Maybe
love is not equatable with the heart at all, he thought, but more
closely allied to the tendons that connect and wrap, keep us together
and allow us to stretch and be elastic at the same moment. And
maybe the poets are wrong about love's season, too. Maybe love is
not solely the province of the young. Maybe it can't even truly happen to the young. We're all callous and hardhearted in our youth
out of simple ignorance: we don't know how much unvarnished
pain is possible. As we grow older, we grow more callous, and thus
brutal, because we do know, and the knowledge itself is so painful
that we shun it, or commit it to ridicule. Maybe we only endure one
taut, one finite moment when we can truly love—between the time
we shed our youthful belief that happiness will come to us out of
sheer deservedness and before we begin the absorbing, ultimately
demeaning pursuit of happiness. A golden, uncomfortable season.
And if it does not last, what of it? Isn't love supposed to be organic—
and like every other living thing, does it not buy its life with the cold
coin of death?

BOOK TWO

Prodigal Daughters

21

IT WAS A DRY summer, 1910, drier than most, but the heat wasn't the worst of it. The worms was the worst of it. If it hadn't been for them worms, it might have been a good summer, what with Gideon graduating from high school—valedictorian, too— and Mother finally giving in, letting Tom Lance call on Afton. Things is always more pleasant when Afton gets her way. Afton says to me, Lil, you see, Mother finally knows that me and Tom Lance have been for keeps from the beginning, and I am going to marry that man, scar down his nose and all. Besides, Lil, that scar was part of a railroad accident, for which the hand of fate must be blamed, and it ain't hereditary, and I think Tom Lance and me will have real nice children.

You don't want to say that to Mother, I said. You don't want to be talking about your children when you ain't even married, Afton.

Afton promised Mother she'd wait to get married, least till she graduated from high school, but Mother just snorted—I got one girl who won't marry and one who can't wait to. Why can't you girls ever do things in their right time?

Eden wasn't there when Mother said that. I was glad, because I do hate a quarrel, and this one was getting bad. Everyone in our family, everyone in this town, knew that Eden Douglass was getting on, twenty now, and still she wouldn't marry Jack McGahey or no one else. Every time Jack asks her, Eden just says the same thing: I am leaving St. Elmo at my earliest opportunity. I am going to Paris, and I won't be back.

Eden keeps picture postcards from faraway places pinned up on her side of the bed so she can see them first thing every morning. Eden reads a lot of novels by W. Somerset Maugham and Hall Caine and Gertrude Atherton and H. G. Wells and anyone else who writes about anyplace that ain't St. Elmo. The farther from St. Elmo, the better. Eden always *says* she is going to Paris and China, but she don't *go* nowhere but to work at the bank.

Afton, she's braver than most. Afton tried to tell Eden that marriage and motherhood is the holiest duties of a woman on this earth. I got to hand it to Afton for taking on Eden like that, but I wished she hadn't done it at Sunday dinner. I guess it was Tom's being there done it to her, made her just bubble on about marriage and how it is so wonderful. Besides, Afton says to Eden, marriage is the only way for a woman to get into the Celestial Kingdom.

Eden says: if you have to have a husband to get into the Celestial Kingdom, then I'll take hell.

Well, that shut them up, didn't it? That just about sewed up the lips of everyone at our table, from Cissa on up. Tom, he don't look up, just asks for the chicken again. Doctor, he burps behind his napkin, and I think he might have chuckled, but he didn't let on. Mother gets real grim and pruny-looking; Mother don't like us to talk about hell. And Arlene McClure, her eyes bugged out so bad they nearly broke her glasses when Eden said she'd rather go to hell.

It could have been a good summer, 1910. Maybe it was a good summer for everyone but Eden and me and the worms. Gideon, he had what he wanted—Arlene come back around after she'd swore she wouldn't step foot in no house that was disgraced by Dr. Lucius Tipton. But by now she was so crazy with love for Gideon, she'd have sat down with Herod if that's who we was having to dinner. And Afton, she had what she wanted. She had Tom Lance to Sunday dinner and twice a week besides. And Mason and Cissa, they was too young to know much what they wanted, 'cept Mason, he hungered after one of them shiny new bicycles, and Mother said he couldn't have one for another year. He stole one from a boy at school. Borrowed it, he said when the boy come stalking into our house after he seen the bicycle on our porch. I only borrowed it, Mason said.

Cissa, she probably didn't want nothing but a new dress now and then, and we could afford that. We were doing fine by then. The Pilgrim was doing fine. You couldn't eat in no finer place in this town. Everyone was doing fine that summer but me and Eden and the worms. And Cissa, who got explained to about the Curse, only Mother didn't call it the Curse. Mother said if you watched your own body and took care of yourself and had a grain of sense, it didn't have to be a curse, but Cissa cried just the same, and Mother said, Cissa, I'm sorry, but you're growing up, and you have to take the good with the bad. Me, I was fifteen and growing up, but I couldn't see much good in it, no matter what Mother said. I couldn't see no point in growing up at all, if all you could do was recognize things you couldn't change or do nothing about. What was the good in being helpless if you wasn't ignorant? That's what I want to know. And after them worms I knew I didn't want to grow up. And after them worms I knew I didn't have no choice.

Them worms was awful. Everything in St. Elmo had them that summer, fat green worms with murderous gnawing teeth. They turned the color of whatever they et, so you couldn't tell them from the leaf or the stalk. It was like a war—Eden against the worms, and the worms was winning. Eden couldn't stand to lose. She signed us up like soldiers and made us fight the worms, but she was losing all the same, and she knew it. When Eden set her mind to a thing, she had to have it and nothing else. She wouldn't settle for nothing partial. Her will was like a muscle she flexed and made stronger. I am not like that. I was ever an accommodator, and if my hopes didn't jelly up just the way I'd like, I'd cry a bit and wipe my nose and get on with it, but Eden, she was always flexing and fighting, and it would sometimes make you tired just to watch her.

She made all of us pick worms in the early morning, 'fore it got too hot. You had to do it before breakfast, or you'd just puke up your breakfast and lose it. We each had our can, and we had to go up and down the rows picking off the worms. They was awful little squeezy things, those worms, with no more body than a silk stocking, and if you picked too hard, it bled green on your fingers, and if you picked too soft, it curled up in a ball and rolled away.

Mason and Cissa got to do the squash and tomatoes, because they was the shortest, and Eden and Gideon did the trellis, because they was the tallest. The trellis was like a huge flowering bedstead of morning glories, and the garden spread out before it like a nubby quilt. Before the worms come, that garden give us enough tomatoes, squash, parsley, peppers, and onions for the Pilgrim and us, too, and it was a real nice sight, especially at twilight. But after the worms, it was awful. You couldn't see one leaf that hadn't been gnawed, some of them down to the marrow, and the vines shriveled

169

and yellowed, and the squashes got puny. Pretty soon you could see through the trellis. Once there was a curtain of morning glories, the flowers all purple at their hearts and the tendrils like little baby fingers clinging to the wood, but no more. It was a losing war against them worms.

We hated worm-picking. Cissa always claimed she was sick and couldn't do it. Cissa said she was too weak to walk, but Eden said, then you'll just have to pick them while you crawl. Mason, he knew better than to try to get out of it, but his worm can was the sparsest. Me and Gideon, we did it without too much complaining, only retching now and then. And Afton, she did it, but she complained all the time. She said we would be better off begging God to do it for us, to send a swarm of sea gulls like He done for the Saints in the Great Basin Kingdom. Or maybe we could scare the worms off by beating tin pans and wooden spoons. And besides, Afton said, everyone's garden had worms this summer, and *they* didn't go around with no worm cans.

After we was done, we dumped all our worms into a little pile at the center of the yard and hotfooted our way to other tasks, all except Mason. He sat on the porch like the curtain was about to go up. He liked to hear them poor worms pop, because Eden always sprinkled a few benzine dewdrops on the pile, struck a match, and lit them afire. She'd stand there, arms crossed over her chest, studying them burning worms, looking pleased for about ten minutes, till she looked back at the garden and saw how the worms was winning anyway. She'd stomp on the cinders, scrape her boots on the step, and come cursing into the house.

Only one day, she didn't.

I was inside when I hear Mason call out: they're getting away, Eden! You better get the rake and scrape them back into the pile.

I heard Eden say: damn their everlasting souls to hell.

And I heard Afton say from the starch tub on the porch: worms don't have souls.

I went outside, using the towel to shade my eyes, because the sun was already brassy and my pupils couldn't shrink up fast enough, but I could see Eden gone back to the trellis with her worm can, picking some more.

Judas Priest All Friday H, says Eden.

Afton's got drawers just coming out of the starch tub, and she carries them over to the line, where they drip in a neat row in the dust. She hangs them up, and then she calls out: the McClures had to till their garden under, their worms was so bad. At least we still got ours.

What do I care about the McClures? says Eden, and we can almost hear the worms ringing in her can, and pretty soon she brings it back to the pile and rakes them all together again, nice and neat. She sprinkles the benzine over them and strikes a match, and the worms burst into flames. There! she says. That's what hell is like!

Cissa comes out and stands on the porch with us, because she wants to see what hell is like, too, and Gideon's violin stops, and he comes outside, too.

Eden don't have no sunhat on, so you could see her face, which was pale, skin laced tight over her bones and eyes reflecting that fire, and I could see her pulse pounding at the base of her neck and her hands clenching tight around the matches and her mouth set like Mother's. To watch her I felt my own innards tighten up. It was like the feeling you have when you are not too young to recognize things, only too young to have words for them. Like when you finally figure out that what you see dogs and pigs doing is the same kind of thing your own parents done to get you, and it makes you weak to think it because you don't have no words to describe it, let alone deny it.

I nudge Afton with my elbow. I said, you better stop her. Eden is going to do it.

What? said Afton.

I don't know.

The worms' funeral pyre dies down, but Eden uncorks the benzine again and takes it to the trellis and sprinkles some over the morning glories.

E-den! Afton's voice sounds like it's got a sugar cookie at the end of it. It's a waste, Eden! It's a waste of a whole garden just for some puny little worms!

It's gone anyway, says Eden. I'd rather burn it to the ground myself than watch these worms defeat me every day.

Eden, please! Afton cries.

But Eden struck the match and threw it at the base of the morning glories, and that parched trellis snapped right up with flames, and Eden pulls her skirts close around her and lights another match

171

and throws it into the stunted corn and another into the tomatoes, and it did seem like you could hear them little worm bodies popping on the walls of hell.

We all cough and watch the fire crawl over the trellis. It starts to plume smoke, and pretty soon it's not a trellis at all, only a wall of flame, and the corn turned to torches and the tomatoes collapsed and the squash burst with the heat. It was like that fire was a glutton and we could hear it gnashing its fiery teeth, devouring our garden before our very eyes. Hungry tongues of flame licking everything. It seemed we couldn't see nothing that didn't wobble with the heat and smoke. Ash got into our eyes and made them water and coated our lips. Eden come back to the porch and joined us, her face streaked with soot and surprise, like she couldn't quite believe the fiery furnace she'd created. The whole yard leaped flames. They wriggled along the ground. They chased each other and snaked and blacked everything in their path, and Afton says: it *is* just like hell.

And I can hear Cissa on the other side of me crying: it's just like in the Book of Mormon when the little children was all encircled by the fire and the angels.

It's just like the fire that killed Father, says Gideon, and he stops and squints into the smoke like he is looking for Father and then he says: Father was burned to death in a fire that took everything. The eight-room house and the barn went, too. He died like this.

The fire roars in our ears and towers over our heads like it might come for us, too, like it did for our father, like he might be dying in there all over again. And what we was too far away to see or stop once, we had to see anyway and couldn't stop again.

Cissa starts to scream: Father! Father! He's burning up alive!

Eden slaps her a good one, and we all start to cry.

Shut up, you fools, says Eden, but it don't do no good, because the tears won't stop. Cissa kicks Eden in the shins and crouches, crying by the empty rain barrel, and Afton sinks to the step and takes Mason in her arms, and Gideon puts his arm around my shoulder so we can weep together and watch what we was powerless to stop twice, knowing that's how it was and how horrible to die like that.

All weeping except Eden. She kept looking at that fire like it was trying to tell her something, something she couldn't quite hear, like she was straining toward it.

I stare into the inferno. I see the can of benzine. I yell and yell, but nothing comes out of my mouth. It takes a long time for that yell to come up from the pit of my stomach, but when it does come out, Eden's already dashing for the can, but it was too late, and the explosion knocked her backward, hands out, as if begging with that can not to burst. Me and Afton run to her and pull her back while Eden clutched her hands and moans.

Afton yells to Gideon to quick call the fire department, but he couldn't because all the telephone wires had caught fire and they snapped overhead, and the wind come up like a mean guest we hadn't thought to invite to a party, and the wind escorts that fire everywhere. Bless God, the wind didn't turn and go back for our house. But the shed, it's gone in a minute, and the clothesline falls, and the burning rag ends of clothes and cornstalks cross the alley and catch in the dry brush growing alongside the neighbors' yard, and their shed caught fire and their outhouse exploded, and you could hear their chickens screaming because they knew they was about to be cooked.

When it was all over, two other yards 'sides ours was burned completely. The leaves seared off trees and trunks blackened and roofs charred and half a dozen sheds and outbuildings gone, too. But the volunteer firemen, three brigades, they come in time to save the houses and the neighbor's horse, though their buggy burned to a rubble.

Even the sheriff rides up after most of it's out. Only little patches that would not be doused, they flamed up and teased the fire brigade. I watch the sheriff question the neighbors, who are crying and angry and swearing and pointing fingers at us. The sheriff crosses our still-smoking and embery yard.

I knew Afton would think of something. I knew I didn't have to think quick or come up with nothing clever, not so long as Afton was there. Because it was always Afton who took charge. It was Afton who took off her petticoat and threw it over the charred benzine can once the fire was put out and who carried that can even while it blistered the cloth, carried it to the starch tub and dropped it in and watched it hiss and sink. It was Afton who threatened Cissa with a slap she'd never forget if she didn't quit her crying and Afton who told me to take off my apron and wet it down and wrap it around Eden's hands and Afton who commanded Mason to hop to it and get

Doctor, and it was Afton who crossed the yard and went out to meet the sheriff.

It was an accident, Sheriff, Afton declares.

The sheriff has to look over his gut to see Afton at all. She never was as tall as Eden or Mother.

Ain't there someone here a little older who can answer for this? Your neighbors over there claim you was trying to burn the whole town down and damn near did it.

The sheriff ignores Afton, walks past her (and nothing's likely to make her madder), and he comes to the porch, where the rest of us are rooted and trembling. Eden gets to her feet, her hands still wrapped in dripping apron, her hair singed and stinking, and her face the color of thrice-used wax. It was an accident, she says, licking the soot from her lips.

The sheriff could not look down on Eden. She was standing on the porch. You burn your hands?

Yes.

How did you burn them hands?

I tried to—Eden stops and looks over his shoulder to Afton—I tried to stop the fire from getting worse.

Who started it? says the sheriff.

I did, but it was an accident.

You say you started it?

I said it was an accident.

Well, how did this here accident start?

Afton comes up to the porch and stands next to Eden. It's August, says Afton. And we haven't had rain all summer.

All spring, too, I say.

Don't read me the almanac, just tell me what happened.

Eden said: I dropped a match and the place lit up. It went wild.

It near burned to the ground, young lady. If the wind hadda changed, you wouldn't be standing on this porch, any of you. Your house would look like that shed over there, what's left of it. What was you doing with a match out here, anyway?

Smoking, says Eden without so much as a flinch.

Smoking! What's the world coming to? Young girls out smoking behind the shed. Mormon girls, too! Well, don't ever let me catch you with a cigarette. Any of you. I'll throw you in jail and throw

174

away the key, and you'll be old and gray before you get outta my jail. Smoking and endangering innocent lives and property!

Sheriff growls some more and threatens and probably would have gone on for days—he was enjoying himself, you could tell—if Doctor hadn't got there. Doctor takes one look at Eden's hands and hustles her into his Flyer and takes her to the office.

I asked to go with him, and he says, get in fast.

I take every chance I get to ride in the Flyer. I like to ride in it, because folks always tell me with my fair hair I look like an angel in a heavenly chariot, even though with all the smoke and stink, sometimes the Flyer seems like it might have come from hell instead.

Doctor called Mother, and she come from the Pilgrim. Fire? Mother says. What burned?

Just the garden, says Doctor.

And the shed, I say, and the neighbors' shed and their outhouse and chicken coops and . . .

I would have gone on, but I can tell she's not listening. She walks over to Eden, who's got big bandages around her hands and her hair is grizzled, and she's sitting in the chair across from Doctor's desk with Blanche looking on.

Your hands, Eden. Mother kneels at her chair and takes her hands.

I've given her something for the pain, says Doctor. Those bandages can come off in a few days.

Your hands, says Mother again.

Eden pulls her hands back in her lap.

Mother stands up. How did this fire start? she says to all of us.

I was smoking, says Eden, before anyone could think of anything else. I was smoking.

I don't believe that, says Mother.

I don't believe it either, says Doctor.

I believe it, I say.

You hush, says Mother. Tell me the truth, Eden.

What for? says Eden. What does it matter? What does the truth matter?

In a few weeks Eden's hands got better and she went back to work at the bank, but Mother couldn't understand why all those weeks we was all having nightmares about that fire. Even Afton. And when we'd come to breakfast and all of us shaky and gray from the

175

nightmares and Mother'd ask why, why wasn't we sleeping well, we didn't say nothing. Just ate in silence, no one trying to explain to her, not even talking much about it amongst ourselves. Not even Afton, who likes a good talking-out. We didn't say much because when we thought back on it, we knew it couldn't have been. Couldn't have been no screams, nobody dying in that fire, no one but a few chickens. Except for the chickens it seemed a silent fire. A quiet inferno in memory. But you could smell it, that fire, for a long long time. The smoke stayed caught in the house for a long long time, even after Afton pulled down all the curtains and washed them and bleached them good.

I think maybe Cissa tried to tell Mother once, how we'd seen Father die all over again in that fire, but she couldn't find the right words. Mother thought Cissa was just weeping from fear and not from a memory she couldn't have anyway, since Cissa wasn't even yet born when Father died. Mother took Cissa on her lap and pulled up her stockings and said: there, there, that fire's all finished, and you mustn't cry.

Cissa, who might have told, couldn't because she didn't have the words, and me, I might have told, because I had the words for the fire. That was easy. I had the words for the fire, but not for the look on Eden's face. I saw the fire, but she saw something else. You could tell from the look on her face that she saw something else, but you couldn't tell what it was.

22

EDEN DOUGLASS KEPT a valise beneath her bed. In the valise she kept an atlas of the world. She studied it, repeating the magical names of exotic places to herself as she rode the trolley to and from the bank every day. At first the names assumed the pattern of a cheerful litany, a long scroll of possibility she kept in her head. She promised herself she would leave St. Elmo within the year. Every year. She blamed her crumbled resolution on her mother, but every time she had the old valise opened and ready to be packed, she knew she was deterred by something more formidable than Ruth Douglass. Eden did not know where to begin: she dreamed of flying all the time she was being shod.

The gnashing teeth of her typewriting machine counterpointed the crashing rain outside. It was noon, dinner hour in St. Elmo, and the bank was very nearly empty, save for those people who had stepped inside its cold marmoreal halls to escape the deluge. She chewed her pencil trying to decipher some shorthand she'd taken down when her mind was not following what the bank's second vice-president had been saying. "It is incumbent on the bank to foreclose under these . . ."

"Eden?"

She looked up to see Jack McGahey. Color lit her face, as if she'd been struck like a match. She wore a suit of gas-jet blue. "I'm working." She looked around quickly, dismayed to see the smirks on the faces of her co-workers. "Please, Jack, not now."

"I have to talk to you, Eden."

"I'm busy."

"Please, Eden." Jack wrung his hat, and water dripped from it to the marble floor. Jack was a big man, stolid, with a halo of tight curls and enormous hairless hands. All the hair had been burned off at his father's forge. He always smelled of singed hair. "Please, Eden, I need to talk to you."

"Very well, then. What do you want?" She capped her fountain pen as if to indicate he had her full attention.

"Not here."

"You might as well say it here."

He pulled up a chair by her desk and leaned forward, keeping his voice low. "I guess it don't matter anyway. I guess everyone knows what I'm here for. I love you, Eden. I always swore I'd marry you or no one."

"Jack, I've told you, I'm leaving here. I couldn't very well leave if I got married, could I?"

"I'll leave with you, Eden. I'll give up my father's business. We'll go anywhere you say."

"And it would still be the same."

177

"The same as *what?*"

"The same as if we stayed." Eden twisted the fountain pen, and ink leaked out over her fingers. She took a pen wipe from her drawer. "I'm leaving very soon."

"You been saying that for three years, and I don't see you going nowhere."

"I don't have to tell you my plans."

"All right. All right. I just want you to know I'm asking you to marry me for the last time. A man's got some pride. He can't go on taking no for an answer, and I'm—we're—at an age when it's time to put away childish things and for a man to cleave unto his wife. I'm ready to marry and take on my earthly responsibilities. I'm asking you for the last time. There ain't going to be no more Jack hanging around after you like a dog."

"No one ever said you were a dog."

"Damnation, Eden! You've always thought you were too good for me. Just because you are the best-looking girl in this town and smart, you're sassy and uppity. Your whole family thinks they're above everyone in this town. Always putting on airs, acting like nothing in this town could touch the Douglasses or keep you—"

"And nothing can. And now, Jack, if you're through degrading my family, I'll thank you to leave."

"This is the last time."

"Then for the last time, no." The pen slipped from her hand, and ink slid out, drowning the words of the bank's second vice-president.

"I'm asking Mabel Norcutt to marry me, Eden. This is the last time Jack McGahey speaks to you as a single man. I know Mabel'll have me."

"Yes," said Eden curtly, "and Mabel knows I won't." She bit her lip. "Jack, I'm sorry, really." He was halfway across the bank before she thought to add, "I hope you'll both be very happy." Then she stared at the indigo stain spreading over her shorthand notes.

After work she went to the library to return her latest collection of novels, pressing them close to her, sheltering them from the rain sluicing through the February afternoon.

The library was a less pleasant place since Arlene McClure had gone to work there after her graduation from high school. Inevitably Arlene cornered Eden and pumped her for information. What did Eden think Gideon might do? He'd thought about going to college, but Arlene was afraid of that—it would be four years before they could get married. He'd thought about taking up accounting, but he had no head for figures. He'd thought about being a carpenter, because he was good with his hands. He'd thought about all kinds of things, but he didn't *do* anything but sit at home and read history books. The life of the mind, he called it. Arlene thought the life of the mind was fine, but after they were married. And now she was nearly frantic because lately Gideon had been taking his duties at church with formidable seriousness, talking about going on a mission.

Arlene assaulted Eden almost as soon as she entered the glass doors, before she'd put her umbrella in the stand. "Oh, Eden," she cried, her pale, round face flushed. "I am sorry. It's all just too terrible."

Eden braced herself; it was entirely possible for the news to have percolated from the bank all the way to the library in the space of an afternoon. "Well, I'm not sorry."

"Well, Eden Douglass, you are a heartless creature."

"And you are a fool if you think I mind one bit. I'm glad. And I don't want to hear another word about it."

Arlene's lower lip trembled. "You don't even know what I was going to say."

"Of course I do. Jack's going to marry Mabel Norcutt. What do I care?"

"He is?" Arlene's eyes wobbled behind her glasses. "Why, Eden, what are you going to do?"

"I am going to exchange these books, that's what I'm going to do."

"But, Eden, you mean you don't know about your grandmother?"

"What grandmother?"

"Mason. The one in Salt Lake. Gideon says your mother just got a letter from your Uncle Albert. She's died."

Eden was surprised, not that her grandmother had died, but that she had lived at all. Vaguely she recalled the scent of camphor and smelling salts wafting from a floating hanky, which seemed to be the only animate portion of her anatomy. Eden shrugged. "I didn't know her. She was a stranger to me. I'm sorry for Mother if she's sorry."

"If she's sorry! Why, you are just as cold as stone."

"And you are just as tiresome as an old hen!" And for the second time that day she bit her lip. Eden left her books off without picking up any new ones.

By the time she arrived at the gate of the little house on L Street, she was windblown and hatless. The windows were steamy, but she could still perceive Mason and Cissa setting the table, and in his room she saw Gideon reading. She took a deep breath and plunged in, as if for battle.

"Supper'll be ready in a bit," Afton called out. "Mother's got to wait for Sister Whitworth, so we'll eat first and keep hers hot."

"Sister Whitworth is an old cat."

"What's the matter, Eden?" Mason said. "Jack McGahey propose to you today?"

"You shut up, you little snake."

"Now, Eden," Afton remonstrated with her, "Mason was out of line, but I don't think—"

"I don't care what any of you think. I'm going into my room, and the first person to open that door will be mighty sorry. I'll have supper with Mother." She marched to the room she shared with Cissa and slammed the door. She took off her coat and unhooked her wet shoes and flung them down. She threw herself on the bed and watched the water slide down the dark window, looking like the indigo ink she'd spilled this afternoon. The postcards she could not see in the dark accused her from the wall. She ripped them off and pressed them to her like small, frail friends, and she wept for her loss.

But loss of what? Not Jack, surely. The loss was more fragile than Jack; it was a matter of nuance and tint: the future had lost its rosy tint. The future, where she had always lived quite happily when she could no longer endure the present, had paled. When she was seventeen, being twenty-one was the future; now that she was twenty-one, twenty-five was the future; and by the time she was twenty-five, the future would very much resemble the present, which by that time would be the past.

She pulled the valise from under the bed and took out the atlas. She began to pack quickly, making mental notes to include some gingersnaps, day-old bread, and apples. She would close out her account at the bank tomorrow and take the eastbound train, because even though she still did not know where to begin, she was certain where she'd end if she did not leave and leave now. She slid the valise back under the bed and lay down and listened to the rain for as long as she could bear the intermittent bouts of doubt and hope.

She ate supper with her mother, their two places set alone and across from one another as if they were meeting for a formal contest rather than weekday supper. "I'm sorry to hear about your mother," Eden said, sliding into her place.

"Yes, well, she was old, my mother. At least, I think she was. She always seemed old even when she was young. I suppose all mothers seem that way to their children. How did you hear?"

"Arlene told me." Eden helped herself to the potatoes. "I went by the library after work."

"Bad news travels fast in this town. Sister Whitworth told me a bit of bad news that might interest you, Eden. She said Jack McGahey asked Mabel Norcutt to marry him."

"Sister Whitworth is an old cat."

"I don't dispute that, but what are you going to do now?"

Eden almost said what she was going to do, but thought better of it. "I'm happy to be rid of him."

"I suppose you think the marriage offers will come pouring in after Jack."

"No, I don't think that. I don't intend to marry, at least not anyone in this wretched railroad town."

"Men are the same everywhere. You're too young to know any better, but they are. Jack ain't exactly inspiring, I grant you that, but he's a sight better than some."

"And a sight worse than others."

"You're being snobbish and stubborn, Eden."

"Am I? And where do you think I learned that from? Where? Who? I'm just like you, Mother. Don't you see that? And if I stay here I'm going to end up just like you whether or not I marry and have six children. It won't matter. Sometimes I look in the mirror and I see your face. My mother's daughter. Well, I'm not going to end up like you, dreamless and full of nothing but old regrets. And

181

I'm not going to do what you did—marry the first man that comes along."

"Your father was not the first man, Eden." Ruth's lips pinched over the admission. "He was the last. I only want what's best for you. That's why I wanted you to marry Jack, or someone like him. At least you know him, you know his family, you know he won't take you off and—"

"I wouldn't marry any man who'd keep me here. I won't be chained to the bed and the cradle. I know what marriage means for a girl—I know what the church thinks—I know what you think—that marriage is wonderful and giving birth is just the grandest thing a girl can do, giving all those little spirit bodies earthly form."

"I think, Eden"—Ruth cleared what felt like gravel from her throat—"that marriage is the only way a girl can get through the world. I am not speaking of the next world and what the Saints believe. But this world. Here. Now. Men write the rules. They make themselves indispensable, and if you're not married—"

"You're free."

"No."

"You can leave whenever you want. Doctor always says he can stand this town because of the train whistle. As long as he can hear the whistle, he knows he can leave, and as long as he knows he can leave, he can stay."

"Doctor is a man," Ruth said dryly. "It's different for a man. He knows it. I know it. And you're going to learn it the hard way. I don't want you to be a desperate old maid."

Eden walked to the dining-room doors and snapped them shut. Then she crossed the room and closed the door that led to the kitchen, making certain that Afton was not there. Then she returned to her place and picked up her fork and said: "If I don't get married, at least I'll never be so desperate that I'll have to kill my husband—invent a fire and kill him off with a lie."

Ruth's knife clattered against the plate and slid to the rug with a muffled thud. "What did you say? No—don't."

"I know Father's not dead. I know there wasn't any fire that burned the house and the barn went, too."

Blood seemed to pop through Ruth's hands. "What makes

you think that?" she said in a voice reminiscent of a razor stropping.

"It was the fire. The one out back last summer." Eden held up her scarred hands. "I knew it couldn't have happened like that. I knew you lied. I just knew it in my bones. I'm like you, Mother."

"You're not like me. There's no reason for you to be like me."

"I'm just as desperate as you were then—"

"That will do. You don't have any idea what you're talking about."

"Do you want to tell? Do you want to tell me where Father is or why you lied?"

"Your father is dead. He has been for many years."

"But not for as many years as you'd like us to think. Why, Mother? What did he do to you?"

Is Samuel a beast, Ruth? Afton Mason's shrill whisper beat in Ruth's ears; the dead woman's question. *Is he a beast, dear?*

"He was a beast," she said, answering her mother rather than her daughter. "He was a beast and a lunatic. I had no choice. I would have had to—" Ruth had never justified her lie to anyone, and looking at Eden's grim face, she did not want to do so now. She did not need her daughter's understanding, and she knew her daughter would not give it anyway. She knit her fingers into a vise. "You listen to me, my girl. You've got three choices in this world, and only three. That's it. A woman can be a virgin, a wife, or a widow, and that's all there is. If you're not one of those three things, it doesn't matter what else you do, what else you are, you're despicable. Despicable, do you hear me? That's the way the world is. You can't undo it, and you'll break your own heart if you try."

"Then why did you insist I go to business school? What was all that eyewash about a woman without skills"—she imitated her mother's formidable manner—"is nothing but the ward of a man, but a woman with skills, why, she can do as she likes."

"You have skills now. You're fortunate, but—"

"But if all I really needed was a husband"—she rose and walked to her mother's chair, and the two women, their faces as alike as coins of the same realm, faced each other intently—"then why didn't you say so in the first place? Why let me believe anything else?"

183

"Because I'm older than you, Eden, I know these things. I learned them the hard—"

"Horseradish. Did you ever once say to me: Eden, take those pictures of Paris down, Eden, your dreams are worthless, Eden, you'd better marry?"

"I thought you'd outgrow your dreams," Ruth replied. "I hoped you would. I hoped you'd marry and be like everyone else. It's easier that way."

Eden went back to her own place and collapsed into the chair. "I hoped I would outgrow them, too. I thought maybe I'd meet someone and fall so in love that going to Paris wouldn't matter to me anymore."

"You couldn't love Jack McGahey?"

"Could you love Jack McGahey?"

"No, I couldn't love him, but if I'd been you, I probably would have married him. When I met your father I didn't love him, but I knew I'd have to marry him just because I had to marry. But the worst is, I've ended up believing in the very thing I hated. Marriage. Family. Duty. It's a lie that's handed down from mother to daughter. Down and down and down." *Is he a beast, Ruth?* "Everyone admires a girl without a husband. Everyone despises a woman without a husband. Men have made themselves essential to getting through the world—and if the church is right, they're essential to getting through the next world, too. It's easier. Everything is easier if you do what people expect of you. It's true."

"Not for me. I won't have it. I'm not like you."

But Ruth had never thought herself to be like her mother either. She realized now that she was. And like her mother she could not tell her daughter how she'd come by all her terrible knowledge, she simply insisted that it pass for wisdom.

23

EDEN DOUGLASS KEPT her eye on the clock. At ten minutes of five, Arthur Whickham came down from his private office and stood, watch in hand, surveying his bank. The vice-president, carrying his umbrella and hat, bade his secretary, Miss Eden Douglass, goodnight. She waited till he had passed through the gate that separated their little domain from the rest of the St. Elmo National Bank and Trust, and then she pulled the contract she was typing out of the machine. File drawers creaked on their runners, tills slammed shut, and locks turned all over the bank.

Eden buttoned the jacket of her double-breasted wine-colored suit all the way up to the lace molding her throat. She pinned her hat to her hair and slid her gloves over her still-scarred hands. Nodding curtly to her uncle, she opened her umbrella and hurried into the rain.

The doctor's house and office was not far from the bank, but a week's rain had turned the streets, even the paved avenues, to mud, and by the time she arrived, her skirt was wet to the knee. She knocked at the study door. It took him a while to answer. "Eden! What a surprise. Come in. I'm just finishing up with a patient. I'll be right back."

He hurried back into the office, and Eden removed her dripping hat and put it on Blanche's head, and she draped her jacket over Blanche's shoulder blades. "Goodbye, Blanche," she murmured. "Be good to Doctor."

Doctor's patient was John Young, who had experienced some inexplicable pain in his missing foot. Nothing but this infernal damp, Doctor assured him. John and Addie both worked for Sister Whitworth now, Addie doing heavy cleaning and John the repair work that didn't require two legs. It pleased Lucius to see them. Lucius was in a particularly good mood that afternoon, despite the infernal damp, because Ruth had been there earlier. Over the past year the underemployed doctor and the busy widow had managed to find more than an occasional moment together. When the rest of the world was up and about, busy at its appointed rounds, the doctor and the widow committed not only adultery, but the equally heinous sin of sloth. Doctor confessed to Ruth that he enjoyed the latter almost as much as he enjoyed the former.

And now, here was Eden, her very presence a tonic infusion. "I thought I might see you before Sunday," he said, moving some papers so Eden could have a chair. "Your mother told me the news— doleful or happy, depending on your point of view. I guess if you're Mabel Norcutt, you think it's happy."

"When did you see Mother?"

The papers slid from his arms, but Doctor recovered them and himself gracefully. "I didn't see her. Just talked on the phone."

"Well, I thought it was happy news." She sat the way her mother did, shoulders straight, back not deigning to touch the chair. "At least now I won't have someone pestering me to marry him."

"You know, Eden, you won't always be young and beautiful and fresh and eager," he said, though he could not imagine her otherwise. "One day you might be old and alone."

"Ye Gods, Doctor! Surely you don't think I should marry now so I'll have someone to hold my hand in forty years. That's no reason to get married."

"At least not for the next forty years." He lit a cigar and peered at her through the smoke. "Well then, you're free of Jack. What will you do now?"

"I'm going to—I want to leave St. Elmo. But I think I'll need you to explain to Mother why I have to leave." She studied her burned hands. "Why I cannot tie myself to someone else's fate."

"Someone else's fate," he said gently. "Sounds like you've been reading too many novels."

"Don't make fun of me," she snapped.

"I'm not. I'm sorry if it sounded like I was. Where will you go?"

"Someplace I could have some adventures."

"What kind of adventures?" He leaned back, letting Eden's voice and the last of the afternoon shadows fill the study. She billowed out freshness like carbonated cologne.

"Well, I'd like to drink absinthe in the cafes of Paris, like they did in this novel I just read."

"Would you settle for a little Burning Bush?" He got out the bottle.

"It's not the same thing."

He poured himself some and watched her over the rim of the glass. "Will you fall in love? It would be a terrible waste if you didn't."

"I might. But I'd rather have a lover"—she colored slightly—"than a husband."

"Oh, you'll get married. All the girls do."

"Don't leap to speak for others, Doctor."

"Excuse me. I only meant—don't all the girls want to get married?"

"That's all Afton wants. She wants to marry Tom Lance so bad it wouldn't surprise me if she got herself in a fix so she'd have to marry him."

"That isn't kind."

"But it's true all the same. Afton will stop at nothing to get her own way. And Arlene! Arlene is just as bad as Afton, but she hasn't Afton's sense."

"You mean to get herself in a fix."

"I mean Arlene just fritters and frets. Now Gideon wants to go on a mission for the church. She can't bear the thought, but all she does is wring her hands. And Gideon! He's insufferable. Every time he comes back from one of his little chats with the bishop or the elders, you'd think he'd been chosen for the Heavenly Host. He can't talk about nothing but converting the heathen and the duties of the priesthood, and he prays so long over supper, it gets cold. Finally a few nights ago, Mother had had enough—she told him to shut up!"

"Your mother is an absolutely unique woman. I never saw such a woman for getting things done."

"How do you think I got my job at the bank? Art Whickham wanted to hire me like he wanted fallen arches. I was the first girl ever to work there. Mother just took me into the bank one day and told me to wait outside his office. She went in, and when she came out, I thought Art was going to break into pustules, he was so red. Mother said to me, go on in, Eden, your uncle will acquaint you

187

with your new duties. And that was that. I don't believe Mother and Art have spoken before or since."

Lucius laughed till tears gathered in his eyes. "Art Whickham never would have married Lily if he'd known he was going to meet his match in your mother."

"Art Whickham is a fool. Everyone in this town—except you—is a fool. They're all a pack of fools. They all want the same thing. They all do the same thing. They don't know they could just look around them and see exactly what they'll be like in ten years. Or twenty. Or fifty. It's enough to make you snort chloride of lime, if you ask me."

"They're particulars, Eden. They can't see themselves as universals."

"Well, I am particular, too, and I'll only marry someone who can promise me more than childbirthing and dullness."

"No one can promise you that."

"No. Anyone could promise, but few could deliver."

"Maybe you've learned more than I thought."

"Maybe you've taught more than you think."

She gave him an arch look he was certain she'd practiced.

Her suit was so becoming, he thought, the deep burgundy contrasting with her pale coloring and high-piled dark hair. She had the aura of a woman with her tickets all punched for the future, even if she was only a girl trapped in a railroad town by circumstances she could not quite understand or deny. Perhaps it was the softening of the twilight or the softening of the whiskey on his brain, but he thought he heard the fetters crack and the essential Lucius Tipton unshackle himself from the gristle and bone of his aging body; the undefeated spirit of the essential Lucius plucked itself clean and free of the corporeal man and sailed toward the essential spirit of Eden Douglass and touched that spirit's cheek and took that spirit's hand.

He rose and lit the gas, and with its hiss and light and odor, both spirits fled, and just as well, he thought. "It's getting late, Eden. They'll worry if you're not home soon. It's raining very hard tonight. Shall I take you in the Flyer?"

"No. I'll take the trolley. I don't mind the rain. I like to stand outside the house in the rain, and I can take my hat off and let my hair blow and listen to the wind whistle through the fence. I like to watch my family when they can't see me. I can see them through the windows, but I only hear the wind and the rain and the branches knocking against one another. I know I can be out of that storm and back to safety if I want it. I can be inside with them and part of the way they all sound and the way they all smell."

"How do they smell?" It was a thing he'd never noticed.

"Like starch, Doctor. We all smell like starch." She gave him a wry grin. "I stand there till I'm soaked through and blown to bits and cold, and then I go inside."

"And once you're inside, you press your nose to the window and watch the storm and wish you could be back in it."

"How did you know?"

"I just know." He took her hat and coat from Blanche, and wondered as she pinned her hat to her hair how it was women didn't stab themselves to death before the age of twenty.

She kissed his cheek. "Goodbye, Doctor."

"I'll see you on Sunday, Eden, and I'll talk to your mother then if you want."

"Thank you. And goodbye."

She flung her arms around him and kissed him again, and he thought perhaps at the edge of the yard she turned and waved, but he couldn't be certain. He stood in the doorway long after, listening for the sound of her footsteps blown back, but he heard only the shriek of the train whistle in the distance. Lucius smiled and took a deep breath. The sky was a moonless indigo, cloud-creped and austere. More rain yet, he thought, the promise of more rain yet on the wind that blew into his study, fluttering the papers, flicking the gas jets, and rattling old Blanche's unresisting bones.

24

WHEN THE RAINS come to the St. Elmo Valley, they are welcome, if occasionally inconvenient, but every ten years or so it floods, and once every half century it rains so damn much in St. Elmo that the water becomes an omnipotent force, like the Old Testament God meting out savage punishments to hundreds of unnamed people who did nothing to deserve His wrath. In 1911 it rained in St. Elmo from January to March, and the desert town was seemingly swept out to sea.

When the flood was over, the Army Corps of Engineers pointed out that in an effort to plant their town near the unreliable springs, the Mormons had settled in the middle of a huge natural wash. Perhaps Madison Whickham believed that the latter days were so close at hand that he need not consider that one day nature would take its predestined course down the wash, sweep through the valley like a mighty brown hand, and leave in its wake enough primordial, turgid, stinking mud to make even Madison Whickham believe in evolution.

In 1911, rain gnawed the earth from under houses and they collapsed; it swept buildings some three hundred yards from their original sites, and people moved their possessions and their families on makeshift rafts. It demolished roads, even the paved testaments to civic splendor. It tore out streetcar tracks that threaded the town's underbelly like an appendectomy scar, uprooted the oak, palm, and eucalyptus and sent them crashing. The hillsides loosened, and mud slid into the valley, burying what it did not budge. Dogsback Ditch split open like a ripping seam, and the bridge collapsed, plunging an eighteen-car train into the river, killing twelve and wounding scores of others; elsewhere track buckled—nothing got in or out of St. Elmo for weeks, and the eastbound route was cut off for months.

Art Whickham's bank building collapsed, and the safe was found in a railway hogpen. The Mormon mill that had stood for over sixty years crashed down as its foundation washed away. The roof of the Ferris Hotel burned in an electrical fire, and the ground floor was a sea of mud. Of the old central district, all that remained was the ground floor of the Ferris, the railway station, the cathouse, and the courthouse. Nearly the entire livestock population of the St. Elmo Valley perished. Stiff, bloated, and stinking, they constituted a menace to public health when the waters subsided in mid-March.

At that time the whole camp following of disaster flowed into town: surveyors and soothsayers, assessors and adjusters, inspectors and examiners, and the Army Corps of Engineers. These, combined with health and financial hazards, promoted goodwill among men and cooperation among the varieties of religious experience for the first time in memory. There were those who pointed the finger of blame at God. And those who cursed the Mormons for their initial bad judgment. And those who swore revenge on shoddy contractors and insurance companies whose costly assurances, by and large, came to naught because there were always clauses people hadn't read and documents they couldn't produce and what had been tangible physical disaster evaporated into symbolic loss: the letter S stabbed through with two parallel lines. And there were those, like Ruth Mason Douglass, who could not sleep after 1911, who could not lie in bed and listen to a tap drip.

Few passengers awaited the early train. They all appeared to be traveling men who had spent the night in the station rather than pay the price of a hotel. They snored lightly on the benches or glanced through damp newspapers. Rain slid down tall windows, and the watery dawn was still an hour away when Eden Douglass came through the door, shaking her umbrella. The skirt of her wine-colored suit was darkened with water and her overcoat flecked with mud. She carried a valise and a maroon carpetbag. She walked to the ticket window and asked for a one-way ticket to New York City.

The sleepy stationmaster regarded her laconically. "Can't do it," he said.

"What do you mean—can't do it?"

"I mean the train don't go that far. You'll have to buy your ticket as you go along."

"Well, how far can I go from here?"

"Which train?"

"This one, of course—the eastbound, the six-ten."

He studied the timetables and said he could sell her a ticket as far as Las Vegas.

"That will be fine," she said, laying out the price from a slender sheaf of bills. She put the ticket and the change in her pocket and took a seat well away from the other passengers.

Discreetly she slid her feet out of her wet shoes and into dry kid pumps with fashionable two-inch heels, though she knew no lady would perform this operation in public. She put the wet shoes into the carpetbag, and as she bent over, the money pinned inside her underwear crinkled reassuringly. The station door slammed, and she jumped, half expecting to see her mother burst in, but it was only the janitor, who made halfhearted rounds of the cuspidors.

She vowed she would not relax until the train pulled out of St. Elmo and she was safe and free. Perhaps you can't be safe and free, she reflected, perhaps you had to take your choice. But she'd almost changed her mind the night before when she had kissed her mother's cheek before she went to bed. She was daunted then. Not by Ruth's opposition, but by the tenderness and suffering that lit her eyes. It had not occurred to Eden before that Ruth could be tender or might have suffered, that she was even Ruth: she had always been simply Mother, uncomprehending Mother. And for one moment Eden wondered about Mother and Father and the fire that never was and wondered if perhaps she, Eden, was the uncomprehending one.

The shriek of the train whistle sliced through Eden's thoughts. Sluggishly the traveling men around her came to life; they collected their things, folded their newspapers, tipped their hats to Eden, and followed the stationmaster outside. She checked her pocket for the ticket, gathered up her baggage, and went outside to the platform, where the roof provided scant protection from the rain. The train snorted and sweated like an overwrought beast, and the passengers waited while the conductor and the stationmaster compared schedules and remarks about the weather and the condition of the track. She missed her mother and family and Doctor and wished there were someone here to give the gallant nod to her departure.

She stood with the little knot of traveling men enveloped in the hiss and steam of the train, and her regrets vanished. There was something bracing about the company of strangers; no younger brothers and sisters underfoot, no mother hovering and impatient, no one making you promise to write and be good and button up and not sass. Miss Eden Douglass was free of all that, thank you, shed of family obligations, allegiance to the Church of Jesus Christ of Latter-day Saints, and fealty to the St. Elmo National Bank and Trust Company. Miss Eden Douglass was responsible only for herself and on her way to New York City. "New York City," she said, as if it were a state of mind and not a geographically knowable place.

The train was dirty and smelled sour. Eden took a seat by the window and set her carpetbag next to her to thwart the attentions of the gentlemen passengers. A needless precaution. They were all half asleep, newspapers covering their faces, before the train pulled out of St. Elmo. She straightened the angle of her hat in the dark window and smiled as she saw the town sliding past, dissolving under the rain and the train's gathering speed. But her reflection was lost before long, because the train headed due east and dawn whetted the clouds with a dull chromium edge.

25

RAIN HAD BEEN coming down for so long, Ruth had ceased to note its presence. It was there when she went to sleep at night and there, an impenetrable caul of wet, when she customarily woke at dawn. She dressed, brushed her hair, and coiled it tightly at the top of her head. She took her boots with her into the kitchen, turned up the gas jets, and sat in her rocker, hooking them tediously. The kitchen was festooned with laundry, since they had not been able to hang anything out for the last three weeks. Petticoats, drawers, skirts, and shirts gave it an oddly festive air of homespun bunting.

She ducked underneath some stockings to fire up the stove. So damp was the wood, it took her twenty minutes to get the stove crackling and the kettle on.

She lit a candle and went into the girls' room. "Eden?" Last night Eden had kissed her cheek, and Ruth had nearly wept. She wanted to tell Eden then, or now, it didn't matter, only wanted to say that she knew that suffering wasn't something you could do for someone else. "Eden?" She moved quietly and held the candle over the bed. Cissa's head on the pillow. Cissa curled up. Cissa murmured and turned over.

Ruth blew out her candle and turned up the gas in the hall and made her way to the bathroom, but Eden was not there either, and then she forced her feet back down the hall. Eden's coat and hat were gone. Lying on the rosewood table was a note, which Ruth read three times before comprehension triumphed over disbelief.

February 15, 1911

Dear Mother—
I'm going to New York City, and when I get there I'll write. I'll die if I stay here one more day. Please don't worry about me. I'm sorry I have to leave like this, but it's the only way. I have plenty of money, and I'm sure I can find work. I have skills, don't forget. You must not worry. I love you all. Doctor, too. I love you, Mother.

Eden

Ruth went to the telephone, but then remembered the phones didn't work this early. She threw her shawl over her head and bolted out the back door into the still-charred yard. Water pulled her skirt till the hem met the mud, and the shawl plastered down across her skull as she made her way through the alleys of St. Elmo, a long, gaunt figure, skirt twitching, shawl flapping, striding the alleys at daybreak through the green-glassy rain.

She came to the back of his house and hurled his name—"Lucius!"—into the rain and against the walls till the second-story window flew open and Doctor cried, "My God, Ruth, it's you!"

194

"It's Eden."

He brought her inside and took the shawl from her head. She handed him the note, but the ink, the very words, had run over her fingers. "She's gone, Lucius."

Lucius grabbed his coat and hat. "Maybe we can stop her. Maybe the train's late."

The Flyer at first refused to start, but finally Lucius coaxed it out of the shed and through the rain and deserted streets to the station, where light burned in every window. Horses and vehicles jostled for position in front of the Moorish monstrosity. Lucius could not quite believe that all these people were here for the 6:10. Ruth followed him into the station, where the telegraph key's staccato punctuated the angry voices around them. They thrust through a crowd of men, men hastily dressed, not passengers or railroad men, Lucius dimly realized, not men in caps and coarse coats. These were civic-pillar men, Art Whickham among them, men whose connection with the railroad was not manual, but money.

The stationmaster wiped his face and came out from behind the cage. "It's no use," he stammered. "It's gone."

"What's gone?" Lucius cried. "Has the eastbound train gone?"

"The train?" cried the stationmaster, blubbering and bewildered. "I'm talking about the bridge, man. The bridge over Dogsback Ditch is gone. Washed out."

"And the train?" said Arthur Whickham, pushing through the crowd. "What about the train?"

"It's gone, too." The stationmaster began to cry. "Gone. The bridge. It was fine last night. The ten-forty crossed," he pleaded as the men dispersed. "The ten-forty crossed fine. The bridge was fine, but the six-ten—it went into the ditch."

A small armada of autos and horses pushed eastward. One by one the cars bogged down in the mud, but Ruth and Lucius forged on when the others turned around. When the Flyer was up to its mechanical belly in mud, they got out and walked, eventually paralleling Dogsback, where the water coursed like brown blood through grossly expanded veins. The channel was gone, and a raging lake had taken its place. Their feet made sucking noises in the mud as they headed silently south in the pewter-gray morning.

They crested a hill that brought them in sight of the bridge. Track dangled uselessly in the air, and the 6:10, water sawtoothing through the windows, eight of the eighteen cars flipped on their sides by the impact, lay like half-submerged stones. The moans of injured livestock mingled with the screams of a few men on horseback, already trying to affix lines on what was left of the bridge's pilings. Lucius felt he had been kicked in the groin; pain bellowed up through his body and roared from his mouth, and beside him, Ruth bent double, snapped like a wishbone.

They supported each other down to the banks, where even the horses were knee-deep in mud. Men pulled the lines taut, but the pilings gave way, floated into the current, ducked under, and bobbed up some twenty feet downstream. "Try the cars!" someone shouted. "Fasten the lines to the cars. Maybe they'll hold."

A man on horseback rode up to them, Avery Patterson, the judge's youngest son. "Doctor, thank God you're here. They need you up there." He pointed to a small rise where a tarp had been strung in a clump of old, misshapen pepper trees, providing shelter for the survivors and the Methodist doctor who ministered to them.

"My daughter." Ruth clutched Avery's leg. "My daughter—"

"Eden Douglass is on that train," Lucius cried. "We think that Eden—"

Avery regarded them stupidly for a moment. "We haven't found her yet," he said, releasing Ruth's fingers. "They need you up there, Doctor." He rode away.

"Found her?" Ruth shook convulsively. "Found her?"

"Maybe she wasn't—" Lucius stumbled. "Maybe—" He watched the ropes thrown into the flood.

"No good!" called the sheriff. "We'll have to take them out to the train and tie them."

"Maybe he's wrong," Lucius whispered. "Maybe she's up there with the others."

They climbed the rise, where the Methodist doctor, soaked and swearing, stood in a writhing mass of broken bones and moaning men. Traveling men they looked to be, railroad men, but no young woman among them.

"Did you bring your bag?" the Methodist doctor shouted. "There's a broken leg over there."

"My daughter," Ruth implored him. "My daughter Eden. Where is she?"

"Your daughter was on that train?"

"She's a tall girl, a beautiful girl. Have you seen her?"

He shook himself free of the pair. "How can you ask me if I've seen anything beautiful?"

Ruth retied her dripping shawl over her chest and pushed the wet hair from her face. She turned to Lucius as they stood in the lacy enclosure of the pepper trees. "She's dead, isn't she, Lucius?"

"No, not Eden."

She was dead, though, and so were eleven others, trapped in the cars that went into the river. They did not even find them all that day; they pulled four from the wreckage but had to leave the others, satisfied that they could not have lived. They did not even find two dead crewmen until weeks later when they were finally able to move the crippled train and bury the livestock in a huge soggy pit.

As Ruth and Lucius watched, the sheriff and his men secured their lines to the cars and, tying themselves to the ropes, made their way out to the sunken train. They broke the windows and lowered themselves and more rope into the cars and pulled the dead out one at a time. One man sliced his hand open on the broken glass, and another lost his footing and was nearly drowned when the current swept over him. They brought the dead out of the flood by binding them in blankets, tying them hand and foot, and pulling them from the river. As the day progressed, wagons arrived from town to take the wounded back, bearing supplies, more rope and tackle, fresh horses, men to take the dead from the river, and efficient women to tend the living.

Ruth and Lucius stood immoblized: the river, the horses, the screams, the men, the mud, the broken bridge, the train lying on its side, all threatened to granulate and dissolve in the rain. Each new body they brought forth was not Eden's. They carried them singly up to the rise and placed them under the tarp, as if they might still be in need of shelter.

At noon Avery Patterson, his gloved hands cupped around a tin of coffee, beckoned to the doctor to leave Ruth's side. "She's in there," he said. "I saw her."

"And?" Lucius moaned. "And?"

"And I think you'd better get her mother out of here." Avery finished his coffee and returned to the diminished bank, which had been trampled by horses and gnawed by rain. He tied a rope around his waist and forged out into the water, clutching the rope as his feet were swept out from under him.

Lucius watched, mumbling the superstitious incantations of the powerless. "Please, God. No, not Eden. Please, God, not Eden." Avery reached the train, and another man followed him. They braced themselves against the car and lowered their lines through a broken window, and Avery himself slowly descended into the car. Lucius knew that the next thing he saw would be the worst there was, the worst that would ever be. Please, God. Not Eden. Eden. "Ruth." He shook the tall woman's shoulders. "You have to leave."

"No," she said without moving her lips.

"You can't watch this. Go back to the wagons. Go anywhere. Please don't stay. I beg you. You can't watch this."

"Can you?"

A man on horseback rode between them and their view of the river. Tom Lance pushed his dripping hat up off his head and leaned down from the saddle, his scarred face twisted with sorrow. "Sister Douglass, you have to come with me. Afton sent me. I'll take you home."

"No."

God, not Eden. Not Eden. The prayer billowed through Doctor's skull as he beseeched her to go with Tom. "Please, Ruth. I'll stay. Isn't that enough? Only one of us should have to—"

"Get up on the horse and come with me." Tom offered her his hand.

Lucius peered around the horse: Avery Patterson was climbing back out of the window. He was shaking his head, pointing to the next window. The other man took a small ax from his belt and smashed the glass. "Ruth, I beg you. Go with Tom. Please, dear God! Don't stay."

Ruth grasped his shoulders. Her eyes were two nails hammered into her face; her voice cracked, barely audible over the rain and raging current. "Promise me—"

"Go. I'll stay."

"Promise me. Only if you promise me no one but you will touch her."

"No one. No one. Now go with Tom. I promise." He pushed her toward the horse, and she took Tom's hand and hoisted herself up. Lucius slapped the horse's flank; the animal bolted, and mud flew from its hooves. "Go!" he cried, watching Avery Patterson's legs and arms vanish into the next window. "Go!" Lucius did not care if Ruth fell off that horse as long as she did not do so in front of what promised to be the worst sight of Lucius's life: Avery Patterson pulling from the train window a wine stain of deep burgundy. Dear God, not Eden.

Eden.

They rolled her body into a blanket, tied her feet together, and secured the lines around her shoulders. From the train Avery signaled to the sheriff and Lucius; he flung the body over his shoulder and slowly made his way off the car into the river. Long dark hair trailed out into the water as he slipped and bobbed in the current. Eden's head went under, and the doctor cried out, but the sheriff maintained his grip on the doctor, and Patterson maintained his grip on the body and the rope and slowly emerged from the flood. "This has to be the last one," he said to the sheriff and the knot of men who greeted him. "The rest are trapped, and it's too dangerous." He knelt and laid his burden in the mud. He untied the ropes.

Had Lucius Tipton been simply Lucius and not Doctor, he might have ridden away with Tom and Ruth, he might have turned at the moment Avery Patterson came out of the water, he might have walked or even crawled through the mud, because he did not think he could bear this, and if he had not promised Ruth, even the Hippocratic Oath would not have stopped his retreat. He would have left and let the Methodist doctor roll Eden Douglass from that sodden blanket, kiss her bruised face, hold her scarred hands, cradle her lifeless head, and weep.

26

THEY DIDN'T BURY my sister Eden right away. They didn't bury anyone for a month. They couldn't dig no graves till the rain let up, and then when the rain let up they buried everyone fast. They took them from the top floor of the courthouse, where they kept all the dead during the flood, and they buried them fast. No black-bordered cards, no mourning calls, none of that. None of that mattered, not when you got a dozen dead on the top floor of the courthouse. They buried the dead all at once in the city cemetery, 'cept for the Catholics, who got their own cemetery and their own way of doing things.

This whole town gathered at the St. Elmo cemetery, Saints and sinners alike, everyone who could walk, they come to the funeral whether they knew the dead or not. They come because it was so nice to walk around outside without a coat or umbrella, without that rain. There's a strong wind and the sky is blue and they go from grave to grave, Methodist and Mormon, trampling the wet grass, their boots caked with mud.

Everyone 'cept us. Me and mine, we wait by my sister's grave by ourselves. We don't attend to words spoken over no one else. Didn't no one else matter to us. Gideon, Lil, Tom, Afton. Mother stands between me and Mason, not looking at anything but the trees, not looking at the grave, nor the coffin. Only the trees. When Doctor come, he slipped in between Mother and me. He had a dirty narcissus tucked in his lapel.

Is that for me, Doctor? Did you wear that flower for me?

I wore it for Eden, Cissa, Doctor says. I wore it because it was the one thing I've seen that spoke to me of any hope, bedraggled as it is. I found it strangling between two fence posts, and I picked it because it spoke to me of hope.

Me, I wondered what that narcissus said to Doctor, but I didn't ask. Wished I could have a flower to smell, wished I could smell something 'sides the black dye in my clothes. Me and Afton and Lil, we all smell of the dye tub. Mother, she don't wear nothing but black anyway, but we all had to dye our clothes. Dye them for the dead, Lil said when Afton hung the black clothes up. Dying for the dead. And Afton looked down at her hands and they were black with dye and Lil cried and Afton cried into her black hands and left her face streaked with black, too.

Afton cut down Eden's clothes for me and dyed them so I could wear them to this funeral. Wished I could have had something new. Afton could have made me something new in the time it took her to take a foot of hem and four or five inches out of the bodice and another four or five inches off the cuffs. It took her a long time, but then, she had a long time. Like I say, they didn't bury nobody during the flood.

Wished I could have had something new, but when you are the youngest, you get used to your clothes being cut down. Afton could have been more careful, if you ask me. She left pins in the bodice and the waistband so I can't sit or stand or move but those little pins jab and stick at me like they were whispering—stand up straight, don't curl your feet, attend to your elders. Wished everyone wasn't my elder.

Least I don't have to wear a veil. Afton and Lil, they are young ladies, so they have to wear veils, and the veils blow out in front of their faces in this wind. Mason, his clothes are always too tight under the arms anyway, and his pants never come any lower than the top of his boots. Mason is popping out of his clothes, but Gideon, he looks to have shrunk in his. His shoulders roll in and he stoops worse than usual and he keeps taking his glasses off and putting them on.

Someone starts to cry, and I look down past Doctor and Mother and Mason and see that it's Lil. Doctor gets out a clean white hanky and passes it to her. Then he takes Mother's arm, but she don't pay him no mind. She keeps her eyes on the trees and the wind blowing water off the leaves. She don't speak. Even to Doctor.

Five days after Eden died, the Pilgrim Cafe washed away. They brung Mother the news. They said everything in that whole block washed away and there wasn't nothing left of it. Mother didn't say nothing. I wasn't surprised. Mother hasn't said nothing since they

201

pulled Eden from the wreck. Not so much as pass the peas. If someone passed her the peas and put them on her plate, she might eat, but she wouldn't ask for them or nothing else. Wouldn't say thank you either. Not even when the bishop and the elders come around to make their condolence calls. They come no matter the rain. They stood in our hall, shaking the rain off their shoulders, and they said to Afton, tell your mother we have come to pray with her in this, the hour of her bereavement.

Mother come out of the parlor and took one look at the bishop and the elders. Get out of my sight, says Mother, turning her back on them. Get those men out of my sight, she says to Afton.

Afton shooed them out on the porch before they so much as took their hats off. Afton said she was sorry.

Mother wasn't sorry. You could tell.

Afton, she took care of everything in the days after Eden's death. Wasn't nothing to do but sit around the house and weep and watch the rain anyway, weep and eat, because we was still mortal, after all. Me and Mason didn't have to go to school, because our school washed away. The high school stood the flood, but all the desks and books was ruined, and so there wasn't no school there either. We stayed home, each of us thinking about Eden lying on the top floor of the courthouse with her hands folded over her chest and her hair probably still wet.

Doctor, he got drunk. I could smell it on him. He didn't come to see us much. Didn't come to see us at all, just come to see Mother. Him and Mother, they sat in the parlor just staring at one another. Like they was cut from stone.

Even today, standing here by this hole, I can smell the whiskey on Doctor, not too bad, just a hint, like maybe he dabbed it behind his ears like eau de cologne. Wished I had some eau de cologne so I didn't have to smell like black dye and starch.

I put my hand in Doctor's, and he takes it, but he don't pay me no mind. He says to Mother: when we put up the stone, what shall we say?

Regret, says Mother. Regret regret regret.

She takes her hand from his and crosses her arms over her breast. Still she don't look down in the hole. The hole is terrible. The walls slough off mud, and down in the pit, six inches of water. I don't want them to put Eden in that hole. It looks cold. I been cold every night since she died. I been getting in bed with Afton and Lil at night because I can't stand the cold beside me where Eden used to be. Eden will be cold in that hole.

She loved you, Doctor says to Mother. You must never doubt that.

She kissed me goodnight, says Mother without taking her eyes from the trees. Goodnight and goodbye. I killed her.

I won't hear you talk like that. It's not your fault, Ruth. It's not even her fault. Who could have known that bridge would come down?

God knew. God did it to punish me. For my lies and my willful pride. God knew it, and He put her on the train anyway.

No, He didn't, says Doctor.

Mother's lips peel back from her teeth. Never thought I'd hear you defending the Almighty, Lucius. I thought I could count on you to spare me that.

I would have thought so, too, says Doctor. He lets go of my hand to get out another handkerchief. He must have known he'd need more than one today. Ruth, he says, Eden was desperate. She was desperate and fearful that her dreams would die inside her, and that's why—

They died inside her anyway, didn't they? God is going to punish me for driving her to that.

We've all been punished enough. No more retribution. I tell you, Ruth, no more wrath and punishment. This is the twentieth century.

Hmph, says Mother, still not taking her eye from the trees. What does that matter?

Doctor don't have no reply. Doctor and Mother both look old and chalky. Doctor looks down in the hole. Mother looks up into the trees. I look down at the others. Afton leans on Tom's arm and weeps beneath her veil. I done my crying. Can't cry no more. I cried myself out when Eden died, and once before, the day she burned the trellis down, when she slapped me because I was crying for Father. I'm glad Father's dead, because now Eden will have someone on the Other Side to greet her. She won't be all alone with no friends in the Celestial Kingdom. But I worry that God won't even let her in. She didn't have no husband, after all. Me, I'm going to get me a

203

husband first thing, so if I die I won't have to worry about getting into the Celestial Kingdom.

They're coming to our grave now. They must be done with everyone else, and now they're coming to speak over Eden. They're all here, folks we know and folks we don't. Even the Pattersons are here, and they been known to change sidewalks if they saw Dr. Tipton coming. Arlene has taken her glasses off so she can cry without seeing, and Mabel Norcutt, she hangs on Jack's arm like she's still afraid Eden might leap up and get him back, and Jack, his whole face looks to be dipped in soot and ash. The bishop and the elders, they don't say nothing about how we have stood apart. They don't dare.

The wind picks up. The pages in Bishop's book ruffle like petticoats hung in the wind. He puts his hand over the page. He don't need to read it. He knows it all by heart anyway.

We are but spirit travelers, Bishop begins. Our souls are pilgrims clad in earthly raiment to travel this terrestrial realm and come at last to the grave whence no traveler may return.

People start to weep. I look across Doctor to Mother. She ain't weeping. She's still looking at the trees.

The bishop says: death is instituted by God for the purposes of resurrection, that day when the body shall be reunited with the soul, when men shall stand before the throne, for that Resurrection Day when the trump shall be sounded and all souls awake!

I look over my family. Lil has near sunk to the ground, and Gideon holds her, and Tom holds Afton, but Mason, he's staring at his shoes. Or the hole. Can't tell which. Mason drops his hat, and the wind steals it, blows it away. The hat leaps over Eden's grave and rolls past the bishop and everyone else there. They stop weeping and snuffling, and they watch Mason's hat like it has terrible bad manners to be rolling and leaping and dancing with the wind when we're here to bury the dead.

Only Mother don't seem to notice that Mason's hat is frolicking amongst the headstones.

On that day we shall rejoice in our salvation, Bishop goes on, heedless of the hat. The Saints shall be given all they were promised and the graves rolled back and the just rewarded.

Finally, for the first time since we gathered at the edge of the hole, Mother brings her eyes down from the trees. She looks into the

204

grave at the mud and the coffin, and past that, if there is such a place, beyond the mud and the coffin. Then she raises her eyes and watches the hat, watches the wind push that hat and pull it, toss and spin it all around the cemetery. Then she turns to Mason. He looks like he might cry.

We will hear the blessed angels sing, assume our celestial estates, and—

Go get your hat, Mother says to Mason.

Mason tears off after his hat, and the bishop, the elders, the mourners, they come undone. Some got their mouths open like they don't believe what they see. Some got their mouths shut up tight like they believe what they see and they don't like it one little bit. But the bishop, he quits talking, and they all turn to watch Mason chasing that hat, running, running on his long, skinny legs, reaching out for that hat at the very minute the wind snatches it from his hand and leads him chasing, dancing, all around the graves, in and out of the chilly shadows, leaping over the headstones, which are still so damp they gleam in the sun.

27

THERE WERE THOSE who said I shouldn't have married the day after I graduated from high school, four months after Eden died. There were those said I owed it to the memory of my dead sister to hold off celebrating a marriage so close upon the heels of death. I told Mother: if you want me to hold off, if you want me to stay at home, if you think I shouldn't marry right now, I won't. I will marry Tom Lance—that don't change. But I'll wait. If that's what you want, Mother.

Mother's skin was hard and dry as nutmeg, and her eyes was hard and shineless as boot blacking. She said: I'll be blasted if I'll use the dead to stop the marriage of the living.

Imagine Mother saying I'll be blasted.

So I got married in June in the parlor of my mother's house. Doctor give me the money for my dress, and I made it myself, sewed in every little tuck and stitch, sewed sometimes till I couldn't see no more, when the whole house was asleep. I stuck my needle in the pincushion and rubbed my eyes and thought of Eden and of Tom, of death and marriage and how they are the two things you can count on to change you forever, and how I hadn't even got used to the one before I'd be living through the other.

Bishop married us—Mr. and Mrs. Tom Lance. What a fine ring that has to it! Makes me proud just to say it. Bishop said yes, it was a fine name, but Bishop also said he thought I should ask my brother Gideon to give me away, because Gideon was the man in our family. Bishop didn't say he didn't want to share no parlor, no ceremony, no very breath of air with Dr. Lucius Tipton, but I held firm. Bishop, I said, it's my wedding, ain't it? And I've chosen the man I want to marry and I've chosen the man I want to give me away and I'm not changing my mind on either count. So it's Doctor gives me away or no one.

There wasn't nothing Bishop could do about it, but he did look pained to share a piece of cake and cup of punch with Dr. Lucius Tipton after the ceremony.

Anyway, Doctor'd sobered up by June. Everyone in this town had sobered up by June. Whether they drank or not. By June, hammers was ringing all over St. Elmo, which was picking up and rebuilding itself northward out of the path of the next flood. In church they said God was rewarding the industry of the citizens of St. Elmo. It was a spring like St. Elmo never seen, but then it was a flood like we never seen either. Grass sprouted in the cindery railyards, and wild sage and mustard blew across the foothills, and in Dogsback Ditch a meadow bloomed where once there wasn't nothing but water and destruction. Yes, in church that spring they was saying that just like Noah's Flood, God was sorry for what He done to us and He was trying to make it up.

Well, I didn't say so, but He couldn't make it up to the Douglasses, no matter what He done. We lost Eden and that was that.

Couldn't no one make that up. Our house stood the flood because we was at the north end of town anyway, but the Pilgrim washed away, along with everything else on that block. Some families lost everything, but Mother'd lost more than everything, not just a daughter and a cafe, but her reason as well. Mother was losing her mind.

I would never say such a terrible thing about my own mother, but it's the truth, and I believe in telling the truth. In my genealogy work for the church, I have folks come up to me all the time and say, Sister Lance, I'm afraid to look back in my family. What if I find a horsethief or an illegitimate child?

The past is the past and can't be undone, I say. Only the future can be altered. And besides, no one's family is perfect.

That's what I tell them, and one night just before we turned out our light, Tom says to me, I'm surprised at you, Afton.

Why is that?

Why, Afton, I thought the Douglasses was perfect. I thought everything they did was just about perfect. That's what you always tell me.

I give him a little kick under the covers and I say: Tom Lance, you are lucky to have married into such a family as mine.

And he says: yes, and you are lucky to have married out of it.

Well, if I hadn't got married and moved into my own house . . . (Rents was cheap in St. Elmo then, because lots of folks left town after the flood.) Me and Tom had just the sunniest little house you can imagine. We had two palms and a morning glory vine on one side and a pomegranate tree on the other. Pomegranates are pretty useless as fruit, but if you cut them open, they're nice to look at.

But if I hadn't left my mother's house I might never have seen she was losing her mind. If I'd stayed with her, I would have got used to it. Might not have noticed the six months of silence. Six months of Mother sitting on the back stoop watching that puny grapevine die. Eden planted that vine after she burned the yard down last summer. After the flood, that vine sprouted to life, but then it just withered up, and Mother sat and watched it wither up, because by August it's so hot here, St. Elmo looks like perdition with the fires out.

So it was August I begun to worry. Mother didn't seem to care about the Pilgrim's loss. She quit going to church altogether and wouldn't see no one from church when they called. Only one she'd talk to was Doctor, and he come when no one else was home, so I don't know what they talked about, because they was both real private about their grief.

So even though Doctor was pretty much sober by August, he was too splintered up with grief himself to be much help to me. And there wasn't no one to be any help to Lil. Lil ain't up to running that house the way I did. Lil's frail and she tires easily, and she don't have my gift for keeping an eye on everything at once. And Mason and Cissa was too much for Lil. Cissa was just as full of sass as an August plum is full of juice. And Mason! He was an armful of trouble. They'd call up from the school when he hadn't been there five straight days, and who knows what Mason Douglass was into? And when I asked him, he just got a smirk on his fat face. Mason is a chubber. Always was. The only one in our family who isn't bone-thin and lanky. Me, now I got a bit of flesh on me, and that's the way Tom likes me, but the rest of them, they don't have nothing to spare.

Specially Lil. She's tiny and frail. She couldn't make Mason stop skipping school, and then when he was there, he was always being drug into the principal's office for smart-mouthing or sloth or something unpleasant. Lil couldn't handle Mason, but I could. I told him: Mason, if I hear one more bad report on you, there'll be no more Chocolate Marbled Supreme Cake for you. And if you're good, I'll bake you one a week. All your very own.

Mason's jaw started working like he already had that cake 'tween his teeth. So that was that.

You'd think Gideon would have took a hand in some of this, but he wasn't no help at all, not after he got this idea he could lay out the world's history from end to end on three-column charts six foot long. He said all that history would take a lot of study, especially since he was beginning with the Creation and ending day before yesterday. He said he had a lot of studying to do.

There's other things to be done here, Gideon, I said, 'sides study. There's no more Pilgrim, and our family coffers will be getting mighty empty mighty fast, and it's time for you to get to work.

Just as soon as I finish the chart, he says, I'll get a job teaching school.

Well, Gideon, I don't think we can wait that long, and you'll pardon me for asking, but how much of this study is taking place in the library where you can see Arlene McClure every day and how much of it is just plain sloth?

Gideon takes off his glasses and cleans them. Arlene is helping me with my Great Timetable, he says, paying no mind to my question about sloth.

So it come to that. By August it come to where I see Gideon's going to be no help. Lil's sinking under the weight of all this responsibility, and I see Mother's got to be pulled from the Slough of Despond and get this family moving again. And it's got to be me pull her from that Slough, because no one else is equal to the task. By August I had nothing left to try in the way of words, and when words fail, you got to pick up the next best thing.

Majic Bitters Tonic. That's what I tried. Majic Bitters Tonic I bought from Mrs. Nana Bowers. I know they say there's nothing heaven cannot heal. And I know they say there's nothing time won't kill or cure. And maybe I should have waited for heaven or time and not gone to Majic Bitters Tonic, but I said to Tom: Mother has drunk too long from affliction's vial, and I'm going to brave this tempest in its den.

Tonics and elixirs was only a sideline for Mrs. Bowers, who come to St. Elmo a child, the slave of Madison Whickham, and stayed to be midwife and owner of the St. Elmo Turkish Baths, which only went out of business with the flood. Me, I didn't care that Mrs. Bowers was a direct descendant of the Lamanites—you could tell by her black skin. She could be Cain's stepsister for all I cared. She was a smart old woman. For one thing, neither Mrs. Bowers nor anyone else in this town knew a Turkish bath from a Spanish grandee, so she decorated the place with whatever come to hand and had her granddaughters—good-looking girls, all of them—dress up in flowing robes, and as Doctor said, people used to come all the way from San Francisco to take a bath in St. Elmo.

There was only one thing wrong with the Majic Bitters Tonic. It had Peruvian bark, prickly ash bark, poplar root, cinnamon bark, cloves, and two quarts each clear worked cider and whiskey in it. Mrs. Bowers knew I was a practicing Saint, and when I come to ask after the tonic she said to me, you can use it or not, Mrs. Lance, but this tonic stimulates the appetite, purifies the blood, restores the brain, and strengthens the bones. She pointed to her own mother as

209

living (but not walking) proof. Her mother was ninety. So I said, how much?

I know it's breaking the Word of Wisdom. I know there's angels taking note, recording my every step. I know it's wrong. But if it would help my mother, I swore I'd do it, and if it didn't help her, I'd take the blame before heaven for that, too.

Tom just looked at me when I come home with that bottle. He don't ask no questions nor make any remarks whatsoever. He's good like that.

I give Mother that tonic just like Mrs. Bowers said, one half hour before supper. I went in her room where she was lying down, and I said, Mother, I got something here for you. But I didn't say what it was.

Mrs. Bowers said six teaspoons to begin with and then if that didn't help, six more every day for a week. But I figured if I was going to break the Word of Wisdom, I'd better do it all at once instead of tiring the angels out making notes day after day. So I bring Mother a cold compress and a nice big cup of Majic Bitters Tonic and talk to her while she sips it. I started off with the weather, which was very warm, even for August.

That tonic stimulated mother all right, but not her appetite. It loosed her tongue, and as I sat with her I knew why she had not been in her right mind since Eden died. I should have thought of it before. One death makes you think of another, just as one wedding makes you think of another and one birth makes you think of another. Eden's death by water brought back Father's death by fire. Only, when Father died, Mother sacrificed the widow's just due—to mourn her husband with the proper interval of grief. Well, Mother didn't get no interval then, not with five little children and Father's last gift to her growing in her womb. Eden's death uncovered Father's. I heard it from Mother's own lips. She wasn't making too much sense, but I figured it from what she said, weeping, about Father going off into the wilderness.

There, there, Mother, I said, you can call it whatever you like, the country of the dead, because ain't no one ever come back from that country to say what it's like. It might be a wilderness, but then, it might not. It might be real nice. Don't you worry about Father. He's safe on the Other Side.

The other side of hell, says Mother.

Hush, Mother, just have another sip. A good Saint has nothing to fear from death. God is specially good to Saints, since we got the Restored Gospel on our side. Saints don't need to fear hell. Mother snorted and choked, and I took the cup back and said she should lie back down and I'd bring her some supper.

It was Father, I said to Lil when I went in the kitchen and picked up her tray. All her old grief for Father was unearthed by Eden's death. Her heart broke all over again like a twice-cracked vessel. After all these years, Mother has never quit loving Father.

Mother nibbled at her supper but threw it up later. She was still vomiting the next day, hot and cold by turns, too dizzy to sit up for long and weak in the limbs. She was so sick I began to doubt the Majic Bitters Tonic and Mrs. Bowers altogether.

But the next day Cissa come to fetch me. You won't believe your eyes! Cissa says. Mother told Mason to mind his manners at breakfast! Mother told me to quit being such a sassy snit! Mother asked Lil to get out the Pilgrim's old account books and bring her some pen and paper! You got to come, Afton, because you won't believe it 'less you see it with your own eyes!

I winged my way to Mother's, and there she sits at the desk in the parlor with the Pilgrim account books and her pen scratching over the page and lots of other papers and letters around her. Her back was to me, but I could see that her hair was done up neat and tight like she always wore it and her back was straight and her mind was working; not wallowing no more. The parlor curtains was parted, and the window was open, and the sunlight poured in over the faded carpet.

I went out on the back porch, and before that blasted grapevine, I blessed God and Nana Bowers.

The next Sunday we was all together for the first time since my wedding. Mother and me and Tom and Doctor and Gideon and Arlene and Lil and Cissa and Mason. We was all doing our best not to look at Eden's empty chair, which was over in the corner by the window. We was all being real pleasant to each other. Maybe—I think to myself—maybe we can go back to being not the family we once was, because I am married now and Eden's dead and nothing is ever the same after death or marriage, but at least go back to being a family united and blessed just the same.

Mother says: Arlene, try some of Afton's peach butter on your

211

squash. And Mason, close your mouth when you chew. And Cissa, sit up straight. Then she says: we are going to make some changes. Some changes—Mother glances at Eden's empty chair—already been made for us, but these changes coming up, we are going to make for ourselves. We have some money coming in. I have some money coming from my dead mother's estate.

Not if Albert has his way, Doctor says, setting down his knife and fork like he has just committed surgery.

Albert knows better than to trifle with me. Albert would put a tollbooth at the gates of heaven if he could, that's true, but he don't trifle with me. I got some money coming from the sale of my mother's house, and I got some money coming from Albert's Providential Insurance Company, because I insured the Pilgrim a few years back, and my brother, Albert, is going to cough me up some money or I'll go to Salt Lake and wring it out of him. And he knows it. And there's another pea-hearted man I got some business with. Doctor and me are going to pay a little visit to Art Whickham next week now that we have reckoned up the damages and the prospects.

Art Whickham wouldn't know prospect if he met it in his water closet, Doctor says, wiping his mustache. Art Whickham knows profits and that's all he knows.

Except he knows not to trifle with me, says Mother.

Yes, he knows that. You got to give him some credit for brains even if he don't have a heart.

I don't care a fig for his brains or heart. He owns a whole block of New Town buildings, and they are almost finished, and he is going to lease me one of them buildings, and we are going to have a new Pilgrim. Better than the last. A real restaurant, this one, with three cooks and indoor plumbing and electricity.

I smile to hear Mother's voice so strong and firm, and her hands don't tremble for the first time in months.

And then, says Mother, we are going to move. We can't stay in this house no longer. Not since Eden—

She couldn't say died. Didn't have to, because the wind come through the curtains and said it for her.

The past is the past, says Mother, it can't be changed, but it don't have to be lived in. I can't stand this house no more.

Where're we going? says Lil.

We're moving into Brother Watterson's house. His dry-goods

212

store was wiped out, and he has left this valley, and we are moving into that house.

But Ma! says Mason in that roostery voice of his. The Wattersons' house is on Silk Stocking Row! Why, it ain't two blocks from Uncle Art Whickham's house!

I know that, says Mother. You don't have to tell me where that house is. It's long since time the Douglasses was equal to the Whickhams in this town.

Are you going to tell Uncle Art we're moving in down the street from him? asks Lil.

Not till I get him to sign the lease papers for the new Pilgrim, says Mother, and then she starts to laugh, and Doctor guffaws into his napkin.

Oh, that'll be a sight, says Doctor. Art'll be more surprised than Moses was when the burning bush started jawing with him.

If you ask me, Doctor's helped himself to the Burning Bush once too often, and he makes pretty free use of the Bible for an atheist, but I don't say none of this, because Doctor has always stuck by us and we will always stick by him.

That house is grand! cries Cissa.

Well, it's time we had something grand, says Mother. I'm sick of the niggling and pinching. The devil can take the hindmost.

If you're smart and fast, says Doctor, that's all the devil can ever catch.

Maybe it's too grand, says Lil, thinking as I was of the two stories of that house with the big staircase, the hall big as our parlor. The Young Women's Mutual Improvement Association would often meet at Wattersons', and I knew that house had a kitchen as big as the Pilgrim's and a little room for a servant, too.

We'll get used to it, however grand it is, says Mother. I know you're all growing up and will leave home soon, but I wanted to be sure we had enough room for Gideon and Arlene to live with us after they marry. Just till Gideon can establish himself, of course.

Arlene McClure turns the color of an autumn sunset, but then she can't face a plate of mush without blushing. She reaches over next to her and takes Gideon's hand, and the two of them just beam at one another like two cupids on a Christmas card.

Of course, that'll be after he gets back from Salt Lake, Mother says.

213

Where? says Gideon.

Salt Lake.

Who? says Gideon.

You. You're going to Salt Lake to learn the insurance trade from your Uncle Albert. I've written to him already, and that's where you're going. It's time you learned something useful instead of sitting around and trying to reunite the tribes of Israel, even if it's only on paper.

But Ma—I was thinking of going on a mission for the church.

Well, you can just forget that.

But I was thinking of teaching school.

You can forget that, too. You're going to Salt Lake, and there's an end to it. I've written to Albert already. He's expecting you.

Arlene boo-hoos into her napkin, and Gideon pats her hand.

You can get married when you get back, Mother says, this time a little gentler. But you have to go. You have to learn something to do with your life.

Oh! Arlene cries. It's just like Jacob and Rachel!

I felt for Arlene. I couldn't have waited that long to marry Tom, so I pat her shoulder and say to Mother: ain't all this a bit sudden?

Maybe. But it would have happened anyway. Eventually. Even if Eden had—

Lived, says Lil, giving Mother the words she was afraid to say. Not lived. Not died. Mother couldn't say neither of those words for months and months.

I think you're hateful and cruel! Arlene cries, shaking my hand off her shoulder. I think you're all hateful and cruel! Always thinking you're right and everyone else is wrong. Always thinking you know what's best and no one knows nothing compared to you. Always thinking you're better than everyone! Gideon's a grown man! Gideon should decide what he wants to do.

If Gideon could decide for himself, Mother says just like Gideon wasn't there, he would have done it already. He would have done it a long time ago. But really, Arlene, she says kindlier, it won't be for long, and—

What do you know? What's long to you? Just because you've always been a widow. You don't know what it's like to be in love! You're hateful and mean, and that's why Eden was leaving you! That's why she died. She couldn't stand to live with you one more minute! Arlene runs from the table, and we could hear the back door slam.

Well, no one could blame Arlene for being mad at Mother, but we was all just shut up with shock. Gideon takes his glasses off and cleans them with the tablecloth, and Doctor, he just wilts. Mother, she don't so much as quiver an eyelid, but her lips knit and purled into grimness and her teeth was clenched when she asked Tom to pass her the salt. Good thing she asked Tom. The rest of us was too dumbfounded to move, but nothing gets to Tom. He passed her the salt like she wanted, and he told her she was welcome to it.

28

PERPETUAL AGITATION KNOTTED the brows of Mrs. Albert Mason, the former Elyse Farnsworth, a prosperous matron and well-upholstered Saint. She perspired under her fur wraps, despairing quietly in the functional splendor of the Salt Lake train station. She wrung her gloves, waiting for the emigration official to call her name so that she might claim the Saint her husband's munificence had brought to Salt Lake City and get home before Albert did. This was the fifth Saint Albert's generosity had sponsored, and though Elyse knew they were blessed to be able to do their part in bringing the latter days to pass, she wished she didn't have to bring strangers to her home. Many of the emigrating Saints were not of the more refined classes. They often lacked manners, and their piety, while unquestionable, made them tiresome over dinner and made Albert cross all evening.

As she watched the procession of shabby, travel-worn emigrants with their harsh accents and pale faces, Elyse dreaded Albert's response to the new emigrant, whoever he was, because Albert had been in a black fury ever since his sister had deposited Gideon with them.

Elyse had only seen a girlhood picture of Ruth: she gazed out from under a fringe of bangs in the fashion of twenty years ago and stood tall and corseted as a steel girder. Albert said that Ruth didn't require corsets, that her very ribs were made of iron, and her heart, too. Elyse had not pursued this discussion of her sister-in-law's innards, but even thinking about Ruth gave Elyse the chills.

Elyse found Gideon studious, well mannered, and unobjectionable, except that he was the offspring of his mother and a lunatic. But he was a burden, and Elyse's burdens seemed to multiply daily: Gideon's arrival, Albert's wrath, and this stranger, this foreigner, who would join her family when it needed no further stress, whatever the rewards that might be reaped in heaven.

Elyse heard her name called and hastened to the greeting committee's table. Her face fell. She was introduced to Sister Katherine Tindall, the newest object of Albert's philanthropy. Elyse protested that there must be some mistake; surely *their* emigrant was a man. The matron at the greeting committee table checked the list. No, Sister Katherine Tindall—about eighteen, pale, plump, dressed in coarse clothing of a serviceable drab that clashed with a high, wild nest of reddish hair and eyes the color of old copper—Sister Tindall was theirs. A battered hat with a drooping, greasy-looking feather perched on Sister Tindall's head. She percolated an unbecoming energy. She pumped Elyse's hand and thanked her profusely in a speech that had obviously been rehearsed in the three-thousand-mile crossing from Liverpool, which, the official said, was where she was from.

"Call me Kitty," said Sister Tindall.

"Oh!" Elyse squealed. "Oh, I hadn't thought to have a girl."

"Well, I'm a girl." Kitty executed a neat two-step and a twirl.

"Oh! Well, hurry. Get your bag, dear. Mr. Mason doesn't like me to keep the car out any longer than I have to."

"The car?" said Kitty with a look of ungarnished alarm. "The *motorcar?*"

Mrs. Albert Mason hustled her out to the automobile, where a handsome black part-time chauffeur stomped his feet in the January cold. Despite Elyse's admonitions to hurry, Kitty stood paralyzed in front of the sparkling chrome, the hard yellow finish, the gleaming woodwork, the black leather seats. The chauffeur took her bag and opened the door. Elyse got in quickly and told Kitty to get a move on. "Please hurry, Sister Tindall. Please."

Elyse was in anguish; passersby were laughing at Kitty's gaping wonder before the car. What if the emigration committee had given her a congenital idiot this time? Albert would be furious.

Miss Katherine Tindall was undone by the sight of the motorcar, the mountains, the solidity and splendor of Zion, but the sight of Albert Mason's house convinced her that she had died and gone to heaven. Surely His many mansions looked something like this one, and God Himself would have to go some distance to improve on steam heat in every room, electric lights, carpets so deep they brushed the ankles, and ceilings so high Kitty thought she might ascend. The staircase was wide enough for three people at once.

In contrast to this magnificence, the room they had reserved for Kitty was a narrow little servant's bedroom behind the kitchen. It was neat and clean, but plain for all that. Kitty thought it was mean of them to give her such a room, but she did not say so. Nor did she mention that in all her eighteen years she had never slept in a room with less than five people in it, or a bed with less than three. She put her coat and hat on the upright chair and checked the sheets for bedbugs anyway, because a girl can never be too careful.

"Surely you don't want to go to bed now!" said Elyse, surprising Kitty in her bug inspection. "I thought you might want to freshen up before dinner. Follow me to the bathroom, and I'll send Bridget up with some towels for you. Please don't use the ones hanging there."

Kitty nodded dutifully, took her satchel, and followed Elyse upstairs. She promised she would not touch the towels, and when Elyse left, she put her satchel down and stood all amazed at the gleaming tiled splendor, the porcelain toilet (which she flushed several times for fun before she used it), the hot and cold taps of shining brass, the six-foot tub with feet curled like lions' paws. She stripped off her clothes, like dry husks, useless blossoms after the fruit has bloomed. The servant, Bridget, knocked, carrying clean towels. Catching a glimpse of Kitty's naked body, she said sourly, "She didn't mean for you to take a bath, just wash up."

"And what's it to you?" Kitty snatched a towel out of Bridget's hands and bolted the door.

As she sank into the tub of hot water, she declared publicly that the Queen of England didn't have it so good, and privately she

217

vowed that she would welcome the return of plural marriage, that she would marry Brother Mason tomorrow if he was as mean as a streetcat and as bald as a bell. She would do anything to live in a house like this.

Kitty lathered and washed and filled the tub again with water so hot her veins pulsated and the mirrors steamed over. She dripped water over to the cabinet, where she found a bottle of Italian hair wash and a jar of French's Fine Cologne. She washed her hair and was just pouring the cologne into the rinse water when Bridget knocked rudely at the door and told her to hurry, because Mr. Albert Mason would be home soon and he might want to use the bathroom. "It is," Bridget added, "his house and his tub."

"Go eat coal and shit cinders," Kitty muttered, pouring the final rinse through her hair. She stepped from the tub and wrapped herself in a clean, soft towel. She regarded herself advantageously, dropping the towel first over one shoulder, then over the other, and smiling coyly into her reflection. Then she dropped the towel altogether and stood on tiptoe to see as much of her body as she could. She'd never seen anything but her face in a broken shard of mirror. She held her firm breasts in her hands. Like twin baskets of apples, someone had once told her, like ripe melons, he'd said, Charley the bill poster, back in the days when she had not been a Saint and had taken pleasure in such sinful things. She was grateful now that she had not granted him the last favor, poor unconverted heathen that he was. Kitty was on her way to the Celestial Kingdom, if this wasn't already it.

"You little pippin!" She tweaked her own fair cheek.

She dried her hair briskly and noticed the old clothes lying dismally where she'd left them. "God's nostrils!" She brushed the weeks of travel from the skirt as best she could and pulled her one other blouse out from the bag. It had permanently petrified along the lines of the bottom of the satchel. She turned her underwear and her stockings inside out and piled her hair back up, tucking in the fake piece that had faded over the years and no longer quite matched her russet-colored wiry curls.

As she slowly descended the staircase into the Mason foyer, she wished the other button-holers at Mrs. Frayling's Corset Company could see her now. They'd know why she had always thought herself a lady of consequence and destiny. They'd never make fun of the Mormons if they could see her now. She wished that her mother and father could sober up long enough to see her, and that her six living siblings and the two boarders who shared their beds in the three-room flat could feast their eyes on Miss Katherine Tindall, who had truly been converted.

She was prepared to deliver her speech of gratitude to Mr. Albert Mason, who had gathered in the parlor with his wife and three daughters, but he hardly acknowledged her presence, more interested in checking his watch and complaining about dinner. At the stroke of six, he shuttled them into the well-lit dining room and bent his head over the longest and most boring prayer Kitty had ever heard. He didn't even thank God for her safe arrival in Zion.

Mr. Albert Mason hollered for Bridget to bring the soup. She swung out the kitchen door bearing a large tureen and slapped a china bowl down in front of each of the five Masons, Kitty, and an empty place. She served Mr. Mason first and Kitty last, dripping a little of the fragrant chicken cream soup on Kitty's skirt. Kitty scarcely noticed. She leaned over her bowl and inhaled. "Oh, God, the Eternal Father," she whispered, "don't take me from this place."

She slathered her bread with butter and drained the soup without pausing. She was about to mop out the bowl with the bread when she looked up into the stricken faces of Elyse and the three Mason girls, staring over their half-finished soup.

"There's more, you know," said Esther, the oldest girl. "You don't have to pig it."

"Esther!" Elyse cried.

Kitty dropped her spoon as if it had caught fire and blushed from every pore. How was she to know there was more? And there was. More than Kitty had ever seen, more than she had ever eaten. More pork chops cooked with apples and a stuffed, savory shoulder of veal, and more potato balls and fried corn and parsnips floating in cream sauce, and more squash fritters and gravy and lots of bright-tinted relishes, catsup and chow chow, grape and tomato jellies, and more hot rusks and rice muffins and endless tubs of butter, and more baked cabbage with grated cheese and pitchers of milk and tapioca pudding and custard cake for dessert.

Judging from his girth and the red veins that littered his balding pate and the vigor with which he applied himself to dinner, Mr. Al-

219

bert Mason had missed few of these sumptuous meals. He ate resolutely, resisting Elyse's attempts to draw him into conversation and ignoring his daughters' forays on his attention. He forgot Kitty altogether till the stuffed veal was going around a second time, and then he wiped his enormous mustache and glared down the table to just opposite Kitty, where there was a place set, but no person present. "Where's Gideon?" he said.

"Now, dear," Elyse interceded, "I'm sure—"

"Isn't it enough that I have to feed him and he eats like a bull in springtime? Do I have to keep his meals hot and the servants on the payroll to make sure he don't faint from starvation? Humph?"

"Now, Albert." Elyse's pretty-puffy face darkened. "Don't work yourself up. I'm sure Gideon will be along any minute now. You know how conscientious he is."

"Not about meals at my table, he's not! He knows we eat at six sharp, and he's late every night. Well, you just tell Bridget— Bridget! You hear me? What Gideon misses, he misses; I won't have it boiling away on the back burner!"

"Pa," Esther said, "you know Cousin Gideon is late every night, and every night you have a fit, and if this keeps up I think you're going to bust a gut."

"Esther!" cried Elyse. "That's very vulgar!"

"Well, I get tired of it. Gideon's always late and Pa is always mad and tonight we have a new boarder—"

"We do not have boarders, young lady!"

"Now, Albert," Elyse crooned. "Esther, Eliza, Edith, Sister Tindall is our guest and she's come all the way from England, and I think we should be a little more polite while she's staying here—just till she can get herself established, Albert, and find some work and be out on her own, paying back her debt to us." Elyse gave Kitty a jumpy smile.

Kitty slid her lips along her fork and returned a puckered grin.

"What kind of work?" asked Edith. Edith was as homely as a day-old cod.

"Bridget!" Albert bellowed, bringing his face up from the trough of his plate. "What kind of fly stickum did you put in the potatoes tonight?"

"What kind of work did you do in England, Sister Tindall?" Elyse inquired sweetly.

Kitty studied her blunt, chunky fingers. "In jolly old England, I didn't work, exactly. I took voice and elocution lessons most all me—my—life so I could follow Mamá on the stage."

A clatter of silverware and crockery erupted from Albert, who choked so hard that Bridget shot through the kitchen door to pound his back. He brushed her away and gawked at his guest. "The stage! Jesus, Joseph, and Emma!"

"Albert, really. Think of the girls."

"Mamá was an *artiste*," Kitty continued. "She played the Empire mostly, but there was lots of other halls—thee-aters—she played. Sang like an angel, she did. You never heard anyone do 'Piccadilly John with His Little Glass Eye' like Mu—Mamá. And poor dead Papá." She looked skyward as if he might be hanging from the ceiling. "He was an *artiste*, too. They could never be parted in life, only by cruel, cruel death, and then their love just broke the hearts of all England. The night they tilled my Papá under, Mamá went on and sang 'My Darling's Crossed Over,' and the Empire near drownt in tears. The barman said he'd never seen the like of it. My little sister, too—God rest her angel's soul—acted in the thee-ater till she caught pneumonia from wearing damp tights and died a few days later."

"Tights!" shrieked Albert.

"She was just eight, and what a voice was lost to the stage. We had to wait a week to bury her, because *artistes* from all over England wanted to be at her funeral. That night Mamá sang—"

"Tights! By great Brigham's wives! Not tights!"

"Albert, please."

"My whole family's been *artistes*. My stepfather is an agent what books lots of wonderful acts. There's this little dog act he manages what's been known to make professional mourners laugh." Kitty studied her plate. "So they say. I never saw it myself, not with my long hours at the piano."

"Do you play?" asked the incredulous Edith.

"Oh, no. My teacher always played for me. 'It's just for you to sing,' he used to say. 'My little lark—you take what gifts God give you, my little dove.' I was known as the Lark of Liverpool. I was born to the stage."

"By God!" Albert roared. "You won't go on the stage till you're out from under my roof!"

"Oh, dear, no, Brother Mason." Kitty gave him the look the reformed Magdalene must have practiced on Christ. "I only intend to lift my lovely voice to God in future as befits a Latter-day Saint."

Elyse let go of a long sigh, and it may have been that one of her stays snapped.

"Cousin Gideon is real musical," Eliza offered.

"He's real smart, too," Edith added. "He wants to teach history."

"You better tell her that Cousin Gideon's got a fiancée," Esther piped up, "and he says *she* sings like an angel."

"Ooooo," said Kitty, "I'm sure she does."

"Gideon can sing for his supper if he don't get here soon," Albert vowed. "Every time I see Ruth or her children, it's to have food taken out of my mouth and money out of my pocket. I have to support that boy's appetite when I can hardly afford three girls, but you can just be grateful to me, Elyse, because you don't know how close you came, madam, you and your children"—he gave the three girls an evil look—"to sharing the very roof over your heads with my sister Ruth!"

The door slammed in the foyer, and the girls and Elyse all said in unison, "There's Gideon now." A tall young man burst into the dining room. He was clean-shaven, with lank brown hair and spectacles, and even-featured, though his ears stuck out slightly. He was bland and handsome, and he apologized three times between entering the room and taking his seat opposite Kitty.

"Nice of you to come," Albert snapped.

"I'm sorry, Uncle Albert. I started reading and forgot the time."

"I suppose any old book is more important than mealtime at my table."

"Now, Albert, please." Elyse turned to her nephew. "Gideon, this is Sister Tindall. She's just arrived from England, and she'll be our guest for a few days while she's looking for work—Albert—only till then."

Gideon took his napkin out of his shirt and stood up. He nodded gravely. "How do you do, Miss Tindall?"

Kitty swallowed a dainty bite and licked her lips. She fluttered her eyelashes as she scrutinized him. He was handsome, but not beautiful. He clearly wasn't as well established as Mr. Albert Mason, but he was single, and moreover—she gave him a rosebud of a smile—he was educated. He had manners, that much was evident, and he appeared before her as if appointed by heaven. She readied herself for a memorable performance so that in years after she could tell her children how her shining green eyes had met those of their dear papá and how Destiny had enveloped them both, how passion and mutual regard had ignited their first, fateful meeting when Kitty murmured, "Charmed, I'm sure," and Gideon Douglass just about fell over, because of course he had never, in all his life, seen anyone quite so beautiful as Miss Kitty Tindall.

29

January 7, 1912

Dear Sister Ruth—

It wasn't my fault. How was I to know? Am I my brother's keeper or my nephew's either? Am I responsible for everything that goes on in this house? Jesus, Joseph, and Emma. If that was so, I tell you the first thing to go out would be that worthless Bridget, who should have been keeping her eye on them in the first place. But she was probably stealing food from my pantry while all this (and I don't need to tell you all what) was going on right above her head. She might have heard the bedsprings and not lifted an eyebrow, let alone a hand. It was all her fault, that overfed mackerel-snapping Mick.

Don't ask me how it happened, Ruth. Ask your Saintly son, but don't ask him till the sun gets through rising and setting on him. Please, don't disturb that natural order of the heavens or the universe, but you might sometime ask him how it happened. I asked him myself, Ruth, I did. I don't want you to think your boy came here and I didn't give him every consideration an uncle owes his nephew and then some. I did. Not only have I let him live under my roof, I have taught him the mysteries of the insurance business, for which, it must be said, he has no gift. But I did ask him. He said he wanted to marry this little English canary, and I said, I thought you were engaged, Gideon, to a girl in St. Elmo.

Well, all he can say, Ruth, is that something come up he hadn't foreseen.

Well, I could have foreseen it. I kick myself, Ruth, that that little drabtail ever darkened my door. That's the last time I'm sponsoring so much as the passage of an immigrant louse. I'd rather cut holes in my pockets and let the money dribble down my legs.

But she was a clever one, Ruth. She wouldn't have fooled you and she didn't fool me, but she fooled Gideon and she fooled Elyse. Elyse danced all around her, asking her when she'd like to find a job. Elyse showed her off to the boys at church like she was a prize rhubarb pie. But why should Miss Kitty Tindall work when she can eat free at my table? She thinks I'm a free ticket to the Celestial Kingdom. They all do. Bridget feeds her whole family out of my larder, and then they all go to confession and tell the priest how they're stealing from me, and the priest says, bless you, my son.

Well, I know you're not going to say that, Ruth, and I don't blame you. I tried to explain to your son that no matter what they done, there's no way that little snippet could *know* anything what had happened to her. Not for sure. I said there's a nice long time between the doing and the knowing. I offered to have Elyse come in and tell him the same thing, but Gideon said he couldn't bear to hear his Aunt Elyse speak to him of women's bodies, even if she is married.

Gideon wrings his big hands out like he expects to see butter drip and then he says—Kitty, Miss Tindall, could not know for certain that she is carrying my child, much as she might suspect it. She hasn't had my education, and she doesn't know things like I do.

I told him that a girl like her was *born* knowing, but he

just cleans off his glasses and says that one afternoon in a bed of sin doesn't necessarily mean that any consequences will follow, but he would be less than manly if he deserted her.

I told him, Gideon (I did, Ruth), I said, young folks do that all the time, Gideon, they just don't talk about it! You don't owe her nothing. Think of your mother! Think of the girl in St. Elmo.

Gideon started to cry, and I thought I'd puke, because, Ruth, if it's one thing I can't stand, it's crying. Where did that boy learn to cry? It wasn't from you, that's for certain. If ever there was a woman with corks in her eyes, it's you, and I don't mean that with no disrespect, understand that.

Gideon said he couldn't leave Kitty alone and friendless, an orphan in the world. It would not be the manly thing to do, he said. He said Kitty couldn't imagine what come over her and put her head on Gideon's shoulder and wept. (I was going to ask him if she put her clothes back on first, but I didn't.) Gideon says—what kind of man would I be if I left her alone?

I told him, Ruth. I told him what you would have told him. Believe me. I did. I said—you'd be a smart man, Gideon, that's what you'd be.

Gideon said she was just a friendless little singer now dishonored in the world of maidens. And you know who told him that! It was her! Of course it was her, the little chit.

Well, it's done now, Ruth, and I blame Elyse. If you want to blame someone for what's happened to your son, blame Elyse. It's her fault. How could she have been such a fool? I cringe to think I'm married to a woman who could hear a little chit like Kitty Tindall say she had a headache and couldn't go to Sacrament Meeting Sunday afternoon and believe her! Elyse is not too smart, Ruth, but then I didn't marry her for her brains, and now I rue it. I confronted Elyse with her stupidity, and she wept. Jesus, Joseph, and Emma! The only ones not weeping in my house that day was Bridget and Kitty, and they was too busy filling their mouths to think about weeping. They was happy!

225

How could I know? Elyse says to me, and I said to her just what you would have, Ruth, I said—if you had a brain to play with, you'd have known, Elyse. That's what I said, and it made her weep all the more.

I suspected right away. The day it happened, I watched them two at suppertime and I knew something was up, and I would have wrote to you then, but I never dreamed it would lead to marriage. I watched Kitty that night at supper. She eats like a she-goat most of the time, but now she's picking over her food and sighing, and Gideon gulps so loud they could have heard him at Temple Square. The two of them was shooting looks to one another across the table that could have fried the chicken if Bridget hadn't overdone it already. I would have written to you then and told you the best thing you could do was call your boy home and forget the insurance trade (for which as I said he has no gift), but I never thought it would mean he'd marry her. I thought maybe they'd just dallied, and though I don't condone that, no indeed, I didn't think he'd marry her. I thought I could talk him out of it.

But I couldn't. I don't know what Gideon's wrote you, Ruth, but I give him the wedding he wanted. The bishop come in to do the ceremony, and I had to give the bride away. If that ain't bad enough, I had to buy the dress on her back and pay for the wedding breakfast, too. But the bishop don't eat too much, and we didn't have no one else there.

Not only that, but because he's your son, Ruth, I paid the first month's rent on a house for them, though I am taking it out of Gideon's wages, because he's a married man now and has to learn that nothing is given to us in this world. We got to buy it all.

Elyse sniveled through the whole ceremony. She must have wanted me to open their little mouths and stuff the wedding cake down so they could just look at each other and not be troubled with keeping body and soul together. Then I had to drive them to their house, which I paid the rent on, in my car, which I earned with the sweat of my brow, and I leave them off, and if Kitty don't have something cooking already, she soon will have. She's that kind of girl. She wouldn't fool you for a minute, Ruth. She's got enough curves for a spiral staircase and a knot of fake hair on top that looks like a mouse in a mop. She wouldn't have fooled any woman except a fool like Elyse.

But I don't want you blaming me for this, Ruth, because it wasn't my fault. I done what I could. I'm doing all that heaven or you could ask of me. I'm keeping Gideon on at the Providential, though he's money through my hands, Ruth, but I'm doing it not for Gideon, who's like Elyse and don't have a lick of sense, I'm doing it for you. You done your part of our bargain, you bought the best life insurance policy we got, and I'll do mine—I'll keep Gideon on.

You are my own dear sister, even if you been nothing but trouble to me since the day you married Samuel Douglass. I know you've had a hard life and I don't deny it, but I wasn't so young when you was married that I don't recall being shut out of my own room and being sent down to the kitchen to sleep like a servant while you and your new husband fogged up the windows. Forgive me, Ruth, for bringing this painful memory back to mind, but you have to understand I'm not to be blamed for what happened to Gideon, and I couldn't help but think, when Gideon told me how he'd been diddling Miss Kitty Tindall, about you and Samuel Douglass up in my room. You know what they say, Ruth, and I don't bring this up to you for any other reason but to absolve myself of any part in this ill-fated marriage. You know what they say. Like father. Like son.

> Your loving and regretful brother,
> Albert

30

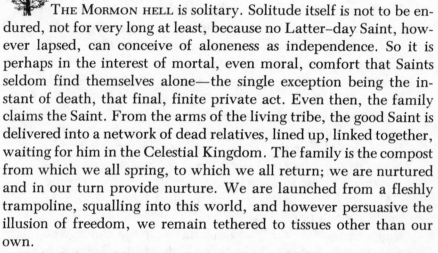THE MORMON HELL is solitary. Solitude itself is not to be endured, not for very long at least, because no Latter–day Saint, however lapsed, can conceive of aloneness as independence. So it is perhaps in the interest of mortal, even moral, comfort that Saints seldom find themselves alone—the single exception being the instant of death, that final, finite private act. Even then, the family claims the Saint. From the arms of the living tribe, the good Saint is delivered into a network of dead relatives, lined up, linked together, waiting for him in the Celestial Kingdom. The family is the compost from which we all spring, to which we all return; we are nurtured and in our turn provide nurture. We are launched from a fleshly trampoline, squalling into this world, and however persuasive the illusion of freedom, we remain tethered to tissues other than our own.

At the behest of family and in accordance with its obligatory rituals, Tom and Afton Lance took the train from the St. Elmo station in August 1914 and rode night and day to Sugarville, Idaho, to bury Tom's younger brother, Willie, and to bring Willie's widow and her two children back to St. Elmo with them.

Willie Lance's widow was the former Lil Douglass, who had married him in 1911 and who, thirty-four months and two children later, found herself with no certainties except grief and family. She had met Willie Lance when he stopped off in St. Elmo, California, on his way back to Idaho after serving a two-year mission for the Saints in New Zealand. He had a fiancée in Idaho.

That is, he had a fiancée until Afton Lance took things in her capable hands and introduced her sister Lil to her brother-in-law Willie. Willie traveled on to Idaho, but he broke off his engagement.

He returned to St. Elmo to claim the sixteen-year-old Lil for his bride if she would have him.

She would have him. She'd made up her mind to that. She was determined to have him. She would have eloped if it had been necessary, but it wasn't. Ruth agreed to the marriage, though Lil was not yet out of high school. If Lil was surprised at her mother's acquiescence, Afton was downright undone, considering the struggle she'd faced for her own marriage. Ruth agreed to Lil's marriage, because her own obstinacy and hypocrisy had pushed her eldest daughter into flight and the arms of death, and she could not, would not, endure any more lost daughters, and if Lil was determined to marry Willie Lance, then, "Marry him," said Ruth, "if that's all you want out of life."

"That's all I want," Lil replied. "To be Willie Lance's wife."

So now she was Willie Lance's widow and the mother of his two children. Afton kept her arm around Lil's shoulders or held her hand all the way back to St. Elmo as they listened to the percussive whisper of the train's wheels Willie Willie Willie oh Willie I get so Willie Willie Willie . . .

"It'll suit you at Mother's, Lil," said Afton. "You'll see."

"Nothing will ever suit me again," said Lil. "I'll live, I expect, but nothing will ever suit me again."

Ruth met them at the St. Elmo station, dressed in her own usual widow's garb. Black was not as becoming to Lil. Lil still smelled of the dye tub, and she was tiny and frail and rumpled-looking, but then there are few nineteen-year-olds on whom widowhood is becoming.

Ruth had a new car, a Locomobile she had bought from the Pattersons. She drove her children and her two granddaughters back to the Douglass home on Silk Stocking Row, a huge, yellow, high-ceilinged, broad-porched, and stiff-gabled affair with thick moldings and high cornices. "There's only Mason and Cissa living here, Lil," Ruth explained, "so there's plenty of room for you and Jean and Rebecca."

Lil had spent her married life in a three-room company house in a sugar-factory town, so her mother's home seemed to her palatial, but a hell nonetheless. She was alone, after all, and without Willie, heaven itself would seem a hell.

Ruth Douglass had bought that house (like many another shrewd

Saint, all the rest of them male) when property was cheap in St. Elmo after the flood. What the flood did not destroy of the old central district, the building of New Town did. The Ferris Hotel refused to move northward with the rest of the town, and eventually it closed its doors. The doors of the new Pilgrim were beveled glass with long-necked lilies and voluptuous (albeit decorously draped) maidens engraved in them. The doors were made of mahogany, and they opened into a carpeted dining room that no longer catered to railroad men and commercial travelers. The Pilgrim's clientele now came from the refined ranks of St. Elmo society: ladies in wide hats and gentlemen with starched fronts frequented the Pilgrim, bishops and bank presidents, and their wives and daughters, awaited their luncheons and dinners at the Pilgrim, where Ruth no longer did the cooking, only kept the accounts and sat in the outer lobby behind the cash box, which registered her success with comforting regularity.

The only matron of any social standing who refused to patronize the Pilgrim was Mrs. Lloyd Whickham, formerly Miss Arlene McClure, who had not spoken to any of the Douglasses since the cryptic telegram arrived that said only: "Please forgive me." It was delivered to the library. Clutching the telegram in her small, fat hand, Arlene went directly to Afton's. "Forgive him for what?"

Three months later she married Lloyd Whickham, and a more baleful bride St. Elmo had never seen.

Ruth felt sorry for Arlene, but she felt sorrier for Gideon, if what Albert said was true. Albert never lied about anything that wasn't costing him money. And in some ways, Ruth reflected with a bitter twinge, she herself had taken her cue from Albert and men of his ilk and had begun asking herself, "What profiteth it?"—the question by which men advanced themselves in this world, and if the Mormons were right, very likely in the next world as well. In answering this question satisfactorily, Ruth, who was always shrewd, became prosperous as well. She hired a Chinese couple to do the cooking at the Pilgrim, and they in turn provided her with a steady stream of reliable help—all of it family. (The Mormons, after all, were not the only ones who believed in the ancestral bond.) The headwaiter had learned his English in a mission school in China, and the other waiters knew "please," "thank you," and the items on the menu, and all the rest of the time they spoke in Chinese. This made some of the Pilgrim's patrons uncomfortable, and it was said in St. Elmo that at the Pilgrim, the help was heathen and the owner was godless.

They deemed her godless because in the three years since Eden's death, the Widow Douglass had not set foot in church. This was especially embarrassing for Afton, who, young as she was, was a leader in the Relief Society, directed the genealogy group, and taught Sunday school and the children's primary. Afton fired every gun in her arsenal of guilt to persuade her mother to return to the church, but her unbelieving mother refused. Afton wondered if her mother had caught atheism from the doctor, rather like the mumps.

The Widow Douglass was too successful to be snubbed and too aloof to be cultivated, but the Saints claimed her anyway in their ongoing struggle with the Methodists for civic superiority. They did not, after 1916, claim, nor wish to be in any way associated with, her youngest daughter, Cissa, who in that year had her hair bobbed in the New Town Hotel Barber Parlor. The barber told Cissa she was the third lady in St. Elmo to have her hair bobbed. He did not tell her that the other two worked at the cathouse.

At sixteen, Cissa first budded and then bloomed, burst out of her prim, girlish frocks like a lilac bush in May. The lilac may be a woody, angular shrub of no particular distinction for eleven months of the year, but in May it reeks of fleeting, cosmic glory that can perhaps be forgotten, but not denied. When the lilac in Cissa burst forth on what was once the woody shrub of her body, Afton admonished her severely for her manner of walking and talking and smiling at men, but Cissa maintained she didn't know what Afton was talking about.

But if Cissa didn't know, every man in town older than twelve and younger than seventy did. Cissa, formerly of the hand-me-down clothes, knobby elbows, and pigeon-pointed feet, was nothing short of a lit fuse, and everyone in St. Elmo wondered when she would explode. And with whom.

But when the Douglasses next outraged St. Elmo, it wasn't Cissa at all, but Mason. By way of contrast with his headstrong sisters, Mason seemed such an indolent boy, overweight and sluggish in school. Possibly because of this, Ruth urged Norton Goodlove to hire Mason part-time while he was still in high school. The stock at Goodlove's Dry Goods was confined primarily to foodstuffs and materials for the home, and its clientele was predominantly female. Mason stocked the shelves and did general cleanup at Goodlove's. He was not happy behind the broom, or kneeling in front of it either, for that matter. He thought it beneath his dignity to sweep up other people's dirt, but he was good and sober and surprisingly industrious. His industry was rewarded in 1916 when Brother Goodlove suffered a stroke and couldn't even come into the store, much less run it. The daily operations of Goodlove's fell more and more to Mason, and soon the job had compensations that Goodlove would not have dreamed of. Nor anyone else.

The women who frequented Goodlove's commented among themselves that Mason was such a nice, friendly young man, meticulous and helpful, and that of all the Douglasses, Mason would be the one to amount to something. He might have. Indeed, he might have amounted to much more than the manipulative petty larcenist he became, except that he was avaricious, congenitally opposed to work, and habitually given to lies, and he stole. He was never, at least not in St. Elmo, indicted for theft. The tale of his malfeasance percolated only in a subterranean fashion through the city, because if Mason had been generally known for a thief, then people he'd victimized would have been generally known for fools.

Mason took a brand-new broom, the most expensive, exclusive broom, the two-dollar variety, and leaned it casually against the shelf next to the cash register at Goodlove's. Bristles down, unobtrusive, ready to go to work. The broom lounged there like an onlooker while Mason, who had a pleasant way with the customers (the weather, the thoughtlessness of automobile drivers, the newest thing in furniture polish—he had quite a repertoire), rang up their goods and wrote their receipts. He added two dollars for the broom. Few customers took the receipt, and only a rare one checked it. In the unlikely instance that the individual noticed the extra two dollars, Mason studied the receipt, his brows dived over his nose, he checked the goods back against it, and he said: "Isn't this your broom?" And when the customer said no, he apologized handsomely and returned the two dollars.

Mason carefully spaced the number of times he used the Old Broom Trick on Goodlove's regular customers. He enjoyed selling it five times to his Aunt Lily Whickham and twice to the former Arlene McClure. He grew so adept that he could measure a potential

232

broom customer from his (or her) demeanor. Every stranger and all male customers bought the broom. Anyone who sent her maid or a child in to do the shopping was bound to be the proud possessor of the fictitious broom. People in a hurry bought the broom. In a year and a half that broom could have bought half a motorcar or kept Mason in spats for the rest of his life. That broom made its phantom way into well-fixed households all over the city, and the profit made its not-so-phantom way into Mason's pockets.

Modest avarice is one thing, but Mason became the victim of galloping greed and sold that broom once too often. At least once too often to Thelma Eubank, who was sister-in-law to Brother Goodlove's niece, Marinda. Mrs. Eubank checked her receipt and complained. Mason checked her goods and said he thought the broom was hers.

"I don't know how you could think that," said Mrs. Eubank. "That broom's been there as long as I can remember."

An older and wiser man would have put the broom away, but Mason only resolved never to sell it to Mrs. Eubank again. (She'd already bought it half a dozen times.)

Sister Eubank mentioned to Marinda Goodlove that the broom always did seem to be in the same place and never to have seen any active service. The two ladies sent their nephew, little Madison W. Eubank, into the store with a list and ordered him to get a receipt. Maddy bought the broom. The two ladies with Maddy in tow made their way straight to Brother Goodlove's house, without regard for his delicate health or his doctor's instructions that he was not to be upset.

Brother Goodlove, stammering, incoherent, blithering with rage, telephoned Mason at the store and told him to come by the house after he closed the store.

Mason was not stupid. He closed the door on the last customer and eyeballed the broom. He put the broom back with the others, opened the till, and helped himself to thirty dollars severance pay, a handful of peppermint candy, a jar of Italian hair dressing, and a new buttonhook; he took off his apron and sleeves and left them on the floor. He wrote "I quit" in bold letters and left the note in the cash drawer. He locked the store, shoving the key under the door.

On the way home he debated telling his mother that Goodlove had fired him unjustly, but Ruth hated injustice and would insist he fight it. So instead he said over his reheated supper, "I quit Good-love's." He said it casually, surveying the evening paper that lay on the kitchen table beside him.

Ruth turned off the tap. "You did what?"

"I quit Goodlove's," he repeated, staring at the screaming head-lines.

"Why?"

Mason wiped his mouth, never taking his eyes off the newspaper, and then he looked at his mother and declared: "I couldn't go on working there, putting money in the till. Let old man Goodlove put his own filthy lucre in his own filthy till! Look at that." He pointed with his buttery knife to the headline. "How can any real man put on an apron in 1917? The whole world is falling to pieces. The Huns have raped Belgium and France! The Limeys and the Frogs are over there defending us! Yes, us! Do you think for one minute that Kaiser Bill will stop at the Atlantic? Not on your life. What are we doing sitting around like a bunch of ducks letting civilization fall under the bootheel of the Huns? War's a man's business, not storetending. You can keep the home fires burning—I'm packing up my old kit bag, and if the army won't send me over there to hang the Kaiser from a sour apple tree, then I'll go by myself!"

The force of Mason's speech was considerably diminished because he had an unpleasant, squawky, high-pitched voice. But he de-clared himself manfully, adopted an all-new military bearing, and marched to his room to pack for his induction into the United States Army, which at that time was in a state of preparedness.

So Mason was training in Plattsburgh, New York, and not at home in the early summer of 1917 when Gideon and his wife and their baby son, Samuel Gideon, also known as Toots, returned to St. Elmo for a visit.

Contrary to Kitty's dire predictions, little Samuel did not make his appearance in this world eight months after his parents' mar-riage. In that first year Kitty's figure thickened only with three meals a day, chocolates, and cheap novels, which she indulged in despite the accumulated mounds of laundry, dishes, and dust, and her husband's despair.

But when the baby did arrive, Kitty gave up cheap novels mo-mentarily and indulged herself in an orgy of contentment. She never tired of studying his little face, gestures, and expressions,

234

stroking his perfect hands; she was proud and possessive of Tootsie, who depended on her exclusively, even as he had in the womb, for sustenance and warmth. Her milk flowed at the mere thought of him, and she lived in a kind of ecstatic union with her son. She was all body and baby—feeding, changing, tending, kissing, stroking, holding the baby's body that had emerged from hers and that responded to her hands, her voice, her breast—all the links of blood and love.

By the time he came to St. Elmo, Toots Douglass could walk and talk like most three-year-olds, but he could also execute a dance routine Kitty had taught him and warble alongside his mother, "Hello, my baby, hello, my honey, hello, my ragtime gal!" Kitty and Tootsie had an act, which they performed for the assembled Douglasses that first night in the parlor.

Lucius Tipton applauded, and the others followed halfhearted suit.

Kitty wiped her face with the hem of her skirt. "Don't my boy have talent, Doctor? He gets it all from me, you know. My family back in jolly old England, we was all thee-atrical as we could be. I was known as the Lark of Liverpool before I became a Saint. I broke the hearts of the North of England when I give up my career for my religion. They was down at the dock weeping when I left Liverpool. But I may go back to the stage—Tootsie and me—'The Dancing Douglasses'! What do you think, Doctor?"

"It has a nice ring to it," said Lucius, sneaking a glance at Ruth, whose face was embroidered with chagrin.

Kitty swooped the little boy up in her arms, nuzzled his neck, and nibbled his ears till he screamed with delight. "Oh, duckie! You are just a pip! Toots looks just like me, don't you think, Doctor? Look at that curly red hair and those green eyes. And he has my own dear papá's nose. Roman, I think they call it. Don't that sound great? Tootsie's lucky he looks like me. I mighta known Gideon'd have a sallow family. Not—" She cast an appraising glance at her mother- and sister-in-law. "Not that I don't think the Douglasses are nice-looking and all that, but Tootsie, he has the complexion of an English rose. Just like me. Don't you, duckie?"

Tootsie beamed.

"Breeding will tell, that's what my dear mamá would say, be-

235

fore she joined the heavenly chorus line. You can put a swan in harness, but that don't make him a mule. Mamá never said that," Kitty hastened to add, "that's what I told Gideon—don't you worry, duck, you are still a swan, even if you are in harness to that loathsome"—she rolled the word out with special relish—"worm, Albert Mason. I told Gideon, Albert Mason is so tight he'd skin a louse for its hide, and what does Albert care that me and Gideon are living in a chamberpot while Albert has a heavenly mansion? I told Gideon—you're lucky, duck, lucky that Albert fired you from that job in that drafty basement. Why, Gideon wheezed all winter. Albert don't heat the basement, and you can just tell that—"

"Albert fired you, Gideon?" said Ruth, still grim and reeling from the shock of her daughter-in-law; Kitty was flighty and vulgar, but Gideon was stuck with her. And now Ruth feared she might be as well. "I thought you said Albert gave you a short holiday."

"A long holiday." Gideon stared at the squares in the carpet, inwardly counting them up. "Albert said I didn't have no gift for the insurance business."

"But how dare he fire you!"

"Albert said there wasn't nothing you could do to him. He said to tell you that."

"Albert is a low buggering toad," Kitty announced. "Gideon's worked his noogies off for Albert for years, and that's the thanks he gets."

Lil paled and Afton flushed and Cissa burst into laughter, till Ruth told her in no uncertain terms to shut up.

"The house," Gideon continued, studying his hairy knuckles, "the house was Albert's, too, and I couldn't pay the rent no more. We sold everything we could." Gideon had big hands, like his father—but Gideon's were long and white and ink-stained.

"Oh, it broke my heart to sell that Victrola! Me and Toots, we loved that Victrola, didn't we, duck?" Kitty bounced Toots on her knee till he squirmed away. "I'd rather part with my drawers than that Victrola, but I told Gideon it don't matter and not to worry. I got all them songs right up here." She pointed to her bright, high nest of coppery hair. "Want to hear me and Toots do 'My Gal Sal'?"

"Not just now, Kitty," Lucius said. "I think we'd better talk about what Gideon's going to do, don't you think so, Ruth?"

Ruth had ossified with rage and outrage, but Afton jumped up and nudged Lil. "Me and Lil will bring some cake. How about some nice cake all around? Cissa, you come help."

"No." Cissa had an eye for the dramatic; she wasn't going to miss this.

Gideon took off his glasses and put them in his pocket. Without them, he could not see the squares in the carpet and the faces around him were a blur; it was easier to admit to failure if you didn't have to see it reflected in people's eyes. "I done the best I could, Mother," he began. "Uncle Albert said I was a sucker for any old widow or orphan, so last year he moved me to the morgue—that's where they keep the files of dead policies and dead people and lost property. There wasn't nothing to do down there, so I brought my books to work with me, and then, pretty soon, I brought the charts."

"What charts?"

"My Great Timetable. I got it calculated now, one hundred years for every inch and seven-eighths."

"Good Lord, Gideon! You're not still doing that, are you?"

Surprise lit his face. "Why, of course. Once I lay it all out, neat and even, then I can start to make sense of the past. I can show how the universal principles work themselves out in particular historical moments, and I can show the relationship of Joseph Smith's revelations to—"

"Please." Ruth looked bilious. "Just tell me what Albert said."

Gideon sank back against the fringed cushions. "I never reckoned Albert to come down to the morgue. It wasn't heated, like Kitty said, and I never did see him, but one day he had some visitors, some men from New York, and they must have wanted to see the files. So he brung them down, and there he sees me with my charts tacked to the walls and my books and . . ." His voice dribbled off.

"What did Albert say?" Ruth's mouth twisted into a fishhook grin.

"He fired me next day." Gideon put his glasses back on and looked to Lucius. "I done what I could after that. I was helping out a builder for a while, doing carpentry work, but my eyes ain't what

237

they used to be, and I cut myself pretty bad, and the builder said he had to fire me, too. Because of the insurance. I guess everybody's got insurance nowadays."

"Everyone but us," said Kitty, glum for the first time since she'd arrived. Tootsie ran out to the kitchen to play with his cousins, Lil's and Afton's children, and with Tootsie gone, the parlor darkened, the clock ticked painfully in the corner, and the high school portrait of Eden hanging on the wall was steeped in shadow. Kitty hummed the sad refrain from "After the Ball Is Over" and discreetly scratched her armpit.

"Well, Gideon," Ruth said presently, "we'll find something for you. You did the right thing to come back here."

"There was no place else."

"Yes. Well, we'll find something for you and your family."

"Maybe we could live here with you," Kitty offered, having appraised the Douglass home as slightly less grand than Albert Mason's but entirely acceptable nonetheless.

"I don't think that would be wise," Ruth said evenly. "I don't think that would do, do you, Lucius?" She turned to him for corroboration.

Doctor quickly lit a cigar, and behind the fragrant cloud of smoke an unchastened smile tugged at his lips. "You're right, Ruth, of course. It probably wouldn't do." He puffed so hard he was all but invisible behind the smoke. "But it would be interesting. It could be very interesting from now on."

Lucius liked Kitty. He was the only one of the family who did. Afton could barely tolerate Kitty's overpowering soprano in church, much less her insistence on telling anyone who asked, and some who didn't, that she was once the Lark of Liverpool and had only given up the stage to marry the man of her dreams and be mother to little Tootsie. And because Afton was disapproving, Lil was, too.

It didn't much matter what Cissa thought of Kitty, because within six weeks of Gideon's return to St. Elmo, Cissa ran off with a young man who had come to town to buy irrigation equipment for his family's ranch in southern Utah. He squandered every nickel of the money he'd been entrusted with on a ten-day honeymoon in San Francisco with Narcissa Douglass, now Mrs. Zeniff Blankenship.

238

Ruth took to her bed for two days, and the family hovered over her with cold compresses and hot bouillon and as much comfort as they could offer when a seventeen-year-old girl runs off with a man she's known four days, five if you count the day they ran off.

Ruth had recovered some ten days later when the new Mrs. Blankenship and her husband stopped in St. Elmo to accept the congratulations—or condolences—of the bride's family before they returned to the Blankenship ranch. Ruth gave them a wedding breakfast at the Pilgrim and flinched visibly when young Zen called her "Mother Douglass."

Cissa's once-bobbed hair still did not quite cover her neck by the time she boarded the train to go to her new life in the bosom of her husband's family. Her mother kissed her goodbye at the station and told her to keep her hat on.

"Why?" said the bright-eyed bride.

"Because when his family gets a look at that short hair of yours, they're going to come after you like a prize hog on slaughtering day, miss."

"Mrs.," Cissa corrected her.

"You made your bed," said Ruth, undaunted by Cissa's impudence, "now you'll have to lie in it."

Cissa blushed, thinking no doubt of the beds she and Zen had already lain in, at the San Francisco hotel and, what was even more fun, in her own virginal chamber at her mother's house. She was married, of course, so it wasn't sin. But it certainly felt as delicious as sin, and Cissa almost wished it were.

By the time Cissa departed for southern Utah, Gideon had a job working for W. C. Early: Insurance with Assurance. Early was a Methodist, but he admired the Widow Douglass and hired Gideon because he thought if her son was half as shrewd as the Widow Douglass, he'd be getting a bargain.

Gideon was not half as shrewd, but he was diligent and painstaking. He promised his mother no books or charts. At least not at work. After work, Gideon walked to the St. Elmo Public Library and renewed his borrowing privileges. The girl behind the desk did not know him. She wrote him out a new card. He took his card and went among the stacks, and there he took off his glasses and wept quietly, thinking of the beautiful Arlene, their shared love of books and learning. Their shared love. He and Arlene had often held hands in the stacks. They'd even kissed.

His vision of Arlene did not dim when he saw her at church on Sunday. She was a stout matron with bad eyes and a shrill voice, mother to three pudding-plain children and wife to Brother Lloyd Whickham. She was still beautiful to Gideon's bad eyes. She was so beautiful, Gideon wanted to take off his glasses, but he couldn't. Neither could he speak. Neither could she. They passed each other like strangers.

Directly after church that Sunday, Mrs. Lloyd Whickham went home and threw herself on the bed and wept for an hour. Her husband glowered to see her. "Dinner needs fixing, and the children need looking after. There's work to be done, and you can't waste your time crying."

"I love you!" Arlene cried as she clutched her husband's arm and pulled him down on the bed, "I love you! I love you!"

Mr. Lloyd Whickham freed himself from her grasp and left the room, and presently Mrs. Lloyd Whickham righted herself, cleaned her thick glasses, tidied her neat bun, and betook herself to the kitchen and her domestic and maternal duties.

After church that Sunday, Gideon Douglass did not protest his undying love to his wife. He and his wife and son returned to the new house on S Street that his mother had rented for him. Gideon wrapped himself in a caul of paper and ink, and barricaded himself at the desk in his bedroom, where his long charts were tacked to the wall like ink-stained banners left behind on a battlefield. The charts rustled in the dry desert wind, and Gideon, with his face to the window and his back to the bed, sat at the desk and applied himself to the Great Timetable, which, to his mind, was the fruit of his faith in the Church of Jesus Christ of Latter-day Saints and fitting enterprise for the valedictorian of the class of 1910. On paper six feet long and eighteen inches wide he laid out three parallel columns, one for Biblical history, one for secular history, and one for Mormon history, beginning with the whole tableau described in the Book of Mormon: the tribes on the North American continent and Christ's appearance before them, and culminating in the battle of Cummorrah, where the tribes wiped themselves out. Mormon history did not start again until many inches down the chart, when the Restored Gospel was given unto Joseph Smith.

Gideon's defenses against life in general and Kitty in particular were manned with calipers and compasses and rulers and ribbons of paper, a whole armada of colored inks, and an army of sharpened pencils. He was safe here, as he saw it, and if every week he was to bleed a little in the Church of Jesus Christ of Latter-day Saints when he beheld Mrs. Lloyd Whickham, he told himself the pain would pass in the fullness of time.

In the meantime he had his library card and his Great Timetable. He had access to Lucius Tipton's library, which he had once scorned for inclusion of Voltaire, Rousseau, and Darwin. He had Doctor's company, Doctor's sense of history, Doctor's vision, all of which he relished more than he would have thought possible, given Gideon's adherence to the Mormon church and Doctor's adherence to the irreverent.

It was the doctor's admiration for the irreverent that drew him to Kitty. Gideon was glad someone liked her, because she took no pains to endear herself, not to the family, not to the church, not to St. Elmo itself. She was, in fact, the horror of the neighborhood, because she marshaled her leftovers between crusts and referred to the dish as Resurrection Pie, and besides, she hung her drawers upside down, inside out, and spread-eagled on the clothesline.

Besides the clothesline, at the back of Gideon's house (which had electricity and hot and cold running water) there was a cottonwood tree and a flowering peach. The church matrons volunteered to help Kitty put up her peaches, and she thanked them and vowed to think about it, and Gideon remarked it would be real nice to have preserved peaches in the winter. But the peaches were never trotted into jars or herded into compotes. Kitty plucked them, raw and rosy from the tree, ate them till the very thought of a peach was enough to make her puke, and then let the rest rot.

Till the day he died, Gideon Douglass remembered the summer of 1918 for its peaches and its promise. The Great War looked as if it might at last be coming to a close; his Great Timetable began to assume a pleasing density of event and structure; he had a plump, exuberant wife and a handsome son, and the world took on the rosy hue of the kingdom of peaches in his backyard. Ever after, with the clarity we ascribe to irrevocable loss, he remembered a hot August day when he returned from Insurance with Assurance to find Kitty in the backyard, lying beneath the peach tree, barefoot and shirtless, her white blouse hanging from a branch like a flag of truce, her hair a burnished wake across the grass, her skin tinting pink, her arm outflung. The half-naked Toots sat beside his mother, splattered with peach meat. Grass stained his drawers, and bees encircled his head; they must have thought him an enormous, ambulating flower. Around them both, fallen fruit rotted into the earth and flies droned. Kitty waved them away, aimlessly singing a tune from her music-hall days.

Gideon's first thought was to yank his son and half-clad wife inside, but he stepped back into the house instead, closing the screen door quietly behind him. Easier to pretend he hadn't seen. He retreated to the bedroom and stood over the desk and the latest timetable, compiled as far as the Punic Wars. From the window he watched Kitty bite into a peach; the juices ran down her mouth into her hair. She flung away what she did not want and went on singing "Piccadilly John with His Little Glass Eye."

Gideon laid his pencils more perfectly parallel and permitted himself a moment of doubt. Perhaps there was something random, crazy, about the begetting and begatting, about history itself, something the Timetable would not be able to express and the Bible didn't explain and the Book of Mormon didn't address itself to. It was only a moment of doubt. He pulled the curtains so he could not see the peach tree. He would never again suggest to Kitty that she preserve from one summer to the next what was clearly to be relished in a single golden moment.

31

TOOTSIE DIED. HE caught the Spanish influenza in the winter of 1919, and then pneumonia, and then he died. They buried him in the St. Elmo cemetery not too far from Eden Douglass REGRET.

Lucius did what he could for Kitty, but her grief was wild and obscene and ongoing, and short of addicting her to morphine, Lucius was powerless before her sorrow.

Three more children were born to Kitty and Gideon Douglass— Eden Louise in 1920 and Ada Ruth in 1922 and Ernest Fred in 1925—but she did not give them pet names, and she did not teach them to sing and dance; much of the time she scarcely noticed their existence. She tended them nonchalantly, with alternating bursts of affection and neglect, as if Kitty's capacity for passion had all been spent in an orgy of love and grief with Toots. She gave up all pretense of Sainthood: let the house go completely to hell, read novels in bed till noon, went to the pictures as often as she could. She took up recreational drinking. She got her gin from Nana Bowers's grandson, who had inherited the elixir business from his grandmother and now supplied St. Elmo with illegal tonics.

Gideon preferred not to notice. He refused the counsel of his mother and his sister Afton. He refused to heed the advice of the Mormon elders and the ward teachers who made monthly calls at each Saint's home. Sometimes they came more frequently than that to Gideon's, because the little home on S Street was a troubled one.

Gideon took the same route every day after work from Insurance with Assurance to the St. Elmo Public Library, where he stayed until the library closed or hunger drove him home. He seldom noticed any of the library's other patrons—though he never quite gave up hoping he might one day see Arlene in the stacks again—and he might not have noticed the old man at his table at all, except the old man was dressed in workingman's clothes and a cap he never removed in the holy precincts of the library. Even with his weak eyes, Gideon could tell the old man looked down every time Gideon looked up. And then Gideon noticed the old man's book was upside down, and then he saw the old man was Fred. The old man pulled his cap over his face and dived into his book.

"Fred? Is it you?" Gideon smelled licorice, and the old man began to cry.

"Never could fool you, could I, Gideon?" He wiped his nose on his sleeve and beamed at his nephew. "You always was a smart one." Fred stood up slowly and embraced Gideon. The bear of a man he had once been had not shrunk, only stooped and loosened. His beard spread like lichen on the tough bark of his face, and he still had the big hands, the long mouth, and the bad vision that were the mark of the Douglass men in general and the blue-eyed kindness that was the mark of Fred Douglass in particular.

"Well, it's good to see you, Gideon, and I can see you're all right, and I don't want to be a burden or a trouble, so I'll be getting along."

Gideon wouldn't hear of it. He insisted on taking Fred home with him. They went through the back gate and sidestepped the peaches, which lay like deflated croquet balls, because it was August again and these were the peaches of 1924 that would never be preserved. Gideon and Fred avoided the garbage bags that lined up at the back door like recruits until they eventually fell over. Gideon ushered Fred into the battlefield of his home: broken toys, open books, dirty dishes, unwashed laundry, unwiped spills, undusted furniture, unopened bills, unmended clothing, unbeaten rugs, unscrubbed pots, unswept floors, unused mops, mismatched socks, misplaced papers—all the carnage of two people equally mismated and ill-fated and bound together forever.

"Well, Gideon, this is real nice. I always knew you'd have a real nice house one day."

"I guess Kitty's at the pictures. I'll call Afton. And Mother! She'll be so happy to see you!"

"Oh, no, Gideon. Don't do that, Gideon. No, not just yet. I can't take too much excitement. The old ticker, don't you know. How is Sister Ruth?"

"Mother's the same as ever. She's got the finest restaurant down-town, and she works sunup to sundown."

"I mighta knowed Sister Ruth wouldn't put her burdens down for nothing.

"And the rest of the family, Gideon, did they all do good as you? Growed up now, everyone is."

Growed up, yes, but not everyone. "You didn't know about Eden, did you? Eden drowned."

"Eden, dead?"

"Yes, years ago. Drowned in a flood." He hadn't expected it would pain him still to say it.

"Not Eden! No."

"Look lively, Eden!" Kitty called from the porch. "And you, Ada, get out of those peaches. Get out, I tell you!" Kitty and the two girls burst into the kitchen and bathed Fred in the commotion of intro-ductions and explanations, and Fred grinned as he jiggled Ada on his knee and pulled licorice from Eden Louise's ears.

"Hotter'n hell's half acre today," said Kitty. She removed her silk stockings carefully, hung them on a towel rack, and peered into the icebox, looking for something that would pass for supper.

"Is there anything I can do, Kitty?" Fred asked, looking up from the children. "In the old days there'd be wood to chop and water to haul, but nowadays there don't seem to be nothing to do. There's still no rest for the weary and the wicked, though."

Kitty remarked that if that were so, three-quarters of the world would find themselves working their noogies off instead of sitting around country clubs sipping forbidden cocktails. Fred sucked con-tentedly on his teeth. "I always knew you'd marry a looker, Gid-eon," he said, "but you are a luckier man than most."

"Well, that's just about the nicest supper I ever et," said Fred, scraping his plate and licking his fork. "The nicest one since I left Sister Ruth's table. Yes, I don't believe I've ever et so good as I did at your mother's house, Gideon. There wasn't nothing she couldn't do, your mother."

"I'm going to telephone Mother and tell her you're here, Fred. She'll want to come see you."

"No, Gideon, no, don't do that. I'll see her. Why, I got days just to spend in St. Elmo. Days. And I'll see her. It's just I look up Doug-

245

lass everywhere I go these days in the city directories, and there you was, Gideon, there you was. I been here a few days already. I've seen your mother. She ain't seen me. Don't think she'd want to. I'm pretty dusty for someone like her. She's still a looker, your mother."

"Of course she'd want to see you, Fred. Think of all those years."

"That's what I'm thinking of, Gideon, and I'll see her. I just need some time." The children bolted outside to play in the long summer twilight, and their voices and a chorus of insects drifted in. Fred cleared his throat. "Well, Gideon, I guess you are still a Latter-day Saint."

"Didn't Gideon show you his eight-foot Timetable of the whole bleedin' world? Who but a bleedin' Mormon would think of that?" Kitty threw the plates in the sink as she spoke.

"I always said Gideon was a smart one, and I always knew he'd be somebody. That Timetable is really something, Gideon."

"Well, it ought to be. He don't go to sleep but he kisses the lost tribes goodnight and ignores his own wife."

"I only asked after the church," Fred stammered, "because I don't want to offend you or nothing. I'm still a Saint in the spirit, and God will remember that when the Last Reckoning comes along, but the flesh—you know what they say about the flesh, Gideon, about its being weak. Well, I have started smoking these here cigars, and well, a man alone, he has to have something, but I'll go outside for my smoke anyway."

Kitty smiled. "You stay right there, Fred, and I'll have a smoke with you." She whisked out to find the cigarette stash.

Fred's jaw dropped. "Well, I guess women do all kinds of things they didn't used to, don't they, Gideon? Well, I guess they just light right up like a man, and there's no place says a woman can't smoke but a man can. No place I know of." He drew out his cigar and struck the match to his boot. "Don't you never take it up, Gideon. Not that you would. You wouldn't need to, not with a fine family like you got. Not with those fine children."

"You ever have any children, Fred?"

"No, I guess the old genealogical tables will look pretty bare when it comes to old Fred Douglass. There won't be no Fred begot so and so on the records in heaven, and I hope God don't hold it against me." He dropped his ash into his coat pocket. "Too bad me and Velda didn't have no children. She was a good-looking girl, that

246

Velda, too good-looking, some might say, but I been thinking the last few years, and you know, I mighta been too hard on Velda. Maybe I shouldn't have hit her around like that. Maybe I shoulda asked her what she was doing in bed with that fellow before I beat him up." He studied his cigar. "Well, that's the past, ain't it, and can't be changed."

"Some things change," Gideon said gently. "You talk more than you used to."

Fred fastened his weak eyes on his nephew. "Well, Samuel, he talked, and Ruth talked, and all you children talked, so there wasn't no reason back then for me to talk, not when I had all those people to listen to. But a man by hisself, well, you got to listen to someone, don't you? I guess I been doing more talking since then. Mostly to myself."

"What about your second wife? Didn't you talk to her?"

"Mavis?" Fred rolled out clouds of smoke. "Well, Mavis died, and she probably got into heaven with her first husband. She was a good woman in her way, but I'm glad I don't have to do eternity with Mavis."

"What about Velda?" Gideon chided him.

"Well, Velda. I guess if she's forgived me, I've forgived her. But I didn't come here to talk about the dead. Awful word, dead. But better'n passed on, don't you think? When Mavis died, the elder just kept saying how she'd passed on, like she'd graduated from high school or something." He made a face. "Afton's married, you say, and—"

"Afton Lance would make the devil dust off his feet before she'd let him walk into hell," said Kitty, entering with a cigarette perched on her lower lip.

"That's not fair," Gideon growled.

"Afton must be like Sister Ruth," Fred offered as a truce. "Sister Ruth didn't give you no choice but to abide by her, and she was usually right anyway. What about Lil—pretty little Lil?"

"Lil's had some hard luck," Gideon said. "She's married again, a fine man, but she's never been too well since her first husband died."

"Never was too well to begin with, poor little thing." Fred clucked. "And Mason?"

"Mason," Kitty announced, "makes his own shit pay a toll to get out."

"Kitty, stop it! I don't like it!"

"I don't like bunions either, but I got them. Mason's nothing but snail snot. Mason come home from the war like he won it himself, and then he didn't do nothing but sit around the Pilgrim and get fat. Mason wanted to be a mining engineer, but the only thing he's good at is mining other people's pockets. Mason's gone to Washington with the St. Elmo congressman, and you can just bet he's busy there, picking pockets." She flung her cigarette into the sink. "You want some music, Fred?" She left them to wind up the Victrola. "Mason's no good. Mason or Cissa either."

"Is Cissa Mason's wife?" Fred asked feebly; he did hate a quarrel.

"No." Gideon cleaned his glasses. Of course, Fred couldn't know. Cissa's life had not begun till Father's ended: the End of Father had been the Beginning of Cissa. "Cissa was born after we got to St. Elmo."

Under his beard, Fred blanched. "You mean, Sister Ruth had another little one after—another little one?"

"Yes, Narcissa's her name, but we call her—"

"Cissa's poor husband don't deserve her." Kitty waltzed back in to the tune of "Pay Day Blues." "Blankenship worked Cissa like a mule, and now she's working Swenson the same way. Poor buggering pan salesman, he didn't know what he was getting when he run off with Cissa. Wouldn't surprise me if Cissa's getting tired of him, got other things up her sleeve, and yes, up her skirt, too."

"That's enough!" Gideon brought his fist down on the table, and the forks jumped. "I won't hear any more. I'm sick of the way you hate my family."

"Why, Gideon, you'll give Fred here the wrong idea. I don't hate the Douglasses, Fred. Why, me and Afton's just like sisters when she isn't buttin' into my life and—"

"Stop it! Don't say another word!"

Kitty's lower lip swelled, and her eyes filled with tears, and she ran into the living room, where the record rasped and hissed on an endless circle.

Fred squeezed his big hands in his lap, staring at the linoleum. "You done real well, Gideon. I always knew you was smart, and you done real well. Well, I better get my hat and go. You thank your wife for that fine supper."

"You can't go, Fred."

"I got to. I got a room at the hotel by the station, and I got to be on that train first thing in the morning. Dawn, in fact."

"I thought you were staying for days."

"Did I say that?"

"What about seeing Mother?"

"Well, I'll be back. I'm always moving around, and now I know you're here. You're all here. I'll be back, but I got this job in Arizona, and if I don't get there, they'll give it away."

"What kind of job?"

"Same kind I always done, anything that would pay and some that wouldn't. I just wanted to see you, Gideon, see how you was doing, and you're doing fine."

"Was it awful?" Gideon gathered up his courage. "Father's death, was it awful?"

Fred popped a licorice bit and sucked it while his eyes grew wide. "Samuel's death? Awful? Well, I reckon death is always awful, Gideon. I got to get now, Gideon. That train leaves at—"

"Mother won't talk about it. Never. But maybe you could tell me. You buried him."

"Holy frijole," Fred muttered.

"I know it's hard, but if you could just tell me what happened—"

Fred studied his boots as if they were today's paper. "Well, there's not much to tell, Gideon. Death's death, and it don't take no for an answer."

"But the fire? How did the house burn down? Why didn't Father escape?"

"Fire?" Fred swallowed his licorice whole. "I got to go, Gideon. The train waits for no man."

Her eyes wiped and face refreshed, Kitty returned to the strains of "Ukelele Lady" and said Fred should stay, but he resisted them both in his way: the train, the job. He wouldn't hear of staying, and he wouldn't even hear of Gideon's walking him any farther than the end of the block.

"I don't mean to make you go through it all over again, Fred, but I have to know," Gideon implored him. "How did Father die? How did it happen?"

They stood in a pool of light under a streetlamp, and Fred watched the moths. "Well, Gideon, who can say? Things like that

249

just happen to some folks, and they don't happen to others. It's real hard to figure out, if you're not too smart, like me. It was Samuel was the smart one." Fred coughed and spat. "But I'll tell you the truth, Gideon, it was an awful thing that happened to your father."

"Did he suffer much?"

"Well, yes, I think he did. We all do, but there's some suffer more than others, and there's those who don't even know they're suffering till the suffering comes to be all they know, and Samuel was one of those. I mean, I think he was." Fred took a deep breath and another licorice bit. "And that house. Well, it's gone, I guess. Long gone, and I don't exactly know how it happened to be burnt, as you say, but anything can burn, you know, given the heat and the flame, and no one could rescue Samuel, Gideon. No one could get to him before he burned up in a fire maybe even of his own making."

"His own making?"

"His own carelessness or thoughtlessness, Gideon. Samuel was often careless and thoughtless. I got to go now. The train. Timetables don't lie. You know that." He reached for Gideon's hand but threw his arms around him instead. "I always knew you'd make something of yourself, and you turned out just like I woulda wished. I couldn't ask for more." He patted Gideon resolutely. "You give my love to everyone, and tell them if it wasn't for this job in Arizona—but I'll come back this way. That's what I'll do. And Gideon, you tell your mother I give her my very best, yes, and that I think she done all the right things. You tell Sister Ruth that I take my hat off to her." He slid his cap down over his ears and stood hatless, as if to impress on Gideon the solemnity of the moment. Then Fred sauntered down the street. "I said goodbye once," he called, "and just look, we found each other again, Gideon, so I won't say goodbye this time. I'll be back. So I won't say goodbye."

But he waved goodbye even if he did not say it, and Gideon watched him till the streetlamps no longer caught his odd gait and he vanished into one of the intersections.

32

EDEN LOUISE'S EARLIEST recollection was a funeral. Her dog, Gyp, died under the wheels of the ice truck when she was about four, and Kitty said Eden shouldn't grieve for Gyp, that he would come back as dust under the bed. Dust unto dust, Kitty said, and that was the reason she didn't sweep more often; the dust might be someone you knew.

Eden was careful not to throw her shoes under the bed and disturb Gyp or, two years later, Lily Whickham, who was the next dead person she knew. She didn't actually know Aunt Lily Whickham, had never met her or spoken with her, but she was careful of the dust just the same.

All Eden's family attended Aunt Lily's funeral. Art Whickham's grand home was filled with mourners commenting on his wealth and good taste. The children had all been shooed into the stifling parlor to wait. They sat sweating in their Sunday-best clothes and Sunday-best silence, all but Eden's one-year-old brother, Ernest, who toddled about the room, bumping into things and talking to himself in a foreign tongue. The parlor was a gallery, mostly of the dead but of some living relatives, too. All over the room, toothless forefathers gazed out from oval frames and long, wiry beards. The forefathers were often accompanied by foremothers whose faces had collapsed around the mouth like rotting cabbages. Sometimes the photograph had been crisply snipped at the man's left or right, leaving only the man and one wife to stare out for time and all eternity. Sallow-looking children also frowned down upon the current generation.

"Your brother's wet his pants and pooped in them, too," said a pert girl of about eleven.

Eden brought her eyes down from the picture of a wrinkled matron to the sassy girl in a navy-blue dress and white stockings. Eden's own dress was a hand-me-down from her Lance cousins; it sagged from her six-year-old shoulders like pillow ticking on a T-square. "How do you know?" she asked, watching Ernest wobble about the room.

"I can smell it. He's walking funny, too."

Ernest beat the settee with his fat hands till the dust flew and then grinned. Nasty smiles lit up the Sunday-best faces of the other children, and Ada looked away, refusing to be related to Eden and Ernest.

"Check his pants, you'll see," the girl insisted.

Ernest maneuvered himself up on the rose-satin settee and picked his nose. Eden wished one of the dusky flowers in the carpet would open up and slurp her down.

"It's my Aunt Lily that's dead," the girl announced. "In fact, these are all my family." The girl waved her arm around the gallery of Saints. "I bet you don't have so many relations."

"Not so many dead ones," Eden admitted.

The girl cast an appraising glance around the walls and tables. "I think they're nice even if they are dead. I think it's nice to have all these relations. Don't you think so?" She flicked a piece of dust from her patent-leather shoes.

"Yes," Eden replied hastily.

"Bet you wish they was your relations."

"Yes, I do." She studied the cinch-lipped photographs. "Well, maybe I don't."

"You don't think my relations are nice?"

"They're nice, but they're ugly."

"Why, you little worm!" The girl dashed across the room and pulled Eden's ears from her head and squashed her nose. Eden gave her a jab in the stomach and a kick in the shins; the girl pummeled Eden's guts, and the two rolled over the floor till the girl was sitting on top of Eden while the other children encircled them, cheering her on.

"Elsie Whickham! What's going on here? Stop it this minute! Look at your dress! What are you doing to that little girl? Elsie!"

Eden bit Elsie's leg and then rolled quickly under the settee, just beyond reach of Elsie's foot. Eden enjoyed hearing Elsie spanked and told to pull up her stockings and march out to the cars. They were ready to see Lily Whickham off to the Celestial Kingdom. At the adult's command, the children filed out of the room. Eden stayed where she was till all the feet had left and she saw her mother's shoes come through the door. "Eden? Eden, where are you?" Kitty called.

"Here."

Kitty got down on all fours and peered under the settee; she brought with her the odor of a freshly smoked Chesterfield. "Come on out, duckie. What happened?"

Eden scrambled out and tugged at her clothes, fighting tears of rage and humiliation. "She picked on me."

"Who?"

"Elsie."

"Elsie who?"

"I don't know, some relation of the dead." Eden ground her teeth in a perfect rage of self-loathing.

"Tell Mother why she picked on you."

"I said her relations were ugly." She looked furtively at the angry photographs.

"Oh, them." Kitty brushed Eden's clothes. "Well, you're right, duckie, they are ugly. Ugly and mean. The whole tribe of them, and that little girl is going to grow up to be just like them."

"I can't go to this funeral, Ma. I can't face them."

"Sure you can. You did all right. That Elsie is bigger'n you, and you did fine."

"I can't face them!" Eden burst into tears.

"Hush now." Kitty handed Eden her handkerchief soaked in My Desire cologne. "This funeral will be over in no time, and we'll all go home and have a nice cup of tea. We'll have a real tea party, us and Ada and Ernest."

"With real tea?"

"Of course with real tea!"

"What about Pa?" Eden rubbed her face dry.

"Oh, your father, he'll be at the library somewheres, working on that infernal Timetable. We'll have the place to ourselves and no one the wiser. And if you're good, I'll tell you the story of the book I just finished. It'll be worth your while, Eden. That was a wonderful book." She fluffed Eden's uneven bob. "Now, let's go to this bloody

253

damn funeral for bleedin' Lily Whickham. I hope she burns in hell, if you ask me."

"Me, too! I hate her!" Eden gulped and momentarily froze: did cold phantom fingers caress her neck? As her mother straightened her skirt, Eden glanced at the settee where Ernest had been sitting. There was indeed a spreading stain. She followed Kitty out and did not look back.

Relieved of her funeral clothes, Eden sat in the kitchen clad only in her underwear, although taking off funeral clothes was not quite the same thing as shaking off the dead, particularly not when at the cemetery Eden had seen her own name—Eden Douglass REGRET—carved on a tombstone. Ada and Ernest and Mother were also in their underwear, though Mother had a wrapper on, half tied at her thick waist. Mother chipped some ice off the block and ran it over her face and bosom. "Wake up, Eden!" She slid the ice down Eden's neck. "Now, here's your tea, duck, and I promised you a story, but you, all of you, got to pretend this ain't mere bread and butter before you, but the food of the gods—breadfruits and coconuts and mangoes—because this here story I got for you today is a tale of the tropics."

"What's breadfruit?" asked Eden, using the last of the ice on her legs.

"Bread that grows on trees, of course. You just peel it off like bark. Now, Eden, we can't have no story without the mop. You go get her."

Eden brought the rag mop in and stood it, head up, its linten locks stained with dirt, against the icebox. She took her place at the table and bit into her breadfruit sandwich.

Kitty heaped sugar in their teacups. "It's too bleedin' hot for tea. Too bad we don't have no pine apple juice like they drink in Pangora, which is where this story takes place."

"It can't be no hotter than here," said Eden.

"Fat lot you know. Mold grows 'tween your toes in Pangora if you don't wash your feet every day and would just about give you black feet, Miss Eden Douglass." Kitty sipped her tea and lit up a half-smoked Chesterfield. "The story goes like this: Lady Diana Stratton comes to Pangora from jolly old England to take care of her aged uncle, Sir Theo Stratton, who is the governor there or something. Anyway, he lives in a big house with fans pulled by servants in every room and mosquito netting hanging everywhere like cobwebs. But none of that don't help Sir Theo, because he's got the death on him, and Lady Diana is there to see to him in his last days. But while she's there she meets Lord Arbuthnot, who is rich. I mean *rich!* Handsome, too. He lives in a white house on a hill surrounded by feathery palms and overlooking his plantation."

"What's a plantation?"

"A big farm where someone else does all the work. And, of course, Lord Arbuthnot falls in love with Lady Diana, but she is engaged to Reginald Percy, who is still back in jolly old England, and she is faithful to her vows." Kitty turned to the mop, who leaned coyly against the icebox; she lowered her voice and held out her arms. " 'Lady Diana, I honor and esteem you above all women and will lay down my fortune at your feet, only say you'll marry me.' "

Kitty flipped her cigarette into the sink and brought the mop up to the table. She addressed it in her best falsetto: " 'Oh, Lord Arbuthnot, you tempt me, truly you do, but I would break Reginald's heart if I was to marry you, and I could not live with that preying on my tender conscience.'

" 'But Lady Diana, what of your own happiness? Have I not reason to believe that you return my affection?'

" 'Oh, Lord Arbuthnot, pass me another of them pine apples. They are just the food of the gods.' "

"What's a pine apple?" said Ada, her mouth full of bread and butter.

"Hush." Kitty stood the Lady Diana mop in front of them, and it addressed the children beseechingly. " 'What happiness could I have here, Lord Arbuthnot? I know there's palm trees and passion flowers and orchids, but if I was to break my troth with Reginald, I would ever feel the pinch.' Here, Ada, you hold the mop a minute." Kitty made her way to the cupboard. Upsetting the oatmeal, she pulled forth a corked and unmarked bottle. She took a long swig and brought it to the table. She opened her arms to the mop and spoke in a rolling tenor: " 'My dear Lady Diana, you know you love me. Write to Reginald and tell him it's off.' "

Kitty sat down and poured from the bottle into her teacup. "The palm trees and the brassy sunsets and the fanning servants was too much for Lady Diana. She writes Reginald his letter and says it's off, and she and Lord Arbuthnot spend many happy hours planning noop-tuals in his big house on the hill while they was being fanned. Only, one day poor Uncle Theo calls Lady Diana to his side and said"—Kitty stuck her feet straight out, threw her head back, and grasped at her own throat—" 'My dear Diana, I have been silent too long, and soon I will join your own dear mother in heaven, and I cannot, nay, I dare not face her if I let you continue in your present course. You cannot marry Lord Arbuthnot. He has a dreadful secret in his stinking rich past, and you must not marry him.' " Kitty picked up the mop, and its head tossed wildly over the table. " 'Why, Uncle, why?'

" 'Because he was married once before, and he *murdered* his wife!'

"Well, when she heard that"—Kitty laid Diana's head against the table and took another sip—"Lady Diana Stratton refused all callers and went up to her room to weep alone."

"What about the servant with the fan?" asked Eden.

"Oh, she let him stay. No white person could live ten minutes in Pangora without someone to fan them." Kitty poured herself some more tea and seasoned it liberally from the bottle. She took two quick snorts and handed the mop to Ada. She stood before it, hand draped at her breast. " 'Lord Arbuthnot,' says Diana, 'I would not have thought you so low and wicked. In short, so hateful. It fills me with undying shame that I have broken the heart of Reginald to say that I would marry you, a beast and a liar and worse.'

" 'But Diana!'

" 'Lady Diana to you, you low, buggering, no-good toad.'

"Then"—Kitty finished off her spiked tea—"she just left him with his tongue hanging out. More bread and butter, ducks? More tea?" She filled Eden's cup and enlivened her own with liquor. She leaned the mop back up against the icebox. "Well, poor Lady Diana, she had her troubles, like we all do from time to time, but hers was worse, because Reginald Percy arrived in Pangora on the very day the old boy—Theo—died. Reginald took her in his arms and forgave her everything, but they didn't have too much time for jawing, because they had to get Uncle Theo in the ground, because you rot fast in Pangora."

"Where's Lord Arbuthnot all this time?" Eden demanded.

"He just went up to his hilltop home, surrounded by feathery palms and silent fanners, and locked himself away. And Reginald—you might want to know—is pressing Diana to marry him quick and come back to jolly old England on the very first boat." Kitty arched her eyebrows. "Ada, close your mouth. You look stupid with your mouth open." She polished off her tea in one gulp. "But Lady Diana is too tore up to leave Pangora right away, so they all gather round while the lawyer reads Uncle Theo's will and the servants pump the fans, and the lawyer says that Theo has left Diana everything, as she was nearest and dearest and the one what came to tend him in his last days. He left her everything, but only on the single condition that she promise *not* to marry Reginald Percy!" Kitty walked over to the mop and flicked it; the stick figure clattered to the floor. "You could have stabbed Diana with a feather when she heard that." She took a quick nip straight from the bottle, and a knock sounded at the door. "God's nostrils! You get it, Eden."

"I don't have any clothes on."

"Well, get them on."

"Ma, let it be. Go on with the story."

"No, you never can tell. It might be good news or money."

It was not good news or money. It was the church's ward teachers, two young men from the local ward who made the rounds regularly checking on the faithful. And the unfaithful. Eden let them in. They wore black suits and black ties, and sweat gleamed under their noses. One suffered from acne, and the other had a smile and beatific good looks that seemed as if they could be removed only with paint thinner.

"Is your mother home?"

"Ma! It's the ward teachers!" It's the damn ward teachers is what she thought, but experience had taught her that whenever she said damn, her Aunt Afton and a bar of soap could not be far behind. She ushered them into the darkened living room and moved some old magazines so they could sit on the couch. She sat across from them hugging a fringed pillow from the 1915 Pan-Pacific Exhibition. "Ma! The ward teachers are here."

257

"Coming, duckie," Kitty warbled from the kitchen.

Ada, still in her underwear, came through the door clutching the mop by what would have been its throat, with Ernest right behind her, and Kitty burst in smelling of ninety-proof eau de cologne. "You gents probably wonder why it's dark in here. It's the heat, don't you know? If I don't keep it dark, I just about swoon. It was never this hot in jolly old England. All sea breezes and London fogs there." She sank into a chair.

The pimpled ward teacher cleared his throat and scooted out of the lap of the couch. He inquired after the funeral of Mrs. Lily Whickham and offered condolences, to which Kitty said dust unto dust, and Eden shivered. The elder then opened his book and said they wanted to talk today about the importance of the Word of Wisdom.

Kitty crossed her knees and inspected her stockings for snags. She considered her fingernails and swung her right foot while the elder spoke. Ada picked up one of the old magazines and stood, fanning the elder.

"Thank you, little lady, but I can't see your mother if you do that." The varnished one took Ada's shoulders and moved her. The pimpled one continued, "The Word of Wisdom is one of the foundations of our faith, and just as everything needs a good foundation, the mother, the wife—in this case, you, Sister Douglass—is the foundation of the family."

"Oh, Lord Arbuthnot!" Eden mumbled into her Pan-Pacific pillow. "You fill me with undying shame."

". . . the mother serves as an example to her family. A bad example, Sister Douglass, can never be undone."

"No indeed," said Kitty, belching politely behind her fingertips. "I've always said that."

"And the Latter-day Saint mother is particularly blessed, and—"

"I've always felt blessed, you know that? I feel really blessed to have this lovely Victrola here, and why don't I just play you gents a little tune?"

"Thank you, no, Sister Douglass. We have only so much time with each family."

"Then how come this is the second time this month you fellas been here?"

The slick youth tried to extricate himself from the couch. "What

Brother McGahey means is that the Latter-day Saint mother should always remember that her duties to her family are the same as her duties to God."

"Yes." The pimpled one nodded. "Our bodies are God's temples, and we as Latter-day Saints are pledged not to do anything that would defile that temple."

"Indeed we are," said Kitty, licking a finger and smoothing her eyebrow.

"Lord Arbuthnot, I shall never forgive you!" Eden pushed the pillow over her face and nibbled on the fringe.

". . . we must remember that we are made in God's image. God has loaned our bodies—His image—to house our spirits on earth, to test those spirits."

"We must not do anything with our bodies we wouldn't want God to see," the pimpled one offered. "It may be your body, Sister Douglass, but it's God's temple."

Kitty flickered her eyelashes and lifted her chin. "Is that so, Brother McGahey? Is that so? Well, what does God think about shit? Is shit part of them temples, too? If God can stand shit, I don't see why He can't stand a little drink now and then."

Papers rained from their arms as the ward teachers tried to get out of the couch at the same time, McGahey falling forward, the other one falling back. Ada and Ernest gawked while Eden threw her pillow in the air and raced to the door, holding it open for the two men, who bounded down the stairs.

"Oh! Did you see their faces? Oh! That ought to hold them, the old pumpsuckers!" Kitty laughed till her face was streaked with tears, and then she collected herself and snarled at the children, "I'll beat you all silly if you so much as breathe a word to your dad that the ward teachers came here today. I won't finish the story if you tell."

"Never, Ma, we'll never tell."

"Well, then, let's take off these bleedin' clothes and go back in the kitchen and finish our tea. Ada, don't forget that mop."

It turned out, of course, that Lord Arbuthnot was as blameless as a lamb as well as being rich as King Midas. It was Reginald Percy who had the soul of a bat. When he had gotten Lady Diana's letter and known he'd been spurned, he'd written Uncle Theo that if he didn't tell Diana that lie about the wife-murdering, he—Regi-

259

nald—would uncover the disreputable story of Sir Theo and the embezzlement of funds from the Bank of England itself, which was the reason the old boy had been exiled to the tropics in the first place. Not wishing his dear niece to know the worst of him, Theo complied, but in the end, he cared more for Diana's happiness than for himself and he let his secret come out. Lady Diana loved her Uncle Theo, no matter what he'd done to the Bank of England. In fact, Lady Diana and Lord Arbuthnot named their first son Theo, that is, after they got married and moved to the huge white hilltop house overlooking the tropical plantation, surrounded by feathery palms and silent servants with a thousand whispering fans.

33

Eden remembered the move to her grandmother's house quite clearly in spite of the reigning confusion. One cold Saturday morning, Tom Lance drove the Pilgrim delivery truck up to their house, and her father and her Uncle Tom loaded the family's possessions. There wasn't much. Most of it had been sold. Most of what they put in the truck consisted of Great Timetable boxes. The Great Timetable had been dismembered and all its respective parts (including hundreds of drafts Gideon could not part with) meticulously packed.

Her parents quarreled bitterly over a sealed box of clothes that had belonged to the long-dead Toots. "It's your fault we have to move in with your bleedin' damned mother!" Kitty shouted in the front yard. "It's you who lost the job! Why should you take them bleedin' damn charts and tell me I can't take my own dear boy's things?"

"They're unnecessary. They're not used," said Gideon tersely.

"And they never will be!" she screamed. "They're Tootsie's things. They're all I have left." She clutched the box and wept.

Eden wandered from empty room to room in the cold house, testing her echo. She breathed on the kitchen window and drew patterns and wrote in her childish hand:

Eden Louise Douglass
February 12, 1927

before the breath faded, and, with it, the words. She stared out to the naked clothesline, the frost-encrusted mop, and the leafless sleeping peach.

That Saturday wrought indelible changes on her life. Grandma's house was big and blissfully empty, since Aunt Lil had remarried some years before and moved to Idaho with her new husband. Eden enjoyed the exclusive domain of a room of her own. She could swim in the bathtub and slide down the banister (when Grandma wasn't looking) and swing on the back-porch swing. At Grandma's they ate in the dining room at a table with massive legs, thick as lions' haunches, and they were required to have clean hands and faces and clothes; they were forbidden to put their feet up. But at Grandma's the mop, alas, served only functional purposes, and the dust was not allowed to collect under the bed no matter who it might be.

Eden sat on two of Gideon's big books in order to reach the table comfortably. Ada sat on three books, and Ernest had been fed and put to bed early. Ruth took her place at the head of table. Though she was still unstooped at sixty-three, Ruth's hair was heavily streaked with white, and she was spare and leafless, rather like the peach they'd left behind at the old house. She frowned at Kitty, who picked at her dinner, slouched, and put her elbows on the table.

"There was a Bible published in 1496," Gideon began without looking up. Gideon had immediately installed his charts, inks, pencils, and books in the small servant's room off the kitchen. "It had blank pages sewn in at the back so the reader could fill in the end of the world for himself."

"So what?" said Kitty.

"They must have thought"—Gideon passed the conversation with the gravy—"that the end of the world was mighty close at hand, or they wouldn't have sewn in the blank pages. They must have thought that everything around them pointed to the end of the world right in their own times."

"So bleedin' what?"

"It makes you think of the Apocalypse, don't it?"

"It don't make me think nothing of the sort. Eden, pass me the butter." Kitty pointed with her knife.

"I can't reach it, Ma."

Kitty stretched across the table and retrieved the butter.

"We always say that in 1492, Columbus sailed the ocean blue, don't we?"

"I don't. I don't give a tinker's damn about Columbus."

"And we always think of that as the Beginning. The Beginning of our world, the discovery of the New World, not the End. It makes you wonder"—Gideon looked up from his plate—"if the end of the world hasn't been going on since the beginning."

"Judas Priest, listen to that!"

"I'm up to the Seven Years' War now. It won't take any time to finish. I could finish real fast, I think. I only have a couple hundred years left to go. Less. I ought to finish first."

"Finish what first?" said Kitty, her mouth full of bread and butter.

"The Timetable. Then I'll get another job."

"Great God's nostrils! You don't mean it! You're so busy diddling the Duke of Wellington, you don't even hear your own weeping children! Suffer the little children!" Kitty implored the ceiling. "Their own father don't hear their cries of hunger."

"I don't see hunger or suffering at this table," said Ruth.

"Not yet."

"Not ever. If you think you can finish your Timetable quickly, Gideon," Ruth said slowly, "then maybe you should devote yourself to that for a while."

"The bloody hell he should! He's got a family, don't he? He's got to get a job, not muck about in—"

"That'll be enough," Ruth commanded her. "I've been thinking that maybe Albert was right and Gideon's got no gift for insurance. Maybe he has a gift for something else that we—I—didn't see or didn't recognize. Maybe I pushed him into something I shouldn't have." Ruth regarded her son with something like regret. "You finish your Timetable, Gideon. It's the least I can do."

"What about the bleedin' rest of us?" Kitty crowed. "How are we supposed to live?"

"Maybe you'd like a job at the Pilgrim, Kitty. You never tire of telling us of your talents. Maybe you need a job."

"You won't find me scraping no one's plates."

"That much was plain in your own home. However," she added quickly, "I'm not thinking of the plates. I'm thinking of making you cashier."

"That's your job."

"I'm getting old."

"You said it."

Ruth's mouth snapped shut quickly as a cash till. "Can you make change, Kitty? Count back the customers' money?"

"I am a lady and an *artiste* what has never sullied her hands with money."

"I'd pay you."

"My own-to-keep money?"

"Yes. Your own to keep. But I'll tell you this, Kitty Douglass, if I so much as hear a whisper about you drinking or smoking in my restaurant, I'll yank you out of there so fast your teeth will chatter."

"A lady with her own money!" Kitty ignored the warning and brightened visibly. "A lady with her own money, Gideon, can do as she likes, and don't you never forget it."

The family was never allowed to forget it. Kitty regaled them daily with stories of what this or that or the other customer said to her, how they didn't believe she was a day over twenty, how her manners and accent were so refined. The puffiness in her face diminished, and she mastered the marcel iron; she still smelled of My Desire and Chesterfields, but not so much of gin and despair. She still wept over romantic novels, but a lady with her own money could go to the pictures as often as she liked.

Frequently she took Eden with her. Kitty liked to arrive at the theater when the box office opened. They bought their popcorn and took their seats in the darkened theater. There was no one else there.

"Why do we have to come so early, Ma?" asked Eden.

"For the smell, duckie. Grand, ain't it?"

"What?"

263

"The smell, duck. It's the thee-ater! Can't you just smell it?" Kitty began to hum "It Had to Be You" in between bites of popcorn, happy in the vaulted, stuffy splendor of the empty theater, the womb and tomb of all her dreams.

If work was Kitty's salvation, leisure was Gideon's. Once relieved of all his domestic, filial, connubial, and fatherly duties, he seldom saw the family except at meals. He remained in the little room off the kitchen working on his Great Timetable. He became like the dust under the bed, friendly, silent, and not to be disturbed.

And so it was Ruth who ordered and tidied and dominated the lives of Eden and Ada and Ernest, Ruth who listened to their childish woes, Ruth who fixed their meals and washed their clothes and scrubbed their necks, who felt their tender cheeks against her dry one when she tucked them in at night, who lavished on them what she had been unwilling or unable to give to her own children. Ruth's attentions were constant, not sporadic like Kitty's nor preoccupied like Gideon's. Ruth would not let them wear frayed clothing or pin up their hems or ink over the holes in their stockings.

Ruth pulled the kitchen matches from her pocket for these children, too. But she no longer used them to illustrate the worth of one's reputation, which she'd come to see not as a standard of excellence, but as a means of discouraging exploration. She lit the match before Eden's small, sallow face (Eden, except for her green eyes, took after the Douglasses). "This match is like your chances in life, and if you once blow it out" —she extinguished it with one gust, and pale smoke wafted between them—"your life will never be the same. This match will never strike with its old spark or usefulness."

She saw in Eden Louise her own chance in life to make circular what had heretofore seemed linear, finalized by death: the reconstruction of lost opportunity. God or Gideon's failures had delivered into Ruth's hands another Eden through whom she might reconstitute the dreams that can sometimes endure past our own earthly tenure, dreams that—with love and luck and work—we need not take with us when we go to the place whence no traveler may return.

Ruth was not alone. From the time Eden Louise was nine, Lucius Tipton took her out to lunch on the third Saturday of every month. Ada fought to go, too, but she was told she was too young, and by

264

the time she was old enough, she'd lost interest in going; Eden's Saturdays with Doctor had become ritualized and had lost their original aura of adventure.

They never lost the aura of adventure for Eden. She wore a fresh starched dress and clean white stockings, and Doctor called for her at her grandmother's house and drove her in his Ford to the Pilgrim Restaurant. There he addressed Kitty as if she were not Eden's mother, and he asked for a table for a lady and a gentleman. Kitty knew a cue when she heard it. "Of course, Doctor. Let me call the headwaiter, and we'll give you and Miss Douglass the best seat in the house. Miss Douglass, you look a little pippin today. Is that a new frock?"

"Thank you," replied Eden, who also knew a cue. "It's not new, but I'm glad you like it."

The headwaiter led them to their favorite table by a window draped with gauzy white curtains and blue velvet drapes. The Chinese waiter always asked her if the flowers on her table were satisfactory to her, and Eden always studied them momentarily before replying yes. In his clipped and foreign-sounding English the waiter told her what the cook had said was particularly good that day, and Lucius always said she should order whatever she wished.

Eden could have stuck with Napoleons and Green Goddess Salad, for their very names if nothing else, but she tried everything at least once. After lunch, Doctor asked her permission to smoke, which Eden thought perfectly entrancing, since Doctor didn't even ask Grandma's permission to smoke. Lucius had not stooped with the years either, but he had grown stouter. He was altogether bald on the top of his head, and the hair that stuck out around his ears was wiry, overlong, and gray. His mustache was equally bushy and gray, but the ardor in his eyes had never dimmed, and Eden consulted Doctor's eyes when she wanted to know if something was true. His eyes never lied. She loved his unique fragrance of soap and tobacco and antiseptic.

Doctor inquired after her family and schoolwork, her friends and her Lance cousins, but Eden felt that any such banal discussion demeaned these lunches. She preferred the high literary plane. She like to discuss her truly intimate circle of acquaintance: Walter Scott, Charles Dickens, and Booth Tarkington. Doctor, after all, had introduced her to these worthies. Every year for Christmas and her birthday he gave her a novel or a book of poetry with her name inscribed in it. (He gave her some books Ruth did not particularly approve of, though she kept her objections to a minimum.)

Eden trusted and admired both her grandmother and the doctor, but Grandma made her points with kitchen matches and strict admonitions. Doctor made his points so that she didn't see they were points at all till after she'd thought about them for a bit. Eden might have confessed her trespasses to her grandmother, but she would confess her dreams only to Doctor. She did, at one of their Saturday lunches when she was twelve, confide over the Napoleons that she would like to write the kind of books she read.

"An estimable occupation, not always lucrative, but worthy," he replied. Eden didn't quite understand him, but at least she knew he wasn't making fun of her. "What kind of writer will you be?"

"Kind?"

"There are all kinds. There are those who tell the truth, though they claim it's all lies, and there are those who tell lies, though they swear it's all truth. Your father and I differ on the subject, but I would put Galileo and Shakespeare into the former category and Joseph Smith into the latter."

"Who's Galileo?"

"On the other hand, lies often have more power than truth, at least in the short run, and who can see past that? Do you mind if I smoke, Miss Douglass?"

"Please do, Doctor."

"And it must be said that a beguiling lie can often beat the dreary truth all to hell. But truths are universals and always bob to the top eventually, and lies are mere particulars. What do you think?"

"I think Grandma's right and you could carve a diamond out of a cabbage the way you talk."

"Your grandma overestimates me. How's the Napoleon?"

"Ex-quis-ite," said Eden, repeating a word she had read and up till only recently pronounced "exquite."

"There's other ways of distinguishing writers from one another. There's those who stay in one place and write, for instance, and those who travel all over the world."

"I'd like to be one of them."

"Where would you like to go? It wouldn't be Paris, would it?"

"I'd want to go anywhere out of St. Elmo, Doctor, and the further the better, and I guess Paris is just about as far as you can get."

Doctor grinned. "Hell is closer to St. Elmo than Paris, dear girl."

"What kind of writer goes there?"

"Hell?"

"No, Doctor." She was determined to look as if she were quite accustomed to discussing hell with cigar-smoking men in restaurants, but she hushed her voice just the same. "To Paris."

"All kinds of writers might go to Paris. But you probably couldn't start out there. You'd have to start somewhere else. That's my guess."

"Where would I have to start?"

"At the beginning, dear girl!"

"Where's that?"

"You'll know it when you get there."

For Christmas that year Lucius gave Eden an Underwood typewriter; it was as huge, to Eden's mind, as a grand piano. He assured her it was rather like a piano in that with a little practice, lovely things could be coaxed from its innards.

On the card he wrote:

Merry Christmas—
This is a beginning. But only one. There will be more
than one beginning. But if you're going to learn to write,
you might as well learn to type. It saves time, and you
won't ruin your teeth chewing pencils.

> With love,
> Lucius Tipton
> Christmas 1932

34

BY NINE IN THE morning the summer sun was already high and poured over the St. Elmo Valley like chlorine bleach; grass faded, leaves paled, bark peeled, and paint blistered with its intensity. Eden lay in bed and felt the sweat gather on the new hair that had disconcertingly sprouted under her arms. She had also recently sprouted pointy little breasts, which were a constant source of mortification. Despite the heat, she put a sweater on over her cotton dress when she got up; she kept the breasts covered no matter what. She brushed her short, unruly bob and made her way down to the kitchen, where her grandmother stood at the sink.

"Where's Ma and the others?"

"Your mother took Ada and Ernest downtown to get their new glasses. She won't be back till suppertime. Once she gets downtown, your mother will make them sit through that new picture twice."

"Is Pa in there?" Eden nodded in the direction of the little room where they sometimes heard Gideon rustling. Gideon often rustled; that's how they knew where he was.

"Probably."

"You think Pa will ever finish the Great Timetable?"

"You'd think so, wouldn't you?" Ruth dried her bony hands on a dish towel and folded it into a neat square. "He's certainly been at it long enough." She sighed and sat down. She wore a dress of serviceable cotton, blue with lavender flowers. She had given up black years before, at Afton's insistence. Afton always got her way.

Eden went to the icebox and got out the jug. "You want some lemonade, Grandma? It's going to be hotter than hell's back burner today."

"You'd best be careful what you say, young lady. Talk like that will—"

Lucius Tipton tapped lightly on the back door, but he didn't wait for an answer, just burst in carrying a newspaper, an enormous armload of purple flowers, and a bag. "Eden, my dear," he said before he so much as greeted them, "get that washpail off the porch and fill it up with ice. Ruth, my dear, good morning, and it is a good morning."

"What brings you here this early, Lucius?"

"Washbucket first." He took off his hat and threw it on the table. He took off his coat and put it on the back of the chair, appearing before them in his suspenders. "Hotter'n hell's back burner today."

Eden brought the bucket and took the smaller cake of ice from the icebox and put it in the bottom. Lucius took the pick and beat the ice a bit till it cracked, and then he drew from his bag a tall green bottle, sealed and mysterious-looking. "Champagne, ladies! We are going to drink champagne this morning."

"Where did you get champagne, Lucius? It's illegal!"

"It wasn't when I bought it. I've had this bottle since 1910."

"Eden and I are Latter-day Saints, and we don't drink champagne," said Ruth unconvincingly.

"Pity, Ruth, because I bought this champagne for you, and I shall insist that you drink it now. That's all." He held up his hand to forestall further objection. "I bought this shortly after that occasion when you and I first imbibed together a little Burning Bush, the spirits forbidden you by virtue of your pruny religion. We did so, you may recall, out of exhaustion and relief, but today it is in the spirit of celebration that I bring this bottle here, to celebrate our collective liberation."

"What?" said Eden and Ruth together.

"You heard what I said." He put the flowers in Ruth's arms.

"Where did you get irises this time of year?"

"At the florist, where else? I told that girl, give me a dozen of the most exotic thing you've got. She had orchids, but you are not the orchid type, so I said, give me two dozen of the tall irises, they are just Ruth's type—regal and with a secret soul gracefully protected by silky petals."

"You are getting old and foolish, Lucius."

"It's true, alas, that I seem to be getting older but no wiser. However, I have not yet parted company with either my brains or my teeth. Now, Eden, you run upstairs and get a vase for these flowers."

"There's a vase right here beneath the sink."

"Go upstairs and get one anyway."

He waited for her to leave, and then he unfurled the Los Angeles newspaper. He opened it and pointed to the bottom of an inside page. "I've been reading the papers for twenty years—more, thirty years—waiting to see this."

NEW CANAAN LOVE TRIANGLE
DEATH IN THE DESERT
PROPHET MURDERED BY APOSTLE
SUSPECT FLEES SOUTH

"Inyo County," said Ruth. "Where's that?"

"Another desert hell north of this one."

"Apostles of the Apocalypse—Prophet Ezekiel—shot twice—found dead. Oh, Lucius—"

"My condolences, my dear Widow Douglass."

Ruth wept into her hands, and Doctor gently stroked her neck. "Looks to me like someone contested his right to prophesy and dictate and take any woman he wanted. Or maybe one of the Apostles took a fancy to one of the prophet's women or didn't want to offer up his wife or daughter to the prophet's clammy hands. Anyway, whoever shot him is clear to Mexico by now, and Samuel's dead and you're free."

"I'm not free." Sobs shook her shoulders. "Look at me. I'm an old woman. I've got three grandchildren to raise, the Pilgrim's not doing as well as it used to, and Art Whickham keeps threatening to call in my note and take it all away from me." She cried into her hands.

"Marry me, Ruth."

"There're no vases upstairs," said Eden from the doorway. "They're all down here." Eden had never seen her grandmother cry, and she'd never seen anyone touch her grandmother in quite the way Lucius Tipton was stroking her hair and neck.

"Hand me that dish towel, Lucius."

"Your grandmother is weeping with joy, dear girl. I ask her to marry me once every ten years, and she's finally consented."

270

"Oh, Lucius, I have not." She wiped her eyes quickly. "There's no marrying for us, and you know it."

"Eden, you see before you a broken man. Spurned by the woman I love. What can I do? Well, I'll just have to ask again in—what will that be?—1943. Yes, I'll ask again in 1943, because foul winds never stopped fair hearts. Isn't that the way it goes?" He went to the cupboard and took out three cups. "Shall we retire to the porch, ladies? Champagne is not meant to be drunk in the kitchen. You may take my word for it—champagne drunk in a kitchen will lose its savor."

Ruth folded the towel back into a neat square and laid it on the table. She picked up the irises and found a vase for them beneath the sink, and Eden reflected that her grandmother did rather resemble the irises, that she was tall and regal, with blue veins throbbing at her temples and a center secret from Eden, from everyone perhaps except Doctor.

Ruth tore the page from the newspaper. She folded it into a cone, took it to the sink, lit one of her fabled matches, and filled the kitchen with the smell of smoke and sulfur. She torched the cone. "Dust unto dust."

"Ashes to ashes," said Lucius.

"It is better to marry than to burn—but not by much." Ruth washed the ashes down the drain. "Now, Eden, let's you and me go out and drink champagne with Doctor this fine Saturday morning."

"Why?"

"Why what?"

"Why are we doing this?" she pleaded. "We've never done it before. What's happened?"

Lucius put his arm around her shoulders. "We're going to drink champagne this morning because . . ." He faltered and looked to Ruth. "Because we're going to celebrate that there are women like you and your grandmother in the world and because women like you *should* drink champagne in the morning. Often. Bother Joseph Smith!"

They sat on the back-porch swing, which groaned on dry hinges. They looked out over the yard, where weeds and wildflowers competed with the hand-planted garden. Foxtails grew golden and knee-high, bees rubbed their furry bodies against responsive sunflowers, and tall, old-fashioned hollyhocks guarded the straggling mint. Honeysuckle climbed over the porch railings and crawled along the roof and dripped scent into the shadows where they sat. Lucius uncorked the bottle with a loud pop and poured them each half a cup of champagne. Eden began to take a sip, but Doctor stopped her. "The first thing you must learn about champagne, Eden, is that you never drink it for itself alone. Not the first sip, anyway. The first sip must always be for something or someone. Shall we drink to your grandmother, for the great and gallant woman that she is?"

Eden had never thought of Grandma as either great or gallant, only Grandma, but she nodded all the same, staring into her cup, where thin columns of bubbles rose and burst across the fragile surface.

"To Ruth, then."

"No," said Ruth, resting her hand on Eden's thin shoulder. "To Eden—for the great and gallant woman she will become."

For the rest of her life Eden could never smell honeysuckle without remembered champagne effervescing on her tongue. For the rest of her life, whenever she drank champagne—and she did drink it later, often, occasionally in the morning and in places far from St. Elmo, places like Paris, where there wasn't any honeysuckle to be seen, only remembered—honeysuckle tickled her nose as it did that hot summer morning on her grandmother's back porch when she was toasted for the girl she was and the woman she might become, when champagne seemed the very tonic of possibility and honeysuckle the elixir of contentment, as if champagne could be distilled from single drops of nectar, and pale light could be squeezed from flowers and wisdom extracted from love.

The three of them sat on the porch, sipping and savoring for a good hour. The champagne seemed to have invaded Eden's veins, and laughter bubbled to her lips. "Too bad Ma's not here," she said when she'd almost finished. "She'd love this. She says she used to drink champagne all the time when she was on the stage in Liverpool, before she became a Saint and married Pa. Pa! What about Pa? We should have asked him if he wanted some."

Lucius looked dubious. "Your father is a good Latter-day Saint, Eden. I don't think he'd indulge."

"Well, we ought to ask him. We ought to give him the chance. If he don't want it, he don't have to have any, but—"

"Go ask him if you want, honey," said Ruth.

Eden found her father with his feet on the desk, his glasses pushed back on his head, rubbing the bones of his nose. All around him, charts billowed from the walls, the long lines drawn in blue, the eras marked off in red. His small study was filled with the smell of graphite and ink.

"Pa? Are you all right?"

Gideon focused slowly on a slender shape in a blue cotton dress and a sweater. He put his glasses back on, but they only confirmed what his bad vision suggested: a girl with dark hair and green eyes and a face as fresh as uncut pages. "Eden?" Surely not Eden Louise. Eden Louise still had grubby hands, didn't she? Bony knees and the hem falling out of dresses that were always too small for her. Didn't she? "Eden Louise?"

"Of course it's me, Pa. Oh, Pa, look, you've spilled ink all over that chart on your desk. Oh, Pa, I think this one is ruined."

"It's all ruined. Leave it be. It's the end."

"But this timetable only goes up to 1900, Pa. This is 1933; you got thirty-three years left to go. It won't take you any time at all to finish now."

"It's the end. It don't take no prophet to see what's going to happen next." With one swoop of his arm he cleared the desk, swept everything to the floor. Books flew open, notes swirled, rulers snapped, red, blue, and green inks spattered across the walls like the blood of rainbows.

"Pa!" Eden cried. "What's come over you? Pa!" She was frightened as he kicked the fallen books and papers. "Pa!"

Gideon sank into his chair and confronted his naked desk. "It was easy before—with the Catholics and the Reformation Protestants," he said, staring at his hands. "Easy with them, easy to see what happened, what was going to happen, even why—but this—I've seen it coming, though. I've dreaded it, but I can't hide from the truth any longer."

"What truth, Pa? What have you done to your timetables?" Carefully she rested her hand on his shoulder.

"I've studied the church from the beginning, Eden, from that first revelation, a new and glorious revelation. And now it's the end. I see what's coming next. I've seen it. I know. There'll be no more glorious visions for us, Eden, just holy writ writ large in dollars and cents. All the ancient records, the holy books, the Restored Gospel,

273

that's all for naught now, because now the church's records will be kept by nothing more than accountants, dim-visioned old men with pencils, with red and black ink. No more golden tablets. They'll forget what God said."

"What was that, Pa?"

"He said to Joseph Smith, go and prune my vineyards, son—didn't He? He didn't say, go count of the flocks or tally the oxen. But that's what they're doing. It's the end."

"You know, Pa, that's just what they been saying in church. Now with this Depression the end is upon us, and we're coming into the Last Days."

"Depression!" Gideon snorted, shaking off her hand and whirling to face her with bright metallic eyes. "Depression? That ain't the end. The end began a long time ago. 1900. Maybe earlier. That's when the end began. We've lost the visionary truth, Eden. We've parked our camels at the door and joined the rest of the money-changers in the temple. The fires are out."

"What fires, Pa?" She knelt among the carnage and righted the ink bottles. "I don't know what you're talking about."

"See?" He grabbed her arm and pulled her to one of the timetables hanging from the wall. "You see the eras I've marked off with red ink? See how each new era is set off by a revelation? See? Look, here's Moses and Copernicus and Galileo and Columbus and Joseph Smith, and here's Darwin—no matter what the church says, he's here, too. The world was revealed to each of them in a new way, and all these revelations, Eden, they turned out to be revolutions, too. Revelation, revolution, it's all the same thing."

"So what, Pa?"

"So what! You sound like your mother!" He tore the timetable from the wall and the two on either side of it and held them in his quaking hand. "There isn't any End coming, that's so what! It's past! The end is past! 1900. That was the end of vision and the beginning of the same old thing. No more revelations, because the church can't stand for revolution! They'll make sure 1900 was the end. They have to! They got to keep everybody happy and comfortable, kept quiet. It ain't the happy man who gets a revelation, Eden, it's the man who's got a hunger on him that money can't cure."

"Pa, I think you're sick. It's the heat. Come outside and have some—"

"*No! No!*" He threw his glasses on the desk and brought his weak eyes up to his daughter's face. "Don't you see, Eden, everyone's got to be lulled now. Lulled so they don't hear no voices but the radio and they don't see no visions but the moving pictures. You mark my words, Eden—prophets and profits—it's come to be the same thing, and in these latter days we'll be led by old men with old dreams and not young men with new visions. No revelations. No revolutions. Just keep everybody happy and stomp out the hunger in the soul, keep them dreaming the old dreams and don't let them see nothing. Compared to real vision, what's the worth of stale old dreams? Nothing! Nothing but the smoke left over when a candle's been blowed out by the wind."

Eden stood horrified and motionless as her father tore all the timetables from the walls, wadded them, and threw them to the floor, where they billowed like paper-crested waves. "I'll be damned," he said without regard for his daughter's tender ears. "I've eaten from the Tree of Knowledge."

Gideon Douglass had devoted himself to his Great Timetable for nearly a quarter century (fifteen thirty-seconds of an inch) when he fell into a morass of doubt from which he could not extricate his beliefs intact. Unfettered from his faith, he was assaulted by fear. At forty he had never experienced such fear, though he'd experienced all the other bodily processes save death; he knew the lusts and hungers, the pain, but he did not know that the old organic chemistries never free us. Or frighten us. It's the physics: the physical, painful process whereby we are released from warm inertia. It's the uncertainty principle, because who knows where you are going—once freed, once set in motion, once you start flying or rolling, defying the laws of social gravity that have held you pinioned, the prisoner of the past and the present.

275

35

IN THE NEXT THREE weeks Gideon found a job, but he was unemployed by Christmas, when Mason came to visit after many years in Washington, D.C., where he had performed a number of civic functions, most recently, lobbying.

"You mean you sat in a lobby like a cuspidor?" asked Kitty as he tried to explain his former occupation to the family. Kitty referred to her brother-in-law, when he was not in her immediate vicinity, as Snail Snot, because, as she told Eden, wherever he went he left a trail of what looked like shiny silver stuff, but if you touched it, you knew it was just old, hardened, sticky snot.

But that grim Christmas, Mason did indeed seem to leave a trail of silver: silver lining the dark clouds of the Depression, silver ringing in his pockets, silver coins and silver veins and silver bells and cockle shells. Opportunities, said Mason as he passed out the gifts he'd brought with him. He mistakenly brought Ernest a doll, thinking that Kitty and Gideon had three girls, but he talked his way out of that (and bought his way out, too, giving Ernest the dazzling sum of five dollars to spend as he saw fit). Mason was the president and founder of the Sunstone Silver Company. He said he had offices on Wall Street and described the view of the city's great skyline from his window. He had a chromed oval desk and a whole fleet of secretaries, their typewriters gnashing like an army on its way to greatness.

Christmas included as much of the Douglass clan as could be assembled in St. Elmo. Lil did not come, because she still lived in National Falls, Idaho, with her second husband. Nor could Cissa come; she was living in Salt Lake with her third husband, a plumbing contractor named Thatcher Stout. Mason returned from Washington with an anemic-looking Gentile wife named

Margaret, who never spoke unless spoken to, and a peppery, unpleasant son named Denton, which was Margaret's maiden name. "Of the Baltimore Dentons," said Margaret, as if that should mean something to the St. Elmo Douglasses. Afton and Tom and their seven children came. Lucius came. Ruth concocted a Christmas dinner almost up to her old standards, though normally she never would have used as much cornstarch. Cornstarch was cheap, and 1933 was a lean year.

For several days they lived on leftover gaiety, food, and hope, some of it flecked with mold. Only Mason kept his sunny equilibrium. He reminded Eden of a sea gull, a squat, puffed-up body on skinny legs, always dressed in sober grays and whites and blacks. His paunch stuck out like the belly on a dollar sign.

Eden stayed in the parlor with the adults after supper, when the other children had been sent in to do the washing-up. At thirteen, nearly fourteen, Eden could choose to be an adult or a child, since she was recognized by neither group. She elected to stay with the adults, because even if her Uncle Mason was a snail snot, he'd been to places other than St. Elmo. He said he could have met the President, but Democrats were beneath him. He talked about all the senators and congressmen he had known in Washington, D.C., for an hour before he came back around to the Sunstone Silver Company.

"Everyone thought the Idaho hills were cleaned out after the big silver boom of the nineties," Mason declared. "But they were wrong. One mining engineer with today's methods and equipment can do by himself what ten men couldn't do back then." He played with his silver suspender snaps. "I wonder that my own father didn't take advantage of the wealth pouring out of those hills forty years ago. You'd have to be crazy to pass up an opportunity like that."

Ruth peered over her bifocals as if they were the rim of a toilet, but returned to ripping out the hem of one of Eden's dresses.

"It'll be up to us to get rich, won't it, Gideon?"

"Someone should," said Gideon, not looking up.

"We'll do it in five years. I got a timetable, and that's what I got it set for. Five years. But I need your help, Gideon. I need your brains. You got vision. I tell you, Margaret, there isn't a man in this country who knows his history like my brother, Gideon."

"Yes," said Margaret. Margaret only ever said yes or no; if there was any equivocating to be done, Mason did it.

"Why, you're just wasted around here, Gideon. You haven't worked in—"

"A long time," said Gideon.

"Well, you can't just sit around here idle. A man with your brains idle! Why, it's just like the old hymn says—'The thought makes reason stare'! No, Gideon, we—the Sunstone Silver Company and I—we need you for vice-president. How do you like that? Your name on a brass plate on the door. Mason Douglass, President, Gideon Douglass, Vice-President. How does that sound? I'll cut you in for half."

"Half of nothing is still nothing," said Lucius, lighting up and coughing. He suppressed the cough, and it rattled through his whole body, shaking his flesh from his bones and silencing everyone save Mason.

"My land has silver veins just about to bust wide open," Mason went on. "I've talked with the geological boys. I've seen the maps. My chief engineer graduated from the Colorado School of Mines, class of '27, and he says to me: 'Mr. Douglass, there's silver in them hills.' "

"Yes, and I'm the bleedin' Queen."

"You are a clever one, Kitty. Don't you think she's clever, Margaret?"

"Yes."

"Too bad you folks never come and visited us in Washington. I'll just bet you would have been the toast of society, Kitty, what with your good looks and quick tongue. Don't you think so, Margaret?"

"Yes."

"Eden, honey," Kitty said, "would you fetch me a glass of water? I think I'm going to puke. And bring my nail paint, too, will you?"

As Eden left the room, Ruth shot her a look that said don't come back, but she did. She must have missed something juicy, however, because by the time she returned, Mason was falling all over Margaret trying to placate her and Kitty looked like a cat who'd just enjoyed a choice filet of mouse.

Mason's face was checked red and white like a tablecloth. "Not

278

just hire you," he blustered. "You'd be important, signing the checks for the payroll. You'd be making money and watching it being made for you. You can do what you want, Gideon, or what your wife here wants, but I'm willing to share this with you: the chance of a lifetime. Money." He rolled the last word off his tongue as if it had grain and texture.

"What I want to know," said Ruth, slicing through the theoretical fat to the meat of the matter, "is three things. Who's putting up the cash for this silver company? How did you come by this land? And have you ever laid eyes on it?"

"Idaho is my home state."

"You were still in wet pants when we left Idaho, so that don't count. Kitty, if you spill that foolish paint on my table, I'll have your hide. Well, Mason?"

"I haven't exactly seen this particular land, but Margaret and I are on our way up there. Anyway, I've seen the silver, and that's what counts. There's men up in Fairwell, Idaho, right now skimming silver like it was cream off a crock. And as for finance, I got people begging me to let them buy stock in the Sunstone Silver Company. I'm not the only one who's sick of being poor."

"I'll have to think about it," Gideon said.

"Well, don't think too long. These are hard times," Mason said sagely, and Margaret said yes.

They were hard times, but the following year was worse, the worst the Douglasses had endured. In February 1934, Lucius Tipton died of a heart attack. He was found in his study by a patient who had waited over an hour for Doctor to inspect a cyst in his armpit. Doctor was slumped over his desk, and Blanche hung speechless and indignant behind him.

So once again the Douglasses stood by a grave of one of their own at the St. Elmo cemetery. The wind came up off the desert that day and whipped Ruth's skirt. She was not wearing black. Doctor had told her once he never wanted her to wear black again. I'll wear it for you if you die before me, she had vowed. No, promise me you won't, he had said. And true to her promise, she wore a dove-gray dress the same color as her hair. Once again she stared into the trees, kept her gaze on snow-sugared mountains so that she would not need to look into the hole where they would put Lucius Tipton. In one hand she clutched a handful of early narcissus, Doctor's favorite

279

flower, and in the other hand she held tight to Eden Louise, and for the first time in more than twenty years she was afraid, not of death necessarily, but of life without Lucius.

Tom Lance read the eulogy and said a few words at the graveside. Tom was not given to speeches, and so his discourse was short and discreetly omitted all reference to religion, noting only that a man like Lucius Tipton could never die as long as there were people to remember him; as long as courage and caring and truth and love were valued in the world, men like Lucius Tipton never died.

The Douglasses—Ruth, Afton and her brood, Gideon, Kitty, and their children—were joined at Doctor's graveside by the entire tribe of Nana Bowers's offspring, most of the Chinese and Mexican population of St. Elmo, the families of railroad men, and every woebegone upcountry miner, sheep farmer, and desert rat who could coax his mule into town that day.

Eden was astonished to see all these people; she'd always felt that Doctor was peculiarly their own—her own, to be more specific—and would not have believed that fragments of him could have belonged to people like the one-legged handyman from the Whitworth Hotel down by the station or his daughter and her children and squirmy, pale grandchildren. Eden held tight to her grandmother's hand and glanced covertly at the grave of Eden Douglass REGRET not far away. She shivered and wondered if Doctor would come back as dust under the bed, but she could not imagine him as anything so insubstantial.

The day after the funeral, Ruth reopened the Pilgrim and life went on. Lucius would want life to go on, Ruth told Eden, inasmuch as it could. She took Eden with her to a lawyer's office that day and handed Avery Patterson an envelope, which she said was Doctor's will. "We exchanged them," she told Patterson. "Whoever died first was to look after things, but you'd better open this and read it. I want all this clear. I like things clear. Lucius liked things muddy and convoluted, but I am not that way."

It was a singularly clear document dated twenty years earlier: Lucius Tipton left everything to Ruth Mason Douglass to do with as she saw fit. He only hoped that Ruth would provide a good home for Blanche.

From Patterson's office, Ruth and Eden drove to Doctor's house in the Pilgrim delivery truck and took Blanche from the study and laid her gently in the back of the truck. Ruth put Doctor's account books on the seat between them. She then relocked the office and slid the key under a loose board on the steps. "I'll never come back here again," she said as she started up the delivery truck.

"What about all the rest of it, Grandma—Doctor's things and books and all that?"

"Someone else will have to take care of that. It won't be me."

And she was right, because two weeks after Lucius Tipton died, the Widow Douglass suffered a stroke that left her speechless and immobile.

Ruth spent ten days in the St. Elmo Hospital, and then the young doctor told Gideon there was nothing more that could be done for her there. "She could live another few months. She could live another few years," he said. "She could surprise us all and regain some of her speech and learn to walk again, but I wouldn't count on it."

So Gideon brought her home, and the family fixed up for Ruth the little room off the kitchen that had once housed his timetables and all his best hopes, because she could no longer go upstairs. She could not eat or move or speak; she could only sit in her wheelchair, knowing and powerless, and watch as the fabric of her family's life unraveled, as if all of them together could not perform the tasks that Ruth had done by herself.

Gideon Douglass might once have laid out the world's history in parallel columns, but he was helpless before the parallel columns of the Pilgrim's account books. And, too, he had to deal with Doctor's estate and Doctor's eccentric bookkeeping, and he was further shocked and helpless before the state of Doctor's indebtedness, till one night Tom and Afton came over and Tom suggested that Gideon forget all the patient fees accruing to Doctor and sell everything—except Blanche and Doctor's library if Gideon wanted the books—and use the money to pay off the debts and be done with it.

Gideon was left with the paperwork, the housework fell to Kitty and Ada, who were hopeless at it, and the cooking became Eden's task. Eden hated the tiresome, cyclic ignominy of cooking; she felt herself the servant of the stove and chopping block. She went to school with grease splatters on her clothes and went to bed with grease odors caught in her hair and the smell of onions indelibly on her hands, and her days seemed plastered to one another with a mucilage of flour and cornstarch. She lost her appetite and lost weight as she watched the endless procession of food vanish into her family's seemingly always open mouths.

Grandma required special concoctions: revolting barley gruels, nauseating milk-and-egg punches. And Ruth had to be fed. Eden tucked a towel in her grandmother's collar and held the spoonful of gruel to her lips. "You got to eat, Grandma. Open up."

Ruth closed her eyes, lips sealed shut.

"Please, Grandma, eat this, will you?" The gruel dripped off the spoon into Ruth's lap. Eden pressed the spoon against the old woman's lips. "You got to keep up your strength. You hear me? Eat it, dammit!"

Ruth's defiant eyes opened, and the index finger on her right hand, all she could move, wagged convulsively in place of the tongue-lashing she was unable to give.

"Grandma, please."

Ruth closed the blinds on her eyes.

Gruel flew across the room as Eden hurled the bowl and spoon. Gruel stuck to the kitchen wall and dripped slowly downward. "Oh, Grandma, Grandma—what are we going to do without you?" Eden slid from her chair and buried her face in her grandmother's lap and wept.

A few days later, Art Whickham appeared in their kitchen bearing long legal documents that he said only needed Ruth's X in front of witnesses to confer on him her power of attorney, to act as her representative in the selling of the Pilgrim.

Ruth's eyes looked like wads of silver solder; she hugged her wheelchair, her skin the texture of cantaloupe rind, her chin jutting out over her knees.

"You hear that, Ruth?" Art yelled. "I say, I'm sorry, but these are tough times, and that restaurant is dying faster than you are."

"She's not deaf," Gideon said, rolling up his newspaper as if Art had become a fly.

"How do you know?" He turned to Ruth. "You sign here. You know you can't run the Pilgrim no more, and you know your son can't either. That's no slur on you, Gideon, don't get me wrong. It's just the simple truth, ain't it? Tell her, tell your mother there ain't been a bill paid since God seen fit to strike her, and there ain't been a day when the ants or the help don't walk off with bolts of flour and bags of butter and whatever else they can carry. Including cash, ain't that right, Kitty?"

"Go eat coal and shit cinders," said Kitty, enjoying Ruth's enforced silence.

Art put the pen in Ruth's hand; it lay there slackly. "You, Eden Louise, you get over here and guide her hand. You sign here, Ruth, and I'll see what I can get for the Pilgrim. Probably not much. Not many folks buying these days. Everybody's bankrupt. Just mark your X right on this line, and Gideon can be your witness. I'll take care of everything, but I got to have your signature."

Ruth moved her index finger negatively.

"You can't mean you don't want to sell! I want to help you, Ruth."

"Judas Priest!" said Kitty. "Help us! You'd feed stones to little children just to hear their teeth crack."

"I'll thank you to keep out of this, madam. This here is a business arrangement between the Widow Douglass and me and no concern of yours."

"You can stuff it where the sun don't shine, Art," said Kitty on her way out of the kitchen.

"If the Pilgrim's sold," Gideon said slowly, "what's going to happen to us?"

"Well, Gideon, you're an able-bodied man, at least I think you are. I don't see no evidence of ill health, death, or dismemberment about you, so I reckon you'll have to get a job like other men. This is still the land of opportunity, in spite of that Bolshevik Roosevelt, and as for your mother here, her share of the Pilgrim's sale—once you sign this paper, Ruth—it should keep you for the rest of your life." Which can't be long—he left unsaid. "There you go, now. Eden will help you. Just wrap your grandma's fingers around that pen and make an X."

Eden put her hand over Ruth's, but the index finger rattled back and forth; Ruth stared at Art from eyes that looked like dirty grates over dying fires.

"What's power of attorney?" said Eden.

"I'm not in the habit of doing business with children."

"I want to know what I'm helping her sign."

"You don't have to know. Just guide her hand."

"Not till you tell me."

Art regarded her like newly sprouted mildew. "It means that I can act as your grandma's agent. Someone has to."

"What does the agent get?"

"Your grandma and I have business, young lady. You just help her sign."

"How much of this money are you going to take?"

"Take! Take? You make me sound like a crook! If Ruth could talk, she'd tell you it was me saved her hide all those years ago. It was me took her in. It was me lent them the money for the first Pilgrim. It was me leased the building for this one! Your grandma owes me, and she knows it!"

"But those were loans, weren't they? She paid the money back, with interest, didn't she pay it back?"

"Not all of it. There's still plenty due on that note, and with the restaurant—" Art tweaked Eden's cheek. "You're just a little girl— what do you know about all this?"

"I know when my grandma's being cheated."

"Cheated!" he screeched. "This ain't the good ship *Lollipop*, miss! You don't get something for nothing! Quit wagging that finger at me, Ruth! I can't stand it! You want something for nothing? Fine. Let Gideon take care of it. I wash my hands. Gideon don't know how to sell mattress ticking, let alone an enterprise like the Pilgrim. Just sign that power of attorney, Ruth. Time is money. You," he said to Eden, "get out of the way. I'll help her sign myself."

Eden took the pen from Ruth's hand and capped it. "My grandmother is not signing anything today." Eden looked to Gideon to see if she'd gone too far, but Gideon had vanished, leaving his glasses on the table.

"I'll be back with the law, you little twit."

"I don't care if you come back with Eleanor Roosevelt!"

At the sound of Eleanor Roosevelt's name, veins popped across Art's skull. He swore as he stuffed his papers back in his case, and he slammed the door on his way out so hard the crockery chattered.

Eden looked at Ruth; her index finger nodded in assent, and pleasure hovered at the corners of her twisted mouth.

Afton took charge. She brought Ruth to her house to live and treated her as if she had the three-day measles, vowing to have her up and about in no time at all. Her children had to quadruple up to empty a room for Grandma.

Afton persuaded Ruth to sign the papers, the power of attorney given to Afton Lance, not Art Whickham, and then she negotiated as best she could for the sale of the Pilgrim and the house, the proceeds to pay off Ruth's note. Afton was shrewd, but she was no match for Art Whickham, for his financial dexterity and resources. The St. Elmo National Bank and Trust bought the house and the Pilgrim, and when all was said and done, notarized, recorded, duly processed, Ruth's portion amounted to $408.42. Art counseled Afton to keep it in his bank, but Afton said she'd rather torch it a dollar at a time.

Afton did well by Gideon, however. The terms of sale included a provision that Gideon keep the Pilgrim's delivery truck and all foodstuffs in the restaurant at the time of sale. Gideon and his family had ninety days in which to vacate the house, and that was when Gideon wrote to Mason in Fairwell, Idaho, to ask if the Sunstone Silver Company still needed a vice-president. Mason wrote back a letter full of promise and opportunity. He said they would all be rich.

The packing began again. There wasn't much. The furniture was sold for what it would bring, which also wasn't much. The family took their clothes and blankets and linens, a few pots and fry pans, the necessities of life. Gideon acquiesced to all the children's requests to take whatever they wanted, including the big Underwood and Blanche, who, after all, was a member of the family. Kitty took her box of Tootsie's things without a word of protest from Gideon. Gideon took his own books and Doctor's, a small parcel of pens and inks and rulers, but he preserved only one of his charts, and that was rolled up, tied securely, and never consulted.

As the living began moving out of Grandma's house, the dead began moving in. Ghosts—inaudible, invisible, intransigent, and ill-mannered—filled the house. Eden and Ada and Ernest assured one another they did not believe in ghosts, but they could not deny that ghosts swung on the porch swing when there was no wind, shinnied up the rainpipe when there was no rain, opened doors, slit windows, made the dust fly, and brought the shrouded furniture to horrifying life. Ghosts crept in under the eaves, eased themselves through broken banisters, and appeared just out of reach or vision

285

or hearing or however it is one is supposed to apprehend creatures one knows are not there.

Eden wondered who these ghosts were. She discounted Lucius Tipton, because he would never have contrived to frighten her. She discounted the dog, Gyp, because Aunt Afton had assured her animals had no souls. She discounted the first Eden, because that ghost would have wet, streaming hair from the flood, and these ghosts all seemed to be of the dry, rustling variety. She wondered about Lily Whickham and Toots and any other of her grandmother's acquaintance among the dead. She concluded finally that whoever they were, the ghosts knew Ruth well enough to wait until she was gone and all but dead. Ruth would never have tolerated ghosts, never allowed them to ruffle the shrouds, rumble in the plumbing, or congregate socially in diaphanous dust curls, rolling under the bed.

36

 ONE SEPTEMBER MORNING the winds again reversed and came up off the desert, parching everything they touched: tough grasses withered, elms bristled, and the morning glories alongside Afton's house closed almost as soon as they opened. The Pilgrim delivery truck pulled up in front, and Gideon and Kitty and their three children got out. Afton wheeled Grandma out of the house and carefully down the porch steps, clucking and fussing over the barely animate piece of gristle that was Ruth Mason Douglass. Gideon and Kitty said goodbye to the Lances and Grandma; the flesh of Ruth's flesh and the bone of her bone kissed her cheek and held her dry, cold hands and promised they would see her again. They did not say when.

Afton gave them a crock of cooked, salted potatoes, a sack of apples, a bag of gingersnaps, and bread still warm from her oven. Gideon and Kitty and Ernest got in the cab, and the truck coughed, snorted, and fired up. Eden climbed into the back with Ada. The girls sat among boxes and blankets and Blanche, who was suspended from the roof between them. Suspending Blanche had been Gideon's idea, but when he saw how strange she looked, he thought perhaps they ought to leave her behind.

"Why should we leave Blanche behind?" cried Kitty. "Blanche ain't no stranger than the rest of your family."

So Blanche dangled between the two girls as the truck pulled away, and Eden Louise last saw her grandmother sitting stolidly in the wheelchair as Afton tidied the blankets over her lap. Eden waved until they were out of sight, and it seemed to her that Blanche, too, might have lifted her arm in a gesture of farewell. As the truck chugged and bounced and chortled away from St. Elmo, Blanche began to click and rattle, as if having been silent all those years she was now prepared to tell what she knew; for a thousand miles she was garrulous and implacable, scolding, nattering, chattering in a bony code that mere flesh is not privileged to comprehend.

BOOK THREE

The Book of Revelation

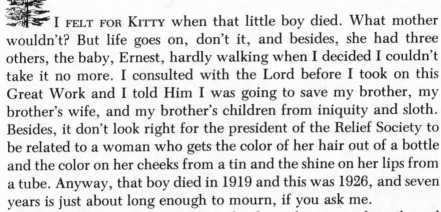

37 Afton

I FELT FOR KITTY when that little boy died. What mother wouldn't? But life goes on, don't it, and besides, she had three others, the baby, Ernest, hardly walking when I decided I couldn't take it no more. I consulted with the Lord before I took on this Great Work and I told Him I was going to save my brother, my brother's wife, and my brother's children from iniquity and sloth. Besides, it don't look right for the president of the Relief Society to be related to a woman who gets the color of her hair out of a bottle and the color on her cheeks from a tin and the shine on her lips from a tube. Anyway, that boy died in 1919 and this was 1926, and seven years is just about long enough to mourn, if you ask me.

Tom, he just smiled to see me load up the car with pails and brushes and rags and Condy's Disinfectant. You got five children of your own, Afton, Tom says to me. That ought to be enough to keep you busy.

It is, I said back, don't get me wrong, but something must be done for Kitty, and I am going to do it.

When I got to Kitty's I found her sitting on the bathroom sink, blowing smoke rings, while them poor children was wallowing in filth, which is the same as sin.

I said: Kitty, you can take off those silk stockings and get a rag to cover your head, because the dust is going to fly.

Well, you can just imagine what I found: gin bottles and empty packs of cigarettes (and some full ones, too) and trashy novels in every corner and webs a spider wouldn't live in and dishes with yesterday's breakfast drying on them and water leading out from under the icebox and the dirty and the clean clothes all mixed up and everything just as bad as it could be. When we was finished I ordered Kitty into the kitchen and pointed to the bottles and I said: Kitty, how could you?

She unwraps the rag off her head and uses it to wipe her nose. Her lips tremble, and she weeps for five straight minutes, plucking at the tablecloth with her fat fingers. I bide my time. Then she looks up and says: I've been just as wicked as I could be, and God ought to knock me off. I don't deserve to live. I don't know how I could have been so sinful. My own dear papá died of gin, ruined his voice and his career and his agent, and left Mamá with us three little angels and nothing but our talent to keep the rent collector from the door. And Mamá with her weak lungs, singing her heart out in all them drafty thee-aters. How could I? Oh, Afton, you have to help me. Lead me to leaner pastures.

Well, Kitty—I patted her shoulder and told her to quit crying— God don't neglect the truly repentant.

Where does she get it? Tom asks me when I come home. Where does she get the gin? Prohibition makes it hard to come by at all, and you really got to want gin to get it in a Mormon town like St. Elmo.

Nana Bowers's oldest boy, I told him. Nana died and left him the elixir business, and he just branched right out when Prohibition come along. But I don't care where she gets it. I'm not interested in arresting her. I want to see her mend her ways.

You'd have more luck mending her children's clothes, says Tom.

Tom was right. Two weeks later I happened over there and hope departed. I stood in that living room, which was a thorny field strewn with tares. I could see Kitty in the bedroom, spread-eagle on the unmade bed, a glass fallen over and dripping to the floor where Gideon's papers had slid from the desk. The baby was screaming himself into a froth and Ada and Eden were playing "sheik" with their dolls and the Victrola was going round and round.

I took Eden and Ada and Ernest home with me and left a note for Gideon, because Kitty didn't bear rousing.

Gideon come for his children the next morning, with Kitty right behind him. Her face was all ashy and her eyes ringed out and her lips a little blue. Does she hang her head and say forgive me for I have sinned? No, she says: was your Aunt Afton nice to you, ducks, and did you have a good time?

And all Gideon says is: I'll see it don't happen again.

292

Tom says to me later: why don't you just let your brother's family be? The children here should be enough.

That ain't the point. The point is that there isn't a sparrow that falls that God don't see, and if God don't let a thing pass, I don't see why I should. The Saint should ask himself daily: have I done any good in the world today? And besides, Kitty's bad habits reflected on my family and, yes, on Saints everywhere, and it doesn't seem fair, but it's so just the same.

Kitty's bad reputation was downright dumped on me one day when Eden's teacher calls up from school and says I should come get her.

I'm not her mother, I said.

I don't care, says the teacher. This girl needs a good walloping and doesn't deserve to be in school with decent children. She said I should call you.

So I left my youngest boy, Douglass, with a neighbor, and I went to school. Eden was waiting for me, sitting in the school corridor, the kind that always smells of stale bread and shoe rubber. She's so little and sad-looking, holes in her stockings and hem falling out, I want to take her in my arms, but instead I say, what's the trouble here, Eden?

You better ask the teacher, she says.

So I knock on the classroom door and out comes the teacher, bristling, flaring at the nose. It seems that she overheard Eden singing about men creeping into her tent and songs like "Hot Tamale Mollie" and "Keep Your Skirts Down, Mary Ann" and "I'm Willing If You're Able" and I don't know what else.

I thanked the teacher—though I don't know why—habit, I guess. And I took Eden home with me and bent her over the bathroom sink and rubbed that soap around her teeth. She twisted and spit and cried, but she must have known I'd do it, so I don't know why she put up such a fight.

Then she went into my girls' room and closed the door and cried. I let her go for a bit, and then I went in and took her in my arms and held her tight and told her she couldn't sing songs like that, no matter what she heard at home, and I'd teach her some good songs like "Shall the Youth of Zion Falter?" Then I kissed her and told her to go wash up and we'd make a nice cake and have it all ready by the time the others got home.

293

While I had her measuring out the flour I said, Eden, why didn't you have the teacher call your own mother?

I didn't know if she'd be all right, says Eden.

Does your father know she's often not all right?

I don't know what he knows, says Eden.

Well, out of the mouths of babes! God pointed me in the right direction. What's amiss in that house ain't just the drinking and the bad music and the cigarettes. It ain't only the time Kitty spends in the picture houses or the trashy books she reads. It's Gideon. He's the trouble. Not because he joins in with her, but because he don't care. That's where I have to begin. With Gideon.

You better stop where you are, Afton, Tom says when I told him of my revelation. You can't go around breaking up people's lives like they was bones and resetting them to your own purposes.

But that's all he said, nothing more. Tom Lance and me have lived together a long time, and I'll say this, Tom knows when to shut up, and I feel sorry for women whose husbands don't.

I left my older children in charge of the younger ones the following day and I drove downtown when I knew Gideon would be getting off work at the Insurance with Assurance and Gideon come out and I toot the horn and he comes over and I say: you don't have to take the streetcar home, I'll drive you.

I'm not going home, he says. I'm going to do some work at the library.

Do that later, I said. This is important.

I drove over to the park and we got out and strolled for a bit and then I gave him both the old barrels. I didn't spare nothing and no one and no details either. If Gideon wants to know what goes on, I told him.

Gideon adjusts his glasses and pinches his nose, uncomfortable but not contrite. (A woman with five children knows contrite when she sees it.) Finally he says: I don't think there's anything in the Bible against jazzy music or picture shows or romance books, and if it's all right with God, it ought to be all right with the church.

Gideon, I'm not here to split hairs. This is common decency we're talking about—drinking and smoking and neglecting the little children God has give you to bring up right. You have to save them,

Gideon, you're their father. Kitty's your wife, and it's up to you to see she changes her ways.

I don't see anything to change. I have to get to the library before it closes. I have work to do there.

We all have work to do, Gideon! That's what we're put on earth for, but you are living in worse than sin. Your own daughter told her teacher to call me up because she don't know if Kitty will be drunk!

I'll see it don't happen again.

Gideon! You don't see anything! This can't go on! You got to weed the field of your own home! God don't believe you don't see, and neither do I!

I don't hardly remember what I said after that. Pretty soon I couldn't believe my own self. There I was, Afton Lance, screaming at my brother in a public park in broad daylight, having lost not only my mind, but every shred of decency, and even when I know I have to stop, that folks are staring at me and Gideon can't believe his ears, I can't seem to stop till I am wore out as well as embarrassed. I drove him to the library in silence.

When I got home, Tom looks up out of the evening paper and says: how was it being thy brother's keeper, Afton?

That done it. I flung my purse across the room and broke the sugar bowl and stomped into the bedroom. I asked God, did I do wrong? Did I? And I knew, even as I asked Him, what it was I done wrong. I'd smothered the voice of conscience that would make each of us blush if we looked at ourselves as hard as we look at others. Then I guess since the recording angels are taking all this down and I'll have to answer for it in heaven anyway, I might just as well pull my face up off the pillow and admit that I hate Kitty Douglass. I hate everything about her. I hate her sin and lies and squalor and smoke, and I especially hate that she is related to me.

And then I had a nice long cry, which wasn't like me. I think I must have had the monthlies.

I had enough troubles without Kitty. I worried after my sister Lil. She had married again after Willie died, to a widower, a good man, but tight. And I worried after Mother, working long hours day in and day out at the Pilgrim at an age when she ought

295

to be settling back and enjoying the fruits of a righteous life. And I worried over my brother Mason, who was married to a Gentile and living in Washington, D.C., and up to no good, because Mason didn't need no bad companions to lead him astray; he was always in the vanguard of that ragtail army. Invest! That was Mason's favorite word. Invest, in Mason's book, meant to spread your money on Mason's waters and he might return it after many days. And if all that wasn't enough to worry about, Cissa cost me some sleepless nights. Cissa'd already been divorced once, and my bones told me she'd do it again.

I had all of that and five children. Bessie was going through what her teacher told me was called puberty. Ornery's what I call it, but she said, no, puberty. She said they had all kinds of new names nowadays from a man named Froid who said that all our troubles in this life stem from desires so horrible we can't tell anyone, even God, desires so low and wicked we don't even know about them ourselves. I told her: miss, you may well tell me about this Dr. Froid, but if you want to keep your job in the St. Elmo schools, you won't breathe a word of this to anyone else.

So I had Bessie to fret over, and Alma, who was plain as a pie plate and cried about it. And I had Lucius and Samuel, who were good boys, and Junior, who was okay, and Douglass still at home, and one more on the way besides, and on top of all that, I hope I get credit in heaven for Eden and Ada and Ernest, too, though I would have done it anyway, because it needed doing.

I cut down my children's cast-off clothing for Eden and Ada and Ernest. I taught them their manners, slapping their hands when they was rude, swatting them when they was mean. I cut the gum out of Eden's hair and scrubbed Ernest's ears. I sent Ada to the dentist, because her teeth come in all crooked and funny. And it was me fed those children two, three times a week, because lots of times Kitty wouldn't cook; she just sent Gideon down to Ming's to bring back heathen Chinese food in slick waxy cartons and made them all talk Chinese while they ate supper. And it was me plucked the trash she was reading out of Eden's hands and put good books there and tidied those children up for Sunday school and took them to church parties, and it was me baked their birthday cakes, though Kitty came over to watch them blow out the candles and make their little wishes.

I stayed friends with Kitty much as I could, because you don't prune the vineyard with a hacksaw. And though I often despaired, I went over there at least once a month and cleaned that house and doused it with Condy's Disinfectant, only by then Kitty knew when to expect me and she had the cigarettes and liquor hid. It was a stab to me one day to see two cold teacups on the kitchen table and only one with a slice of lipstick on it. I knew my brother was ever weakening.

Well, it wasn't too long after that that Gideon lost his job and the lot of them had to move back in with Mother. I wouldn't say I was glad he lost his job, but the Lord works in mysterious ways. At least those children got looked after good at Mother's. Even Kitty improved. Mother taught her how to make change and gave her a job at the Pilgrim behind the cash register. She was like a new woman. But what I didn't understand, what I said to Mother, was, how can you trust her with a job like that?

And Mother says, she only skims a little off the top. She don't dare skim more than a little, and besides, with her at the Pilgrim, I can look after those children. I know what they're reading and I know what they're eating and I even know what they're thinking.

Mother seemed to have it all nailed down, all right. She was devoted to those children. In fact, her devotion to Eden and Ada and Ernest startled me some. Mother never waxed such affection on us when we was growing up, never pulled us into her arms and called us little made-up names or made our favorite things to eat or costumes for school plays. Well, the six of us didn't have no time for any of that when we was growing up. Hard days, back then. Mother had all she could do to keep us fed and clothed.

I guess Mother's devotion shouldn't surprise me, especially when Eden Louise was the image of our Eden. Oh, she had Kitty's green eyes, but she was Eden, all right. She was even smart like Eden. Ada and Ernest was good, obedient children, but they wasn't smart. Eden was always good in school, writing little poems and stories, always reading. Mother swore that one day Eden would make us all proud, that she would be somebody, amount to something. I didn't say nothing, but I wondered if that meant Mother thought the rest of us had come to naught.

Living with Mother was the very thing Gideon's children needed. At least Mother taught them a little respect for the truth, which

Kitty never would. Couldn't no one get the truth out of Kitty. I needed to know about her parents for my genealogical records, and she couldn't remember nothing about them. First she said her father's name was Charles and then one time she said it was Edward and then it was Reginald, and when I called her on it, she said it was all three.

Well, there was one name Kitty ain't likely to confuse with any other, and that's because she can read it on a tombstone:

SAMUEL GIDEON DOUGLASS
March 5, 1914—January 7, 1919

You could fault Kitty on a lot, but you couldn't begrudge her devotion to that dead little boy. Half a dozen times a year I'd drive her to the cemetery where he lay buried, and finally one day when we was almost there, I said to her: Kitty, you shouldn't mourn so after twelve long years.

He would be seventeen now, she says. A young man. A beautiful young man.

You've got three other children. You should think of them.

You never lost a child, Afton. How could you know what it's like?

Kitty, the dead go on living with God, progressing through the Celestial Kingdom, inhabiting worlds without end forever and ever.

That's fine for the dead, she said, but it don't help the living, does it?

I had never thought of it like that.

Anyway, she says, sometimes I think I'd rather be dead than live in this old burg. You know, Afton, I been thinking I might go back on the stage.

The stage!

Or maybe I might try the pictures. The stage can be so wearisome. The same old lines every night and the same old songs. An *artiste* needs more.

I just about drove up the sidewalk. Kitty Douglass! I shout. You must have lost what's left of your mind to talk about the stage and the pictures. You better wake up! You better have a look at yourself. You are thirty-eight years old and you haul around thirty more pounds of flesh than your bones was made for and you're getting wrinkles and you—

Don't forget, Mrs. Afton-Hoity-Toity-Lance, I was once the Lark of Liverpool, and talent don't die or get old like some other things.

Well, let me tell you, Kitty, I don't believe for one minute you were the Lark of Liverpool or anywhere else. And I don't care what lies Gideon or your children believe. I don't. Lies stick in my craw. I only mince pies, not words, Kitty Douglass, and I am going to tell you, you don't have one shred of talent.

Stop this car! Kitty commands me. I shall walk from here, and I shall walk home, too. I shall not ride with no one who would say such things to me. I am going to see my own dear little boy, my sweet Toots, and I will not trouble you again. She raises her chins, opens the door, gets out, and walks away.

Well, I left her. If that's what she wanted, she got it. As I was driving home, I thought about all the reasons I was in the right, and I was, of course, but I just couldn't rinse off the feeling that I'd been mean-spirited and maybe even nasty. I almost went back to pick her up, but my pride kept me from it.

They say your spirit never ceases to learn through this world and the next. And I learned. Even from Kitty Douglass. I learned that there are some things which defy faith and zeal. And sometimes even armed yea unto the teeth with righteousness, you meet defeat. Naturally no right-thinking person would believe that, lest they'd lived it like I did. In my heart I know God will not suffer the righteous to fail, but finally I had to give up with Kitty, because I knew that even if I was to succeed with her, the victory was too far off for me to see or care about.

Anyway, I didn't see Kitty or her family very often after that, because in 1934 Mother had her stroke and come to live with us, and Gideon packed them all up and took them up to Fairwell so he could work with Mason, who naturally didn't have no job at all. Mason has disgraced the noble name of Douglass with his schemes and frauds. Mason always claimed he had vision where the rest of us was just blind to the possibilities, but I said, Mason, if you got vision, then how is it all you can see is dollar signs?

Well, I could have used a few dollar signs myself by 1934, because that gutless, thankless railroad laid Tom off after nearly thirty years of service. They were letting everyone go, but that don't make it any easier when it's your own family going to go hungry.

We're not going hungry, Tom says to me, we're just going to do something else.

How can we start over at our time of life? I asked him.

But we did. And we didn't do too bad, either. We sunk all our savings in some acreage east of town with orange groves on it. We put in a big garden and got a cow and some chickens, and we never did go hungry. And Tom, who never grew so much as a tomato, he made them orange trees sing with fruit.

Soon as we moved there, Tom started building, and over the years he built us—with his own two hands and his sons' help—a brand-new house, as nice a place as anyone's. And when Lil come to live with us in '43, he built her her own little room, with bath, out back, because Lil ain't used to living with boys, Tom says, and she should have her own place.

Even though our children growed up and left, that house stayed full. We had Mother with us till she died, and we was cramped but happy. We always had grandkids in. They all came and some stayed.

The orphaned boys of my son Lucius, they stayed. Lucius joined up with the navy before Pearl Harbor, and that's where he was when the Japs struck. He lived through Pearl Harbor, but he died at Guadalcanal, leaving a wife and two little boys. His wife remarried soon, a man who didn't care for her children by Lucius, and so I said, give them here. No grandchildren of mine are going to grow up in a house where they're not wanted. Give them here. She went off, and I don't expect she saw them again but three or four times, but they didn't seem to miss it. They was happy with us.

And I had a couple of Junior's kids once when he and his wife split up for a bit, though bless God, none of my children ever got divorced. I took Douglass's brood, too, when he and his wife went off into the desert to do some mining—one of Mason's fool schemes. Once my children grew up, Mason had a whole 'nother generation to sucker into his schemes, and it seemed like all he had to say was Get Rich Quick and off they went. You'd think they was never brought up to believe in the value of work. Look at your father, I said to Douglass when he was packing for the desert, your father is up every day at dawn for nearly fifty years and never a word of complaint. Ain't you ever heard of work? And Douglass says to me: that's all I've ever heard, and I'm sick of it.

300

Junior lost his shirt on one of Mason's schemes, and Douglass lost three years out in the desert, and my youngest boy, William, went down to Florida on one of Mason's land deals and ended up owning a motel and not seeing me and Tom for seventeen years. But Tom would never let me say to them boys, I told you so. Tom said they were grown men and bad enough they should look like fools in front of their children, much less their parents.

So my sons was a disappointment to me and my daughters broke my heart a couple of times. Bessie's oldest was born just six short months after the wedding. And Alma, she married a man I disapproved of, though it worked out all right in the end. And my youngest, Constance, she died in 1962, just thirty-four, died of something I couldn't even pronounce, and I took her four kids in till her husband remarried a good LDS woman who loved them like her own.

I felt Constance's death, but by then I had so much acquaintance with death, it didn't shrivel me up the way I thought it would. I felt it, but I kept on living. It was Lucius's death at Guadalcanal I thought would kill me, and once I survived that, I guessed I could survive anything.

After Lucius died I couldn't help but think of Kitty and how she was never the same after her Tootsie died. I thought about all the mean things I'd said to Kitty and how I'd hated her. But when my son died at Guadalcanal, a revelation came on me and I understood what happened to Kitty. I wished I could have gone to her and begged her forgiveness, said, forgive me, Kitty, but how could I have knowed? Maybe Kitty should have put away her grief and got on with the business of living like I wanted her to. But it wasn't till Guadalcanal that I could see that the business of living wasn't ever again going to be as interesting as it once was.

In the midst of life we are in death, and in the face of death we are commanded to go on living. But the day that telegram came about my Lucius, I dropped to the kitchen floor. I crawled out on the porch and sat and I didn't move. Pretty soon all around me they was all weeping and wailing and on the phone, but I stayed on the porch and I did not move. Tom come home in the middle of the day, and my daughters and daughters-in-law and sons come over and begged me to eat or talk or leastways to cry. Tom told them to leave me be. They cooked and fed everyone else and cleaned up the supper dishes and packed up their kids and begged me to go inside.

301

And Tom said: leave her be. And after they had all left and the house was shut down and quiet, then I let the tears come and didn't try to staunch or wipe them. I just cried out to the night and the stars and the sliver of a moon that lay cradled like a baby in its own arms: I had lost my boy, and even though it was a good cause, I knew that God could be unjust.

And finally, when the moon was down, I heard Tom. He was sitting in the dark in the living room, and I heard him get out of his chair and come out to the porch, and he stands beside me for a while till he takes my hand. He says: let's go to bed, Mother. Today's going to be both yesterday and tomorrow quicker than you know, and the grief ain't going to pass any other way.

They don't make them like Tom Lance anymore.

38 Lil

THAT LIL OUTLIVED them all. She outloved them all, too, except Afton, who could never be outdone. She was tiny and frail and beautiful to begin with, and tiny and frail and wizened at the end. She lived her young life and her old age in her older sister's shadow, because it was more fun to be bossed around by Afton than to be catered to by anyone else. After Afton passed on, it wasn't so much fun anymore, and it wasn't any fun at all when her children removed her to the Vegas Gardens Rest Home in 1965, but she lived there eleven years all the same, just to go on living.

She had three children, two girls by Handsome Willie and a son by Mr. Walsh. They came to visit her regularly. On holidays and her birthday. Sometimes they missed her birthday. Afton never missed her birthday, no indeed. Even in the thirty years Lil and Afton lived apart. When Lil came to live with Afton and Tom in 1943, she had her own nice little room, almost an apartment, just out back of Afton's place, and what a good time they had, because Lil knew that Afton was never really happy unless she had about twenty-five claims on her attention and about twice that many on her time.

"Afton never forgot my birthday," Lil said to her daughter Jean, who came to visit five days after her birthday in 1972. "Afton never forgot a thing. If the time came to remember a good someone done, Afton remembered it, and if the time came to remember a harm, well, Afton remembered that, too."

"Aunt Afton was a wonderful woman," Jean replied. "God rest her soul."

"Oh, God's the only one who'll rest Afton's soul," Lil declared, her head bobbing up and down. "That Afton, she was just like Mother: her hands was never empty and her heart was always full. Afton's in the Celestial Kingdom, all right, and probably telling everyone up there what to do, too."

Jean grimaced. "Yes, well. How do you feel, Ma?"

"How'm I supposed to feel? I'm seventy-seven years old." Lil let go of the wheelchair to scratch her nose. "Afton always said she'd like to get as old as Methuselah so long as she could hold on to her brains, her stomach, her liver, and her feet—all the rest of it could go and she wouldn't care. I got my liver."

"You're doing all right, Ma."

"If you call this all right, then you're a fool, Jean." Lil smoothed out a wrinkle in her cotton dress and pulled up her long socks, wheezing under the strain. "Afton always baked me a cake on my birthday. I never had the heart to tell her that I hate cake. I always threw it up afterward, but she never knew. Can't stand the sweetness. It makes me sick, but Afton always enjoyed baking those cakes, and she did it real well, so I couldn't tell her, could I?"

"No, Ma."

"Afton never forgot no one's birthday. Even if they was dead. Never forgot when they died, neither. Me and Afton, we used to get wore out going back and forth to the cemetery on everyone's birthdays and some on the days they died. We went for Eden and Mother and Doctor. Afton even took flowers for Kitty's little boy when Kitty left St. Elmo. That Afton, she never forgot no one or nothing. How could she forget, with her bones reminding her all the time? That Afton, she was just like Mother. Mother's bones

303

was always talking to her, too. Afton never forgot nothing. I do sometimes."

"I'll say you do."

"Not too much, though. I don't forget too much."

"It's all relative."

"That's what Afton used to say—they're all your relatives, even if they are dead. They're all waiting for me on the death train."

"The what, Ma? Ma? Ma?"

I'm the last passenger. They're all waiting for me to get on the death train. First one to get on was Eden. Eden was the first passenger. She gets on, no luggage or nothing, and she sits there for a long time, looking out the window, rocking through country where there ain't no scenery. I can see my sister Eden in her smart burgundy suit riding that train all by herself till Willie got on. Then Willie and Eden, they have a good time talking about me and all the foolish things I done, laughing over me and crying, too. Then pretty soon, someone else gets on—Doctor, I guess. Doctor gets on, and then Mr. Walsh, and then Mother, and then they all get on, one after the other, and pretty soon the death train is so filled up there's no room to sit down, because I know more dead people than living. And now I'm the last passenger, and when I get on, then that train can get to wherever it's going. And not before. I wave to them now and then, and I say—just a little longer! Just give me a little more time.

> *"What are you waving at, Ma?"*
> *"I'm not waving."*
> *"I was talking about Eldon's new job, and you just start waving."*
> *"Did not."*
> *"Do you want to hear about Eldon's new job?"*
> *"Sure."*
> *"He works so much now, Ma, he doesn't have any time at all."*

I didn't have any time either, only thirty-four months. That was all. But even if I didn't have any time on earth with Willie, I'll have all eternity, and I guess that ought to be enough. Handsome Willie. He was a looker. Handsome Willie and Dandelion Lil, that's what they always called us. Look at Jean. How did she get to be so fat? Neither me nor Willie had an ounce of fat on us, and Afton always used to say, Lil, how can you work in a bakery and keep your figure? And I laughed and said someone like Mason coulda got fat anywhere. Even in jail. And Afton said, yes, he came real close to that, didn't he? But she didn't say anything more, because she held her tongue when there was only mean things to say about a body, especially family. Afton always said Mason could sell tapwater in Niagara.

> "What's so funny, Ma?"
> "Nothing. Did you bring the funny paper with you?"
> "I did, but I was telling you about—"
> "Read me the funnies."
> "It's Friday, Ma. Didn't you get someone to read them to you on Sunday?"
> "If you'da come on my birthday like you was supposed to, you coulda read them to me on Sunday, but now it's so long ago that I can't remember."

I can remember Monday, September 18, 1911, when I first met Willie Lance. He was visiting his brother, Tom Lance, and his new wife, my sister Afton. Afton drives over to Mother's in the morning—you could always tell it was her, because no one in St. Elmo tooted a horn like Afton Lance—and she says to me, Lil, I have your man. You just wait till you see him.

I was cleaning Mother's black kid gloves with a little sweet milk and soap, and I was rubbing every inch of those gloves like they was the last pair on earth, and I remark to Afton how hot it is for September, and then I say, what man?

Afton does her favorite little cakewalk around the table and peeks into our pie cooler, and I can't figure out why she's so happy today, but she surely does have a little devil in her eye, and Afton says: Tom's younger brother, Willie. He's just back from a mission to New Zealand, and he's stopping here for a few days before he goes back home to Lilac, Idaho.

305

Same place Tom's from? I say, giving those gloves the final once-over and laying them out on the towel and thinking to myself, well, Afton's Tom is a good man and a good man for her, but I'd die of the silence if I was to marry a man like that. Afton's a talker, and she don't even notice that Tom don't have a word to say, but I'm not like that; I am more shy.

But, of course, I have to go over to Afton's and see this man, but before I do, Afton combs my hair out for me, and she says, you have such beautiful gold hair, Lil, too bad there ain't more of it, but she makes do with what there is and borrows Mother's tortoiseshell comb and tells me to take off my apron and pinch my cheeks and off we go to Afton's.

Afton's got two stunted palms at either side of the lawn and two pillars at either side of the porch, and they are like a frame for that picture of Tom and Willie Lance, which I will carry to my grave. Both men in open collars and their sleeves rolled up, and they are sitting on thin kitchen chairs in the inky shadows of that porch while everything else is white and hot, flat and ironed out by the noonday sun. It must have been Willie doing the talking in that low, sweet voice of his, because Tom almost never talked. Afton don't even pull around to the back, but stops right in front and urges me out, and together we walk across the burning grass, up to the porch, and Afton says, Willie, this is my sister Lil.

I stand there, and I can feel the sun beating down on my head and sweat pricking up under my bodice, and I look at Willie Lance and I have to smile, because I hope with all my heart that Afton is right and this is the man for me.

God passed emery paper over Willie Lance's face. Bright eyes that look right at you and a narrow mouth with a fine, firm smile. He was so smooth and clean-shaven and chiseled-looking he reminded me of the statue in the park, the beardless man on horseback, and how I always longed to crawl up into that man's lap and rest my head on his stone shoulder and touch his smooth stone face. But I shouldn't be comparing the living man to the statue, because there wasn't no way you could have mistook Willie Lance for a statue. He had those Fourth-of-July-blue eyes, and he said, I'm pleased to meet you, Miss Douglass, Miss Lily Douglass.

Willie was promised—more or less—to a girl in Lilac, Idaho, a Sarah Briggs. That never bothered Afton. I said, Afton, if he's *promised*, maybe I shouldn't even— But Afton just pooh-pooh'd that, because he wasn't *married*. And anyway, says Afton, the church don't favor long engagements.

Willie himself told me that this Sarah Briggs had gone on a mission, and that gave me pause, because it was so few girls who went on missions in those days—unmarried girls almost never—and I thought, Miss Sarah Briggs must be a lady to be reckoned with if she could talk the church into letting her go on a mission. I didn't think I could come close to outshining a girl like that, and when I told Afton so, she just called me a goose and told me to step back out on the porch and talk to Willie, because she'd be there forever and he wouldn't.

I spent just about that whole week at Afton's with Willie. Mother never asked me no questions about Willie or anything, even when I brought him home one night so she could meet him. She said, he's a fine young man, and that was all she said. Well, I wondered if she'd think he was such a fine young man if she'd known I was crazy with love for Willie Lance, but I didn't say anything, because he was promised to someone else, even if he wasn't married.

Willie didn't talk much, but he talked more than Tom, and we spent many hours that week—was it only a week?—on Afton's front porch, talking, calling each other Mr. Lance and Miss Douglass, and I asked him all about the mission field in New Zealand, and he asked me all about me. I don't have much to tell, I said, I'm just in my last year of high school, and there's nothing too interesting about that. Willie said: Miss Douglass, how can you say that? You do yourself an injustice. I think you are one of the most interesting persons I have ever met, and certainly the most beautiful.

Well, that would have been enough, right there. If the train came by and swept him off the porch and carried him off forever, I still could have died happy, because words (and Willie had a way with words) can always be remembered. Any old time you want them, they're there. They can be pressed like flowers and fingered anytime you want. All the rest of it turns into empty memory if it's not in words, and you have to wait for memory to summon *you*, you can't hasten or stop it. But words, they can be remembered easy, and you can put them away fast, too, if someone comes up on you and startles you. You can have words whenever you want. You get hungry for the past? There they are, a box of word chocolates. Just choose.

307

Don't know why I thought about chocolates. I could eat them and enjoy them in those days. It wasn't till later that I couldn't stand sweets, that they made me sick, vomitous, when I lived at Mother's after Willie died. I worked at Cotton's Bakery then. I didn't need the job, but I needed the work. When I just stayed at Mother's I didn't do nothing but cry all day for months, and finally, Doctor, he says, Lil, you're going to float downriver if you keep this up. You got to stop. You got to do something else.

So that was when I went to work for Cotton's Bakery ("Nice Making and Nice Baking—our Cakes Crown Any Meal"), and it kept me from crying, but I started throwing up instead. I'd come home and throw up every day, but I never let anyone know. Not Mother. Not the children. The two children Willie left me with when he died. Left a widow with two small children. Every time I'd think it was more than I could bear and that I'd leap into the grave and join Willie if I could, I'd say, Lil Lance, at least you don't have it so bad as Sarah Briggs, who I heard married a widower fifteen years older than her who had five children by his first wife. Then he died and left her the care of those children, who weren't even her own. At least mine were my own. Mine and Willie's. The fruit of our love.

Willie said he couldn't stay in St. Elmo but just that one week, because his mother—and others—were expecting him home, and Tom didn't press him to stay, but Afton did. She made it just about impossible for him to leave, till I think Tom let her know she was managing things too much and she should let them be, but that was never her way. Willie got all packed, and she drove him to the station. I went, too, of course. I was wearing my best peek-a-boo blouse, which was very daring, but Afton said it was perfectly respectable and if anyone didn't think so, it just went to show what they were thinking. Afton often said stuff like that.

Willie, he looked beautiful, his hair slicked down, his tie straight, and his jacket buttoned even if it was hot as hell's suspenders that day. He held his bag on his lap and didn't look any too comfortable with Afton's driving. When we got to the train station, Afton said, well, Brother Will, I expect we'll see you back here before too long, and Lil, I'll come pick you up later. You get out and wait for the train with Willie. I have to go to my genealogy group. It was about an hour before that meeting, and I knew it, but I didn't say so, just got out of the car like Afton said, and Willie gave me his arm and we went in to buy his ticket and wait for the train.

Well, I have all those words, too, all those that passed between us when we sat in the St. Elmo station, waiting for his train. I have them all pressed and perfect. I think I listened extra hard, because I thought: the next time I see Willie Lance, he will be a married man, and I'll marry, too, I guess, someday, but I'll never love a man like I love Willie Lance. I knew that in a week.

He knows it, too, Lil, Afton said, and don't you worry. He'll be back.

> *"I'll be back next week, Ma. And Rebecca*
> *said she'd come just as soon as her daughter*
> *has had her baby and the car's not acting up.*
> *It's a long ride from Reno to Vegas. Ma?"*

Well, it's a long ride from St. Elmo, California, to Lilac, Idaho, too. And Willie told me later that my face was before him all the time and he heard my voice calling to him, come back, Willie, come back. (And I did say it, too, over the washtub, to the stove, and in my school books, which I filled up with his name, Willie Willie Willie.)

Willie got to Lilac, Idaho, and saw his people, and they welcomed him back from the mission field. In fact, they had a special gathering to welcome back Brother Lance and Sister Briggs and hoped they'd have another announcement—a *happy* announcement—to make about Brother Lance and Sister Briggs real soon. Willie said he could hear my voice, Willie, Willie, said my voice was so strong in his heart that directly after that gathering he took Miss Sarah Briggs home and said to her: I know I have not been back but less than a week and perhaps I should have spoken before this. (I imagine Sarah Briggs here—small and dark and pink-cheeked with anticipation, wearing a nice, serviceable gray and probably no ribbon at all, her lips all ready to say, yes, Willie, I do, Willie, thinking how Willie brought her home especially to have some courting time with her.)

But my heart has been in turmoil, Willie continued. I have prayed for guidance and I have wrestled with my feelings for days, like Jacob and his angel. My time in the mission field has only served

309

to impress upon me the responsibilities and the duties of the holy state of matrimony and the heavy burden of free will in a world that is full of temptations. Believe me, I do not do this lightly—but I would be less than manly if I waited one more day, one more hour, before telling you that my feelings for you have changed. I will always love you in my heart, but it is the love of a brother for his sister, of one of God's Latter-day Saints for another, not, alas, the love of a man for his wife.

Well, I can just imagine Sarah Briggs here, too, after her face had drained, leaving it long and sourish, because I met her years later in a general meeting of the Relief Societies of Idaho, after I had married Mr. Walsh. This woman comes up to me (she was small and dark and wearing serviceable gray and no ribbon at all, but then I wasn't wearing no ribbons either in 1925), and she said, you're Willie Lance's widow, aren't you? Well, I'm glad I didn't marry him, because I would hate to be left a widow with two small children. And I just stood there, my tongue tied down at both ends, and it was only later I wished I'd been smart enough to say: at least my children are my own. But it was always Willie had the way with words.

Willie left Lilac right after telling Miss Briggs he couldn't marry her. He went to Sugarville, Idaho, and got a job in the sugar factory there, and he said he'd be back in two weeks: he was going to California to get married. The foreman was a Latter-day Saint. He said, all right, I'll give you two weeks, but then you better come back.

> "I'll be back, Ma. Ma? You don't hear me at all, do you?"
> "What did you say?"
> "I said I'll be back."
> "I'm not going anywhere."
> "You want me to leave you the funnies?"
> "No. Didn't you just read them to me?"
> "Well, I thought you might like to see the pictures."
> "I can't make out the pictures. Stay awhile, Jean. Please."
> "I would, Ma, but I don't think you're

listening to a word I say, and how's that
supposed to make me feel?"

I reach out my hand to touch Jean, and I notice that my hand has got blue flour dusted all over it. Jean takes my hand in hers and pats it like I am three. Once I thought I would die of happiness, that my spirit would soar out of my body, when I put my finger out and little Jeannie grabs it and her little hand is so soft and tight for such a baby. And Willie, he puts his finger out for her other hand, and then he touches my face. Willie says, she's going to look like you, Lil, she's going to be fair and lovely like Dandelion Lil.

But the truth is, she don't look like either of us. Sometimes when I look at my grown children, I think the church might be right and they are only spirits I clothed in flesh, and barring that, why, there's no connections at all. Jean sits here and pats my hand because I gave her spirit a body to come to earth in. What does it matter? If I hadn't done it, someone else would have.

"I am listening, Jean. I hear every word
you say. You stay, and we'll talk some more."
"Okay, Ma. What do you want to talk
about?"

I don't want to talk, of course. I don't even want to listen. I just want to *hear*. Jean could recite the *Doctrine and Covenants* and it would all be the same to me. I smile and take my hand back from her and watch it shake till I can't stand it no more, and then I hold on to the wheelchair.

"I don't care."
"Let's talk about you, Ma."
"Me! What's there to talk about me? I'm in
the checkout line."
"Who are you going to vote for for
President, Ma? Nixon or—"
"What do I care who's President? Tell me
something about someone I know. Tell me
what Lily Annetta's doing."
"She has turned out vain and empty-

311

headed, if you ask me. All she cares about is clothes."

Mother always said it was Kitty would be condemned by heaven for her vanity. Mother always said if Kitty got to heaven first she'd be on the lookout for you just to see what you was wearing and how she could criticize it. Kitty wasn't the only vain one. You can't have people telling you your whole life that you're beautiful and not have little seeds of vanity planted in you, though I fought it, and I haven't been beautiful for fifty years, so that makes it easier. (Age never made no difference to Kitty. She always thought she was a nineteen-year-old belle when two nineteen-year-old belles could have fit inside her clothes.) I was beautiful once. There wasn't no one more beautiful than me in my wedding dress on my wedding day. That was the happiest day of my life.

We didn't have no time to spare by the time Willie got down to St. Elmo. We had to be married right away and be back on the train and back to Idaho and Willie's job. I was scared, not of Willie, but of Mother. I told myself I'd run off and elope if I had to. Afton went with me to ask Mother about marrying Willie, 'cause Afton was sure there'd be trouble, too.

But Mother said: marry him, Lil, if that's all you want from life.

I just about fainted clean away at that. I wasn't yet finished with high school, and I looked at Afton, and I have never but that once seen Afton Lance's mouth drop with sheer surprise.

I said: that's all I want is to be Willie Lance's wife. That was all I wanted, and I got it for thirty-four months.

Dr. Tipton gave me the money for my wedding dress. Lots of money. I said, I cannot accept such a bountiful gift, but Dr. Tipton, he just smiled at Mother and clapped Willie on the shoulder, and he said, that's the best wedding present I could give you. I could buy you a whole wagonload of china, and pretty soon you'll be married so long it'll just be the same old plates you stare at every day in the scummy dishwater. You'd forget eventually that they were ever once new and young—like your love.

Me, I looked at Willie, and we smiled.

But that dress, Doctor went on, you'll never forget that dress, and no matter how old it gets, it will always be precious and new. You never forget your wedding, isn't that so, Ruth?

312

Mother coughed and said it was so, and then she said Doctor seemed to have a heap of knowledge of these things for never having had the experience.

You don't always need experience, he said. Some things you just know. And I thought I saw Mother squash a smile. No, Lil, he said, you let me buy your wedding dress, and I know you'll never forget me. I'll know there'll be one young woman, even one old woman, who'll remember Lucius Tipton every time she looks at those little crimps and ruches, and that satin chiffon and mousseline and silk and—

We all stared at him. Who would have thought Doctor would know all that?

All those lovely names women give their lovely things, he said, but he did color a bit, and then he gave me the money and left.

Afton and me had a great time with that money. None of that sprigged muslin for you, Lil, says Afton. Let's take Doctor at his word. So we bought the best there was: ninon silk over chiffon with a deep snowy-silk yoke set about with pink pale flowers and a long rose satin sash. I had lace a foot long dripping from my elbows and a froth of tulle over my head, and when Dr. Tipton walked me into Mother's living room to face the bishop and Willie, I thought Willie was just going to fall over, and the whole family just sucked their breath in. I could hear it then just like I can hear Jean talking now, but I didn't pay it any mind then and I don't pay her any mind now, because I was then and I am now thinking about Willie Lance. Handsome Willie.

I left instructions that I'm to be buried in that dress. Shipped to Rexburg and buried next to Willie. There is money for all of it. I brought the dress and the money and the instructions, all of it, to the Vegas Gardens with me, because I knew when they brought me here I'd never leave but in a box, and I can't imagine how it is I've lived so long.

Thirty-four months. That was all we had. From our wedding day till he drew his last breath, Willie Lance and I had thirty-four months.

*"And Martha said she was a fool to spend
so much money on Lily Annetta's graduation*

313

*dress, because she'd be getting married soon
and then she would have—"
"Who said that?"
"Martha."*

Martha? Martha?

*"Martha Walsh. Owen's wife. Your
daughter-in-law, Martha, Ma."*

Who's Martha, Afton?
*That little piece of khaki that married your Owen, Lil. Owen
don't take after the Douglasses one bit, Lil. He is a Walsh through
and through.*
Owen does take after Mr. Walsh. Mr. Walsh was a good man. I
could have done worse. I had to do something after I couldn't work
in the bakery no more. I couldn't just go on living with Mother my
whole life or till my babies grew up. What would I do then? What
could I do, anyway? There wasn't nothing I was fit for. I wished I'd
gone to business school like Eden or at least graduated from high
school. All I could do was keep house, and that was all Mr. Walsh,
the widower, wanted, someone to keep house and look after his
motherless children. Two of them. They were all right, but pretty
colorless children and no beauties.
I met Mr. Walsh when he was visiting his sister in St. Elmo. He
liked me. He asked me to come up to National Falls and keep house
for him.
Don't go, said Mother.
But I had to go. After I fainted in the bakery, there wasn't no
choice for me but to go with Mr. Walsh.
It wasn't the first time I'd fainted, but it was the first time anybody knew about it, because usually I could get to a chair before it
happened, but this was a Saturday morning like no other. There
was six of us girls and Mrs. Cotton. We had a wedding cake to get
out and delivered, and it went bad. One of the girls opened the oven
door to put in some ginger cakes, and the wedding cake fell, but we
had to let it finish baking before we knew if we could cover it up
with frosting or if we'd have to make a new one. Mrs. Cotton was
plenty mad at that girl and fired her and said she couldn't leave till

the end of the day even if she was fired, and that girl just took off her apron and cap, threw them on the floor, wiped her feet on them, and flounced out. So that left the rest of us with her work, too, and Mrs. Cotton felt bad because she knew she shouldn't have been so sharp.

I didn't blame that girl for walking out, but at the time I was up to my elbows in cake dough. I had the flour and butter all rubbed together and was just about to add the sugar when I felt the weakness coming over me, but I didn't dare sit down and collect myself, because Mrs. Cotton might just have fired me, too. Anyway, it wasn't real hot yet, and I thought maybe it would get better if I thought of something else, something cool and moist, not like that kitchen, the air dried out with flour and parched with soda and crawling with sugar grains. If I could think of something cool and scentless, not like the smells around me, teasing me, the nutmegs and gingers, lemon and chocolate, and that thick, gasping sugar everywhere: in my nose, my hair, over my face, and billowing up in stiff peaks out of Mrs. Cotton's icing bowl, flying around the room because she beat it with such fury. It started to pour out of the oven, too, that smell, sweet and solvent on the tongue maybe, but packing in around me, pressing my head into my shoulders. But I just kept pouring in that sugar, when I had to stop and hold on to the table for a minute: I know I can make it pass, I say to myself. Pass, I say to it. And it came to pass that the weak were uplifted and made strong, but it didn't do no good. Down I went, and when I open my eyes, I'm on the floor in Mrs. Cotton's office, watching the light come in through the flour-caked window.

Well, I go back to Mother's, and she's stone-eyed and her lips twitch with worry, and she calls Doctor, and he says to Mother: this girl has fainted clean away because she's malnourished.

No, Mother, I say, it was the smell. That awful sweetness. The sugar. It's getting me like it got Willie. I can't stand the smell.

Smell, hell, says Doctor, and then he sends Mother out of the room and he takes my hand and he says, Lil, are you pregnant?

Doctor! I am a widow!

I didn't ask you that, says Doctor.

I am a widow, I say again, and then I start to cry all over again, and Doctor takes me in his arms and holds me, and I tell him: it *is* the smell. I can't keep anything down. I haven't been able to for months. It's that terrible sweetness. I come home from the bakery and I'm covered with that confection, and it lodges in my craw till all I can do is vomit. It stays with me all the time.

There, there, dear girl, says Doctor. Don't cry. Hush. But this is the end of the bakery job, Lil. This is the end of that.

In being the end of one thing, it was the beginning of another. It was the beginning of Mr. Walsh.

Don't go with Mr. Walsh, says Mother. Don't go to Idaho with Mr. Walsh.

Mother, I said, Mr. Walsh is a good, respectable man, a Latter-day Saint who needs a housekeeper, and I need a home for my two children. Every adult mortal has to have duties if they want to claim the right to knock at heaven's gate.

Don't go, says Mother.

But I went, and I lived there seven years before I knew why she didn't want me to go. In 1927 I made the journey she must have feared I'd make all along. I didn't go meaning no harm or out of idle curiosity. I went for Mother, to do what she couldn't do for herself, and once I went, I knew why she couldn't do it, but there wasn't no way to go back and unlearn what I knew by then.

I took Mr. Walsh's car and drove to Healy. It was my first and my only trip by myself. I explained to Mr. Walsh that I wanted to go by myself, to pay my respects at my father's grave.

But there wasn't any grave. I asked at the cafe, and there wasn't anyone who remembered Samuel Douglass, but a man there said I should check with city records on Monday or ask at the Mormon church. I paid my nickel and thanked him, but I couldn't wait till Monday, and when I drove by the church there didn't look to be anyone there. I didn't remember Healy, and just as well. It was one of those grubby towns too far from the railroad to live, but just enough folks to keep it from dying. At the filling station I asked after the old Douglass place, but it meant nothing to the man. Then I said, there was a brickyard. And the man said, oh, yes, there was a place with an old brickyard six miles from town.

So I drove out, and there it was. Well, some of it was and some of it wasn't. The fruit trees were old and gnarled; the ones that weren't dead dripped fruit, and there was a young man and his wife who lived in a little wooden shack near what used to be the barn. I stopped Mr. Walsh's car and got out and walked up to the charred

316

foundation of our old brick house, and the wife come out. She naturally wanted to know what I was doing poking around there, standing at what had once been my own front door.

I used to live here, I said. My father planted those fruit trees. My father built that brickyard. My father homesteaded this land, came to it when it was nothing but a howling wilderness, and I was born in a dugout that used to be over there somewhere. We used it for a chicken coop after my father built this brick house, this burnt-up brick house here.

The woman's eyes filled with tears at that, and I couldn't imagine what I'd said to upset her so. She wiped her eyes with her apron, and she said: we lost everything in that fire.

What fire?

When the house burned down. We lost everything we had in it, we never—

Well, I hated to be rude, but I said: that house burned down a long time ago.

Five years. She sniffs. It seems like forever.

That house burned down a long, *long* time ago. In 1900.

Well, that changed her tune. That house, she snaps at me, just about burned over my head in August 1922, and don't tell me that I don't remember what was the worst thing that ever happened to me.

Well, I stalked through those ruins without so much as another word to her and stood there and kicked at some of the dirt and charred bricks and beams and disbelieved that woman. My father died in that fire, and he couldn't have died just five years before. Could he? Could someone have got it wrong? Could this be the wrong ruins? I tried to remember Father, but it had been so many years since I had even said the word "father" that it didn't seem to have no meaning for me. I could hardly remember the word, let alone the person who once filled it up.

I drove back toward town and then passed through it. I was no sooner to the Healy city limit than I knew I had to go back. I knew I would never return to Healy again, but I had to go back now, even though I ought to let it lie. I had to know however much there was to know, or could be known, or would ever be known. So I went to the church and found someone and told him who I was looking for, and he got on the phone and called up an old man who came over

317

presently, an old man shaking dander wherever he went. He told me my father was a lunatic and my mother was a liar.

He said Samuel Douglass was a false prophet who had run off to Mexico with another woman. Samuel Douglass thought he was a new prophet, and the Church of Jesus Christ of Latter-day Saints wasn't good enough for Samuel Douglass. He said if my mother told me Samuel Douglass died in a fire, then she lied, and the only fire either of them would see was in hell. He barked on about my father, and I just sat there. Lil Walsh. Grown woman, wife to two men, mother to three children, I cried into my new gloves. But when he started on Mother, when he said Mother run off and left Father and her pride drove him crazy, that's when I quit crying. I stood up. I said: you are a low, lying dog. Only a worm-hearted creature would say such things about the best mother any children ever had. You got worms in your soul, you old goat! And then I left. Didn't give him no time to call me no names back. I left quick.

When I got home that night, Mr. Walsh said to me, did you pay your respects to your father? I said, yes, yes, I did. And I reckoned that was at least fifty percent of the truth and it would pass.

Then I went to bed, and I lay awake in the darkness, long after Mr. Walsh come to bed and the house lay in silence. I wanted to take that silence and stuff it in my ears, but you can't unlearn the truth. I wonder what Eden did when she couldn't unlearn it, when that fire, that other fire, talked to her. It was talking to the rest of us, too, but it was lying. The trellis alight, the whole yard afire and lying—*this is the way it was when Father died and the eight-room house burned to the ground and the barn went, too.* But it wasn't that way at all. And Eden knew it. Eden had a revelation, and now I have the revelation, only I don't know what to do with it.

I thought about sharing it with Afton, but I didn't. Afton's the best there is, but it's not her way to let things lie. And some things you have to let lie. And I thought about writing a letter and saying: Dear Mother—I have thought about going over to Healy and paying my respects to Father, but I've decided against it.

But then she would know I'd gone, so there wasn't nothing I could do but keep shut about that knowledge, not share that revelation with no one from that day to this.

Mother never let on the real reason she didn't want me to go with Mr. Walsh, but she was just full of reasons why I shouldn't go to

Idaho. When none of the others worked, she said to me: I don't see how you can bear to go back to the place you lived with Willie and keep house for another man.

Well, I said, me and Willie lived in Sugarville, and that's a long ways from National Falls, and so it isn't as though I'll have to think of Willie all the time. Or ever, really. Besides, it's 1920, and Willie's been dead six years, and sometimes I can hardly remember him.

That was a lie. But I thought it would make her feel better. I said Mr. Walsh was a nice man. But I didn't say that he was certainly no Willie Lance, and I didn't say that there was nights when I'd lie abed and I'd dream Willie'd be there. I'd hear a child crying in the night and I'd stir, and Willie'd say to me in my dream, stay here and talk to me, Lil. Stay here in this dream and talk to me. I get real lonely. Oh, Willie, *I* get so lonely without you.

Then there was other nights when Willie would do more than talk to me in my dreams and I'd wake up aching in all the places Willie used to touch and having thoughts no woman should have even if she is married, much less if she's widowed. And there was other nights he'd reach out to me and say, Lil—Dandelion Lil—it's me, Willie. Come with me, Lil.

Those nights were the worst, because I'd have to rouse myself and remind myself how Prophet Joseph Smith said to tell a good spirit from an evil one. You ask him to shake hands with you, and if he does and you feel his hand, then you are all right, because your messenger is an angel and you better hear him out. If he shakes hands with you and you don't feel it, you tell him to scat! Because *that* is the devil. But if your visitor is a just-man-made-perfect, he will sigh and he will be sad and say that God won't let him touch the hands of mortals, only give messages. And that's how you can tell the good from the bad.

Well, it never worked, because I could never remember it in time. I know the real Willie would never be begging me to join him in death and shake off my earthly responsibilities before my Heavenly Father calls me. Then I wonder what business the Heavenly Father had calling Willie when he was so young and handsome and loved and needed.

I always hoped He'd call me just as soon as my children were grown, but He didn't. Look at Jean. She's grown. And Rebecca, and even Mr. Walsh's Owen. All grown with children who are

319

grown with children. I don't know why I'm here. Don't serve no useful purpose. And look at me. I'll just die if when I get to heaven I look like this and Willie looks like the day they laid his beautiful head on the satin pillow. I made that pillow myself. Cut it from the sash of my wedding dress and put it into the grave with him. He was still beautiful. Even death couldn't mar the face of a good man like Willie Lance. Handsome Willie. He was indeed a just-man-made-perfect.

> *"I have to leave now, Ma. It takes me a while to do that drive."*
> *"At least you come to see me. Rebecca never even comes."*
> *"No, Ma. Rebecca comes when she gets the chance."*
> *"If I'd a come to her needs when I got the chance, I can tell you, Jean, Rebecca'd still have dirty diapers."*
> *"Sometimes you shock me, Ma."*
> *"The truth hurts. Afton always said if it didn't hurt, it probably wasn't the truth. Good thing Afton's passed on. She'd shriek to see the way my children treat me."*
> *"Mother, you know Rebecca's daughter is about to have another baby. Another great-grandchild. What do you think of that?"*

What's one more? I don't care. Why should Rebecca care? She done her time on her back. I did mine. Mother did hers. This young lady (what's her name, Afton? You never forget anything), she can do her time, too, because I don't care if you have the Sons of Zion lined up outside, it don't make one shred of difference: you're in there by yourself. Just you and that baby getting itself birthed, and that's it. Every mortal person comes into the world the same way—whether you plop out on a silken coverlet or into a bog; it's all done the same. Come in the same way. Go out the same way. Alone. What does it matter? What's one more? When I die, what will it matter? What's one less? It all amounts to the same thing.

Of my children, Jean married Eldon, who is a dolt. Rebecca married Homer, who can't hold a job. Owen married what's-her-name, who is selfish and won't let him come see his own mother. But now—now I wonder if it all might have been different if I hadn't been pregnant fully half of those thirty-four months. Maybe I could have done something to save Willie. He worked his hands to the bone for me. He'd come home from working in the sugar factory and he'd say, you sit down, Lil, and put your feet up and let me finish getting supper, and you just talk to me while I'm doing it, and don't let me hear of you doing any heavy work around here, either, Lil. And when my children was nearly due and I was big and ugly, Willie would say, if we have a girl, we'll name her Lily like her mother and hope she will be half as beautiful.

But I never did have a Lily. I expected to have lots and lots of children so I could pick out names for them at my leisure. But who knows God's plan for their life? Who knows?

What I always wanted to know was how Willie got his jaw so clean-shaved, so smooth. Unblemished. Not a pock or a pit on him. After he died I tried to shave him, and I cut him. I'd never seen a cut on his chin. None of those angry little sores you see on men all the time. I cut Willie, and I started to cry, and I bent my head over him, close to his cheek, and he was as cold as that stone statue in the park. I cried into his hair, and then Afton comes in. She takes my shoulders and she says: Lil, I'm taking over here. You do exactly what I tell you from now on. Afton takes me out of the room where Willie lies, and she takes me to the sink and pumps some water into my hand and puts some on the back of my neck and then she gets something out of her suitcase, a little brown bottle of something foul-smelling, and then she says, Lil, you take a snort of this.

Afton Lance—surely this isn't whiskey!

It's Majic Bitters Tonic, says Afton, and it'll do you good, and you just do what I say.

I do, because after the first few sips, the stuff don't taste bad at all, and it's so nice to have Afton sit there beside me; she smells so nice and starchy. And it's so nice to have her say that she'll do everything and all I have to do is just say yes and sink into that bed that doesn't even smell like Willie anymore, because Afton changed all the bedding and washed it and beat it all clean, because she said it would be easier for me if I didn't have to smell Willie still in bed with me.

Afton says, go to sleep, and I do. She says she'll take care of Willie, and she will. She says I'm not to go into the room where Willie lies, and I won't. But my heart aches, because one day Afton will leave and I will have to face the world without Willie.

I have my children to think of.

"I can see you're not even listening to me. Anyway, it's getting late. Shall I wheel you into your room or into the main hall? Where would you like to be?"

I'd like to be in the Celestial Kingdom, reaping the rewards of a just life, and not down here rotting in this carcass. What if I get into heaven looking like this? No bright dandelion halo of hair, no smooth skin or cupid's-bow mouth or dimpled chin. The only thing that's the same is my eyes are still blue, and I'm not even sure about them, because I can't see well enough to know if they are blue or not. Well, I try not to believe that *all* the good die young, because I've been trying, doing my best for seventy-seven years.

"Let me tie your shawl around your shoulders, Ma, and let's go in."

Jean pushes me just exactly like I'm in a baby carriage. So it is all the same thing. We're all the same at the beginning and at the end. Just like that cake Afton used to make. Same on top. Same on the bottom. But you could never guess what she'd put in the middle, and it was always different. Such a hand she had for things like that. My wedding cake was the delight and marvel of St. Elmo when Afton made it. Three perfect layers with everything: chocolate, almonds, citron, apricots, one dozen eggs, thank you, one dozen macaroons, layered with jellies and fluffy custard, and everything made with the nicest sugar and the finest flour. That Afton didn't spare no pains. You're only going to have one wedding, Lil, she says to me, her eyes just snapping the way they do when she's excited. You could see how happy she was for me and Willie.

Afton was wrong, though. I had more than one wedding, and when I had the second, when I married Mr. Walsh, I wept. Not because of anything to do with Mr. Walsh, who was nice and all that, but because my heart went back to Willie Lance and that glorious wedding day of ours, that day Dr. Tipton gave me away to Willie and I looked so beautiful the clock in the parlor stopped ticking for a full minute and the smell of Afton's wedding cake was all over our house and filling us all with surprise and gladness. Yes, only one wedding like that, to Willie Lance, the best-looking, the sweetest, the gentlest man in the West. I never could quite believe that Willie chose me, that Handsome Willie fell in love with me. It was enough to make me humble, but it passed.

Well, I can see there's no keeping Jean now. I wonder if she ever pulls away from the Vegas Gardens thinking: I wonder what Ma's doing in there? I think she might have asked me once, or maybe that was someone else. Someone asked me what I do. Well, me and Brother Russell, we sit up nights and watch the late movie, but I'm the only one who stays awake. Then the night nurse comes in and she says, Mrs. Walsh, you should be in bed. You need your sleep. And I say, what for? I have the longest sleep of all waiting for me, and I don't need it while I'm here and I have the choice. But these nurses, they never listen to a word we say. They repeat the same thing over and over like we don't have no memory at all.

Look at them nurses smile at Jean as she rolls me past the slot machines. And Jean smiles back. It's enough to make you puke. Jean is going to park me in front of the TV with the others, and then she'll get in her car and leave, and I'll bet she don't spare one thought backward when she leaves the Gardens. That's the difference 'tween me and Jean. I scarcely spare one thought forward, because I know I'll never leave Vegas Gardens alive. Sometimes I do get scared, though, like when they come for my roommate, Sister Staunton, one morning. To think, just the night before I said, goodnight, Sister Staunton, and she said, goodnight, Sister Walsh, and those must have been the last words to cross her lips. I've lived too long now and I've got real used to it and I'm not real anxious to cross that Last Threshold, but on the other hand, if I knew for sure I'd meet Willie—

*"Well, here you are, Ma. Can you see the
TV, or shall I push you up a little closer?"*

323

"Push me back. I don't want to sit too close
to all those people. They smell bad."
"Ma, they'll hear you!"
"No, they won't. They can't hear no better
than I do. Push me over in the corner."

I can't stand those smiling nurses. They say hello to Jean. They
know her. They know everyone's children who comes to visit, and
they know whose don't. Every day for five years, Mrs. Kimball asks
them, did I get a letter from my son? And every day they say, no,
not today, Mrs. Kimball. Like maybe tomorrow or the next day.
Whew. Afton would never have tolerated such foolishness. Afton
would have said, did that worthless no-good boy of mine write to
me today? And if they said no, Afton would say, well, you get him
on the phone, yes, and get the President of the United States on the
other line and the president of the church and all the apostles, too,
and I'll talk to them all at once. I'll direct that erring boy back to the
Book—I'll say, you look here, you little pea-brained ingrate, there's
something amiss in the world if there's no precious link 'tween the
parents and the children, you little growed-up monster. Afton
would have put that nurse in her place. I chuckle to think of it.

"What's so funny, Ma?"
"Nothing. You haven't told me what
you're going to do tomorrow, Jean."
"I can't possibly come back tomorrow."
"I know that. I don't ask that. Just tell me
what you're going to do tomorrow."

That'll keep her here for a while. That's what Mr. Walsh would
ask young Owen and my girls and his own two children every night
after prayers. Tell-me-what-you're-going-to-do-tomorrow. You
must have a plan. Each day must have its purpose and its plan, and
you should know it in advance.

Well, that's fine, Mr. Walsh, I said to him one night, but it don't
allow for something. Something's lost if you do it that way. You
might go through the whole day and do everything you said you'd
do, but you'd miss the one thing that might make it a day worth remembering.

Every day is worth remembering, Mr. Walsh said. But if he had lived as long as I have, he'd know that was just plain rockbound wrong. Every day isn't. Take yesterday, for instance. I don't remember a thing about it. The nurse knows if my bowels moved and what I ate, but I don't remember and I don't care. Not that day or the day before or the day before that either. Mr. Walsh was wrong.

On June 18, 1939, Mr. Walsh said to me, tomorrow I'm going to change the oil in the Ford and ring up Brother Lindstrom to tell him his hooks are in and I'm going to fix the rickety rainpipe that rattles next to the bedroom window. Well, Mr. Walsh did call Brother Lindstrom, but that was all he did, because Mr. Walsh just up and died on June 19 and there was nothing he could do about it.

It was his heart, the doctor said. I was pretty heartbroke myself, because we'd lived together all those years, and I don't much like living by myself. All my children was gone, even Owen. I knew I'd have to spend a lot of years looking at just one cup and one dish and one fork on the drainboard. Mr. Walsh was a nice man, and it was nice to have him in the house.

I sent him up to Bozeman, Montana, to lie next to his first wife. He never did say so, but I expect he looked forward to eternity with her, though we'll always be good friends, Mr. Walsh and me, and we was pretty good husband and wife, too. Afton came up for the funeral. She wore her black gabardine that got such a workout later during the war. We was pretty solemn, but Afton said to me, at least Mr. Walsh went quick and painless. And as the train that took Mr. Walsh's body to Bozeman pulled out of the station, I said to Afton: you're thinking of Willie, aren't you? Willie's death. Afton nodded, and the two of us fought back tears for Willie as we went back to the funeral breakfast for Mr. Walsh.

> "I must go now, Ma. So kiss me and I'll be off."

I'm not letting Jean go that easy.

> "Come on, Ma. I have to get home. It's late enough as it is."

So I kiss her cheek. Let her leave. What do I care? But I can't remember what she said she was going to do tomorrow, and now I'm afraid Jean will just dissolve for me like mildew under chloride of lime.

> "Who do you have at home now, Jean?"
> "I tell you, Ma. I've got to go."
> "Just tell me who's at home and who's not."
> "I tell you that every time I see you."
> "That ain't very often. Somebody might have growed up and left home in the meantime."
> "Only Eldon and me. Eldon Junior and Barbara and Eliza are all married."
> "And your other one, your youngest boy. What's he doing?"

Jean don't like to talk about this one. I can see it in her eyes. Even with my eyes I can see it in her eyes.

> "Douglass is divorced, and he's gone to California. Going to school out there to be a Ph.D. in history."
> "A what?"
> "A Ph.D., Ma, so he won't have to work like his father. It's not bad enough that he had to get a divorce, he has to get a doctorate, too."

Divorce must be harder than death. I remember when that boy Douglass got divorced. (Can't remember who he married though— can you, Afton?) I don't blame him for leaving. He couldn't stay and be divorced, because he was living around everyone he'd married. I told Jean that in the first place, and in the second place I said California ain't such a bad place. Places are only as bad as you make them. I remember during the flu epidemic after the Great War, it was bad. People dying like flies. It was so bad the doctors in St. Elmo put out a call for volunteers to help nurse the sick. I'm able-bodied, Afton said, I'm going. She had to go to a house in town—

the kind you always knew was there and had to pretend wasn't. Afton told me on the porch the following summer when everyone was in bed and asleep and it was only us two on the porch, Afton said: the Methodist doctor put his hand on my arm, Lil, and said, Mrs. Lance, you can't go in there. That's a bad, wicked place; I will not allow a respectable woman like you to go in there. Well, I just shook off his hand, Lil, and I didn't say—because he was a doctor, after all—I didn't say, I don't take advice very well, Doctor, and I don't take it from men at all!

Me and Afton just laughed into our hands at that, just like a couple of girls. No man except my husband, says Afton, straightening up and clearing her throat. But I didn't tell him that, Lil. I just take his hand off my arm and remind him that we're not to be spreading infection by touching, and then I tell him: that bad place don't scare me in the least. I am a Latter-day Saint. I love the Lord. I love the church, and as long as I have that, Doctor, you'll pardon me, but I could walk into hell and fear no evil. And besides, Lil, it wasn't so different from other places. Those girls was just as sick as the righteous. We're all mortals, after all, and heir to death.

Every night when Afton come home after nursing the sick, she'd strip down on the back porch and Tom and the children would have a tub of hot water waiting for her and she'd scrub down, and not one of Afton's brood caught that flu or got sick or died. Not then.

But I reckon she was right. We're all mortal. We all go, don't we? Eden. Willie. Doctor. Mother. Mr. Walsh. Gideon. Kitty. Afton. Tom. Mason. Cissa. Me. Even you, Jean.

> *"Jean? Jean! Where's my Jean? Nurse— where's my daughter? She didn't leave without saying goodbye, did she? Where is she?"*
>
> *"Hush, Mrs. Walsh. I'll check. You just sit here a minute, and I'll be right back. She probably just went to the bathroom."*

I could stand to go to the bathroom myself, but I can wait. Don't want to miss Jean or keep her here any longer than I have to. I maybe pushed my luck this time. Where was I? Oh, yes. I don't think she should be so rough on young Douglass just for divorcing.

Afton's bones told her that marriage was all wrong, too, and Afton's bones never lied.

So that boy got divorced, so what? And why should Jean be so upset that he's going to be a doctor? Doctoring is a fine profession. There's no better one for helping your fellow man. Just look at Dr. Tipton, wasn't he just about the best man in the whole world? But I wondered about that other doctor. Dr. Henderson, the one that saw to Willie in his last days.

Willie had been dying for a long time, young as he was. Well, how could I know? I had two tiny babies and never a moment to myself. When I'd get into bed those last few months of our thirty-four, I'd fall right to sleep, hardly hear a thing, hardly feel a thing except Willie's warm body giving off heat under the covers. Goodnight, Willie, I'd say. Goodnight, Lil. And I'd be so exhausted that it was months before I realized that Willie got up in the middle of the night to cough. One night he come back to bed, and I put my arms around him and brought my lips to his mouth and the sides of his nose where it sloped down to his smooth cheeks, and I said, Willie, you have to go to the doctor.

I will, Lil, he says.

You sound awful, Willie.

I know.

Willie—

Don't talk now, Lil. Unbraid your hair. It's so beautiful. You keep your golden hair up all day and braided all night. Let it go.

All the time I'm unbraiding my hair I can feel Willie's hand rubbing my back, and I can feel all the happiness he gives me beating through my body. Willie Lance's hands was enough to make you bless God you had a body, and I hope I don't have to wait till Resurrection Day to feel his hands again. I hope I can feel his touch when we meet on the Other Side. . . .

Dr. Henderson wasn't what you'd call a real doctor, but he was as good as we had in Sugarville, and he was a practicing Latter-day Saint, and that was in his favor. He'd been two years to medical school, which was two years more than anyone else in Sugarville, so Willie went to him. Willie told me Dr. Henderson peered down his throat and looked into his ears and thumped his kneecaps. (Your kneecaps, Willie?) And then Dr. Henderson said to him: this is probably nothing, Mr. Lance. Latter-day Saint men are known to live the longest of any Americans. They live clean, eat well, do right. You just got a little something settled on your lungs, and you just keep coughing it up and it will go away. It's not TB. I know all the symptoms, and I can assure you, it's not TB.

Well, that was a comfort, because TB was a killer, and I felt better, but by now I'd wake up whenever Willie started coughing, and I said, you might just as well stay in bed and cough, Willie. The doctor said it was good for you to cough and get it all out. The doctor said it wasn't TB.

It wasn't TB. It was sugar. When Willie died the doctor had another look at him and said it was sugar. Willie had coughed himself off forty pounds by then and his nice jaw was gaunt, and he could hardly string two sentences together without coughing, till finally the foreman at the sugar factory sent him home to cough, because they feared it might be catching.

It ain't catching, one of the Gentiles at the factory, a Mr. Fletcher, told him. You got sugar on your lungs, Willie. Mr. Fletcher worked at that sugar factory for fifteen years, and he must have known whereof he spoke, because Willie came home and said: I think Mr. Fletcher's right, Lil. It's the sugar. I've got sugar dust down my craw, up my nose, and sugar caked on my skin so I can hardly sweat but it turns to sugar water, and I bet I cry sugar tears, not salt.

Sugar on his lungs, Dr. Henderson said after he died. He came into the kitchen where I was waiting, and he said: Willie Lance couldn't get a breath for all the sugar coating his lungs. The good die young, Mrs. Lance.

He washed his hands in the sink, and he said: I've tended the men from that sugar factory for years, and I've seen them, the Gentiles, the drinkers, the smokers, the sinners, they live forever. They coat their lungs with the cigarette smoke, so their lungs get slippery and foul. Nothing can stick to lungs like that. And when they drink that rotgut whiskey, the body gets used to fighting off poison. But Willie was too good a man, too good a Latter-day Saint, to do any of that. He hadn't any tobacco in his lungs or bitter coffee or acid tea or rotten liquor in his body to fight the poison off, and so it just collected there, stuck, and choked him to death. He lived a clean, upright life, Sister Lance. A virtuous life. A good life.

A short life, Doctor. That's what I say.

So I cut up the sash of my wedding dress and I made the pillow for his head. Afton took care of him. And Tom, tears streaming down his scarred face, lifted his brother, Handsome Willie, into that box, and we put him away. Like wedding cake.

I tried to save some of my wedding cake in a cool, dry place in our first house in Sugarville, but I come back to it a year later on my anniversary and cried my eyes out to see it—black and white and green with mold. Willie said, Lil, that cake don't matter. That cake was meant to be eaten the day of our marriage, not saved up and stored for later. You forget that cake, Lil, and go put your wedding dress on and I'll marry you all over again to-day. I couldn't have fit into my wedding dress then, because I was seven months along with Jean, but what did that matter? All that mattered was Willie's words that he'd marry me all over again.

Well, I'll float in that dress now, won't I? I've wasted away so, that dress will just hang around me. But what do I care? I don't have to waltz in it, just lie and wait for Willie to take the veil of death from my eyes and wake me on the Other Side.

They'll put me in my wedding dress and pack me up like molding cake and ship me up to Rexburg, and some stranger will lay me down beside Willie. Too bad I can't have a stone that says, here lie Handsome Willie and Dandelion Lil, the fairest girl, the sweetest man, the handsomest couple in the West.

The sweetest, most wonderful man, who died young because he wouldn't coat his lungs and save himself like the Gentiles. Well, I'm too old not to tell the truth now, and if I had my choice of a live Gentile sinner or a dead Latter-day Saint, I say give me the live sinner, Willie.

Well, Willie would never have agreed to that. Never. And he'd be ashamed of me for thinking so. No wonder the good die young. Oh, but that Willie was a looker!

Mrs. Walsh
Mrs. Walsh
"Mrs. Walsh."

"What?"

"Mrs. Walsh, your daughter left. The nurse at the desk saw her leave hours ago. She says she saw you say goodbye to your daughter hours ago."

"I never did any such thing."

"Well, I'm sure your daughter will be back, Mrs. Walsh, but she's gone home now. Why don't you let me wheel you back to your room?"

Wheel me anywhere you want, you lying ninny. I never did say goodbye to Jean, and that nurse up front is a lying little snit if ever there was one. Jean never left any long time ago. Don't try to tell me that. She was just here a minute ago, telling me about—someone or another—someone or other of the flesh of my flesh and the bone of my bone. Wish I had bones like Afton and Mother. Sometimes Afton's bones talked to her so much, she declared she couldn't get a word in edgewise. I'd never get lonely if I had my bones to talk to.

39 Narcissa

IN 1916 THE FAT fell away from Narcissa Douglass and she emerged like the fair, fragrant flower she was named for, out of the burlap swaddling of the bulb. Of all the Douglass children, she looked the most like the father she never knew. She had the lank, fair hair of Samuel Douglass and his long mouth, wide-set eyes, and high cheekbones. She would never have known that her ears stuck out like her father's, too, if she hadn't stopped one cold afternoon at the New Town Hotel Barber Parlor and had her hair bobbed.

"Holycheeses!" Mason screeched when she came in the back door. "What did you do to your hair?"

"I had it bobbed," she said, patting her newly naked neck. "There's a New Woman now, Mason. We're going to get to vote and do all the things men do and not waste time with a lot of useless hair." She took herself to the darkening window for a better look.

"Well, you better go back to being the Old Woman when Mother gets home. Holycheeses, Cissa."

"I just wish my ears didn't stick out so." She frowned at the prominent ears. "Maybe if I wore ear bobs . . ."

Mason scurried from the room and decided to absent himself from supper that night. He didn't, though; he could never resist a spectacle.

The Douglass dining room with its gay rosebud paper and massive oak table rang only with the monotonous sounds of eating. Lil could hardly pry her eyes from Cissa's exposed neck. Cissa kept her eyes on her dinner. Mason kept one eye on his mother, and Ruth kept her eyes on the salt till she could bear it no longer. "Have you lost your mind, Cissa? Have you completely lost your mind? Have you any idea how ridiculous you look with your neck all bare and your ears sticking out?"

Cissa hung her bobbed head.

"You look like a plucked chicken. Worse, a half-plucked chicken. Why didn't you shave it all off? What am I going to do with you? What will people say?"

"They'll say she looks like a plucked chicken," said Mason, with his mouth full.

"You shut up," said Ruth.

"It will grow out," Cissa said weakly. "It will."

The whole Douglass family agreed that it would grow out, but in the meantime they gave Cissa hell. Everyone maintained that it would grow out, but no one seemed to believe it. Cissa's short hair caused her untold grief. She had to endure a long session with the principal of the high school, who said it was the school's policy to expel students who could not follow the rules of good conduct and good taste, and did Cissa think she was some kind of Broadway Baby? Cissa stored the term away for future use and assured the principal that she'd been ill the day she'd had her hair bobbed, suffering from a high fever that fried her brain.

He let her stay in school, but directed her to the girls' gym instructor, a Miss Livingston, who gave Cissa a lecture on the proper hygiene, daintiness, and modesty that all young ladies should strive for. Even the bishop of Cissa's ward asked her to come around for a little chat and insisted that the Latter-day Saint girl must ever maintain her high standards and vigilance; perfection of soul and person were one and the same for the Latter-day Saint girl, especially since she would one day have the care of little souls and persons under her hand. No female Latter-day Saint could hope to achieve these goals with short hair.

These cheerless interviews and the sight of her ears sticking out under the unruly fringe punctured Cissa's bravado. She accepted the rebukes contritely. She might have succumbed altogether and worn some Hester Prynnish cap till her hair grew out except that Cissa came to realize that even if everyone hated her hair, everyone noticed it—and not everyone hated it.

There were several boys, one might say many, who took her aside at church dances and in the high school halls to say how much they liked her hair. Certain men, grown men, liked her hair and took the trouble to tell her so. Mr. Drummond, a regular patron of the Pilgrim, told Cissa in front of Ruth he thought her hair was most becoming.

Maybe she was a Broadway Baby. She practiced a syncopated Broadway Baby walk. She became quite proficient, and when she walked into a store in this fashion, it was very gratifying to see the wordless, emphatic admiration given her by the man behind the counter. By lots of men, in fact.

After school she unbuttoned the triangular chemisette that kept her sailor blouse demure, and with that gone, a thin, delicious crack was visible down her blouse. She knew it was delicious because of the look on the face of the man behind the soda fountain. She liked to watch boys pale at the view down her blouse.

If she hadn't bobbed her hair, neither Cissa nor anyone else would have known what a nice pearly neck she had or that her hair dovetailed at the back into the tiniest triangular point of downy hairs. Edward Goodlove would be her willing slave if she would just let him touch that triangular patch; he'd crawl to Arizona on his hands and knees if she'd let him kiss it. She let him kiss it now and then and did not require him to get down on all fours but once.

333

Her ears sticking out mattered less after the initial shock of her bob died down, and it did in fact grow out a bit.

Cissa hoped it would not grow out too fast, because she found that she could gather her rosebuds anywhere she chose and that her bobbed hair was actually rather becoming. She buttoned the chemisette back into the sailor blouse before coming home, but even when Cissa was at her schoolgirl best, it did seem that men noticed her: the ice man, customers at the Pilgrim, male pedestrians, boys at school, men at church. They noticed. They didn't say as much; they didn't have to. Cissa knew. They knew that Cissa knew. And Cissa knew that they knew that she knew.

Ruth suspected. But a woman with a full-time restaurant to run and accounts to tally and meals to cater and a hundred other claims on her attention can't be expected to know everything. The elders of the church knew. They all hoped that young Sister Douglass would marry sooner rather than later, and they wiped their moist palms on black coats after they implored God to visit Narcissa Douglass on someone else's son. Gideon knew, and remarked to Kitty that perhaps Mother ought to tie Cissa to the bedpost for a while, and Kitty replied that the bedpost was the worst place Cissa could be tied.

There was, in short, that finite ephemeral moment in 1916 and 1917, not given to every young girl, when Narcissa Douglass fairly oozed some earthly substance, some extreme unction, some lip-quivering, mysterious, elemental compound that could out-attar the rose and out-suckle the honey and that would several generations later be unceremoniously dismissed as hot pants.

Mr. Drummond came to Ruth's house, hat in hand, to apologize in person, disclaiming his role in the lovers' elopement and professing his ignorance as to the true nature of Zeniff Blankenship. Young Blankenship seemed like such a nice boy, one of ten children, just down from his family's southern Utah ranch with his new bowler and some crispy greenbacks in his pocket, money from a fat army contract for his father's beef. He had been sent to St. Elmo to buy irrigation equipment, pipes and flumes and gauges and whatever else it would take to launder up the red land of his family's ranch. Mr. Drummond had innocently introduced Zeniff Blankenship to Cissa on the street when Cissa was coming home from school. How was Mr. Drummond to know that young Mr. Blankenship, with his clean-shaven, sun-tanned face, was a vile seducer, a viper, and a snake?

Ruth heard Mr. Drummond out, and then she told him that if he ever set foot in the Pilgrim again, she would cut off his ears.

Mr. Drummond's visit took place two days after the lovers had departed. Five days later Mr. Blankenship, Sr., showed up, red-faced, sweat stains looped to his waist, yellowed underwear poking out of his unbuttoned shirt. When Gideon answered the door he leaped into the front hall, swearing the revenge of Nephi on all Douglasses living and dead and eternal hellfires on that ungrateful, black-hearted, chicken-brained boy of his who had taken money that was meant for the ranch and the good of the entire Blankenship clan, taken that and Narcissa Douglass and run off to San Francisco to get married.

Gideon forcibly restrained Mr. Blankenship from going upstairs and confronting Ruth. He tried to use tact and reason with Mr. Blankenship; he tried to commiserate, to no avail. Gideon, however, would probably never have used force if Mr. Blankenship had not cast foul, filthy aspersions on the virtue of Gideon's sister, Mr. Blankenship's new daughter-in-law. He physically ejected the old man from the front hall and manually instructed him on the use of the steps.

Gideon dusted his hands of Mr. Blankenship, who left behind a cloying, ubiquitous red mesa dust and the too-fresh smell of fertilizer. Gideon would never have thought that such a rickety old man would put up such a fight; welts rose on Gideon's forearms from the old man's fingernails. Gideon rolled his sleeves down. Poor Cissa. She didn't know what she'd gotten into. Poor Cissa. She should have married some nice local boy and not married into any family that included that old man. Besides, it was bad business to marry a boy who'd squandered his family's cash on a fling in San Francisco, even if that fling included lawful marriage. Then Gideon found himself hoping that Zeniff Blankenship had made an honest woman of his sister. Then he hoped he hadn't.

Cissa's hair had not grown out by the time she and her new husband boarded the train east for the return to Utah. They slept on each other's shoulders and ate apples and sandwiches, because

335

they'd exhausted their money in hotels and restaurants and on new clothes, shows, and other extravagances in San Francisco.

From underneath the eye-level veil of her hat, Narcissa Blankenship first glimpsed her in-laws. Zen's taciturn brother drove them, jolting in the springless wagon, up Devil's Finger Canyon to the Blankenship ranch. Cissa realized that her San Francisco finery, a suit of deep, plum-colored silk, clashed violently with everything around her, the ocher and umber, the brick-red hues and mesas and mountains.

Zen's mother was almost uniformly cinder-gray except for her eyes, which were bloodshot and red-rimmed, as though the facing of her eyelids had been turned inside out. She was a tiny woman with hands so bony as to appear webbed. She regarded Cissa as if Zen had plucked her out of Babylon, but she was not as bad as Zen's father, who threatened to take the strap to him, and she was better than his sisters, Effie and Florence, who fingered Cissa's plum-colored silk every time they passed her.

Cissa closed her eyes over supper (beans, the same red color as the land) and thought back to the gray fogs and ribbony streets, the ultramarine Pacific, the aquamarine hillsides of San Francisco. She pictured the high white cornices of their hotel room and the sounding brass of their bed. Those two glorious weeks in San Francisco: icewater days and champagne nights (even if they were Latter-day Saints, Zen and Cissa vowed never to tell on one another). They had gorged themselves on oysters and love.

"You pregnant?" Florence hit Cissa's elbow.

"What?"

"I say, you got a little one cooking? You look sort of sick."

"Yes—I mean, no. I mean I—"

"Eat up and shut up," said Zen's father.

In San Francisco, Zen had assured Cissa that once his father laid eyes on the prettiest little girl in the West, he would relent and forgive. But that did not happen. Then Zen promised her that when her hair grew out, the family would open their numerous arms to her. Cissa's hair was pulled back in a tight (if puny) bun when she told Zen she was expecting, and that, he promised, was all the family needed to come around. But there was another child after that, and Cissa's hair grew back to its old long, lank, unwieldy mass, and there was no forgiveness forthcoming. Zen's father and the entire

Blankenship clan laid their every conceivable setback at Zen's feet and the young couple's doorstep.

It wasn't much of a doorstep. One step up to a two-room shed with a tin roof, paper siding, and a four-foot stove. Close enough to the rest of the clan so the dogs still had their scent.

Narcissa Blankenship had little leisure in which to repent her hasty marriage, but she was not a Mormon girl for nothing, and what was done was done and had to be lived with. In two and a half years she birthed two children; she fed, clothed, and cleaned up after them, her husband, hired men, and a tribe of in-laws. Even her severest critics admitted that Cissa did a good day's work. She cleaned out chicken coops, mixed horse mash, made soap, sat up with sick hogs and sick children. She made up liniments and put up peaches, apricots, and pickles; she tried to keep a kitchen garden, but lost it to locusts and land so dry it cracked open. She wrung chickens' necks with her own hands, and with those same hands she kneaded as fine and light and substantial a loaf of bread as anyone. She wielded ten-pound fry pans and twenty-pound horse collars, and when she fell and broke her arm, she saddled a horse and rode ten miles to the nearest doctor to have it set.

Cissa worked like a dog and slept like the dead, and as those days in San Francisco slipped relentlessly backward, she tried to remember each one as separate and distinct from the ones that followed or preceded it. She wanted to wrap each day in tissue of sorts, crisp and singular, still sweet like aging violets, still brilliant like the stiffening plum-colored silk.

As for Zen, he quit promising forgiveness and began eyeing her as the author of his doom. His father threatened weekly to cut Zen out of his will, saying that Zen had already squandered his portion and making comments about the ten foolish virgins and the stupidity of the father in the Prodigal Son story. Zen worked hard to ingratiate himself with his father, and his father made certain Zen worked hard, so hard that when he came home at night he could scarcely crawl from the supper table to the bed, which was not a very long crawl. The handsome young man who had gazed at Cissa over a single hothouse rose in a San Francisco restaurant dried up and blew away on the wind.

Southern Utah, they say, is God's playground: the place where the Lord gave His imagination free rein. God scooped out the val-

337

leys with His fingers, bolstered yellow mesas against the red sky, and fashioned stone turrets of amber and orange. God sculpted God-size statues in blue-black smoldering rock; He scraped canyons out of brimstone and threw up geological balustrades. Southern Utah inspires wonder, but it will break the heart, it will desiccate the skin and hair and soul of anyone who tries to live there.

Given the hostility of such a land, what happened to old man Blankenship and his wife was bound to happen. What happened to Zeniff Blankenship was bound to happen. But what happened to Narcissa was not inevitable. The girl who ran off to San Francisco in 1917 died in a Beverly Hills hospital suite in 1974 as she was applying her eye makeup. She was surrounded by flowers and soft-center chocolates. When they found her, only one eye was done and she looked downright surprised, as if Death had burst in where he was not wanted and where Cissa had paid good money to keep him out.

Cissa's path from southern Utah to the Beverly Hills hospital suite included three husbands after Zen, beginning with the pan peddler with whom she eloped in 1920. When she showed up briefly in St. Elmo with the pan peddler, she indicated to her mother that she had left Blankenship because of his sexual inadequacy, thinking that Ruth would not pursue the subject. Ruth said: then where'd you get those two children?

The two children she left with Blankenship; she never saw them again. She had two more by Arnie Swenson, the pan peddler, and she took them with her when she left him in 1928. In 1929 she married Thatcher Stout, a plumbing contractor who was virtually untouched by the Depression because he not only installed faulty plumbing in the Salt Lake government buildings but had the contract to repair that plumbing for time and all eternity as well. In 1942, Thatcher Stout was approached by a small-time entrepreneur and local builder, a Mr. Asa "Sport" Holliwell, who had the fool idea that the deserted towns in the mountains above Salt Lake could be revived for skiing. Thatcher Stout bowed out of the project, thinking it a losing venture. Cissa did not bow out. In 1944 she married Sport Holliwell, and by 1949 it was clear that Sport had a knack for these things. Wherever Sport thought folks might like to ski, they did, in Utah and Idaho and Colorado and Wyoming, and

Sport and Sis (as he called her) found to their great joy that there was nothing that money could not buy.

Narcissa Douglass Blankenship Swenson Stout Holliwell stuck to old Sport like shit to a shovel, only now the spunky lady who'd ridden ten miles to have her broken arm set could hardly lift a glass of Moët champagne to her lips without tiring. She couldn't cruise the Caribbean without sunstroke. She couldn't eat *pâté de fois* or *petits fours* in Paris without requiring a Suez root canal. She had her teeth replaced and her gall bladder removed, her heart and glands and liver and kidneys tuned up, her face and breasts lifted, and the equivalent of an oil change three times a year. Even her mind got an expensive overhaul. All those divorces, it seems, had left her a neurotic wreck. For about eight years she went to a shrink, who concluded that all Cissa's problems were Ruth's fault. If only Ruth had remarried, little Cissa wouldn't have spent her life searching for her father.

Whoever she was searching for, Cissa was one of those women who successfully made herself over, created herself anew for each new man in her life. She was as sensitive as a tuning fork to the needs of men, and she lacked the introspection and imagination that might have forced her to align the woman she became with the woman she had been. She was spared introspection and imagination, but even Cissa could not quell memory. Perhaps, even in that last moment before she was attacked by her own heart in 1974, she might have remembered the beginning, that October night, the moment of revelation that precedes all rebellion.

DIXIE EXPOSITION
Saturday, October 4, 1919
ALL THE ARTS OF DIXIE
Prizes to be given for every aspect of domestic excellence
The Homes! The Hearts! The Hands!
of
DIXIE
Ladies, Bring Your Best
Independent Judges

The high school gymnasium was decked with buntings and beehive banners and crepe paper curling in the heat generated by electric lights. Men, women, children came from all over the

339

southernmost section of Utah, known as Dixie. Those who came the longest distance were put up in the church hall overnight and fed at the tables of the local Saints. The Blankenships came in three separate wagons. They brought their dinners in pails and their children in droves. Zen and his father and brothers enviously eyed the automobiles glimmering in the afternoon sunlight. They made their way to makeshift livestock pens, where their shrewd eyes puckered at the corners and their dry hands fingered dirty bills. (All except Zen's hands; he never touched cash after San Francisco.)

Cissa and the Blankenship women entered their goods—preserves, jams, jellies, cakes, confection breads, and pies—in the competition. The judges were indeed independent, middle-aged, well-fed men from the Stock and Dairymen's Association, Salt Lake City.

Cissa entered a loaf of her bread and a box of her sugar-dusted translucent Papered Peaches. She placed them in a basket and balanced it on one hip with the weight of the baby, Janis (after Elsie Janis of Liberty Bond fame), on the other. She told the toddler, Wilbur, to hold tight to her skirt and not get lost. Cissa had lost weight in the time she'd been married, and the skirt lay loosely around her bony hips. Whatever effulgence and abundance Narcissa had threatened the world with at sixteen, it had dried along with her hair and skin. At nineteen, pouches and squint lines surrounded her eyes and her lips threatened a permanent pinch.

She entered her goods and saw them duly tagged and whisked off to designated tables. She spent the afternoon making the promenade of the gym with her female relatives, discussing the handiwork displayed. That or various aspects of childbirth and preserving.

The prizes were to be announced after supper, and then the hall would be cleared for dancing, as essential to Mormon gatherings as prayer.

Zen held Wilbur's hand and Cissa cradled Janis as they stood deep in the restless crowd, their eyes glued to the crepe-papered platform and the prize-winning goods under a huge sheet. Half a dozen chairs awaited the dignitaries, and finally those worthies took their places. The bishop introduced Brother Ephraim B. Watkins, who would give out the prizes. Brother Watkins hove to his feet like the full-rigger he resembled. "Brothers and Sisters! Let me say first that when we return to Salt Lake, I, for one, will send my wife down

340

here to Dixie to see how things are done best. Everywhere the eye turns it beholds stalwart men, healthy children, and girls who are the finest flower of Zion!" Brother Watkins got a gratifying round of applause. "I have supped at the tables of senators in Washington, D.C., and I must tell you I have never eaten so well as I did today judging the koo-linary arts of the ladies of Dixie." More applause. Janis woke and began to cry, and Cissa bounced her in her arms.

"The other judges agree with me that the goods here displayed ass-wage all doubt that the domestic arts of Dixie are the best in all the world." Applause rattled the gym. "First and foremost. First Prize for Bread."

Janis sent up a wail and resisted Cissa's attempts to calm her. "Hush," Cissa whispered.

"Go in the bathroom and feed her," said Zen.

"Let her wait."

"Get her out of here," Zen hissed over Janis's angry squalls.

"I have a loaf of bread entered, and I'm not leaving until I find out who won. Hush, Janis," she crooned to the bellowing baby.

". . . a loaf of perfect bread is the acme of civilization, a duty, nay, an art practiced to perfection by the ladies of Zion in general and the ladies of Dixie in particular. Your reward, Sisters, besides coming in heaven, can be seen in the grateful wreaths of smiles on . . ."

"Cissa, take that screaming brat out of here."

"I'm not leaving till I hear who won. Shh, Janis. Shh."

". . . we consulted our hearts and our palates, and the decision was not easy, but we all concurred. There can be no doubt which is the finest loaf of bread upon this podium. Never before have I . . ."

"Cissa, shut her up."

"First prize for bread goes to Sister N. D. Blankenship. N. D. Blankenship, that's all it says. I hope it's a Sister and not a Brother!" He got a laugh and more applause.

"Zen, did you hear? I won! Take Janis so I can go get my ribbon."

"She wants you. You feed her."

"Zen—"

"Sister N. D. Blankenship?" Watkins called.

Zen folded his arms over his chest. Cissa tucked the squalling Janis under her arm like an overgrown sausage and made her way slowly up through the crowd; she tapped their shoulders and their flanneled backs; she plowed through their bony elbows and stiff, sun-bleached cottons, through bearded men and faded women, all reeking gently of red mesa dust and sweat.

"Going once! Going twice! First Prize for Bread to N. D. Blankenship!"

She stood at the foot of the platform and tugged at Brother Watkins's cuff. "I'm Narcissa Blankenship," she said over Janis's wailing.

Brother Watkins peered at her over his enormous gut. He looked at the tag in his hand and rehooked his glasses over his ears. "Where's your mother, little lady?"

Cissa's mother was in St. Elmo, and for one terrible moment she thought she might have misheard. "I'm N. D. Blankenship. Did I win?"

Brother Watkins's face fell, and the lips that had supped at senators' tables went slack. He held the first prize ribbon just out of her reach while he ogled her dubiously. An audible titter rippled through the crowd, and Cissa's cheeks burned as she heard her exchange with Brother Watkins being whispered to the farthest reaches of the gym.

"Did I win first prize or not?" she demanded.

"Why, yes—Sister Blankenship. Forgive me. Dear lady. It's just that I expected to see a much older . . . that is, the judges—I mean, the quality of the bread, we thought—I mean, you're so young. You're just a girl. This is quite a surprise! Allow me to present you with the ribbon." He coughed and regained his oratorical balance. "Just goes to show you, folks, they grow them young in Dixie!"

Weak with embarrassment, Cissa took her ribbon and her screaming baby and made her way through good-natured guffaws to the girls' bathroom as Brother Watkins launched into "The making of a fine pickle . . ."

She closed the door behind her and slammed into one of the two stalls, locking it. Janis shrieked with outrage and hunger. Cissa seated herself on the closed toilet seat, and her fingers trembled as she undid her blouse. She pushed aside the straps of her shapeless undergarment and lifted her breast to the baby's open mouth. Janis made greedy slurping noises.

The breast in Cissa's right hand sloped down to the baby's round head, buttony nose, and chafed red cheeks. Cissa's breasts were sallow, striped with stretch marks. Cissa stood up, unbolted the stall door, and, cradling Janis, walked to the oval mirror that hung above the solitary washbasin. She stared at herself in the unsoftened light of the girls' bathroom. "He thought I was just a girl," she whispered. "He thought I was no more than a girl up there to get the award for my mother. Just a girl, not the mother of two children." She searched her reflection; her eyes were red-rimmed like her mother-in-law's, her hair sun-bleached to a straw color. "It's only been three years since I bobbed my hair."

Balancing the baby, she tried to recapture the old syncopated Broadway Baby walk and thought how men had fallen over themselves to have a look down her dress. At these? These two drooping dugs? How did they get that way? How did she get this way? How did she get here with this baby who was sucking her dry? She felt light-headed and disconnected, as though more than her blouse were undone, as though her mortal seams were undone and all the stuffing falling out. "I must still be pretty," she murmured, returning to the mirror. "If he thought I was just a girl, then this mirror is wrong and I'm still pretty. I must be." *You're only nineteen*—she heard the echo, though she didn't know who had spoken. "I'm only nineteen."

But you'll live to be eighty, said the woman in the mirror, *and this will be the high point of your life. First Prize for Bread. Nothing will change but you.*

Cissa leaned over the washbasin looking for the eighty-year-old crone that lurked in the reflection of the bare-breasted young woman.

"Cissa! What are you doing?" Florence Blankenship burst in on her. "Get back in that stall. What if someone comes in and sees you?"

Cissa did as she was told. She sat on the toilet seat and finished feeding the baby. Then she gave Janis to Florence while she pulled her clothes back up and buttoned them. She picked up her First Prize for Bread ribbon, and the two Blankenship women left the bathroom. They moved along the walls of the well-lit gym, past the fiddlers, who were tuning up their instruments, past the high school boys wheeling in the upright piano, past knots of flowering girls in pink bows and yellow sashes. They passed through the gym doors, out into the night and the chill wind that snapped women's skirts and bent the rim of Zen's hat.

"Ma got your basket for you, Cissa," said Zen, hitching the horses up to the wagon.

"Zen! Listen to the music! It's the first music we've heard since San Francisco! Look at the lights, Zen."

"She's got your basket, but your bread and your Papered Peaches got et."

"Zen, remember the lights and the music and the dancing? San Francisco. Zen, remember?" she pleaded, grabbing his arm. "Let's stay for the dancing. Let's not go home yet. It's early. Let's stay. We're young. Zen, I'm only nineteen."

"Are you out of your mind? We got to take Ma and Pa and Effie and Archie and Florence and their kids home, too, you know."

"Let them go by themselves. Let's you and me stay. Let's just dance a few and go home with someone else. Oh, Zen, listen to the music!"

The fiddlers, tuning up, played broken shards of recognizable songs, greasing their bows, tightening their strings, and someone executed a long, graceful run on the piano. Cissa clutched his arm till his coat bunched in her fingers. "Please, Zen, let's stay and dance."

"Get in the wagon, Cissa. You're too old to dance, and so am I. What'll we do with our kids? Hold 'em while we kick up our heels like fools? Archie! Florence! Effie! Everyone who's coming with me, get in, because I'm leaving. Ho there, horse."

"Please, Zen, please. It's the first lights and the first music since San Francisco, and I only—"

"Don't pester me, Cissa."

Assorted Blankenships piled into the wagon. Zen lifted Cissa up to the seat and took his place beside her. He hit the horse's high back, and they pulled away from the Dixie Exposition, from the lights and music, from the be-ribboned girls and clapping hands and tapping feet ringing on the gymnasium floor. They moved northeast along Devil's Finger Canyon. The only light shone from the lantern that swung at the back of their wagon, and the only music was created by the wind whistling through grasses, and you had to be very still to hear it at all.

40 Eden Louise

PROTESTING THE LONG haul up to the northern tip of Idaho, the Pilgrim's delivery truck wheezed and spluttered and complained even as Gideon killed the engine in front of the Paris Chop House in Fairwell. Long iridescent threads of twilight clung to the mountains, but working people had long since finished their suppers, and the Paris Chop House was empty except for the combined cook and waiter.

Eden went in with her father to inquire if the cook knew a Mason Douglass and where he might be reached. The man gave them a look that could only be described as fishy, the way a dead fish keeps its opaque eye on you, following you around the room, daring you to cut off its head. His expression did not improve when Gideon put a nickel in the pay phone and talked to Mason briefly. Nor did he look any less dubious when Gideon called Kitty and Ernest and Ada into the Paris Chop House and told them to take a table, that Mason had said he'd be there directly and buy them all supper.

They shared a much-thumbed menu, and Kitty commented on the flyspecks in the sugar and the watery ketchup. She said she'd have to write Afton and get her recipe for Poor Man's Cake, because you only had to look at the Paris Chop House to know that no one ever got rich in Fairwell.

Mason surged in like a sea gull, flapping around them, asking after Ruth, glad to know she was in Afton's capable hands. He made extensive inquiries into the health of each and every one in the family and gave detailed descriptions of his own dyspeptic condition and—

"Well, Mason," said Kitty, "where's that big pillow of silver we have only to split open and spill to the ground?"

345

Ah, that. Mason threw his head back and studied the flypaper hanging from the ceiling. That.

It seemed there was a court order tying up the Sunstone Silver Company right now, and temporarily—only temporarily—the silver would have to stay in the hills. The court order had been slapped on because of an investigation launched against Mason by the Securities and Exchange Commission, which was run by rich Jewish lawyers.

It came out later—not over the beefsteak and onions, grilled potatoes, canned beans, and peach cobbler in the Paris Chop House—that certain deeds and trust deeds had been made out to certain individuals discovered to be dead, and further, the evidence suggested that Mason had gone about selling stock as if the Sunstone were a huge pie that could be divided up for time and all eternity, and that in short, the Sunstone Silver Company was richer on paper than it was in fact. All that came out later. What came out in the Paris Chop House was that Mason was about to hotfoot his way out of Idaho's back door for a little holiday in Canada. Mason said over supper—he didn't eat, just drank a cup of coffee—that it was too bad Gideon couldn't have come up earlier in the summer so they could have enjoyed this magnificent wilderness before they went back to St. Elmo.

"We're not going back," said Gideon.

That was fine with Mason, though he was sorry he couldn't stay to see them properly settled, and it was a pity that the Get Rich Quick Timetable had to be revised because of the litigation the lousy Jews had slapped on the Sunstone. Mason explained the litigation, using words that were spellbinding if unintelligible and drawing graphs on napkins and adding up figures that only ever made subtotals with arrows pointing to other arrows. Mason paid for their dinner; he said it was the least he could do.

Gideon picked his teeth after Mason had left them. He made sucking noises around the point of the toothpick. "I don't understand it."

"I do," said Kitty, lighting up a Chesterfield. "Mason's buggered us. If I was a man I'd string him up by his thumbs and paint his noogies blue."

"Well, it's not the end of the world." Gideon snapped his toothpick in half.

"Oh, no? Just direct me to our hotel suite, Gideon. Sprinkle my sheets with French cologne. Call the porter to unload the delivery truck, and then you and me can have a little chat about the end of the world while the maid is drawing my bath."

"That's enough."

"I told you Mason was a snail snot."

"That's enough."

"Hey, mister," the man with the fish eyes called out. "You better finish up. I got to get home tonight."

Gideon ambled to the counter. "Is there a Mormon bishop in this town?"

"Does the devil live in hell?" The man shrugged. "Bishop Whickham. He's in the book."

Gideon took a nickel and walked to the phone. The fish-eyed man rested his baleful, pitying gaze on the Douglass family, and color crawled up Eden's neck as she realized he recognized them for what they were: poor, pathetic, and prospectless. She writhed for their collective humiliation. She wished herself severed, surgically removed, from Ada, who was engaged in a fork duel with Ernest, and from Kitty, who, still muttering about snail snot, smashed her Chesterfield in the leftover ketchup on her plate, and from Gideon, whose face never changed expression as he talked to the local bishop, casting his entire family on the church's mercy and goodwill.

Gideon Douglass later swore that the nickel he'd used to call Bishop Whickham was the best investment he ever made, because the bishop said the church took care of its own and invited all five Douglasses, sight unseen, to stay with his family. Gideon said it just went to prove what he'd thought all along: the end of one thing is the beginning of another. It was the very night of their arrival in Fairwell that the high school history teacher ran off with the bank teller and an estimated $677 of the bank's money, which the teller had stolen. They fled in a fit of passion and adulterous larceny that rocked Fairwell for months.

Bishop Whickham saw to it that Brother Douglass, who was an educated man, moved into the teacher's hurriedly vacated post, and so with that one nickel, Gideon found his way to what he'd wanted

347

for twenty-five years: teaching the history of the world to students who couldn't remember the day before yesterday.

Her father's job, their new stability, and the rented six-room house interested Eden less than the bank teller and the history teacher. What had they done, said to each other, before they ran off? To say nothing of after! Four years later, in Eden's senior year at Fairwell High, the teller was extradited back to stand trial. The *Fairwell Enterprise* carried the story in lurid detail. When questioned about the teacher, the teller claimed to have no knowledge of her whereabouts. He said she had run out on him, but the evidence suggested otherwise. The teller and a woman who fit the teacher's description had checked into an auto court as Mr. and Mrs. some days before the teller was apprehended for passing bad checks. The teller stuck to his story, though, despite his lawyer's urging to divulge her whereabouts.

"What's 'divulge' mean, Eden?" Kitty called from the living room.

"It means to tell," Eden replied. She was flushed with the heat from the iron and concentrating on the sleeve of the dress she would wear that night when she went out with her boyfriend, Madison Jefferson Gates, better known as Emjay.

"Well, why don't they just say 'tell' instead of mucking it up with words no one knows?"

"Did the jury decide yet?"

"No, they're still trying to get him to rat on his lady love, the poor bloody fool. I say, good for him, protecting her like that."

"Fasten me up, Ma, will you?" Eden's cotton dress was starched within an inch of splintering, and she'd ironed the buttonholes shut.

Kitty dropped the newspaper and stuck her cigarette in her mouth, squinting against the smoke. "There, that'll do it. Let me have a look at you. You've turned into a real beauty, duck. Yes, I never would have thought it, you was always such a skinny kid, but here you are, a real beauty. 'Course, you could use some meat on them bones, and it wouldn't hurt to stoop a bit, Eden. You look like a bailiff's pike."

"I stoop for no one," Eden announced. "Besides, Emjay doesn't care that I'm taller than him."

"Well, you're not taller than him when you're not standing up,

348

are you?" Kitty grinned. "You're not taller than him lying down, are you?"

"I'm sure I don't know what you refer to."

"She don't know what I refer to!" Kitty crowed. "Well, all I can say is it's a good thing for you that Emjay Gates is a practicing Saint, that he's been a deacon since he sprouted hair. His old man has him all marked out for a mission for the church, and his family's the meanest bunch of no-nonsense Mormons in town, because if I didn't know Emjay Gates, you'd be heading for a fall, Miss Vanity-and-Vexation Douglass."

"Leave off, Ma."

" 'Leave off, Ma'! You better leave off! Your dad is as blind as a beggar, but I'm not, and I know what's happening."

Eden turned to her mother; she towered over the henna-haired, overweight Kitty and glared at her. "What do you mean? Why don't you just tell me if you know so much?"

Kitty shuffled back to the couch and opened a bag of peppermints she had stashed under the pillow. The peppermint bulged in her cheek. She picked up her latest novel, *The Wealth of Ages*, and shook it at Eden. "I'll tell you what I mean, miss. You ought to leave off reading all them Russkies and Frenchies and read some good books. Now just look at Victorine St. John here."

"Judas Priest, Ma. Who's Victorine St. John?" Eden stalked into the bedroom and dug her gloves out of the dresser drawer. Then she carefully tested the stockings that were hanging from Blanche's ribs to see which ones were dry. Blanche had become a kind of bony valet and indoor clothesline. Underpants often hung from her clavicles, and slips were draped over her arms, which Eden had tied to the curtain rod so that they were outstretched as if Blanche were always offering a welcoming embrace.

Eden sat on Ada's unmade bed and slid the gloves over her hands and the stockings over her legs.

"You waste your father's money on them stockings, Eden."

"You wasted his money on them for years."

"We're poor now."

"We've always been poor. Just because you don't wear stockings anymore don't—doesn't—mean I can't."

Kitty had long since given up silk stockings and all her other vanities except for henna-tinted hair. Kitty wore wool stockings in winter and went bare-legged the rest of the time.

"Victorine St. John could afford to wear silk stockings. She was a rich girl, which you sure ain't. She was a smart girl, too—which you also ain't—never mind the Russkie writers and Flowbert and that French grammar book I seen you poring over. Victorine knows there's always men trying to persuade girls to do wicked things, but Victorine knows enough to say no. Victorine is smarter than you—Miss Parlayvoofransay Douglass—because she knows that a girl what resists overtures—"

"Overtures! God's nostrils, Ma, where'd you learn 'overtures'?"

"Right here!" Kitty wagged the book in front of her face. "Right from this book and others! A girl what resists overtures gets asked to get married and a girl what don't, don't."

"I'm not getting married for a long time."

"You ain't telling me what I don't already know. I'm surprised Emjay's family lets him take up with you at all, because you can just bet that old Brother Gates heard all there was to hear about you and that surveyor who come through here last year. You can just bet he knows, and I'm s'prised he lets his boy out with you at all."

"I love Emjay and he loves me, and no one—not you or his father or anyone—is going to tell us what to do."

"Who, me, tell you what to do? Perish the thought, Eden. Was you in love with the surveyor, too?"

"I only went out with him for a while."

"Long enough for you to be caught in his hotel room sitting on the bed with his hand on your knee."

"He didn't have his hand on my knee."

"Oh, yeah? What do they call it in French?" Kitty picked up Eden's brush and applied it to her bright mop, the color of an unfingered penny. "Don't tell me, Eden. I know he had his way with you, and that's why he never asked you out again."

"Ma." Eden snapped her garters into place and slid her feet into high-heeled shoes. "He didn't ask me out again because he left town with the surveying team. Now, will you leave off?" A knock sounded at the front door. "Will you go out there and get that, or do I have to?"

"Emjay ain't coming for me. Emjay don't speak no French or read no Russkies—I don't see why you have to. Emjay don't—"

350

"Will you go get that door and leave me in a little peace?"

Kitty slouched out, and Eden could hear her welcoming Emjay Gates as if he were Solomon, offering him a peppermint and a seat on the couch.

Eden sat at the mirror and brushed out her short, dark hair till it shone and electrified. She powdered her face and sparingly applied rouge. She was very nearly the only girl at Fairwell High to use makeup. Of course, it was forbidden to her, too, but Eden's father was so blind he couldn't tell and her mother seldom looked that closely. She surveyed the finished woman in the mirror: she was without a doubt the prettiest girl in Fairwell. The prettiest and the smartest. Part of Emjay's attraction was that he had not failed to notice her superiority, and part of his appeal was that he never tired of telling her so.

Instead of joining the rest of Fairwell's youthful population in the close, dark confines of the Bijoux, sighing over *In Old Chicago*, Emjay and Eden drove out of town toward the old, narrow unpaved road to a ridge that overlooked the scattered lights of Fairwell. Emjay stopped the car, doused the lights, and took Eden in his arms, kissing her tenderly at first and then with accelerating hunger. Eden closed her eyes and gave herself up to Emjay's lips and hands. She lived for these moments; she could endure the banal school week, the sticky chaos of her life at home, because on Saturday nights Eden and Emjay drove his father's car up into the hills, a journey, for all intents and purposes, to a foreign land. Forbidden. Exotic.

Emjay rubbed her breasts roughly, squeezing them in either hand. The warmth from his hands seemed to penetrate her very tissues. Her nipples puckered, and shivers radiated between her legs. "Oh, Emjay, I love you."

"I love you, Eden, more than anything in the world. I'll always love you." He slid his hand just under her skirt and reached for the flesh just above her stockings. His fingers grazed her underpants and found their way into the moist grotto. They traded places so that Eden's head could lie under the steering wheel. Otherwise, they'd discovered, her knee kept hitting the horn.

Emjay lay on top of her and pushed and pressed and fondled, and Eden smiled to herself. Tomorrow morning in church her breasts would ache, and every time she walked or sat or stood, her body would remember tonight. She took a guilty sense of pleasure in Sunday's discomfort, in knowing that the Saints would probably not smile on Eden and Emjay's young love if they knew how well acquainted they were in the Biblical sense.

Eden got home late that night, dismayed to find her mother still curled up in the chair, devouring the last of the peppermints and *The Wealth of Ages*. Kitty remarked that her stockings were falling out of her purse and her dress was buttoned up wrong in the back.

Eden had planned to give her virginity to Emjay for a graduation present, but thought better of it. In the weeks just before and following graduation there were a great many weddings hastened by considerations other than love. Eden had believed herself to be the only woman of the world among her acquaintance, and she was disappointed to discover that other girls had visited that same exotic country, albeit in different company.

Besides, there were other things to think about in the weeks following graduation. Emjay had a terrible row with his father when he refused to go on a two-year mission for the church and instead went to work for the mining company that had taken over, reopened, and improved upon the old Sunstone holdings. He put at least half his check in savings every month so that he and Eden could get married.

Eden went to work, too. The only person other than Lucius Tipton to whom she had confessed her wish to write was her high school English teacher, Mrs. (Sister) Staunton. Mrs. Staunton, in turn, convinced her brother-in-law, Mr. (Brother) Oakes, editor of the *Fairwell Enterprise*, that the *Enterprise* needed a society writer to keep up with all the activity in a booming, though respectable, town like Fairwell. Mrs. Staunton took with her a sheaf of Eden's high school essays as proof of her talent and suitability for the job.

"Can you type?" Mr. Oakes asked when she came in for the interview.

"I've been typing since I was twelve," Eden replied.

"Well, you can write, I'll say that for you, but we don't have much call for this sort of thing." He held up one of her high school essays. He was a portly, grizzled man of about fifty. "I'll pay you four dollars a week to write up the weddings and engagements and births, the church events—all faiths, we don't play no favorites here—and another dollar if you'll do the obits. I been doing the obits now for six years, and they get real tiresome. They're all the same. What do you say?"

"Yes. And thank you. And you won't regret it."

"If I expected to regret it, I wouldn't hire you in the first place."

When Eden went to work there in 1938, the *Enterprise* came out twice weekly. The office was a two-room affair, one for the writing of the paper and one for the printing of it. All of the other employees were male, and she got along well enough with them, except for the reporter, who covered the courts, the mines, and local politics, a Mr. (Brother) Redbourne. Ned Redbourne continually teased her, asking when she would marry and exchange one *Enterprise* for another. "When are we going to read your wedding announcement, Eden?"

"You won't ever read it, Mr. Redbourne, because I don't plan to write up my wedding till I write up your obit." Across the room, Eden could hear Mr. Oakes laughing. Mr. Redbourne blushed and growled.

"You better watch out, Ned," Mr. Oakes called. "She's after your job, and she just might get it. At least her copy comes in on time."

The new society writer was indeed prompt with her copy, conscientious, hardworking, and thoroughly enamored of her name on the masthead.

She wished she could have clipped the *Enterprise* masthead and sent it to Lucius Tipton so he would know she had indeed recognized a beginning when she got there. She did clip and send it to her Aunt Afton and her grandmother, who against all the medical predictions was making a slow but dramatic recovery. Afton wrote long, cheerful letters about how Grandma's speech was gradually returning, and the use of her hands and legs, too.

Eden clipped everything she wrote and pasted it in a scrapbook. The scrapbook got thicker and thicker, but the bank account didn't. Eden tried to put some of her wages aside toward her marriage, but with the dollar and a half she paid her parents weekly and the cost of silk stockings, the savings account dwindled and vanished.

"You'll have to be more careful with money once we're married," Emjay grumbled, "especially after we have babies."

"Hush, Emjay. Don't talk about babies. It's bad luck."

"Why?"

"You know why," she said emphatically, because for his nineteenth birthday in July of 1939, Eden had given Emjay her virginity for a present. A month later she was frantic with fear, and when God saw fit to bless her with her period, she vowed she'd never do it again. She was chastened by the experience, but not to the point of chastity.

Her sister, Ada, was not so fortunate. Ada had a little one well on the way when she got married in her last year of high school. Kitty wept all through the wedding preparations. She moaned about virtue priceless beyond rubies and wondered in one breath how Ada could have been so weak and in the next how she could have been so stupid.

"Oh, leave off, Ma," said Eden as she let out the seams in Ada's wedding dress. "She's marrying him, isn't she?"

"A girl of sullied virtue don't have no virtue at all. There's no in between. Either you hang on to it or you don't. And once you let it go, there's no getting it back, and you're cast on the mercy of your lover."

"Judas Priest, Ma. How can you believe such tripe?"

"Sneer if you wish! I have ever been a lady with standards."

"You mean to say Pa didn't sully up your virtue just a little before you married him?"

"I was a lily of the valley."

"Then how'd you know you loved him enough to marry him?"

"Why, duck—we was soul mates from the beginning. Your pa loved me from the minute his eyes met mine. He begged me to marry him. He said his life would be nothing but tarnish and ash if I didn't marry him." Kitty picked up her book. "When are you going to marry old Emjay? The dew is off your virtue, Eden. A blind man could see it. If you're smart, you'll grab Emjay Gates and grab him fast, Miss Eden Sneersalot, because no other man will have you. No man will have nothing to do with shopworn goods." Kitty lit up a Chesterfield and blew out the match. "And there's many a night you come home shopworn."

"You remind me of Grandma and her blasted match. She always said your chances in life were like a match and you only got one chance and you'd lose it if you struck it wrong, or too late, or too early."

"Or not at all, Miss Society Writer. You better grab Emjay Gates before you get in a fix like Ada."

> Mr. and Mrs. Gideon Douglass announce the engagement
> of their daughter Eden Louise to Mr. Madison Jefferson
> Gates, son of Mr. and Mrs. Rex Gates. The wedding is
> tentatively planned for March 9.

She inserted the "tentatively" at the last minute, added it to the galleys before the page was printed. Though she had been informally engaged to Emjay for two years, they had agreed on a wedding date shortly after Ada got married. Afton was right: one wedding makes you think of another. Eden had been the maid—if not maiden—of honor in her sister's wedding, and Ada's happiness was so contagious that Eden pictured herself as a beaming bride, imagined her own wedding, heard her own voice pledge solemn vows as she laughed in the shower of rice and caught Ada's bouquet. The next wedding would be hers.

One wedding makes you think of another. After she pasted her own engagement announcement in her scrapbook, Eden leafed back through it. Her announcement read like all the others, universally the same; only the names were different. Different names participating in all the same acts: announcing, will be married, were united in marriage, gathered to celebrate, was held on, at, or in. These entries were inevitably followed by "was born to," and eventually, of course, long years later, the final announcement: died.

On February 20, 1940, Ruth Mason Douglass died. Afton called them that night; she was tearless but shaken, because Grandma had been making such good progress that they were surprised one afternoon to find her simply dead in a chair in the living room. "Died peacefully as she lived," Afton added, "but don't you let Mother's death put off Eden's wedding. No indeed. Mother wouldn't have agreed to that—never use the dead to stop the marriage of the living, that's what Mother said to me when I wanted to get married, and I know she'd feel the same way about you, Eden. We're going to bury her in three days' time if all of you want to come down. We're going to bury her by Eden. The other Eden."

Eden Douglass REGRET. Ever since Lily Whickham's funeral when she'd first seen her own name carved across a headstone with REGRET after it as if it were her married name, Eden had had infrequent but vivid nightmares in which a girl with wet, streaming hair floated up to her like the fat on the top of a stew. As a child, Eden had longed to be Ginger or Dot, a name not once worn like clothes that still smelled of someone else. "Why couldn't you give me my own name?" she once demanded of her mother.

"It wasn't my idea, duck. I wanted to name you Violet Lamont, like the heroine of the book I was reading, but your dad insisted. He's like all the other bleedin' Mormons—never waste a thing. Hoard and preserve! That's all they know. Save it all, every bit of string and crust of bread. If a shirt don't get worn out on one back, put it on another; if a name don't get its full sixty years' worth of use, pin it on another body."

If a fate don't get used up, rearrange it for someone else. Eden Douglass REGRET.

The elders of the church came to pay a condolence call as Gideon and Kitty were packing to attend Ruth's funeral in St. Elmo. Eden hid out in her bedroom with a book, but their well-meaning drone pierced the very walls. They sounded cheery rather than doleful, as if Ruth had bought a ticket for some foreign land and though she wouldn't exactly be sending postcards, the family shouldn't worry, they'd all be reunited one day in the Celestial Kingdom, where they could inherit property and marry and carry on just as they had on earth. A bit more refined, that's all. And since everyone was resurrected in the flesh anyway, death didn't even matter. Only a momentary wind blowing troublesome mortal dust off the shoulders.

"Your grandma will be real disappointed you're not coming to the funeral, Eden," Gideon said when she drove her parents and Ernest to the station. "You was always her favorite. She never took no pains to cover that up."

Eden began to say that Grandma had always been her favorite, too, Grandma and Doctor, but thought better of it. "I have a job, Pa. Grandma would understand." Eden was not sure she understood quite why she did not want to say that last farewell, did not want to stand at the St. Elmo cemetery close to Eden Douglass REGRET. She wrote a mental obit for her grandmother. It was quite

356

commonplace like all the others: born, married, died, as if life were a track and once you got on, you could get off only by derailing, and even at that, you ended up dead.

After their train left, Eden drove back home to change before meeting Emjay at the Paris Chop House. Once inside her house, whispers and snuffling gathered, seemingly around her ankles. Just the wind through these old newspapers, she assured herself as she picked the newspapers up off the floor and folded them. Mice in the walls, perhaps. Or snow. Snow falling outside. She marveled that she could hear it inside. If it was the snow. She trespassed from room to room; the house, always in disarray, bore all the scars of hasty packing and departures. At first Eden righted things and put them away, but then she gave up and let the awful solitude oppress her: Eden had never been alone in this house, this house or any other. She had always been surrounded and supported and stifled by family, and now it seemed they had loosed her. Like a balloon she floated aloft and alone, surrounded not by fleshly family, only by disembodied weeping, distant laughter, hollow, indistinct voices. Had the ghosts just arrived like unwelcome tenants, or were they always there, submerged beneath sounds of the living? She checked under all the beds. There was plenty of dust, but none of it animate.

She took off her coat and hat and gloves and washed her face brusquely. Going into her own room, she pulled her clean socks from Blanche's ribs. Blanche chattered, chiding Eden for her silly fears and uneasiness, for her generally bad habits and untidy approach to life. Blanche's boney protest was somehow comforting.

"I wish you wouldn't wear trousers," said Emjay as they studied the menu in the Paris Chop House.

"It's the very latest thing."

"Girls don't wear pants. Look around you. Do you see another girl here in pants?"

Eden looked around. The Paris Chop House was crowded, the mirror behind the counter fogged with cooking steam and human warmth, and the windows smudged with dirty snow. The coatracks bulged like obese scarecrows, and the air rang with the unmuffled sounds of heavy crockery and cheap flatware. Sister Staunton and her husband and an elderly couple came through the door, added their coats to the pile, and took a table by the window. Sister Staunton waved at her, and Eden waved back.

"What do I care what other people wear?" she said. "If everyone here was in sackcloth and ashes, does that mean I have to put them on, too? Anyway," she said, changing the subject deftly, "I'm picking up my wedding dress tomorrow. All it needs is a hem."

Sister Staunton made her way to their table. "Eden, I just wanted you to know how sorry I was to hear about your grandmother. I guess Gideon and Kitty and Ernest have took off for her funeral already."

"This afternoon."

"How come you didn't go?"

"I have to work. Remember? You're the one who got me the job."

"Best thing I ever did for this town! And I'm real happy about your wedding, you two. I feel like I'm a part of it, since you met in my class. You're getting quite a peach here, Emjay. Quite a peach. When's the Big Day?"

"A week from Saturday."

"Well, me and Earl'll be there with bells on. Well, dear, I have to go. Earl's parents are visiting, and we thought we'd take them out tonight. I just wanted to say I'm real sorry about your grandma, Eden. Death's always a blow." She glanced back at Earl's parents. "No matter how old they are."

Eden watched Sister Staunton rejoin her in-laws. They were both elderly, but the wife was considerably younger than the old man. He looked like a cotton boll with tufts of white hair on his dry brown head and white hair tufting out from his ears. He had twigs of arms, and his cuffs hung around his wrists. In the huge booth he was tiny, dwarfed by his wife and son and daughter-in-law.

Eden and Emjay ordered—ham steak with potatoes. Emjay wanted to know all about the wedding dress, but she said he'd just have to wait till the wedding. Emjay said the company bungalow they were renting would be ready March 1. "We can start moving our furniture in then. We'll go out and do some shopping next Saturday. I know it's important for a girl to have new things in her first home."

The noise and steam and human heat in the Paris Chop House

were almost unbearable. Eden's skin felt clammy dry. She took a drink of water. Emjay reached across the cracked linoleum table and took her hand. "You're real sad about your grandma, aren't you, honey?"

She started to tell him something of the ghosts, about the weightless, rising, freed, and yeasty feeling that oddly complemented the oppressive solitude, but her tongue tripped over the words. "I was always my grandma's favorite," she said finally and let it go at that.

The fish-eyed cook finished fixing their ham steaks and potatoes and brought them to the table. Emjay cut into his. "I've been thinking, Eden, maybe we could afford to go to Salt Lake for our honeymoon. Would you like that?" he asked, chewing with relish.

"Fine," said Eden, watching the cook deliver food to Sister Staunton's table. The old man's wife cut his meat for him, but otherwise the three of them ignored the elder Mr. Staunton altogether. He hunkered down between his wife and son, watching his wife cut his meat into tiny pieces. Birds watch worms with less concentration than that old man gave his food.

"Or maybe we'll just go to Coeur d'Alene like your sister did. It'll be cold, though, this time of year."

"Yes."

The meat once cut, Earl Staunton's father began shoveling it in, but not all the food made it into the old man's mouth, and some of what went in dribbled back out, down his chin. His wife took her napkin and wiped his chin, and the three of them went on talking. Sister Staunton waved when she saw Eden looking at them. Eden averted her eyes, overcome with fleeting, inexplicable nausea.

"Eat your potatoes, Eden."

"I don't think I'm hungry."

"You sick?"

"No."

"Upset about your grandma's dying?"

"Yes." And no. Eden watched the old man; she watched Emjay devour his supper with gusto. A beginning and an end? The beginning, the end? The end of the beginning? Eden shifted her weight uncomfortably. It wasn't her grandmother who came to mind there in the Paris Chop House, but Lucius Tipton, his geniality, his mischievous curiosity, his affection for the convolute, his ability to carve a diamond out of a cabbage. What would Doctor have made of Earl Staunton's father? Of Emjay Gates?

"You look real pale, Eden."

She smiled weakly. "Actually, I was just thinking about the doctor, Dr. Tipton. You remember—I told you about him, my grandmother's friend."

"The atheist."

"Yes. And now I think maybe he was more than her friend. Maybe he was her lover."

"Her lover!" Emjay washed down his surprise with some water. "You mean like—"

"Yes, like that."

"Then why didn't they ever get married? Your grandmother was a widow."

"I don't know why. As a child it never crossed my mind that they ought to get married. They were just Grandma and Doctor to me. One morning he brought a bottle of champagne over and we drank it on the porch. He brought some irises, too, because he said they were like Grandma, and the two of them were celebrating something that didn't have anything to do with me, but they included me. They toasted me—the woman I would become, they said."

"You drank champagne? You know that's against the Word of Wisdom."

"It didn't seem to matter then."

"Can I have your potatoes if you're not hungry?"

"Sure." The old man across the room mopped his plate with bread, and a chunk of wet bread dropped into his lap. His wife picked it up, breaking her sentence in midair. Gingerly she tucked the soggy bread beneath her own plate. *Let's go.* Eden distinctly heard the old man say, *Let's go.* "Dr. Tipton used to take me out to lunch," she continued. "At my grandmother's restaurant. There were flowers on all the tables and white cloths and napkins and blue velvet drapes and wonderful things to eat like Napoleons and Green Goddess salad dressing."

"Sounds heathen."

"The cook was Chinese. So were all the waiters and the help."

"Don't sound like the Paris Chop House."

"No. And now I'm wondering if the Paris Chop House is as close as I'll ever get to Paris."

"I never could figure out why you wanted to go there anyway. They don't speak our lingo."

"I had a year of French in high school," she reminded him.

"Aren't you going to eat anything at all?"

Eden frowned to watch Brother Staunton's father. The old man wanted to leave badly; he tugged insistently at his wife's sleeve. His wife murmured something to him, and he shook his head. Probably she wanted to know if he had to pee.

"Care if I eat your ham, too, Eden?"

"No. Take it all."

The three Stauntons went on chatting. The old man looked up and caught Eden staring at him. His blue eyes focused on her like spinning dimes; his face twisted into a grin, pulling his lips back from what should have been his teeth and wasn't. Eden looked away. She concentrated on Emjay's knife flashing through the pink, tough, resistant ham. Emjay trimmed the rind of fat and separated the flesh from its bone, and Eden flinched to see it sundered so roughly, without regard for its corporeal nature or the limits of its elasticity, and the limits of her own elasticity throbbed painfully as the Stauntons quickly vacated their table. Brother Staunton fumbled for his wallet while the two women hurriedly escorted the old man outside. They turned to the right, and in front of the window, his head framed by the arc of words proclaiming PARIS CHOP HOUSE, the old man vomited into the snow. His family tugged at him and tried to lead him back from the window, but he would not be moved; he vomited and vomited, more than he could possibly have eaten.

Eden glanced quickly around the Paris, but no one else so much as noticed the Stauntons, so engrossed were they in their own lives and suppers. Eden's gaze returned to the Stauntons, and when the old man finished vomiting, he looked up and met Eden's eyes. This time he did not grin. His face crumbled, and Eden blanched with unendurable pity and horror.

"What are you looking at?" Emjay turned around just as the Stauntons led the old man away. "What's the matter? What's going on here?"

Eden began to weep. She covered her face with her hands and cried till the tears ran down her wrists and shudders shook her bones as if she'd no more flesh than Blanche. "Doctor said you'll know the beginning when you get there," she sobbed incoherently, but what if the beginning was also the end, what if you returned helplessly, flesh unto dust, a dog to his vomit? Eden Douglass REGRET.

In the week that her parents were gone, Emjay had hoped to use their house for a little prenuptial practice, but Eden contended they were so close to their wedding day, they ought to wait, to give themselves something to look forward to, and Emjay agreed. In truth, Eden looked forward to having the house to herself; she came to enjoy the solitude that had first so disturbed her. The voices that rustled, murmured, creaked, and bristled were not unfriendly, and if they were ghosts, they seemed harmless, downright benign. But they vanished when Kitty and Gideon and Ernest returned.

"They was all there," said Kitty, throwing off her coat, kicking off her galoshes, and sinking into the couch, which was as bulging and overweight as she was. "My dogs are killing me. Ernest, push that ottoman over this way, will you? They was all there, Eden, all but Snail Snot. Afton wrote him somewheres in Florida, but I think he's in jail."

"Mason is my brother. Please do not call him Snail Snot."

"Oh, yeah, Gideon? Well, I have an arse, too, and just because it's mine don't mean I call it a lily pad."

"You've always been jealous because you don't have any family," Gideon returned.

"No family, he says! I got the Douglasses, don't I? Do they ever let go? Never."

Eden and Ernest glanced at each other; they had listened to this too often not to know what was coming next. "Think I'll go down to the high school and see what I've been missing this week," Ernest said, jamming his hands in his pockets. He slammed the door as he left.

"Ernest is such a good boy. He'll be the only one to take care of me in my old age," Kitty said, sighing. "Ada will always be too busy, and Eden won't care about anybody 'cept herself, but Ernest will take care of his old mother."

"I'm going to take a nap," Gideon announced. "It's been a long trip, and I have to go back to work tomorrow."

"I'm sorry about Grandma, Pa," Eden offered, strangely moved to pity by her father, who seemed rather more spare and gray than he had the week before. "I know how you felt about her."

"I don't even know how I felt about her, Eden. Afton is the only one who's certain of everything."

Kitty waited till Gideon went into the bedroom to continue. "Ruth got a nice sendoff, duck. Albert Mason come all the way from Salt Lake. He's a snake, though, Albert is, and I knew it the minute I first laid eyes on him. He only come so he could tell everyone how he flew down there in an airplane. And Cissa only come so she could wear her new fur coat. She said as much. It was a real nice coat."

"Did you try it on?" Eden picked up her mother's threadbare jacket and put it on the chair.

"Oh, once. Maybe twice. I never let on to Cissa, though, no indeed. That coat was a little too small for me, and she never would let me forget it. That's the trouble with the Douglasses, they never forget. The whole tribe of them never forget a thing. There's Afton and Lil after the funeral rattling on about some fire happened a hundred years ago when Eden burned her hands, just like it was yesterday. Or tomorrow. Not you, the other Eden."

Eden Douglass REGRET

"Open that suitcase there, will you, duck, and hand me *The Purloined Lover*. It's right on top. Just the saddest story ever put to words. It's about this girl what—"

"I have to go to work now, Ma. I'll take the truck, if you're not going to need it."

"I don't need it. I got *The Purloined Lover*."

When she arrived at the *Enterprise* office, Ned Redbourne turned his back to her, and Eden returned the favor by not speaking. She hung her coat and hat up and sat in front of the Underwood. She was working on the announcement of her own wedding, which would appear in the paper the week she was gone on her wedding trip to Coeur d'Alene. Like Ada and her husband.

One wedding makes you think of another.

Mr. Oakes came in from the pressroom laden with galleys. He stopped by her desk and read over her shoulder:

Miss Eden Douglass and Mr. Madison Jefferson Gates
were united in marriage Saturday, March 9, in the

363

Church of Jesus Christ of Latter-day Saints. The bride
wore . . .

"Well, Eden, I'll come to your wedding, but my wife's made me
promise to sew my lips shut and not speak up when they ask if anyone here can see why these two shouldn't be united in marriage."

"And why shouldn't we?"

"Because I'll be losing the best writer the *Enterprise* ever had.
This stuff"—he pointed to the wedding and social events lying all
over her desk—"is bilge, of course, but those articles you wrote last
month when old Ned over there was sick, the ones about the mine
accident—they were gems. You can write, honey. Make no mistake
of it. You can write. And nobody knows it better than me—except
maybe old Ned there. He knows it, too." He winked and took his
long galleys and ambled back to his desk.

a gown of floor-length white satin with a face insert . . .

She found a pencil and scratched out "face" and wrote in
"lace."

the bride is the daughter of . . .
were united in marriage . . .
pleased to announce the birth of . . .

One birth, one marriage, one death, they all make you think of
the others. Particular lives submerged in the universal experience,
lived out in kitchens and bedrooms and bathrooms and backyards,
over stoves and sickbeds and washtubs, soothing children only to
have them cry again, washing them only to watch them get dirty,
feeding them only to clean out their pants, loving them only to have
them grow up to be Eden Douglass REGRET.

"Judas Priest All Friday H! Get that wedding dress off that
bleedin' skeleton!"

Eden took the pins out of her mouth. "Ma, I have to do up the
hem, and Blanche is just about my height."

"Look at Blanche grinning out of that wedding dress. My skin
crawls, Eden. Haven't you got a lick of reverence?"

"Blanche is a friend of the family."

"Not my family, she ain't."

"Then don't look."

Kitty covered her eyes with *The Purloined Lover* and stretched her hand out to Eden. She wagged a fat envelope at her. "Here, take this, and I shall depart."

"What is it?"

"How do I know? It's from that snake Albert. He said I was to give it to you. Did you see the wedding presents I brung back with me? I'll say this, Lil and Afton, they done all right by you, Eden. Nice presents." She lowered the book. "Well, take this and see what Snakewad Albert has got to say."

Eden stuck the needle in the hem and took the envelope from her mother. It had only her name on it, and the return address in flourishing script was the Providential Mutual Life Insurance Company of Salt Lake.

Eden slit the envelope with her scissors. She withdrew a letter and twenty fifty-dollar bills. New ones. Crisp ones. Fragrant with ink and promise.

"God's almighty nostrils!"

"Judas Priest, Ma! Where is this from? What's it for?"

"Do I look like I know? Open the letter." She read over Eden's shoulder.

Dear Miss Douglass—

I address you thus because I am unknown to you, though we are members of the same family. I am carrying out the last wishes of my dear sister, Ruth Mason Douglass, who was also an insuree of my company, whose letterhead you'll note above.

You can thank me for the enclosed bounty, because if it wasn't for me, Ruth Mason Douglass never would have bought insurance. Ruth never believed in insurance, scoffed at my profession, but when she wanted her boy Gideon (your father) to go into my profession, I told her I'd take him only on the condition that she buy the best, the biggest, the most expensive life insurance policy we offer. I was only thinking of her own good. She called me

365

a thieving cheat, and that's the thanks I get, but you will live to reap the bounty of my foresight.

Three months ago Ruth wants me to rewrite the policy like it was no trouble at all. She wants her five living children removed and your name put in as sole beneficiary. And naturally, being Ruth, that ain't all she wanted. She wants me to come to her funeral and deliver that money to you. In cash. She won't have it no other way. She claims if I do this for her just like she says, it will be the last thing she ever asks of me. Ruth and me go back a long way. I told her to swear that in writing and I'd do whatever she said. Since you are not here, I will give the money to your parents and ask that they keep their wits about them long enough to give it to you.

Cash seems foolhardy to give to a young girl, but if you are a smart girl, you'll take these bills right down to the bank and put it in, and if you are as smart as they say, you'll send me back some of it and I'll write you up an insurance policy, as I understand you are getting married, and insurance is the one thing a newly married couple must have. You can get by with used furniture, but insurance is a necessity, because who knows when Death's untimely hand will snatch us from our loved ones and carry us off?

Your loving Uncle,

Albert Mason

"Well, I'll be damned," said Eden.

"Not with no thousand dollars, you won't! Gideon!" Kitty cried. "Gideon! Get in here and have a look at what Eden got from Albert!"

"From Grandma."

"From heaven, honey, and don't you forget it. 'Your loving Uncle'! I know Albert Mason. He wrestled with the angels before he coughed up that money. Who'd know the difference? He must have been afraid Ruth would come back and strangle him in his sleep if he didn't do it. And she probably would have. Gideon—look at this."

Gideon put on his glasses and read the letter. "How much money is it?"

"A thousand dollars."

"A thousand? A thousand!"

"You better go call Emjay quick, Eden. Oh, that money will set you two up for the rest of your lives! No company bungalow for Mr. and Mrs. Gates, no indeed. You can have all new furniture and new clothes and a new car, too. You can go to San Francisco for your honeymoon if you want. Why, Eden, you and Emjay could go to London if the Krauts wasn't bombing the bejesus out of it."

"I could go to Paris."

"No, the Krauts are there, too. You better settle for San Francisco and a new car and some furniture. What's the matter with you, duck? You sick?" Kitty put her hand on Eden's forehead.

"Oh, Ma!" Eden burst into tears, and Kitty put her arms around her. Crying into Kitty's shoulder was like weeping into a marshmallow.

"Now, Eden." Gideon patted her shoulder. "I told you you was always your grandma's favorite. I wonder why she didn't tell no one she was doing this. I know she didn't tell Afton. Afton couldn't have kept shut about something like this."

"Now, duck, don't cry. Your grandma was old. She was ready to go."

"It's not that."

"Then what the bleedin' hell is it? You ought to be dancing a jig. You're just starting out in life. Why, duck, this is just the beginning. We'll take that money to the bank first thing tomorrow. I love to think of it. Oh, won't this set their noogies on fire!"

"Whose noogies?" Eden wiped her nose on a handkerchief her father gave her.

"Why, this whole town, Eden, and the Douglasses, too! I'm going to write to Afton tomorrow. She'll take to her bed. I bet she don't get up for a week."

"Come on, Mother. Let Eden get some rest. You call Emjay in the morning, honey. The morning's plenty soon. Your wedding dress looks real pretty, Eden, even on Blanche."

"Thanks, Pa." She closed the door after them, put on her flannel nightgown, and counted the money once more before putting it beneath her mattress and turning out the light. A thousand dollars.

Cash money. Oh, it would be fun to take that money to the bank to-morrow, to snap those bills on the counter while everyone gawked. She and Emjay would be more notorious than the runaway teller and the teacher. Of course, she reflected in an afterthought, we will be married and they were not. But even as she relished the spectacle she would create, the money seemed to crunch audibly beneath her body, to murmur, to question, to demand: why the injunction to deliver it in cash? Why had Grandma changed the beneficiary, ex-cluding her own five children in favor of one grandchild? Why was there no scribbled note or suggestion? Only Grandma could answer those questions, and she was dead and in that foreign country whence no traveler may return. But there was one question all that cash money posed that only Eden could answer: what if Grandma had died after her wedding?

Eden sat up and clutched her knees, regarding Blanche, who glowed in the half-hemmed wedding dress. "What if that money had come to Mrs. Emjay Gates, Blanche?" Blanche's bones seemed to rattle with a passing wind that shuddered the thin windowpane behind her. Eden got out of bed, pushed the curtain aside, and gazed out to the snow-quilted yard. She put her arm around Blanche and her young cheek to Blanche's lower mandible. "Why, Blanche? Why did Grandma do it?"

And Blanche, or perhaps Eden's own bones, replied: *Because she thought you could be something besides Mrs. Emjay Gates. That's why. That money is a revelation in greenbacks. Take it and . . .*

In the distance a train whistle ripped through the cloudless night sky.

Go. Go.

Eden rummaged in a drawer and found some paper and a blunt pencil.

> Dear Emjay—
> I don't want to get married, even though I know I
> ought to. I haven't wanted to get married ever since that
> night at the Paris Chop House when I watched the old
> man vomit. You didn't see him, but I did. He was trying
> to tell me something, but I didn't have the words for it
> then. I just watched him vomit, and I knew he was telling

me something, but I didn't know what it was. And now I've got this money and it's my one chance and I'm going to take it.

To where? Anywhere that wasn't Fairwell, Idaho, or St. Elmo, California, or all the dreary places in between.

I hope you'll understand and not be too angry with me.

Eden

She folded the letter and slid it into an envelope. On another sheet she wrote to her parents:

Please don't worry about me. I'll be fine and I'll write to you often and I'll always be your daughter, but I know that Grandma would want me to do this, and Doctor would, too. I know it. That's why the money was in cash. You can be sensible with a check, but cash talks, and I am going to heed it.
I love you all.

Eden

As she tiptoed across the living-room floor, Eden Louise Douglass could see a light under her parents' door, but they made no sound, and she assumed her father was asleep and her mother deep in the arms of *The Purloined Lover*. In the kitchen she took a loaf of bread and some apples and gingersnaps, which travel well and keep a long time. On her way back to her own room she picked up one of the suitcases, which still lay where Gideon and Kitty had put them down that afternoon.

In her own room Eden emptied her parents' things onto the bed and began to pack the clothes she had bought for her honeymoon: dresses, underwear, stockings. She tossed in some woolly socks and as many of her other clothes as she could cram in. She took off her flannel nightgown, threw that in, too, and snapped the suitcase shut. She went to the closet and took out the navy blue gabardine traveling suit with brass buttons and padded shoulders. She dressed as she would have for her wedding journey—the shoes and gloves, the suit and coat and hat with a small, fashionable veil—but this was a journey she was making by herself to that place from which she had no wish to return: the future.

Eden pulled the money out from under the mattress and put one fifty-dollar bill into her purse. She stuffed all the rest of it into her bra, where it lay starchy, delicious, and uncomfortable against her narrow breasts. She left her two notes stuck in Blanche's clavicles and impulsively kissed the bride's cranium. Then she walked softly across the living room and out the door. She put the suitcase in the Pilgrim delivery truck and slid in after it, took the brake off, and coasted downhill.

Eden drove to the station and put the keys under the clutch. The stationmaster was asleep with the *Fairwell Enterprise* over his face when she rang the bell. "When's the next train through here?"

"Eleven-thirty."

"Which way is it going?"

"Eastbound."

"Give me a ticket."

"To where?"

"How far can I go?"

"Chicago on this line."

"Give me a ticket to Chicago." She took out her fifty-dollar bill and laid it in the dish.

"Where'd you get this kind of money?"

"Who are you? Dick Tracy?"

"Last time someone handed me a fifty, it was the teller who robbed the bank."

"Mind your own bleeding business and give me the ticket."

"You're all alone, girl?"

"You see anyone with me?"

The stationmaster peered over her shoulder as if indeed they might all be lined up behind her: Grandma, Doctor, Eden Douglass REGRET, Afton, Lil, Gideon, Kitty, Cissa, Snail Snot, Ada and Ernest and Emjay. Eden had a look over her shoulder as well.

Her high heels clicked over the near-empty lobby as she took her ticket and chose a seat facing the grim station clock that read eleven-fifteen. She hoped that the train would be on time and that she would have but fifteen minutes to consider more closely what she was doing and to whom. Revelations, after all, are effervescent and compelling, but they are fragile and wither under scrutiny.

370

Fifteen minutes later the train pulled in, heaving, enveloping Eden in steam and smoke and soot. She chose a dim car that held a sleeping commercial traveler and a tired conductor absorbed in punching tickets and checking timetables. She put her suitcase on the seat beside her, as if to assure herself that the ghosts who hovered in the station had not boarded with her. Eden was determined to travel light. They had come with her, of course; they were that remnant of her past she would take to the future because one can escape the past only if one is willing to forgo the future as well; it's all of one thread, wound on one spindle, the way flesh is wound around bone. The train slowly pulled out of the Fairwell station.

"Ticket, little lady?" The conductor smiled at her. "All alone, are you?" He punched her ticket emphatically.

"Yes. I think so anyway."

"Well, you got a long ride to Chicago. You better try to get some sleep." He returned the ticket to her and ambled back to his seat and his rustling timetables.

Eden Louise Douglass enjoyed the sensation of the stiff money crinkling against her breasts as she removed her gloves and rolled them carefully, tucking the thumbs in. The train gave a long, plaintive whistle, and when its familiar shriek died, she heard another familiar sound, a scratch, and the indelible scent of a just-lit match wafted nearby. She glanced over to see the conductor casually lighting a cigarette. Briefly, brilliantly, the match burned blue and gold. Eden smiled at her reflection in the darkened window as the winter-whitened world slid by.